Praise for
THE SECOND SLEEP

'A wake-up call of a novel . . . an ingenious tour de force that is also a timely alert.'
Sunday Times, BOOKS OF THE YEAR

'A gripping and topical evocation of civilisation's fragility.'
Spectator, BOOKS OF THE YEAR

'Human complacency and the urge to endure and inquire frame this masterly tale.'
The Times, BOOKS OF THE YEAR

'[An] absorbing, thought-provoking thriller.'
Daily Express, BOOKS OF THE YEAR

'Ingenious.'
Daily Telegraph, BOOKS OF THE YEAR

'He gives his imagination full rein in a gripping thriller that tells us a lot about our past, present and future.'
Sunday Express, BOOKS OF THE YEAR

'A classy blockbuster from a wily old hand.'
Mail on Sunday, BOOKS OF THE YEAR

'A gripping mystery.'
Tablet, BOOKS OF THE YEAR

'A truly surprising future-history thriller. Fabulous, really.'
Evening Standard

Also by Robert Harris

FICTION

The Cicero Trilogy

Imperium

Lustrum

Dictator

Standalone novels

Fatherland
What if Hitler had won the war?

Enigma
Secrets and intrigue in wartime Bletchley Park.

Archangel
The discovery of Stalin's notebook prompts a mission to
uncover a secret chapter of Russia's history.

Pompeii
A thrilling depiction of one of the most famous natural
disasters in human history: the explosion of Vesuvius.

The Ghost
A former British prime minister's secret past comes
back to haunt him.

The Fear Index
A legendary financial genius, who generates billions of dollars
for the super-rich, is hunted down – by whom?

An Officer and a Spy
Dreyfus has been exiled to Devil's Island. But someone is still
handing secrets to the Germans.

Conclave
The Pope is dead. Over the next seventy-two hours of secret
voting and rivalry, one cardinal will become the most
powerful spiritual figure on earth.

Munich
Hitler is determined to start a war. Chamberlain is desperate
to stop him. Is any price too high for peace?

NON-FICTION

A Higher Form of Killing (with Jeremy Paxman)

Gotcha: Media, the Government and the Falklands Crisis

The Making of Neil Kinnock

Selling Hitler

*Good and Faithful Servant: The Unauthorized
Biography of Bernard Ingham*

Robert Harris

THE SECOND SLEEP

arrow books

1 3 5 7 9 10 8 6 4 2

Arrow
20 Vauxhall Bridge Road
London SW1V 2SA

Arrow is part of the Penguin Random House group of companies whose
addresses can be found at global.penguinrandomhouse.com

First published in the United Kingdom by Hutchinson in 2019
First published by Arrow in 2020

www.penguin.co.uk

A CIP catalogue record for this book is available from the British Library.

ISBN 9781787460966 (paperback)
ISBN 9781787460973 (export paperback)

Typeset in 12.85/15.2pt Spectrum MT by Jouve (UK), Milton Keynes
Printed and bound in Great Britain by Clays Ltd, Elcograf S.p.A.

Penguin Random House is committed to a
sustainable future for our business, our readers
and our planet. This book is made from Forest
Stewardship Council® certified paper.

To Sam

Until the close of the early modern era, Western Europeans on most evenings experienced two major intervals of sleep . . . The initial interval of slumber was usually referred to as 'first sleep' . . . The succeeding interval was called 'second' or 'morning' sleep . . . Both phases lasted roughly the same length of time, with individuals waking some time after midnight before returning to rest.

A. Roger Ekirch, *At Day's Close: A History of Nighttime*

It was impossible to dig more than a foot or two deep about the town fields and gardens without coming upon some tall soldier or other of the Empire, who had lain there in his silent unobtrusive rest for a space of fifteen hundred years. He was mostly found lying on his side, in an oval scoop in the chalk, like a chicken in its shell; his knees drawn up to his chest; sometimes with the remains of his spear against his arm; a fibula or brooch of bronze on his breast or forehead; an urn at his knees, a jar at his throat, a bottle at his mouth . . . They had lived so long ago, their time was so unlike the present, their hopes and motives were so widely removed from ours, that between them and the living there seemed to stretch a gulf too wide even for a spirit to pass.

Thomas Hardy, *The Mayor of Casterbridge*

CHAPTER ONE

The hidden valley

LATE ON THE afternoon of Tuesday the ninth of April in the Year of Our Risen Lord 1468, a solitary traveller was to be observed picking his way on horseback across the wild moorland of that ancient region of south-western England known since Saxon times as Wessex. If this young man's expression was troubled, we may grant he had good cause. More than an hour had elapsed since he had last seen a living soul. Soon it would be dusk, and if he was caught out of doors after curfew he risked a night in jail.

He had stopped to ask directions in the market town of Axford, where a group of rough-looking fellows had been drinking outside an inn beneath the painted sign of a swan. After grinning between themselves at the strangeness of his accent, and imitating the refinement of his *yeses* and *yous*, they had assured him that to reach his destination all he needed to do was to ride straight towards the setting sun. But now he was beginning to suspect this might have been another piece of local mischief. For no sooner had he passed the high walls of the town's prison, where three executed felons hung rotting from their gibbets, and crossed the river and entered open country, than heavy clouds had blown across the western sky, obliterating the sunset. Behind him the tall spire of Axford's church had long since submerged below the horizon. Ahead, the road twisted and dipped between unpopulated ridges of dark woodland and stretches of wild heath daubed with streaks of yellow gorse before dwindling into the murk.

Presently, in the way that often in those parts signals a change in the weather, it became very still. All the birds went quiet, even the huge red kites with their incongruous high-pitched cries that had pursued him for miles. Chilly veils of sodden grey mist drifted across the moor and draped themselves around him, and for the first time since he set off early that morning, he felt moved to pray aloud for protection to his name saint, who had borne the infant Christ on his back across the river.

After a while, the road began to ascend a wooded hillside. As it climbed, so it dwindled, until it was little better than a cart track – ridged brown earth covered loosely by stones, shards of soft blue slate and yellow gravel braided by the running rainwater. From the steep banks on either side rose the scent of wild herbs — lungwort, lemon balm, mustard garlic — while the overhanging branches drooped so low he had to duck and fend them off with his arm, dislodging further showers of fresh cold water that drenched his head and trickled down his sleeve. Something shrieked and flashed emerald in the gloom, and his heart seemed to jump halfway up his throat, even though he realised almost at once that it was nothing more sinister than a common parakeet. He shut his eyes in relief.

When he opened them again, he saw a brownish object up ahead. At first he mistook it for a fallen tree. He wiped his sleeve across his face and leaned forward in his saddle. A figure in a hessian smock, cowled like a monk, was pushing a handcart. He dug his knees into the flanks of his mount and urged her on. 'God be with you!' he shouted down at the curious apparition. 'I am a stranger here.'

The figure pushed ahead even harder, pretending not to have heard, so that he was obliged to pass it once again. This time he wheeled around to block the narrow lane. He noticed the cart was piled with wool bales. He loosened the neck strings of his cape. 'I mean you no harm. Christopher Fairfax is my name.' He pulled down the wet fabric and lifted his beard to show the white cloth tied around his neck. 'I am a man of God.'

A damp thin male face squinted up at him through the rain. Slowly and reluctantly the hood was drawn back to reveal a head entirely bald. Water ran off the shiny dome, upon the crown of which curved a blood-coloured crescent-shaped birthmark.

'Is this the road to Addicott St George?'

The man scratched at his birthmark and screwed up his eyes as if making a great effort of memory. Eventually he said, 'Ye means *Adcut*?'

Fairfax – dripping water, losing patience – answered, 'Yes, very well, then – *Adcut*.'

'No. There's a fork, a half-mile back. Ye needs t'take t'other.' The man looked him up and down. A knowing expression crept across his face – a slow, rural slyness, as if he were measuring a beast at market. 'Ye're young for the work.'

'And yet old enough, I think!' Fairfax forced a smile and bowed. 'Peace be upon you.'

He tugged at the bridle and turned his elderly grey mare around, riding her carefully back down the watery track until he found the place where the road forked. It was almost impossible to spot unless one had been warned to look for it. So those wretches in Axford had indeed been trying to get him lost – a trick they'd never have dared attempt had they known he was a priest. He ought to tell the local sheriffs. Yes, on his way home he would do exactly that. He would bring the whole weight of the law down upon their stupid rustic numbskulls – imprisonment, a fine, a day in the stocks being pelted by stones and shit . . .

This second track was even steeper. Ancient trees on either side, already in full leaf, leaned in no more than a couple of yards above his head as if to confer. Their entwined branches shut out the light. Inside this dank tunnel night seemed already to have fallen. His horse skittered and refused to carry him further. He wrapped his arms around her neck and whispered in her ear, 'Come on, May!' But she was a grumpy beast, stubborn with age, more mule than horse, and in the end he had to dismount and lead her.

On foot, he felt even more vulnerable. He had twenty pounds in his purse for expenses, counted out a coin at a time by the dean the previous evening, and many were the travellers who had been murdered for half as much. His boots slithered in the mud as he dragged at the bridle. Oh, but this was a fine joke, he thought bitterly. The bishop might rarely smile, but that did not mean he entirely lacked a certain sense of humour. To send a man off thirty miles, to the furthest edge of the diocese, on such an errand, and on a clapped-out horse . . .

He pictured his colleagues gathering for their customary early supper – seated on the long benches in the chapter house in front of the huge fire, the bishop bowing his narrow grizzled head to say grace, his face in the blaze still the colour of an oyster, a flicker of malicious merriment in those small dark eyes. 'And lastly we pray for our brother in Christ, Christopher

Fairfax, serving our holy mother the Church tonight . . . *in a far-off land*!'

Some wretched nearby brook seemed to gurgle with laughter.

But then, just as he was despairing, a pale glow appeared at the end of the overgrown lane and after a few more minutes of weary dragging, he emerged into what was left of the day's light to discover himself on the crest of a hill. To his right the land fell away sharply. Small fields with low dry-stone walls enclosed a scattering of cows, sheep and goats. Ramshackle wooden stalls had been weathered by the winter to the colour of pewter. At the bottom of the valley, about a mile distant, was a river with a bridge. Next to it, a small settlement of mostly thatched roofs was centred around a square stone church tower. Here and there, feathery lines of white-grey smoke rose and bled into the darker grey of the sky. The clouds above the enclosing hills were low and racing, like waves fleeing a storm out at sea. It had stopped raining. He fancied he could smell the chimneys. He imagined light, warmth, company, food. In the wet fresh evening air his spirits revived. Even May's mood improved sufficiently that she consented to let him remount her.

It was nearly dark by the time they trotted into the centre of the village. May's shod hooves clattered over the arched stone bridge that spanned the river and splashed along the muddy narrow street. His high

6

vantage point enabled him to peer into the white-washed cottages on either side. Some had small front gardens with white wooden fences. Most opened directly on to the road. In a couple of windows, candles glowed; in one, he glimpsed the full pale moon of a face, quickly eclipsed by a curtain. He halted at the lychgate and looked about him. A cobbled path led through the graveyard to the portico of a church that he guessed must have stood square on this land for at least a thousand years; more likely fifteen hundred. Wrapped around the middle of the flagpole on the top of the tower, the red and white standard of England and St George hung damply at half-mast.

On the far side of the graveyard, beyond the wall, was a tumbling two-storey building with a thatched roof. On the threshold, now that he looked more closely, he could just make out the gaunt figure of a woman dressed in black, holding a lantern, watching him. For a few moments they regarded one another across the lichened tombstones. Then she lifted the light a little and moved it back and forth. He raised his hand, spurred the mare and rode around the perimeter of the churchyard towards the waiting figure.

CHAPTER TWO

Father Fairfax makes the acquaintance of
Father Thomas Lacy

S HE TOOK HIM upstairs to see Father Lacy right
away. He barely had time to lay down his bag in
the passage, shed his dripping cape and pull off
his muddy boots before he was following her, stiff and
bow-legged from his hours in the saddle, up the narrow wooden staircase to the landing.

Over her shoulder she informed him that she was
Mrs Agnes Budd, housekeeper, and that she had been
watching out for him all day. Beneath her deference
he detected an undertone of reproach.

He had to dip his head to pass through the low
doorway. The bedchamber was cold and smelled of
chloride of lime. The window was open wide to the
bluish dusk; on the floorboards beneath its leaded
panes, the rain had puddled. A black coffin lid was
propped against a chest of drawers. The coffin itself

was on the bed. Candles stood on the nightstands on either side of the heavy wooden bed frame, along with a book and a pair of spectacles, as if the dead man had just finished reading. The flames of the candles flickered in the draught.

Cautiously he approached the coffin and peered down. The corpse was long and thin, packed in sawdust and bound up tight in a papery white linen shroud, like a chrysalis ready to hatch. A white lace handkerchief covered the face. He glanced at the housekeeper. She nodded. He took the two upper corners of the handkerchief between his thumbs and forefingers and lifted it away.

In his short existence he had seen plenty of corpses. They could scarcely be avoided in England at that time. They hung suspended in iron cages, like the wretched convicts in Axford, to deter the unlawful. They turned up overnight in doorways or on patches of wasteland, especially in winter, and lay there until someone could be bothered to pay the night soil man to remove them. During the recent outbreak of the putrid fever he had administered the last rites to babies even as he had closed the eyes of their grandparents. But never had he beheld a body such as this. The nose was broken, the eye sockets bruised. A deep gash ran across the forehead. The right ear was mangled, as if it had been chewed half off. Although an attempt had been made to mask these disfigurements with powdered white lead, the wounds shone greenish through the dust. The effect was grotesque. Unusually for a cleric, Lacy had no beard, merely grey stubble.

Bending to touch his head in benediction, Fairfax detected the maggoty stink of decay and drew back quickly. The old priest ought to have been in his grave some while ago.

'He died how long since?'

'A week, Father. The weather has been warm.'

'And what hour is the burial?'

'Eleven, sir.'

'Well, I fear it cannot come too soon.' He replaced the handkerchief over the broken face, stepped away and made the sign of the cross. 'Peace be upon him. May the Lord's faithful servant rest in the arms of Christ. Amen.'

'Amen,' said the housekeeper.

'Come, Mrs Budd — let us cover the coffin.'

Between them they carried the heavy lid over to the bed and laid it on top of the box. Good plain carpentry, Fairfax thought — honest English oak painted black, the brass handles set along its sides the only ostentation, and a tight enough fit to hold in the stench. Agnes pulled a cloth from her belt and wiped it clean. They contemplated it for a few moments, then she noticed the puddle beneath the window. She muttered under her breath and went over and mopped it up, then wrung her cloth out into the garden below.

As she reached to close the window, he said, 'Best maybe to leave it open.'

On the landing, he took out his handkerchief and pretended to blow his nose. He could still taste the smell. 'The marks upon his face . . . ? Poor fellow! How did he sustain such wounds?'

'He received 'em when he fell, sir.'

'It must have been a rare fall.'

'A hundred feet, or so they says.'

'They?'

'Them that found him, sir – Captain Hancock, Mr Keefer, the church clerk, and Mr Gann, the blacksmith, among others.'

'What time of day was this?'

'He left the parsonage last Tuesday afternoon with his trowel in his hand and his strong boots on and never came back. A search was raised and his body carried home on Wednesday evening.'

'He walked much?'

'Aye, sir. He walked most places. Seldom rode. Gave up his horse a few years back.'

She led him downstairs and into the parlour, where a meagre fire burned in the grate, insufficient to take the chill off the room. A table had been laid for one.

'Ye'll be wanting supper, Father?'

An hour earlier he had been ravenous. Now the thought of food turned his stomach. 'Thank you. But first I should attend to my horse.'

He went back along the stone passage. Already he was calculating his escape. He was trying to remember the name of the inn he had stopped outside in Axford. The Swan, that was it. If the burial was at eleven, he could leave the village at one, and easily be at the Swan by supper time.

The front door had a heavy lock, shiny with newness. He opened it and stepped out into the small garden. The damp and glassy evening was fragrant with the scent of wet grass and woodsmoke. May had gone. He had left her tethered to the gatepost. Had he not tied her properly? He peered around the darkened village. No light showed. The deep country silence pressed like wadding against his ears.

Behind him Agnes said, 'Don't bother thyself, Father.' Her voice in the quietness made him jump. 'Rose will've stabled her.'

'That's kind. Please thank her for me.'

He felt obscurely irritated, for reasons he could not rightly specify. He picked up his bag and followed the housekeeper back into the parlour.

'Now, Mrs Budd,' he said, trying to be businesslike, 'a few questions require settling, if I may.' He set his bag upon the table, rummaged through it and pulled out his pen case and a few sheaves of paper. 'First matters first . . .' he smiled at her, trying to set her at ease, 'is there ink in the house?'

'What questions might those be?' She looked wary.

He wondered how old she was. Fifty, perhaps. Sallow, plain-faced, hair already grey, eyes raw, presumably with weeping. How grief ages us, he thought, with sudden pity; how vulnerable we are, poor mortal creatures, beneath our vain show of composure.

'I am charged, as part of my duties, with the delivery of Father Lacy's eulogy – a task seldom easy even if one knew the deceased, but trickier still if one had never met them.' He made it sound as if it was a problem with which he was familiar, although in truth he had never conducted a burial or composed a eulogy in his life. 'I stand in need of certain simple facts. So – ink? I imagine a priest must have had ink?'

'Aye, he had ink, sir, and plenty of it.' She sounded affronted and went off, presumably to fetch him some.

He sat at the table, gripped the edge of it and took stock of the room. A plain wooden cross hung above the fireplace. The walls were a dull orange brown in the candlelight. The sides leaned in markedly and the ceiling bulged in the centre. Yet the room had a feeling of great solidity and antiquity, as if it had settled centuries before and nothing now would shift it. He imagined the generations of priests who must have sat in this very spot – scores of them, probably – quietly doing God's work in this remote valley, unknown and forgotten. The thought of such unsung devotion humbled him, so that when Agnes returned, he tried to display some humility himself, by bringing over a chair so that she could sit opposite him, and talking to her in a kindly tone.

'Forgive me — I should know this — but how long was Father Lacy priest here?'

'Thirty-two years this January.'

'Thirty-two years? Well nigh a third of a century — a lifetime!' Fairfax had rarely heard of so long a tenure. He dipped his pen in the ink pot and made a note. 'Did he have family?'

'There were a brother, but he died years back.'

'And how long were you in his service?'

'Twenty years.'

'And your husband, too?'

'No, sir, I am long widowed, though I has a niece — Rose.'

'The one who looked after my horse?'

'She lives here in the parsonage with us — with me, I must learn to say.'

'And what is to become of you both now Father Lacy is dead?'

To his dismay, her eyes filled with tears. 'I cannot say. It's been so sudden, I has given it no thought. Perhaps the new priest will wish to keep us on.' She looked at him hopefully. 'Will ye be taking the living, sir?'

'Me?' He nearly laughed out loud at the absurdity of the idea of entombing himself in such a place, but realising how rude it would seem, he managed to stop himself. 'No, Mrs Budd. I am the lowliest member of the bishop's staff. I have duties to attend to in the cathedral. My task is to conduct the burial only. But I shall inform the diocese of the situation.' He made another note and sat back. He sucked on the end of his pen and studied her. 'Could not some local priest have taken the service?'

He had asked the same question of Bishop Pole the previous day when the task of officiating had first been entrusted to him — had phrased it diplomatically, of course, because the bishop was not a man who expected to have his orders interrogated. But the bishop had made a thin line of his mouth, then busied himself with his papers and muttered something about Lacy being a strange fellow and unpopular with his neighbouring colleagues. 'I knew him when he was a young man. We were at the seminary together. Our lives took different paths.' Then he had looked Fairfax straight in the eye. 'This is a good opportunity for you, Christopher. A simple task, yet one that requires some discretion. You should be in and out in a day. I'm relying on you.'

Agnes looked at her hands. 'Father Lacy had no dealings with parsons in t'other valleys.'

'Why not?'

'He went his own way.'

Fairfax frowned and leaned forward slightly, as if

he hadn't quite caught her words. 'I'm sorry. I don't follow you. "He went his own way"? There is but one way, surely – the true way? All else is heresy.'

Still she refused to meet his gaze. 'I cannot rightly answer, Father. Such matters lie beyond me.'

'What about his relations with his parishioners? Was he popular with his flock?'

'Oh aye.' A pause. 'Wi' most.'

'But not all?'

This time she made no answer. Fairfax laid down his pen and rubbed his eyes. Suddenly he felt weary. Well, this was a just chastisement for his pride in the bishop's favour: to ride eight hours to bury an obscure cleric, a heretic possibly, whom a good proportion of his parishioners apparently disliked. At least his eulogy could be short. 'I suppose,' he said dubiously, 'I might speak in general terms – of a life well lived in God's service, and so forth. How old was he when he died?'

'Old, sir, yet still fit enough. He were fifty-six.'

Fairfax calculated. If Lacy had been here thirty-two years, he must have arrived when he was twenty-four – his own age exactly. 'So Addicott was his only parish?'

'Aye, sir.'

He tried to picture himself in the old priest's place. Planted in so quiet a spot, he was sure he would go mad. Perhaps over the years that was what had happened. While Pole had risen to eminence, Lacy had been left to rot out here. An idealistic heart shrivelled to misanthropy by loneliness. 'A third of a century! He must have liked it here.'

'Oh aye, he loved it. He would never leave.' Agnes stood. 'Ye'll be hungry, Father. I've prepared you something to eat.'

CHAPTER THREE

*Fairfax has an early night, and makes
a disturbing discovery*

S**HE SERVED HIM** a simple supper of rabbit and
sheep's heart stew and a jug of strong dark ale,
which she told him Father Lacy had brewed
himself. He invited her to join him, but she excused
herself. She said she had to prepare the refreshments
for the wake. Of the girl Rose there remained no sign.

To start with, Fairfax picked at the food. But by
some strange paradox of digestion, with each tentative
mouthful his appetite revived, so that by the end hc had
eaten the lot. He dabbed at his mouth with his handkerchief. Every experience had a purpose, knowable
only to God. He must make the best of this situation.
The bishop would expect no less, and he would at least
have a good story to tell over dinner at the chapter
house.

He threw another small log on the fire in an effort

to soften the cold, then returned to the table, shifted his plate to one side and took out his Bible and prayer book. He struck a match, lit his pipe and sat back in his chair. For the first time he took notice of the ink pot — ink bottle, in fact. He picked it up and held it to the candle flame. It was of a curious design, three inches long and an inch wide, made of thick clear glass with ribbed sides. It had a hollow angle inset two thirds along the base so that the ink could be pooled conveniently at the smaller end in a reservoir. He had never seen one like it before. It was obviously ancient. He wondered how the old priest had come by it.

He set it down and began to write.

Nothing disturbed the silence save the ticking of the long-case clock in the passage. He became absorbed in his task. Christ's final instruction to the Apostles before his Ascension was that they should stay in the city and await, in contemplation, the arrival of the Lord. Wasn't that what Lacy had done? Stayed humbly where he had been placed and waited for God to show Himself? He could make something of that.

After an hour or so, Agnes returned to clear the table. When she came back from the kitchen, she announced that she was turning in for the night. 'I've made thee a bed in Father Lacy's study.'

She went around extinguishing the candles with a snuffer. He wondered what time it was. Nine? Usually at that hour he would be gathering with the others in the lady chapel for compline. But although it was an earlier retirement than he was used to, he did not complain. He could finish his eulogy in the morning. Besides, he had left Exeter not long after dawn, and his bones ached with weariness. He put his possessions back into his bag and knocked the bowl of his pipe empty against the side of the fireplace.

The study was smaller and more cluttered than the parlour. Agnes carried in two candles and set one down for him on the edge of the desk. The homemade tallow hissed and spluttered. Its yellow glow lit a couch with a thin pillow and a patchwork quilt, doubtless sewn by the housekeeper over the interminable winter evenings. In the shadows beyond its gleam he had a vague impression of well-stocked bookshelves, papers, ornaments. The curtains were already drawn.

'I hopes ye'll be comfortable here. 'Tis but two chambers upstairs – Rose and I shares one, and the parson lies in t'other. Mind,' she added, 'we could move him to the floor if ye'd prefer.'

'No, no,' he said quickly. 'This will do me well enough. It's only for one night.' He sat on the couch. It was hard and unyielding. He smiled. 'After such a day I swear I could sleep standing up. God keep you, Mrs Budd.'

'And ye, Father.'

He listened to the sounds of her locking the front

door and the creak of the boards as she went upstairs. Her footsteps passed above his head. He said his prayers (*Into Thy hands, O Lord . . .*) and lay down on the couch. A minute later, he sat up again. At least a quart of the old priest's strong ale was pressing on his bladder and he was in urgent need of relief. He groped around under the couch for a chamber pot, but found only cobwebs.

He took the candle and went out into the passage. He retrieved his boots from beside the front door and carried them past the parlour and the study towards the rear of the house. In the kitchen, the warm smell of baking lingered. Muslin cloths covered various dishes that Agnes must have made for the wake. He sat on a chair beside the back door and pulled on his boots.

Outside, the blackness and the silence were absolute. Accustomed to the hourly bells and lights of a cathedral city, to the night-time prayers and shuffling feet, to the sounds of the sailors up from the docks on the English Channel running from the patrolling sheriffs, he felt almost dizzy at such nothingness – as if he were poised on the edge of eternity.

And the Earth was without form, and void; and darkness was upon the face of the deep.

It was hopeless to try to find the privy. He ventured forward a few paces, placed the candle-holder on the damp grass, hoisted his cassock, pulled down his drawers, planted his feet apart and pissed into he knew not what. The strong stream made a noise — percussive, unmistakable — that must have been audible on the other side of the valley, let alone upstairs, where he imagined Agnes and Rose cowering in alarm. Again it was all he could do not to burst out laughing.

He shook himself dry, rearranged his clothes, picked up his candle and stumbled back over the grass to the door. The timber was as old as the house, but the lock was new he noticed, as it was at the front. Like many townsmen, he had a romantic notion that country folk never locked their doors. Apparently this was not the case in Addicott St George.

He went back into the study, took off his cassock, threw himself down on the couch and fell immediately asleep.

Something woke him. He was not sure what. The room was in such darkness that between his eyes being shut and open there was no difference. The sensation was alarming, like being blind, or buried alive. He reasoned that if his candle had burned out, it must mean that several hours had passed and that his body had woken him as usual after the first sleep.

He thought he heard a man's voice, muttering something he couldn't quite make out. He strained to listen. There was a pause, and then it came again. He propped himself up on his elbow. Now the first voice was interrupted by a second. Two men were talking – the rolling local dialect, *ye, thee, thou*: low, indistinct, almost musical, like the droning of bees. They were just outside his window.

He rose from the couch and stood swaying for a moment, trying to find his bearings. He edged forward, and at once his knee struck the edge of the desk. He started to utter an oath, quickly stifled it, rubbed his knee, then reached out and began feeling along the wall until he touched fabric. He burrowed his hands into it, mole-like, searching for a gap, parted the curtains, ran his palms over the small diamond-shaped panes of cold glass, found a handle and opened the window. He stuck out his head.

The men had moved on. Away to his right and slightly below him two lights bobbed in the darkness. He guessed he must be looking out at the lane that ran along the side of the parsonage towards the church. Beyond the two lanterns were other, fainter lights, some stationary, a few moving. Far in the distance, a dog barked. He could hear the trundle of cart wheels.

Above his head, the floorboards creaked.

He shut the window and felt his way across the room to the door. He threw it open just as Agnes turned the corner at the bottom of the stairs. She was carrying a candle. Her hair was in curling papers. Over her nightdress she wore an outdoor coat, which she pulled tight around her as soon as she saw him. 'Oh, Father Fairfax – what a fright ye gave me!'

'What hour is this, Mrs Budd? Why does everyone wander about in this strange manner?'

She turned slightly and held her candle to the face of the long-case clock. 'Two o'clock, sir, same as normal.'

'In Exeter, the custom between the first and second sleeps is to stick to our rooms. Yet the villagers here are abroad. What of the curfew? They risk a whipping, surely?'

'Nobody here gives much mind to curfews.' She was carefully avoiding looking at him, and he realised he was wearing only his drawers and undershirt.

He took a pace back into the study and called out through the doorway. 'Forgive my lack of modesty. This middle-of-the-night wandering – the practice is new to me. Might I take another candle? Two, if they can be spared?'

'Wait there, sir, and I'll fetch them.' Her head still averted, she went past him into the kitchen. He searched around in the darkness for his cassock and fastened a few of the buttons, his fingers clumsy with sleep.

'Here's your candles, Father.' She placed them on the floor just outside the study.

He collected both, closed the door and set one upon the desk. Rather than his usual nocturnal meditation, he decided that he might perhaps seek some fresh inspiration for his eulogy. What better way to take the measure of a man than by the nature of his library? He began an inspection of the shelves.

Father Lacy had a hundred books or more, some plainly of great antiquity. In particular, he had a remarkable array of volumes produced by that army of scholars who had dedicated their lives to the study of the Apocalypse. Fairfax ran his finger along the titles — *The Fall of Man* . . . *The Great Flood of Noah* . . . *The Destruction of Sodom and Gomorrah* . . . *God's Wrath Against Babylon* . . . *The Ten Plagues of Egypt* . . . *The Locusts of the Abyss* . . . *The Lake of Fire* . . . What a gloomy fellow he must have been, he thought. Little wonder his fellow priests had shunned him.

He took down a volume at random, *Pouring Out the Seven Disasters: A Study of Revelation 16*. It fell open at a well-marked passage:

> And he gathered them together into a place called in the Hebrew tongue Armageddon.
>
> And the seventh angel poured out his vial into the air; and there came a great voice out of the temple of Heaven, from the throne, saying, It is done.
>
> And there were voices, and thunders, and lightnings; and there was a great earthquake, such as was not since men were upon the Earth, so mighty an earthquake, and so great.
>
> And the great city was divided into three parts, and the cities of the nations fell.

He closed it and replaced it on the shelf. Such a collection would not have been out of place in the bishop's library; to find it in a small parsonage in an isolated village struck him as peculiar.

He took up his candle again and moved along to the second bookcase, where his eye was immediately drawn to a shelf of small volumes bound in pale brown leather. He held the flame up close to the spines — *The Proceedings and Papers of the Society of Antiquaries* — and in that instant he became wide awake, for he recognised the name at once, even though he had been but a boy at the time of the trials. The organisation had been declared heretical, its officers imprisoned, its publications confiscated and publicly burned, the very word 'antiquarian' forbidden from use. He recalled the priests in the seminary lighting a bonfire in the middle of Exeter. It had been midwinter, and the townspeople had been as impressed by the heat as they had by the zealotry. And yet here was a set of the society's works still extant — and in Addicott St George, of all places!

For a few moments, Fairfax stared at the shelf in dismay. Nineteen volumes, with a narrow gap where the twentieth had been withdrawn. What did this mean for his mission tomorrow? Lacy was a heretic: there could be no question of it now. Could a heretic be knowingly buried in consecrated ground? Ought he to postpone the interment, however ripe the corpse, and seek fresh guidance from the bishop?

He considered the matter carefully. He was a practical young man. Not for him the fanaticism of some of his fellow younger clergy, with their straggling hair and beards and their wild eyes, who could sniff out blasphemy as keenly as a water hound unearths truffles. His instructions were to be quick and tactful. Therefore, the wisest course would be to go on as planned and pretend he knew nothing. Nobody could prove otherwise, and, if necessary, he could always square his conscience with God and the bishop at a later date.

Thus resolved in the matter, he resumed his inspection of the study. Two more shelves were entirely devoted to the same perversion. He noted monographs on burial sites, on artefacts, on inscriptions, on monuments. It amazed him that the old priest had displayed them so brazenly. It was as if the valley, with its singular geographic isolation and its contempt for the curfew, existed somehow outside time and law. There was a thick volume on the ruins of England entitled *Antiquis Anglia* by a Dr Nicholas Shadwell, 'President of the Society of Antiquaries'. He passed his candle quickly along the titles, tempted to linger but forcing himself not to look at them too closely, then turned his attention to the display cabinet in the corner of the room.

This was chest high, wood-framed, with a front of glass — ancient glass, he could tell, because it was completely clear and smooth, with none of the rippling effect produced by modern glazing. It was cracked in the top right-hand corner. The shelves were also made of the finest glass, and by the light of the candle the objects they supported seemed to hover magically in mid-air. All of them it was illegal to possess: coins and plastic banknotes from the Elizabethan era, keys, gold rings, pens, glassware, a plate commemorating a royal wedding, thin metal canisters, a bundle of plastic straws, a plastic swaddler with faded images of storks carrying infants, white plastic cutlery, plastic bottles of all shapes and varieties, toy plastic bricks all fitted together of vibrant yellows and reds, a spool of greenish-blue plastic fishing line, a plastic flesh-coloured baby from which the eyes were missing, and, on the topmost shelf, propped up on a clear plastic stand, what seemed to be the pride of the collection: one of the devices used by the ancients to communicate.

Fairfax had seen fragments of them before, but never one in such a perfect state of preservation. He felt drawn to it, and this time, despite himself, he could not resist opening the cabinet and taking it out. It was thinner than his little finger, smaller than his hand, black and smooth and shiny, fashioned out of plastic and glass. It weighed quite heavy in his palm, pleasingly substantial. He wondered who had owned it and how the priest had come by it. What images might it once have conveyed? What sounds might have emerged from it? He pressed the button on the front, as if it might miraculously spring to life, but the glossy surface remained resolutely black and dead, and all he could see was the reflection of his own face, ghostly in the candlelight. He turned it over. On the back was the ultimate symbol of the ancients' hubris and blasphemy – an apple with a bite taken out of it.

CHAPTER FOUR

Wednesday 10th April: an unexpected
incident at the burial

H E BLEW OUT the candles and went back to
bed, pulling the patchwork quilt up to his
chin. In the darkness he found it easier to
put the symbols of the old priest's heresy out of his
mind. Indeed, such was his weariness that, despite his
various perturbations, the hard couch soon seemed to
dissolve beneath him and his breathing became deep
and regular.

His second sleep was more dream-filled than his
first, although afterwards he could not remember any
of them, apart from the last, a recurrent nightmare
that had started soon after his parents and sister had
died of the sweating fever and around the time he
had been sent to live with his elderly uncle. He imagined himself pursued barefoot through a strange
neighbourhood, searching for a particular street, a

certain house, a special door. Only when he found it, after hours of searching — a mean, shabby building in a poor district — and broke open the lock and tumbled over the threshold did he see his family again. Silently, they held out their hands to him, and always in that instant he awoke.

His eyes flickered open. The room was grey with the early light. He felt an ache of unease at the back of his mind, turned his head and saw dimly the glass cabinet with its floating objects. The memory of the night returned.

He threw off the cover and kneeled by the couch. He clenched his hands in prayer so tightly his knuckles shone white. *Dear Father, I thank thee for sparing me to see another day. Grant me I beseech thee the strength to resist temptation, and the piety to serve thy glory today and for ever more. Amen.*

Keeping his eyes from the bookshelves and the cabinet, he stood, drew back the curtains and opened the little window. The air was cool and damp, silent, still. At the bottom of the lane he could see the church with its limp flag, the village behind it, and further beyond that, rising like waves, the steep green sides of the valley dotted with foamy white sheep beneath a low grey threatening sky.

On the table next to the windowsill a jug of water had been put out for him, together with a basin, a small mirror, a towel and a piece of old-fashioned black soap that stank of potash. He couldn't bring himself to use it — to carry around that chemical smell all day would remind him too much of chilly mornings in the seminary, queuing shivering in his underclothes to use the pump.

He splashed his face with the cold water and ran his wet hands through his hair and beard, then inspected his appearance in the mirror. He had let his beard grow as all priests did. Like his hair, it was thick and dark. He was careful to keep it cut square in the modern fashion. And yet it seemed not to impart any sense of gravity to his appearance. His skin, pallid after a winter spent mostly in the cathedral, was too smooth. There was too much youthful eagerness in his eyes. He tried frowning at his reflection, but decided he looked ridiculous.

The clock in the passage showed just after seven. From the kitchen came the sound of pots and pans being moved. He called out, 'Good morning!' and went through into the parlour, where the table had been laid for his breakfast. The window here looked directly along the cart track that served as the village's main street. A woman was carrying a heavy pitcher carefully on her head, presumably on her way back from a communal well. A man in a smock was leading a mule. They greeted one another and walked on together. Fairfax stood watching until they were out of sight.

He heard a noise behind him and turned to find a young woman at the table in the act of setting down a plate. He had not heard her enter. For some reason he had imagined Mrs Budd's niece to be a plain, rough country girl. Instead she was slim, with a pale oval face, large blue eyes, and abundant black hair tied up by a blue ribbon that emphasised her delicate long white neck. The fact that she was dressed in mourning made her appearance all the more striking, and he feared he must have stared too hard at her, for when, after a pause to recover his surprise, he said cheerfully, 'Good morning, you must be Rose – a welcome sight to brighten a drab day!' she turned and fled without a word.

When it was clear she would not be returning, he sat at the table and gazed with regret at the plate of cold mutton and cheese. Such was his tragedy: to possess an ardent nature and yet be denied an outlet for it. In consequence he lacked any aptitude or experience with women. The society at the cathedral was exclusively male: chastity was the prime constraint placed upon the clergy. He could not deny to himself that he regretted the prohibition, but he struggled to observe it and had certainly never thought to question it. And yet it was said that in England before the Apocalypse most priests had been married, and that in the final decades, women themselves had actually been permitted to celebrate Holy Communion! Surely that was not the least of the blasphemies that had brought down God's wrath upon the world.

The door opened again and he turned eagerly in

the hopes of making amends. But it was only Agnes carrying a teapot. 'Good morning, Father.'

'Good morning, Mrs Budd.'

'Ye'll take some tea? Father Lacy favoured Cornish, but we've Highland if ye prefers.'

'Cornish suits me well enough.' He watched her pour it carefully into the bowl, one hand grasping the teapot handle, the other holding the lid. 'I fear I may have startled your niece.'

'Oh, pay her no mind. She's shy as a fawn.'

'Still, I would have liked to have had some conversation with her.' He added, 'About her sadly altered circumstances.'

'Ye'll never do that, more's the pity.'

'Why not?'

'She speaks not.'

'What — never?'

'No, she were born without the talent for it.'

Now he felt his clumsiness even more keenly. 'I am very sorry to hear it.'

'God's will, Father.'

'How old is she?'

'Eighteen.'

After Agnes had gone, he cupped his bowl of tea and tried to imagine what would become of the poor girl after her home was taken from her. Would she return to her family? Would they even take her back given that she was dumb, and presumably hard to marry off, despite her looks? Perhaps, after all, he should ask the bishop if there was any chance he might be able to take the living. He pictured the three of them sharing the house together. By his gentleness he would gain her trust. In the long winter evenings he might even teach her to overcome her affliction. And in his daily struggle to master temptation he would move closer to God. Would it really be such a bad life?

By the time he had finished his tea, Fairfax had almost convinced himself that his destiny would take this improbable — indeed, self-torturing — twist, and he found he was able to set to work on his breakfast with gusto.

He fetched his bag from the study, closed the door firmly, crossed himself, and returned to the parlour to finish writing his address. This had become a much more challenging task since his discoveries between the first and second sleeps, and for the next two hours he struggled to reconcile the teachings of the Church with what he now knew of Father Lacy. He blew on his hands to warm them. He lit another pipe. From time to time he broke off to stare out of the window. The light was not improving. If anything, it was getting darker. Eventually it started to rain — not the soft, misty rain of the previous day, but a real downpour that hammered on the roof and cascaded in waterfalls over the edges of the gutters.

Agnes spent the morning ferrying dishes to the church. Eventually she brought him a candle. From somewhere far in the distance came a heavy boom that rolled around the valley. He looked up. 'Thunder?'

'Can't be thunder with no lightning, Father. That'll be blasting in the quarry.'

'Even in this weather?'

She didn't answer. Something beyond the window had distracted her. A group of five hooded men was coming out of the side gate of the churchyard, their heads bent against the rain. Four looked uncomfortable in their dark Sabbath suits; one wore the red surplice of a parish clerk. They hurried across the road towards the parsonage.

Agnes spoke in a flat voice. 'So they've come to take him. Must be almost time.'

She went to the front door to let them in. He heard their voices – hushed, respectful – and their boots stamping on the flagstone floor to knock off the mud and water. Footsteps clumped up the staircase. Agnes reappeared in the doorway with the red-clad figure behind her. Fairfax got to his feet. She said, 'Father, this is George Keefer, the church clerk.' She stood aside to let him past.

Fairfax recognised him at once by his bald head with its sickle birthmark. Keefer stuck out his hand. 'Ye found us then, Father.'

'Evidently.' Fairfax shook his thick damp palm.

Agnes regarded them with surprise. 'Thee knows each other?'

'We met on the road yesterday,' said Fairfax.

'I'd've guided thee myself,' said Keefer, 'but I'd wool to deliver to the mill before dark.' From upstairs came a noise of hammering. He glanced up at the ceiling. 'I've instructed the coffin should be closed. He's lain a week since, and those as wanted to pay their respects has done so by now. Is that not right, Agnes?'

She said coldly, 'Thou's the clerk, George.'

Such was the effect of his baldness, Fairfax found it hard to estimate Keefer's years. Doubtless he was younger than he looked. Middle twenties, perhaps? Whatever his age, the priest did not care for his attitude, and was of a mind to reproach him for his unfriendliness the previous day, especially given the man's status as a clerk of the Church compared to his own as an ordained minister. He must surely have realised Fairfax was on his way to bury Father Lacy. But the muffled hammering from upstairs reminded him he had weightier matters to attend to than his dignity.

'Well, I suppose we should settle the service, Mr Keefer.' He consulted his notes. 'For hymns, I have chosen "Of the Father's Heart Begotten" and "A Mighty Fortress Is Our God". Unless Father Lacy had some special song he favoured?'

Keefer shrugged. 'Don't know as he did.'

'Then it is decided. And for the lesson, the First Letter to the Corinthians: "We shall not all sleep but we shall all be changed." It is traditional and well fit for the occasion.'

'As ye wish.'

'Who will read it?'

Keefer scratched his head. 'Doubtless Lady Durston'll be there. The Durston family takes first pew by tradition. She knew the parson well as any.'

'Good, then ask Lady Durston. Might there be others who will wish to say a word?'

'We're not folk for talking much before others.'

The first reverberation of the death knell ended their conversation. If there was a more sombre sound in Christendom, Fairfax hoped never to hear it. Between each muffled toll stretched an interval lasting three or four moments, and then it came again – the call for the dead: insistent, inescapable, remorseless.

Fairfax said, 'What time is it, Mrs Budd?'

She looked over her shoulder into the passage. 'Three quarters past ten, Father.'

'We had best begin. Leave me, please.'

After they had withdrawn, Fairfax opened his bag and took out his vestments. He tugged the white alb over his head and smoothed it down to his ankles. Over his shoulders he donned the green and gold chasuble. He unfolded the stole, kissed it, and draped it round his neck. The heavy embroidered material was stiff and unfamiliar. He had only been ordained the previous Michaelmas, and he felt a prickle of nerves, which he immediately suppressed. If he could not conduct a straightforward service in such a backward little spot as this, what hope was there for a career in the priesthood? He gathered together his prayer book, Bible and notes, and went into the passage.

The pall-bearers were still struggling to manoeuvre the coffin down the narrow staircase. They were having to lower it almost vertically. It banged against the walls and banisters and looked as though it might burst open at any moment and spill the old priest in a shower of sawdust down the stairs. Agnes was standing further back along the passage, her hand pressed to her mouth. Rose was behind her. Both had put on black bonnets.

Fairfax pushed past Keefer, who was attempting to supervise, and went halfway up the stairs. He took the edge of the coffin. 'Which way is his head? The head must leave first!' When the box was steadied – two men standing on the bottom stair to hold the rear end, two at the front – he let go and opened the door.

He prayed to God to let the Holy Spirit enter him – for it most certainly was not with him at that moment – and stepped into a blast of rain. On a count of three, the pall-bearers hoisted the coffin up on to their shoulders and swayed out after him. Keefer came next, then Rose and Agnes, who locked the door behind her, and together the little burial party made its way slowly down the garden path and weaving across the muddy lane, skirting the puddles, towards the lychgate. Fairfax could see a couple of horses tethered to hooks set into the wall; a pony and trap waited nearby, and a covered wagon with a team of mules. The bell tolled. The wind whipped his vestments like a sail. He felt as if he had been stranded by the tide and was struggling to reach the shore.

Under the lychgate they went, between the dripping stones, past the waiting mouth of the freshly dug grave towards the shelter of the porch. After a brief pause to shift the load of the coffin, they descended through the open door, down a step worn concave by centuries of use, and into the little church. His impressions were of hushed silence punctuated by an occasional cough; of coldness and a greyish gloom; of a mass of candles at the periphery of his vision; of various faint smells – wax, frankincense, wet clothes, sweat. He walked ahead of the coffin towards the altar and opened his prayer book. The congregation stood.

Centuries earlier, as part of its rejection of scientism, the Church had rooted out the heretical modernised texts of the time before the Apocalypse and had returned Christian worship to the language of the King James Bible. Its twelve thousand words formed the basis of the Authorised National Dictionary – although other words had found their way into common usage, the

Biblical lexicon alone was taught in school. Thus it was English as it was meant by God to be spoken – rich and majestic and purged of all expressions that might permit even the concept of science – that rang around St George's that morning, exactly as it must have done in the olden time before the Fall.

I am the resurrection and the life, saith the Lord: he that believeth in me, though he were dead, yet shall he live: and whosoever liveth and believeth in me shall never die.

Fairfax had a good strong voice. He was aware of heads turning to examine him as he passed. In the crepuscular light it was hard for him to make out the small print, but it did not matter. Lives were short, burials were frequent; he knew the service off by heart.

We brought nothing into this world, and it is certain we can carry nothing out. The Lord gave, and the Lord hath taken away; blessed be the Name of the Lord.

He halted at the altar step and turned. The nave was narrow, the walls dotted with niches containing images of saints – an unusually large number for so small a church. The offertory candles beneath the carved figures flickered starlike in the shadows. The pall-bearers came to a halt beside the waiting trestles, carefully set down the coffin, and bowed towards the altar. Keefer, Agnes and Rose took their places in the second pew. Keefer leaned forward respectfully to whisper in the ear of a woman seated in front of him, who nodded and began looking through her Bible.

Fairfax lifted his arms. 'Let us pray.'

The congregation kneeled.

Lord, thou hast been our refuge: from one generation to another.

Before the mountains were brought forth, or ever the Earth and the world were made: thou art God from everlasting, and world without end.

Thou turnest man to destruction: again thou sayest, Come again, ye children of men.

For a thousand years in thy sight are but as yesterday: seeing that is past as a watch in the night . . .

At the end of the prayer, to his surprise, it was Rose who stood and walked past him to the organ. Somewhere, unseen, the bellows wheezed and clattered. She played the opening bars with delicate precision, then paused. The mourners rustled through the pages of their hymn books. The ancient tune began.

> Of the Father's love begotten,
> Ere the worlds began to be,
> He is Alpha and Omega,
> He the source, the ending He . . .

As he sang, Fairfax let his gaze travel across the congregation. Despite the foul weather, upwards of a hundred people had turned out to pay their respects – ragged, skinny, weather-coarsened country folk, drably dressed, with an ugly scattering of disfigurements that told of hard births, heavy work and poor diets. Nevertheless, their voices rose in tuneful acclamation. The rain thumped down on the roof.

At the end of the hymn, he nodded to the woman in the front pew, whom he took to be Lady Durston. She rose to her feet with her Bible open. She was at least a person of quality. He could tell at once by the upright way she carried herself, as well as by her costume. She wore a tailored jacket and ankle-length skirt of dark green velvet, both somewhat frayed and faded but obviously expensive and doubtless once fashionable. Her hair was russet, gathered up beneath a matching velvet bonnet. She mounted the pulpit with confidence and took a moment to gather her concentration before she spoke.

Behold, I shew ye a mystery: We shall not all sleep, but we shall all be changed, in a moment, in the twinkling of an eye, at the last trump (for the trumpet shall sound), and the dead shall be raised incorruptible, and we shall be changed . . .

She read the lesson faultlessly in a clear and pleasing voice and returned to her place. The man next to her — her husband, presumably — patted her gloved hand approvingly. Fairfax climbed the few steps to the pulpit and placed his notes on the lectern.

'Friends, we have come together this morning to bid farewell to Father Thomas James Lacy, cut off at the age of two score and sixteen by an evil chance—'

Somewhere at the back a man said loudly and mockingly, 'Evil chance!'

Fairfax stopped and looked up to see who had spoken. The congregation stirred and turned. A few muttered in annoyance; some told the man to hush. He was seated at the back, half hidden by a pillar. Fairfax tried again. 'Father Lacy, cut off at the age of two score and sixteen by an evil chance. His death reminds us—'

' "Chance" is falsehood, pure and simple!' The accent was educated, the voice loud, albeit thinned and tuned to a higher pitch by old age. 'No, I shall not hush!' he protested irritably to someone nearby. 'It's you who all should hush and wake up to the truth!'

A murmur of conversation broke out all around the church. Fairfax could hear his heart beating in his ears. 'Please, friends, recall the gravity of our purpose—' But his voice was lost in the hubbub.

Suddenly the man sitting next to Lady Durston threw down his hymnal and sprang from his place. His face was rough and his muscular shoulders and neck were out of proportion to the rest of his body, red as brick. He put Fairfax in mind of a minotaur. As he stalked towards the back of the nave the congregation fell silent. He reached the cause of the disturbance, leaned down and communicated something briefly and quietly. His bulk obscured Fairfax's view of what was happening. There was a noise of movement. A few moments later, two figures passed through the shadows at the back of the church, one apparently leading the other. The door opened and then closed again. Lady Durston's companion watched them go, arms akimbo, then let his hands fall loosely by his sides, turned and marched back up the aisle. He retrieved his hymn book, resumed his place and nodded to Fairfax to continue.

Fairfax ploughed on through the remainder of his address. 'His death reminds us that the Lord may call us to His judgement at any moment. *So teach us to number our days, that we may apply our hearts unto wisdom . . .*'

He spoke of the sacredness of service, of the long and quiet value of being planted in one place, of the shepherd and his flock, and expounded various other pieties, and when it was over, he realised his hands were clenching the lectern so tightly they were spread stiff as griffin's claws. He came down out of the pulpit and announced the second hymn. It seemed to him to be sung with a certain collective defiance that was intended to show disapproval of the heckler. When it was finished, the coffin was lifted back on to the shoulders of the pall-bearers and Fairfax led the procession out of the church. He looked around for the mourner who had interrupted his sermon, but apart from the sexton and his boy, there was no one in the churchyard.

The rain was still falling, chill as winter, cold as death. It spattered the pages of his prayer book. Wooden planks had been laid around the open grave. They sank beneath his weight. Mud oozed up between them. Water was running down the mound of excavated earth and pooling in the bottom of the pit. He worried that if he left it much longer, the coffin might end up floating, and decided he should make a start on the committal prayers even before the last of the mourners had arrived at the graveside.

Man that is born of a woman hath but a short time to live, and is full of misery. He cometh up, and is cut down, like a flower; he fleeth as it were a shadow, and never continueth in one stay . . .

The pall-bearers laid the coffin across two lengths of rope and inched it over the open grave where it hung briefly suspended before they started to lower it in a series of jerks. When it was about halfway down, one of them paid out his rope too quickly. The slippery hemp ran through his hands, the coffin tilted and dropped the last couple of feet and landed with a splash. Had he not been responsible for the ceremony, Fairfax might have conceded that the scene had a certain grim comedy.

The mourners filed past, each taking a handful of soil to throw into the grave. Lady Durston paused the longest, tugging off her green calfskin glove and digging her hand, regardless of the dirt, into the chalky earth. She let it trickle through her slim fingers on to the coffin lid, gazed down at it for a moment or two in profound contemplation, then lifted the bottom of her skirt and stepped away.

Forasmuch as it hath pleased Almighty God of His great mercy to take unto Himself the soul of our dear brother here departed, we therefore commit his body to the ground; earth to earth, ashes to ashes, dust to dust; in sure and certain hope of the Resurrection to eternal life, through our Lord Jesus Christ . . .

He gabbled through the Lord's Prayer and the collect and by the time he came to intone the blessing, most people had abandoned decorum and were running for cover. The instant he closed his prayer book, the sexton and his boy began shovelling soil into the grave pit, working with such haste that within less than a quarter of an hour the mortal remains of Father Thomas Lacy were entirely buried – vanished to join the millions of other bones that had lain ten thousand years or more beneath the ancient Wessex ground, and whose voices had called to him so urgently while he was yet alive.

CHAPTER FIVE

In which Fairfax's plans are thwarted

THE WAKE WAS held in a two-storey thatched building that belonged to the church and stood on the opposite side of the graveyard to the parsonage. The church ale-house, as it was known, like the priest's house, was many centuries old – leaning sideways, its sagging walls shored up by timber buttresses along a southern flank that was a patchwork of ancient yellow stone, pale cement and modern brick, the whole edifice licked by tongues of dark green ivy. And yet it too felt solid, as if it had finally settled and would stand for several more centuries yet.

A large log fire was burning in the open hearth. Beside it stood an iron spit, long enough on a feast day to roast an entire pig. The room was fuggy and noisy. Mourners crowded around the fire to dry themselves. Clay pipes had been lit. Smoke mingled with the steam issuing from their wet clothes. Agnes and Rose were bent over a trestle table, uncovering dishes of food. Beneath the table, children played. A queue of mostly men and some women waited to fill pewter tankards from barrels of ale and cider.

Fairfax observed the scene from just inside the doorway. He was looking for Keefer. Certain formalities needed to be completed before he could get away – filling out the register, signing it, having it witnessed – for which he needed the assistance of the clerk. Then he would take to the road. The weather was foul, but so be it: he was young and fit and unafraid of a drenching. More than ever he was determined to be in Axford by mid afternoon.

Unable to locate Keefer, he took a few paces into the room, and for the first time his presence was noticed. The volume of conversation dropped, as if they were ashamed of their levity. Faces turned sombre. Heads were briefly nodded.

'Father.'

'Father.'

' 'Twere a fine service, Father.'

' "A word fitly spoken is like apples of gold in pictures of silver." '

'Thank you. My blessings upon you.' He tried to acknowledge them all with a single gracious turn of his head. 'My lord bishop wished me to convey his sorrow at the loss of so long-serving a priest. May he now enjoy the rest he deserves.'

'Amen.'

'Amen to that.'

He crossed himself.

'We was just discussin' that feller what cried out in church, Father.'

'Oh yes,' said Fairfax. He swung round to the speaker, an old man with a mass of white whiskers. 'Who *was* that?'

'None knows.'

'He weren't from round 'ere.'

'He's buggered off now, whoever he were.'

'Not just one man. Two of 'em, 'twere.'

'Anyways, Captain Hancock soon sorted him out.'

Fairfax wished he had got a proper look at the interlopers. 'What do you suppose he meant when he said that Father Lacy's death was no mere chance?'

The old man said cheerfully, 'Oh, that he were taken by the devils, no doubt about it.'

'The devils?'

'The devils that sit in the Devil's Chair.'

'And what is the Devil's Chair?'

'The name of the place he fell — a lonely, fearsome spot.'

One of the women cut in briskly, 'Pay him no mind, Father. He's just a nervy old fool.'

'I ain't nervy! Devils exist and 'tis heresy to say otherwise! Is that not so, Parson?'

'There is evil in the world, no doubt of that, sir,

whatever form it may assume.' Fairfax was suddenly anxious to extract himself from the discussion. 'I mustn't interrupt you any longer. I was looking for Mr Keefer.' He was met with shrugs and blank faces. Nobody had seen the clerk since the burial.

He went over to Agnes, who was cutting a pie. 'A handsome spread, Mrs Budd, most fit for the occasion.'

'Ye'll take a piece of pie, Father?'

'Thanks, but no. I must be on my way. That was beautifully played, Rose.' The girl smiled faintly and glanced down. Fairfax turned back to Agnes. 'Where is Mr Keefer?'

'Gone to church, sir, to fetch the register.'

'Ah,' he exclaimed with relief. 'So that is where he is! In which case, while I wait, I will indeed take a piece of your pie, if I may, to fortify me for the journey.'

'Will ye say a few words of grace for us, Father?'

'Gladly.' He banged a knife against a glass jug and the noise of conversation quickly ceased. He bowed his head. 'Bless, O Lord, this food for thy use, and make us ever mindful of the wants and needs of others. Amen.'

'Amen.'

The chatter resumed. He picked up his plate and dug a fork into the pie. He was hungry; he was always hungry, yet he remained as thin as a stray dog. His body seemed determined to make up for all the food it had missed during the years when he was at the seminary. And a very good pie it was, of game and hard-boiled egg, and to wash it down he consented to take a tankard of ale, which Rose went and fetched for him.

Seeing him standing there, eating and drinking, the local people became emboldened, and more of them began edging over to him to thank him for the service — one or two, very shyly, at first, but after a while a small crowd was gathered. Agnes introduced them: George Revel and George Rogan, who were farmers; John Gann the blacksmith, who had served as one of the pall-bearers; Alison Kern and her sister Mercy, who were wardens of the light before the statue of the Virgin Mary; Jacob Rota, the night soil man; Jack Singer, a shepherd, his face browned by a long life lived outdoors, and his friend Frank Waterbury, the rat-catcher, who tended Our Lady's sheep on behalf of the Church; John Lusty and Paul Fisher and Paul Fuente, weavers . . .

Fairfax didn't catch every name and occupation, but it was clear their lives had all been touched by the old priest in some way — christened by him, taught by him at the village school, married by him, their parents and their siblings and even — tragically and quite commonly — their children buried by him; and slowly, as they reminisced, Father Lacy began to come alive, to assume a personality, and he regretted that he had not had the opportunity to collect their memories before he wrote his eulogy.

'He loved this valley – knew every inch of it . . .'

'He were a great one for walking . . .'

'Went everywhere on foot . . .'

'Can't recall as I ever saw him on a horse . . .'

'It were that what did for him in the end, of course.' This remark, from Gann the blacksmith, was greeted by wistful nods.

'A very learned sort of a gentleman . . .'

'Never without a trowel and a little bag to put his discoveries in . . .'

'Best of all he loved the little ones in school . . .'

'Do ye remember when we was little how he used to give us a shilling if we brought him a treasure?'

'Half a crown if it were something good . . .'

Fairfax's interest was aroused. 'What manner of treasures were these?'

'Oh, anything from the ancient time – coins with Old King Charles's head on 'em. Bottles. Bits of glass. Rubbish mostly.'

'Remember that old doll I found in Tremble's meadow? He loved that! Gave me a pound for it.'

'I suppose he could come over as a little bit strange, if ye didn't know him . . .'

'More so latterly . . .'

'Not all liked him for it . . .'

Fairfax interjected. 'In what regard?'

'Well, there's always folks that talk – more so in a cut-off little place like this.'

'What sort of things were said of him?'

There was a hesitation, glances were exchanged.

'It weren't my opinion, but some said he neglected the Scriptures in favour of his own ideas . . .'

'It's true his sermons were of a peculiar sort . . .'

Rota, the night soil man, who had a bad case of the cross-eye, folded his arms and said significantly, 'I heard tell the bishop sent a priest in deep disguise to spy on him for heresy . . .'

'I heard t'same . . .'

Fairfax looked from one to the other. The bishop had mentioned no such investigation to him. He fell silent as he pondered this, and someone else – it was the blacksmith, Gann – began pressing him to try a pull of tobacco. Fairfax waved it away politely, but the blacksmith was insistent: 'I grows it myself. Ye'll not smoke better this side of Axford.'

Reluctantly he took the grubby long-stemmed pipe and wiped the tip. The tobacco was strong – too strong: it burned his mouth and made his eyes water. He started to cough like a schoolboy trying to smoke for the first time, turned his head away and blindly handed it back.

'Now, John Gann,' came a loud, stern voice, 'don't ye go poisoning the father with your noxious weed.'

The effect of the intervention on the little group was immediate. They glanced behind them and parted – as if by Aaron's rod, thought Fairfax — turning away and returning meekly to the fire without another word.

'I trust they've not been boring ye with their local tales.' It was the man who had risen from his place in church to silence the disturbance. He advanced and stuck out a strong, square-wristed hand. 'John Hancock. And this,' he said, with the flourish of a collector presenting a prized possession, 'is Sarah, Lady Durston, of Durston Court.'

'Why he must always mention my house in the same breath as my name I cannot think.' Lady Durston smiled at Fairfax and offered him a gloved hand. 'Sometimes I believe he regards it as my principal attraction.'

'Ye know very well that's not the case!' Hancock seemed irritable, as if this was the continuation of some earlier quarrel. 'I don't know why ye say such things.'

She ignored him and continued to stare at Fairfax. Her eyes were a striking bluish-green; her features firm-jawed, sharp-cheeked; her complexion pale, freckled, in keeping with her red hair. She was in her thirties: married, he assumed, but not apparently to this man. Her glove concealed her wedding ring finger.

'It was kind of you to come all the way from Exeter to our little church.'

'The visit has been most memorable. And thank you, your ladyship, for your reading.'

'She did it well. I told her as much, did I not, Sarah?'

'Will you be staying long in the valley, Mr Fairfax?'

'Alas, I must leave today.'

'Then the loss is ours, for we are short of educated company.'

'Not that short!' said Hancock. He laughed to show he meant it as a joke, revealing a gold tooth, but there was no humour in his face. 'If ye mean to go, go now, sir. There's but one road out this time of year, and a treacherous way when the rain is heavy.'

'I'm sure that's wise advice. And thank you for quelling that noisy fellow in church. He seems entirely unknown in the village.'

'Never seen him in my life before, and never shall again, I'm confident.'

'Why is that?'

'Because I told him if he could not hold his tongue I'd put my fist between his teeth and hold it for him.'

Sarah Durston caught Fairfax's gaze. Her eyes widened slightly in shared amusement. Fairfax said, 'Well, if you'll forgive me, I must attend to the register and then be gone. Lady Durston.' He nodded to her. 'Captain Hancock.'

He went back out into the rain. He hoisted up his vestments with one hand, tried to shield his head with the other, and ran across the graveyard towards the church. From the distant quarry came another boom, which trembled the air and reverberated around the valley. He reached the porch and turned the heavy ring handle of the studded oak door. The noise clattered in the deserted nave.

'Mr Keefer!' He advanced up the aisle towards the altar, looking about him for the clerk. 'Mr Keefer!' The parish's guardian saints stared out at him from their niches and tabernacles. Their expressions seemed to shift in the light of their candles. Some he recognised – St George, of course, the patron saint of England, with his spear plunged into the belly of a rearing dragon; St Anthony with his pigs, the healer of animals; St Anne, the patron saint of childbirth, pointing to the infant in her womb – but others were unknown to him: obscure icons, all male, their significance lost in history, who must once have had some local meaning but whose worship would nowadays be considered idolatrous. The bishop would have apoplexy if he saw them.

He reached the altar rail. To the left a small door stood ajar. He heard a crash followed by a groan.

'Mr Keefer?'

He went forward cautiously, pushed open the door and descended a step into the little low-ceilinged vestry. Keefer was on his knees with his back to him, muttering to himself. At first Fairfax thought he was praying or performing some kind of lamentation, but then he saw that he was emptying a wooden cupboard. Scattered across the floor around him was a profusion of prayer books, candlesticks, chalices, vestments, communion wine bottles and wafers, dusty papers.

'Mr Keefer? What is this?'

Keefer gave a panicky glance over his shoulder. All his former cockiness had disappeared. 'The register's gone.'

'What?'

'Should be here,' he said helplessly. ''Tis always kept here, under lock and key with t'others.'

'Perhaps it has been put somewhere else in the church?'

'But I've searched all over!'

To his surprise, Fairfax saw that the clerk had tears in his eyes. 'Well, do not weep about it, Mr Keefer. I am sure it will be found. Who else has the key?'

'Only the parson.'

'Then he must have removed it somewhere – to the parsonage, perhaps.'

''Tisn't only the current book that's gone, though – 'tis all four of them that's missing.'

'Four?'

'The older volumes go back more than a thousand year! "Books of great antiquity and value", he called them. I has a terrible feeling we've been robbed, Father.'

'Surely not. Does the place look as though it has been broken into?'

'No — not as I can tell.'

'Then it's almost certain that Father Lacy must have been the one who took them. Make straight this mess, and I'll go directly and ask Mrs Budd for the key to the parsonage.'

Fairfax retraced his steps to the door of the church and out into the downpour. This time he did not bother to cover his head or hoist his vestments above the mud. He marched past Lacy's newly heaped grave towards the church ale-house. Someone had taken up a violin and was playing a lament, and the combination of the plangent tune floating through the rain and the headstones and the drenching grey sky created within him a sensation of the utmost melancholy. He went inside, ignored the enquiring eyes that greeted his reappearance, and beckoned urgently to Agnes.

'Did Father Lacy take the church registers back to the parsonage?'

'No, sir. They always stays in church.'

'And yet he must have moved them, for they aren't there now. May I have the key to the parsonage?'

'No — it can't be. Those're big old books. I'd've seen if he'd brought them home.'

'Well, they must be found, wherever they are, and quickly.' He could see Lady Durston and John Hancock watching him. 'They are important legal records. I shall look for them myself. His study's the likeliest place. Please give me the key.'

'I'll come with ye.'

'No, you are needed here.'

'No, sir, I should come. Rose can manage.'

He threw up his hands. He liked to think of himself as an equable man, but he was losing patience. 'As you wish.'

Keefer was waiting for them, sheltering in the porch, and together they half walked, half ran out of the graveyard and across the lane to the parsonage. Agnes pulled out a new iron key from beneath her bodice and let them in.

The house felt peculiarly forlorn, its silence emphasised by the long tick of the clock, as if the physical removal of the old priest's corpse had severed its connection with the living world and robbed it of its purpose. Fairfax said, 'Mrs Budd, why don't you look upstairs? Mr Keefer, if you take the parlour, I shall search the study.'

Once he was inside, he closed the door, leaned his back against it and surveyed the room. There were so many books, there must be a chance that the registers – which would be large, in his experience, like merchants' ledgers – might be concealed among the others. But a thorough examination of the shelves yielded nothing. He turned his attention to the desk. The drawers were unlocked and crammed with objects – pens, a penknife, twine, rulers, pins, writing paper, a magnifying glass, sealing wax and a small pocket telescope in one; fossils, pieces of flint, bits of metal and glass, bottle tops and yet more coloured plastic straws in the other – mere gewgaws, he thought with a frisson of distaste, like a jackdaw's nest. There was no space for large books, only a yellowing bundle of Lacy's old sermons tied up with a black ribbon. He looked under the couch, behind and beneath the display cabinet and the little table. He even got down on his hands and knees and examined the floorboards in case one was loose and concealed some secret cavity. Nothing.

He sat back on his heels and tried to settle upon a course of action. It would be a black mark against him to return to the cathedral and confess that on his very first assignment as an ordained priest he had been unable to complete the legal formalities. That suggested he ought to stay and get to the bottom of it. On the other hand, 'be in and out in a day' had been his instruction. And the disappearance of the registers was hardly his responsibility, but rather part of a pattern of irregularities – the heretical texts, the obsession with antiquities, the apparently bizarre sermons, even the obscure saints – that pre-dated his arrival and was far beyond his competence as a junior priest to investigate. He should stick to his original plan, and go.

He returned to the passage, where both Agnes and Keefer stood empty-handed. 'Nothing?'

They shook their heads.

'Well, this is a mystery, and a serious one. I shall have to disclose it to the bishop, and no doubt he will want to pursue the matter further.' He saw the fear in their faces and hastened to reassure them. 'None of this is your fault – I shall make that clear. Keep on looking, by all means, but lose no sleep over it. Soon there will be a new priest, and a fresh start, and I am certain God will continue to hold His faithful children in this fine valley very close to His heart.' He pressed his hands together in what he hoped was a suitably pious gesture, then rubbed his palms. 'Now, Mrs Budd, I need to pack up my things, and I should be obliged if Rose could be sent back to fetch me my horse.'

She bowed her head. 'Very well, Father.'

'Good. Thank you both for all you've done. I hope that perhaps one day we may meet again in happier times.' He shook hands with each in turn, and blessed them.

When the door was closed he went into the parlour and began to disrobe. His outer vestments were soaking, but his cassock was dry enough. He folded the alb, chasuble and stole inside out and replaced them in his bag, along with his Bible, prayer book, pipe and pen. He had not long finished fastening his cape when he heard the sound of horse's hooves in the road outside.

He paused in the passage with his hand on the

doorknob and took a last look round before stepping outside.

Rose was waiting at the gate, holding the bridle of his horse. She was standing like a sentinel, oblivious to the rain, which had drenched her black dress so that it clung to her slim figure as a second skin. Strands of dark hair were plastered to her face. She flicked them away with her free hand, and for the first time when he spoke to her she looked up straight into his eyes.

'Thank you, child.' He took the bridle and squeezed her hand, and then on a sudden impulse that afterwards made him blush with shame, and which he would never have succumbed to had he not been sure he would never see her again, he raised her cold white fingers to his lips and kissed them. 'God bless you, dear Rose.' Then he pulled himself up on to the horse and without looking back set off down the lane.

As he rode past the church ale-house he could hear the violin distinctly. What had once been a lament now sounded remarkably like a jig, and it occurred to him that the burial had become a day's holiday for the village — a gathering that by the sound of it would probably go on until nightfall. He could still hear the tune as he reached the end of the main street, and it was not until the road began to climb out of the valley that the music was at last drowned out by the incessant rush and hiss of rain.

The track steepened and became a stream. Torrents of brownish-yellow water ran downhill. May would go no faster than walking pace. It must have taken the best part of half an hour to reach the point where the lane finally curved towards the ridge of the hill, and it was only as they rounded the corner that Fairfax glimpsed, above the trees to his right and up ahead, a lateral brown scar where a part of the steep slope had sheared away, taking the trees and rocks with it. They had tumbled down as if they had been tipped out of some giant's sack – a narrow glacier of mud and stones, roots and splintered timber that spilled out of the wood and lay across the road.

He rode up to it and stopped. The barrier was at least as high as his head. It blocked his way entirely. He dismounted and began to climb it, sinking up to his calves in the wet mud. He clutched at protruding branches and hauled himself out of the sucking mire, toiling to the top, where he stood like a general surveying a battlefield, with his hands on his hips, squinting into the rain. The obstruction was not very wide – ten feet, if that – and beyond it the road was frustratingly clear. The reality of his situation slowly settled upon him. There was simply no way past. He bowed his head in resignation to his fate.

The journey back down to the village was as

laboured as his ascent, but worse, for he knew what awaited him. He hitched his mare to the wall of the graveyard, slung his bag over his shoulder and slouched towards the church ale-house. His reappearance was greeted with knowing looks. They were familiar with what the road was like in this weather. A chair was fetched for him and placed in front of the fire so that he could dry himself. A tankard of ale was put in his hand. The violinist struck up another merry tune, a song from the olden days. People began to dance. He looked around for Sarah Durston and John Hancock, but both had left. Rose would not meet his eye. Oh God, he thought, oh God . . .

He drained the tankard and was urged to take another. How friendly everyone was! He ate more pie. At some point, Mercy Kern asked him to dance. She was passably pretty, despite the hairy mole on her chin. It seemed churlish to refuse.

> Here's a health to the King, and a lasting peace.
> May faction end and wealth increase.
> Come, let us drink it while we have breath,
> For there's no drinking after death.

He had a vague recollection of people standing in a circle and clapping and stamping in time with the music as the tempo increased and he whirled her around the floor.

And he that will this health deny,
Down among the dead men, down among the dead men,
Down, down, down, down;
Down among the dead men let him lie!

The walls seemed to detach themselves and spin faster and faster. After that, his memory was hazy.

CHAPTER SIX

A hand reaches out from the past

A MATCH STRUCK, flared blue in the darkness. The brilliance of it pierced his eyes. He squinted. His fingers trembled as he touched it to the candle wick. The yellow flame stuttered and swelled. The shadowed unfamiliar room danced into view. His nostrils detected chloride of lime and he realised he was in the old priest's bedroom – that he was in fact lying in Father Lacy's bed – and that he was naked. The match burned down to his fingers. He dropped it and collapsed back on to his pillow.

Oh God, oh God . . .

He struggled to sit up and immediately felt an ominous roiling in his stomach, as if he had swallowed some writhing serpent or a fat black maybug with flailing legs. He lurched to the window and managed to open it just in time to retch into the front garden. His mouth was full of bile and fragments of half-digested game pie. He coughed and spat and rested his hot cheek against the cold panes.

The rain had ceased at last. He could smell hawthorn, parsley, wet grass. Above the church was a bright half-moon that outlined its square tower. Lights were moving in the village. He could hear the wheels of a cart. It must be that strange perambulatory hour, he thought, between the first and second sleeps.

When he was confident he wasn't going to be sick again, he stepped back carefully into the room. Now that he had voided his stomach, he felt surprisingly sober, apart from a desperate thirst and a dusty throb behind his eyes. He ran his hands over his body. He could find no bruises or abrasions. How had he ended up here? Try as he might, he could not recall his journey back from the wake. And where were his clothes? In a belated attempt at modesty, he dragged the sheet from the bed and wrapped himself up, then took the candle and searched the room. There was not much to see. A small wardrobe. A plain wooden chair. A chest of drawers with a basin, jug and mirror on top of it. His bag was by the door, with his purse still in it. But there was no sign of his cassock or underclothes. His humiliation was complete.

He lifted the jug of water to his lips, took a few deep gulps, then bent his face over the washbowl and emptied the remainder over his head.

He lay down on the bed and stared at the raftered

ceiling. He suspected they had got him drunk on purpose, in order to make a fool of him, but he had no one to blame but himself. *Dear Father, forgive me for the shame I have brought upon thy holy office* . . .

For several minutes he remained without moving, pondering how best to make his escape from Addicott St George. Once he had recovered his clothes, he could try to leave on foot — scale the mudslide in the road and walk to Axford; it would take him four or five hours. But how would he get from Axford to the cathedral? And how would it look to return without May? Perhaps he could find some way through the woods and lead her? It did not strike him as a realistic prospect. Eventually he rolled over on to his side, meaning to try to go back to sleep, and instead found himself eye to eye with Father Lacy's rimless spectacles. They were lying on top of a small book bound in pale brown leather and had a steely, reproachful look that reminded him of the bishop. He moved the glasses gingerly to one side, picked up the book and held it close to his face. *The Proceedings and Papers of the Society of Antiquaries*, Volume XX — the volume missing from the shelves downstairs.

He hesitated, sniffed the leather and ran his thumbs over its scratched surface, then toyed with the cover. It was another sin he was contemplating: sin upon sin, the serpent's apple. *Ye shall not eat of it, neither shall ye touch it, lest ye die.* Yet he was curious, and youthful inquisitiveness, despite his indoctrination, on this occasion overcame his training. He sat up and rearranged his pillow to support his back and opened the book.

At first he was disappointed. It was soon apparent that the volume consisted merely of the minutes of the society's meetings over a period of four years, bound together in book form. The paper was of poor quality, the type small and crooked, like a row of bad teeth, the binding loose; it looked and felt like an amateur production. The members assembled quarterly at a London tavern, the Crown and Garter in Pall Mall, and their meetings invariably followed the same pattern. First they would discuss the business of the society: correspondence, approval of minutes, admission of new members, the acquisition of objects offered for sale, the exhibition of antiquities belonging to the society, which archaeological projects should be funded and which abandoned. Then they would listen to a paper presented by a member. The same names recurred: Mr Shadwell (President), Mr Quycke (Secretary), Captain Stewart (Treasurer), Mr Shirley, Colonel Denny, Mr Howe, Mr Berkeley, Mr Fauquier . . . Perhaps four dozen men in all. The papers reported on excavations of grave sites, of houses and factories, and of a great wide straight highway to the north of London that was almost a hundred feet across; they catalogued discoveries (fragments of travelling machines constructed of metal that were now barely more than rust stains in the earth, instruments for communication, household utensils, public statues and memorials); and they aired theories ('How did the ancients make music?', 'What was lost in The Cloud?', 'Tombstone inscriptions of the late pre-Apocalypse era', 'The Great Exodus of London').

Much of it was too arcane for him to understand, and he leafed through it quickly until about two thirds of the way through he came across the striped feather of a partridge protruding from the top of the pages. It drifted down on to his chest. The meeting it marked had been held at the end of spring some thirteen years previously. After the approval of the minutes, matters arising and correspondence, the fourth item on the agenda was a report by the President.

Fairfax rolled on to his side and held the text closer to the candle.

Mr Shadwell begged leave to notify the society of a most significant discovery that had recently been made in the course of the excavation of the mass grave at Winchester.

A plastic box had been uncovered containing correspondence addressed to a Professor Geoffrey Chandler, a fellow of Trinity College, Cambridge. Unfortunately, there had been an ingress of damp that had destroyed, or rendered indecipherable, the bulk of the material. One letter, however, had been sealed in its own plastic wallet, and this was found to be in near-perfect condition. Mr Shadwell had made a copy, and asked permission to read it aloud to the society. His proposal was approved unanimously.

Imperial College, London, 22 March 2022
Dear Colleague,

Forgive this impersonal form of address. I am sending the same letter, as a matter of urgency, to a number of highly placed individuals — mostly in the scientific community but also some involved in industry, medicine, agriculture and the arts — whose work I esteem, and with whom I hope to communicate on a more personal level at a later date. For reasons that will become obvious, I would be grateful if you would treat what I am about to say as confidential.

Three months ago I formed, with a group of like-minded colleagues, a working party to consider what contingency measures should be taken to prepare for a systemic collapse of technical civilisation. If you do not share this concern, and especially if you regard such a notion as alarmist nonsense, please discard this letter now!

We have broadly identified six possible catastrophic scenarios that fundamentally threaten the existence of our advanced science-based way of life:

1. *Climate change*
2. *A nuclear exchange*
3. *A super-volcano eruption, leading to rapidly accelerated climate change*
4. *An asteroid strike, also causing accelerated climate change*
5. *A general failure of computer technology due either to cyber warfare, an uncontrollable virus, or solar activity*
6. *A pandemic resistant to antibiotics*

Our purpose is not to propose counter-measures to avert any of these potential catastrophes — a task that, in the cases of 3 and 4, is in any case impossible — but to devise strategies for the days, weeks, months and years following such a disaster, with the aim of the earliest possible restoration of technical civilisation.

We regard our society as having reached a level of sophistication that renders it uniquely vulnerable to total collapse. The gravity of the threat has increased vastly since 2000, with the transfer of so much economic and social activity to cyberspace, and yet there has been no corresponding contingency planning at government level.

A prolonged general interruption to computer networks, for example, would lead within twenty four hours to food and fuel shortages — especially in urban areas — a dramatic curtailing of money supply (due to the loss of ATMs, credit card transactions and online banking), communications and information breakdowns, transport shutdown, panic buying, mass exodus and civil disorder. Interruption of food distribution in particular, which relies upon computer-based information networks for round-the-clock resupply, would have serious consequences within a matter of hours. Thirty years ago, the average British household contained enough food to last eight days; today the average is two days. It is no exaggeration to say that London, at any time, exists only six meals away from starvation.

Our fear is that an initial collapse could spread exponentially and at a speed that might rapidly overwhelm any official response. Vital workers might desert their posts, or be unable to reach them. Data might be lost irretrievably. Key sectors and technologies could be affected to such an extent that our chances of finding our way back to the status quo ante could diminish alarmingly quickly.

I have myself made repeated representations at the highest levels of government and the civil service, and have been met effectively with a shrug. The general level of understanding in Westminster and Whitehall of the impact of new technologies is abysmal. Rather than do nothing, therefore, we have decided to take matters into our own hands, and attempt to devise practical steps to safeguard our present highly developed way of life.

All civilisations consider themselves invulnerable; history warns us that none is.

If you wish to play your part, I invite you to contact me, by letter, at the above address, at your earliest possible convenience. For security, all communications will be paper rather than electronic. I stress again the need for strict confidence: we have no desire to attract media attention and cause a general panic.

Yours sincerely,

Peter Morgenstern

Mr Shadwell stated that ever since the discovery of the document he had been endeavouring to find out more about Morgenstern and his group, so far without success. It was impossible to say whether they had continued to meet, or done anything more than talk. Morgenstern himself was clearly an eminent figure of the late pre-Apocalypse era, for his name appeared upon a list of winners of the Nobel Prize that was extant in the hands of a private collector. (Mr Shadwell explained that this was an award made once per annum for over a century to figures of the greatest renown in the sciences and literature.) Morgenstern had received the said prize for the science of physic. But as far as was in Mr Shadwell's competence to discover, no published work of his had survived.

Mr Shadwell proposed that he should continue his researches, and to that end requested the award of a sum of £100 to defray his expenses. After a discussion, this was agreed, and the Treasurer was instructed to make the necessary funds available.

The business of the society having been concluded, the meeting was adjourned at half past nine.

Fairfax slowly laid the book face down on his chest. The language was difficult, the words obscure. It was the first time he had encountered the strange, abrupt, forbidden rhythms of pre-Apocalypse writing. And yet he felt he had been able to penetrate it sufficiently to grasp the essence of it. He felt quite faint — as if the solid wooden bed frame beneath him had dissolved while he was reading and he was plunging through the air.

From the moment he could first begin to understand his lessons — from the moment he could read — he had accepted without question the teaching of the Church: that there had once been a time when Satan had been in control of the world; that God had punished the ancients for their elevation of science above all else by bringing down upon the Earth the four terrible riders of the Apocalypse — Pestilence, War, Famine and Death — as foretold in the Book of Revelation; and that thanks to a revival of the True Faith, they were blessed to be living in the time of the Risen Christ, when order had been restored to the world. He had never stopped to consider that there might be six possible scenarios that had led to the

Apocalypse, let alone that there could have existed people misguided enough to wish to find their way back to the very system that had brought God's punishment down upon their heads in the first place. Here in his hands was the mortal sin that the Church was determined to guard against: that what pretended to be a harmless interest in the past was in truth a disguised form of scientism that aimed to restore it. The book was heretical, pure and simple: it rightly deserved to be burned.

And yet he found something about Morgenstern's letter profoundly moving, even if much of it lay beyond him. What was 'cyberspace', or an 'ATM', or 'antibiotics'? He picked up the book again, went back to the beginning of the passage and read it with close attention for a second time, snagging his mind on the difficult words, struggling like a captured Ephraimite to pronounce the tongue-twisting shibboleth, then began turning the succeeding pages in search of any further reference to Morgenstern.

There was none. Shadwell had also vanished. He had sent his apologies for missing the next two meetings of the society, which were devoted to a monograph on the weathering of concrete structures and the excavation of a tunnel under the Thames at Blackwall, and after that the entries ceased. It was the final volume of the series. At that point, Fairfax presumed, the society must have been proscribed.

Shadwell? He ruminated on the name. He wondered what had become of him. If he was still alive, he must be getting on in years — he did not sound as if he were a young man even thirteen years ago — and in that instant it flashed into his mind that perhaps Shadwell was the elderly mourner who had shouted out in church. It was absurd, of course. The likelihood that the former president of the Society of Antiquaries was still alive, let alone that he would have found his way to Addicott St George in the middle of a rainstorm, was infinitesimal. He told himself his imagination was becoming overstimulated. Still, the thought was unsettling.

He reinserted the feather in its original place, closed the volume and replaced it on the nightstand. Then he put Father Lacy's spectacles back on top of it exactly as he had found them, as if by so doing he could pretend they had never been disturbed, and blew out the candle. This time oblivion did not come so easily. He felt as if a hand had reached out of the distant past and brushed its fingers across his face. He wished he could unsee what he had read, but knowledge alters everything, and he knew that was impossible.

CHAPTER SEVEN

Thursday 11th April: The Piggeries

H E FINALLY FELL asleep just before dawn, and was woken shortly afterwards by the sound of knocking — gentle but persistent and increasingly urgent. The day had broken and for the first time since he had arrived in the valley there was a suspicion of pale sunlight beyond the leaded window.

A woman's voice came through the closed door. 'Father Fairfax?'

'Yes, Mrs Budd. Good morning. Is all well?'

'Ye're needed quickly. Please may ye come at once?'

He threw off the covers, then glanced down at his nakedness. 'Willingly I would. But I fear . . .'

'Thy clothes were filthy, Father, from when ye fell over. I took 'em away to wash 'em. Ye can use Father Lacy's.'

He had fallen over? Had she undressed him? Oh God, oh God . . .

'Thank you. I shall be down directly.'

'As fast as ye can, Father, please.'

In the chest of drawers, he found neatly ironed underclothes and a pair of old-fashioned long black woollen socks. Worse even than sleeping in the old man's bed was the prospect of having to wear his clothes. At the first touch of the fabric his skin puckered into goose flesh. But he set his jaw and put them on. In the wardrobe was a simple black cassock, stinking of camphor and frayed at the hem and cuffs. It fitted him well. Let it be my hair shirt, he thought. My penance. A reminder of my sin.

He went out on to the landing, looping Father Lacy's white cotton stock around his neck, and tied it as he descended the stairs.

Agnes was waiting for him in the passage, together with Rose, who was dressed to go out in a long brown coat that looked as if it had once belonged to Father Lacy. Between them stood a thin young man, bareheaded, twisting a felt cap in his hands. He was wearing an old black worsted suit, the trousers held up by twine. On his face was a look of such anguish that Fairfax instinctively reached out his hand and clasped his shoulder. 'My good fellow, what is it?' The man gaped at him, red-eyed, speechless.

'His wife's birthed and the babe's not fit to last the morning,' said Agnes. 'The poor thing must be baptised.'

'Yes indeed. I'm sorry. Allow me a moment.' He ran back upstairs to his bag and retrieved his prayer book. At the front door he pulled on his boots, and Agnes kneeled to lace them. The young man was already waiting in the road. 'His name's John Revel,' she whispered. ''Twill be the second they'll have lost. Their house's in The Piggeries. Rose'll show thee back after.'

He hurried down the path to the gate, which Rose held open for him, and together they set off after the man as he strode towards the village. Rose kept a few paces ahead of him. Now that the storm had passed, daily life was resuming. A woman was hanging out washing in her garden. Another carried pails of milk in either hand along the centre of the street, her shoulders sloped by the weight. Both stopped as Revel passed, and Fairfax could tell they knew what it meant to see a new young father at this hour of the morning trailed by a priest.

The central arch of the bridge was almost entirely submerged. Barely a foot beneath the parapet a thunderous spate of yellowish-brown water foamed against a dam of broken branches. The spray drenched their faces. A hundred yards beyond the river, Revel abruptly disappeared into a narrow lane, itself a torrent, so that Fairfax and Rose were obliged to clamber up on to the grass verge and limp along it, occasionally slithering down into the water up to their ankles.

Beyond the high hedge, a half-dozen spindly columns of smoke rose from invisible chimneys. Revel opened a barred wooden gate and they went after him into a yard. Chickens ran towards them in the hope of food, swaying from side to side like clerics with their skirts hitched up, while the pigs that had presumably given the place its name – all pink and grey with caked mud – snuffled at a pile of dung. On three sides of the yard were what Fairfax took at first to be dilapidated sties. But then he noticed that children were running in and out of them, and he realised with a shock that they were human dwellings – tumbling hovels with tiny windows and low doorways, into one of which they followed Revel.

In the dimness, he registered a floor of bare earth spread with straw and sawdust. Clearly the animals must be brought in at night for their security and to provide a little heat. A ladder led up to a loft. On one side of the gloomy chamber, wet logs hissed in a small brick fireplace. Beside it an old woman seated on a stool sucked a short-stemmed pipe. The stink was tangible – human and animal, piss and shit, boiled food, woodsmoke and tobacco smoke, ammonia from the straw. Children clustered behind them at the door, blocking the daylight.

As his eyes adjusted to the shadows, Fairfax made out a mattress in the corner heaped with rags. Revel went over and kneeled next to it. 'The priest is come, Hannah,' he said gently.

The rags stirred and a thin white face appeared. 'Parson Lacy?'

'No, I am Father Fairfax.' He approached the mattress, his hands outstretched. Rose lingered at the back, watching him. 'May I see?'

Revel gently pulled back the sheet. She had the child clasped to her chest. It was slate blue, the same blue as the veins on her bare white breasts, heavy with milk. She hadn't the strength to lift it herself, so Revel took it and handed it up to Fairfax. It was as cold and light as a dead bird. He glanced around in despair and caught Rose's eye. She looked away. He should have stopped the ceremony then. A proper priest would have explained the mystery of God's will, not offered false comfort. He knew it, but he had not the courage to do it.

Hannah whispered, 'She ain't gone, please God, tell me?'

'No, no. We are just in time.' Fairfax nestled the corpse in his left arm and fumbled with his prayer book. 'Might I have some light, please? And a cupful of water? Children, why don't you come in and join us?'

Four of the young ones gathered round. The old woman came wearily from her stool, handed him a wooden beaker of water and held up a candle behind his shoulder. He could hear and smell her rank wheezing breath.

'What is to be her name?'

Revel looked at his wife. She said, 'Judith Elizabeth.' He nodded.

Fairfax poured a little water over the wrinkled face. 'Judith Elizabeth, I baptise thee in the name of the Father, and of the Son, and of the Holy Ghost. Amen.'

'Amen.'

'Shall we kneel together?' He twisted his prayer book to the candle, but he knew the words well enough – too well, indeed. *We yield thee hearty thanks, most merciful Father, that it hath pleased thee to regenerate Judith Elizabeth with thy Holy Spirit, to receive her for thine own Child by adoption, and to incorporate her into thy holy Church. And we humbly beseech thee to grant, that as she is now made partaker of the death of thy Son, so she may be also of his resurrection; and that finally, with the residue of thy Saints, she may inherit thine everlasting kingdom; through the same thy Son Jesus Christ our Lord. Amen.*

After a few moments of silence, one of the children said, 'She's dead, ain't she?'

'I think she may be now, God rest her soul.' Fairfax placed the baby back in her mother's arms. 'But we were in time.'

He stood in the centre of the yard, his hands hanging loosely at his sides, face tilted to the sky, and breathed in the smells of the farmyard. The poorest quarter of Exeter always shocked him, but somehow the quietness and isolation of rural poverty struck him as much worse. No wonder in the centuries after the Fall people had turned back to God: they would have needed to believe there was a life better than this one, whereas the ancients, with all their comforts, had been able to exist without faith. But then he corrected himself. Peculiar, barely comprehensible phrases from Morgenstern's letter were coming back to him. *We regard our society as having reached a level of sophistication that renders it uniquely vulnerable to total collapse . . . Key sectors and technologies could be affected to such an extent that our chances of finding our way back to the status quo ante could diminish alarmingly quickly . . .* Oh yes, the ancients had had faith right enough, he thought. Their God had been science, and it had deserted them.

His presence in The Piggeries was creating a stir. People were watching him from their open doorways. He recognised some faces from the wake. Scrawny barefoot children, the tallest no higher than his chest, ran in circles round him, shouting and waving their arms. In their upraised hands they flourished wooden crosses, which they swooped and spun. After a while, he started to pay them more attention.

'What's that game you're playing?'

'Flying machines!'

'How do you know of flying machines?'

'The parson told us!'

'May I see that?'

The toy was crudely carved out of a single piece of wood, its wings swept back in the style of a swallow's, its tail raised like a magpie's. Tiny holes gouged along either side of its body seemed to represent portholes. In their imaginations the children were high above the puddled farmyard, flashing through the clouds. He had never observed such a game before. He turned the carved flying machine back and forth in his hands until Rose tugged at his sleeve. She nodded to a fair-headed girl, barely more than a child herself, yet her belly already swollen by pregnancy. The girl curtsied.

'Beg pardon, Father.'

'What is it, child?'

'My mother'd like communion, sir. 'Tis a while since her last and she feels the lack most keenly.'

'Can she not come to church?'

'She cannot leave her bed, sir. Been a widow these last ten year.'

'Alas, I fear I have no wafers with me; nor wine . . .'

Rose touched his arm again. She unbuttoned her vast brown coat, fished into an inside pocket and pulled out a small black cotton bag, tied with cord. She undid the neck and showed him the contents: communion wafers and a stoppered half-pint jar. He took it from her, surprised and somehow chastened. 'Thank you, Rose. What is your name, child?'

'Alice, Father.'

'Very well, Alice – show us the way.'

They followed the girl across the yard, and Fairfax braced himself to his vocation: *to visit the fatherless and widows in their affliction, and to keep himself unspotted from the world* . . . He could see now that the warren of hovels was more extensive than he had first realised. One yard led on to another, and another. The numerous threads of smoke rising beyond the thatched roofs suggested a settlement at least as large as the village itself. The thin walls were made almost entirely of cob—that mix of clay, straw and gravel, washed with lime, that provided shelter for such a large percentage of humanity. He passed a man with a knife whittling a stick, and felt a moment of unease at being in such a rough spot, until he remembered that he had nothing of which he could be robbed, save his prayer book and the old priest's cassock.

A mangy dog, its ribcage showing, was chained to a doorpost. It struggled up on to its hind legs, growling. The girl ignored it and went inside, and he plunged in after her with Rose behind him, ducking through a low doorway and into a dwelling exactly like the last, dark and filled with straw. A sow lay on her side suckling her young in front of a cold black hearth. A ladder led up to a second storey.

'Does she lie up there?'

'Aye, Father.'

'What is your mother's name, Alice?'

'Matilda Shorcum, sir.'

'Who looks after her?'

'Me, sir.'

'Alone?'

'Aye, sir.'

'She has no other family?'

'My brothers has all been took by the army, sir, to fight the Northern Caliphate.'

Fairfax nodded encouragingly. 'Brave lads, I'm sure.' That was a war that had gone on all his life – and for centuries beforehand, or so it was said – ever present but oddly distant, its occasional lulls punctuated by lurid reports of horrible atrocities that aroused a fervour of public outrage and set the whole thing off again. Mostly it involved dreary garrison duty in some isolated Yorkshire moorland outpost. But the regular punitive raids to keep the Islamist enclave in check always carried with them the risk of capture and beheading, which the government took care to publicise. 'I'll be sure to pray for them as well.'

He tucked his prayer book under his arm and put his foot on the rickety first rung of the ladder. He hauled himself through a trapdoor and came up into a loft. Rose climbed up after him. The only light was provided by a filthy broken skylight. In the corner, beside a plain wooden table, was a cot on which lay the skeleton of a woman. Her hands and feet were bandaged. Around her head was fastened what looked to be a soiled napkin. Her eyes were unusually large and dark and glittering, full of intelligence. Rose kneeled beside her and stroked her face. He tried not to notice the smell.

'Mrs Shorcum, I am Christopher Fairfax.'

She turned her head slightly. ' 'Twere good of ye to come, Father.'

'I would do no other. When did you last receive communion?'

'A fortnight since.' Her voice was very weak. He had to bend low to hear. 'Just afore the parson were murdered.'

He smiled at her, reassuring. 'He was not murdered, Mrs Shorcum. His death was an evil chance, I promise you.'

'No, sir, he were murdered by the devils in the woods. I did warn him, sir, never to walk up there. I told him!' She was becoming agitated. 'I saw 'em when I were a girl.' She tried to rise.

'Well, he is at peace now, whatever happened. Do not distress yourself.'

Unsure exactly what was expected of him, he set out the wafers and wine on the table and opened his prayer book.

'You are ready to receive the Lord?' He found his place. 'Shall we pray together?' *Almighty, ever-living God, Maker of mankind, who dost correct those whom thou dost love, and chastise every one whom thou dost receive: We beseech thee to have mercy upon this thy servant visited with thine hand, and to grant that she may take her sickness patiently, and recover her bodily health (if it be thy gracious will).*

She was too ill to swallow the wafer. He dipped his finger in the wine and moistened her cracked lips. When the ceremony was over, she rested her bandaged hand on his and closed her eyes.

For the remainder of that morning they went from place to place, fulfilling the old priest's duties, neglected in the week since his death, visiting the sick and the bereaved. Rose knew exactly where to take him, moving swiftly across the yards, down the narrow alleys, lifting the lines of washing to let him pass.

The hours became a blur of squalid beds, wailing wall-eyed children, gloom, bad smells, mud and straw, dogs and cats and pigs and chickens wandering in and out. He administered the sacrament, heard whispered confessions, uttered words of comfort, accepted hospitality – water, tea, bread – whenever it was offered, not because he wanted it, God knew – he had to suppress a grimace each time he swallowed – but for fear of causing offence. Throughout he was conscious of Rose watching him, and he realised he was doing it as much for her approval as out of a sense of duty. He wanted her to see he was a serious man of God, and not some fanatical young zealot who would object to seeing her out unaccompanied, or an aloof theologian from the cathedral city who shrank from contact with the poor. It was absurd, but there it was: at that moment he preferred the good opinion of this simple country maid to that of his powerful, worldly bishop.

Once the wafers were all used up and the wine jar was empty, they made their way back along the water-logged lane into the village's main street and across the bridge. This time she walked at his side rather than in front of him, which he took as a sign of favour, and as they reached the church, he said, 'Thank you, Rose, for your help. I have felt closer to God this morning than I have for many a month.' She did not react, so he talked on into the silence. 'I also felt a kin-ship with Father Lacy – sensed something of his spirit in those poor places. He was a good priest, I can see that now – a truly holy man, despite what some in the village may say of him.'

She glanced at him and pursed her lips as if she did not entirely agree. But surely that was his imagination.

When they reached the parsonage, she indicated that rather than go in through the front door, they should make their way around to the side. A wooden gate in the grey stone wall led into the small stable yard. There was a vegetable garden, an orchard, a chicken coop, an earth closet – all the things he had been unable to make out the other night, all very neatly kept. In a small paddock beyond a fence of post and rail, a cow the colour of caramel grazed on the lush grass. The air had been washed clean by the rainfall. In the distance, the hills and woods were sharp in the sunlight.

The stable's door was divided in two. The upper part was open and May was looking out. Rose rubbed her own pale cheek against the grey muzzle, made a soothing noise — the first sound Fairfax had heard from her — and kneaded the horse's ear. Then she opened the lower door. She went past the mare and returned carrying Fairfax's saddle, leaned it against the wall and disappeared inside again.

He gazed at the hills. Of course, she was right: he should leave at once and take advantage of this break in the weather to find a way out of the valley. Nevertheless, he felt disappointed that she should make it so obvious she was keen to see him gone. He heard the swish of straw being swept. After a while, when she had still not reappeared, he went into the stable. She had just finished clearing a space at the end of the stall. She set aside the broom, kneeled, and began working bricks free from the wall, arranging them in a stack beside her. Finally she reached into the cavity and pulled out, one by one, four bulky, flat rectangular objects wrapped in centuries-old black plastic sheeting.

CHAPTER EIGHT

The registers yield a secret

ROSE WENT AHEAD of him, checking the way was clear, pausing to listen before opening the back door, the kitchen door and then at last the door into the study. The packages seemed as heavy as gravestones. He carried them clasped awkwardly to his chest and dropped them on to the desk with relief. Already he felt uncomfortable, as if he was being drawn into a conspiracy. Nevertheless, he was careful to close the door quietly and keep his voice low.

'These are the church registers, I take it?'

Her eyes were wide and fixed on his. She nodded.

'Why were they taken to the stable? Was it you who hid them?'

She shook her head vigorously.

'The parson, then?'

A reluctant nod.

'With your help?'

A shake.

'But you saw him do it?'

Nod.

'Did he know you were watching him?'

A slight narrowing of the eyes; a bite of the lip; a slow, somewhat guilty shake of the head.

'So you saw him carry them from the church without him knowing? How long before he died was this?'

She held up a finger.

'A week before his death?'

She stared at him without responding.

'A *day*?'

She nodded.

'The day of his death?'

Another nod.

'But that is an ominous coincidence!' He ran his hand through his hair and then tugged at his beard as he considered the implications. 'Why would he have done such a thing?' He rephrased the question. 'Was something troubling him?'

A shrug, another shake of her head.

'Think carefully now, Rose.' He wagged his finger at her. 'The matter is important. Father Lacy did not seem discomfited about anything at all?'

She creased her brow in concentration, then pressed the tips of her thumb and forefinger together and turned them clockwise. She had to repeat the mime a couple more times before he understood.

'He changed the locks on the doors?'

She nodded.

'Did you notice any strangers in the village?'

Again she held up a finger.

'One? A man? When?'

She pointed to the registers.

'On the same day he hid the books?'

A nod.

Before he could ask any further questions, a volley of loud knocks resounded through the house. 'Are you expecting visitors?'

She shook her head. They glanced at the ceiling. Agnes was descending the stairs.

'I suggest we say nothing of this matter to Mrs Budd — for the present, at least. It would only add to her cares.'

She nodded emphatically.

'Good, Rose. You did well to tell me.'

He opened the door and ushered her out into the passage.

Agnes, drying her hands on her apron, had reached the bottom of the stairs. She noticed them, and surprise flickered briefly in her face — followed closely, or so Fairfax thought, by a look of suspicion. But then came another burst of knocking, and she turned away to open the front door.

John Hancock's massive shoulders filled the frame. He removed his hat — a battered pie-shaped object with a parakeet's bright green feather in its band – and bowed. 'Good morning to ye, Agnes. Is the priest in?' He drew himself up to his full height. 'Ah, yes – I see him there!' Without waiting for an invitation, he stepped over the threshold. He wore a heavy brown frock coat and an old pair of knee boots spattered with mud. In his right hand was a riding crop. 'Good morning, Father! I heard ye had to turn back last night.'

'I did, Captain Hancock. The lane was entirely blocked. I should have heeded your warning and set off sooner.'

'Well, no matter now. I've good news for ye. My men have cleared the road, so ye can leave whenever thee wishes.'

'That was swift work.'

'I set a dozen of my strongest lads upon the task at first light. I can escort ye myself, if it pleases ye.'

'Thank you, but there's no need to burden yourself with me.'

'It would be no burden. I'm returning that way in any case. Indeed, it would be my pleasure. If we made but a small diversion, I could show ye my mill.'

'You are a mill owner? I had taken you to be an army man.'

'In my youth I was, but these days I'm a weaver. Fifty men employed and the finest cloth in the county produced. Come and see it – I insist.'

'A tempting offer, sir, but I have one or two matters to detain me here before I leave.'

'One or two matters?' Captain Hancock seemed to find the notion amusing. 'And what *matters* might they be?'

'Church business.'

'Ah! Church business? Is that how it is?' Hancock struck the top of his boot with his riding crop and twisted his head this way and that, as if he hoped to discover these obstacles to an immediate departure and flatten them. But Fairfax stood his ground, and finally the captain gave up. 'Well then, I suppose I must allow ye to make your own way. But I'd not leave it so late this time – not if ye wishes to make Axford before curfew. The sheriffs are mighty strict there. Ladies. Fairfax.' He touched the crop to his temple, nodded, jammed his hat back on his head and stamped off down the garden path.

Fairfax watched him go. 'He seems in a rush about something.'

'John Hancock was born in a rush,' pronounced Agnes, closing the door, 'and he will die in a rush. Now then, child,' she said, turning to Rose, 'I know not where ye've been all morning, but there's work needs doing – fetching back the dishes from the church ale-house and washing them all up, for a start. And ye'll be wanting feeding, Father?'

'That's kind, Mrs Budd, but I fear I must take

Captain Hancock's advice and leave quite soon. Yet I should like to do just a little work in the study beforehand.'

Seated alone at the desk, the door closed, he lifted the package that lay on top of the pile and examined it more closely. He saw now that the register had been put into a large black plastic sack, which had been folded around it several times to provide extra protection. This time he felt no hesitation as he unwrapped the volume and pulled it out. On the contrary, his curiosity thoroughly aroused, he was keen to discover more. It had a thick leather binding and a tarnished broken brass lock in the shape of a trefoil. At some point, many years before, it had been damaged by water, and as he opened it he inhaled the sharp fungal odour of the past – a compound of mildew, dust and what might have been a lingering trace of frankincense. The lines of ink had faded to a pale brown, scarcely darker than the yellowing parchment on which they were written. He lit a candle so that he could see them more clearly. The script itself was full of sharp angles and daggered down-strokes, hard to decipher. Here and there the letters were invisible. But he made it out roughly.

Maius IV sepultus MDXCVII antequam nascantur morien-tium filius Francis Tunstall, Agricola, et uxor Jane

VIII Iulii MDXCIX, et accepit Thomam Ann Shaxton
Turberville de hac parochia
   Ianuarii Robynns Nicolaus IV baptizatus MDCIV Ali-
ciam filiam Rogeri Halys, Agricola, et uxorem, Margaritam,
natus December XXXI MDCIII

Latin had been revived by the Church as another bulwark against scientism; consequently, its vocabulary and declensions had been beaten into him at the seminary, and once he had caught the hang of the abbreviated style, he found he could follow it well enough.

Buried 4 May 1597 stillborn son of Francis Tunstall, farmer, and his wife, Jane
   Married 8 July 1599 Thomas Turberville and Ann Shaxton of this parish
   Baptised 4 January 1604 Alice daughter of Nicholas Robynns, farmer, and his wife, Margaret, born 31 December 1603

The dating was all done according to the calendar that had existed before the Apocalypse, which made it at least a thousand years old. Apart from a gap in the 1640s, the volume had been kept up continuously, by a score of different hands, until the beginning of the ancients' nineteenth century.

He set it aside and unwrapped the next. It was

similar to the first, but without a lock, and written in an altogether sharper, clearer, blacker ink.

> Buried 4 October 1803 William George Perry, son of George, blacksmith of Addicott St George, and Caroline, aged 14, drowned, double fees

He turned the heavy pages and the life of the parish materialised before him. The same surnames again and again. Baptised-married-buried. Baptised-married-buried. The staccato rhythm reminded him of the stick figures he used to flick into life when he was a child. It told one nothing of who they were, or what they thought or felt or looked like.

As he read on, he realised how little he understood or had even bothered to think about the past. It was not a subject that was encouraged by either Church or state: on the contrary, an interest in what had gone on before the modern era was established, even if it did not touch on the heresy of science, was considered a step on the path to Hell. Besides, what was there to know? History was a patchwork of voids. The great university libraries and public archives had mostly rotted away or been used as fuel in the Dark Age. An entire generation's correspondence and memories had vanished into this mysterious entity the antiquarians called 'The Cloud'. The few records that remained were mostly to be found in the ordinary parish churches — buildings made of stone and intended to last, which had continued to stand even as the newer settlements around them crumbled into ruins. Lacy had been right in what he had said to Keefer: these were books of great antiquity and value.

He unwrapped the two remaining volumes and chose the oldest-looking to examine next. The register opened in 1927 and had been kept consistently until 2025. The final entries were for September and October of that year and consisted solely of burials — twenty in all, mostly of children: an astonishing number, he thought, for such a small community — and then there was nothing but blank pages until an entry made more than a century later, dated according to the new calendar, scratched in charcoal, in a shaky hand, and in the crude capital letters that were a feature of early post-Apocalypse writing:

BAPTISED 8 MARCH ARD 795, JOHN SON OF PETER KERN, FLETCHER, AND HELEN, HIS WIFE, OF ADCUT, THIS PARISH

The calendar had been reset after the Apocalypse so that it started in the year 666: the numeral assigned to the Beast of Revelation, whose appearance in the New Testament had foretold the ruin of the world at Armageddon. *Let him that hath understanding count the number of the beast: for it is the number of a man; and his number is six hundred threescore and six.* So if this entry had been made in ARD — *Anno Resurrexit Domini*, the Year of Our Risen Lord — 795, it meant that the recorded life of Addicott St George had restarted 673 years ago, 129 years after civilisation had collapsed into chaos.

The entries that followed were intermittent — sometimes one a year, sometimes none — roughly written by a stick of charcoal to begin with, and then by what looked to be a blotchy quill pen dipped in some kind of home-made ink — a mixture of soot and glue, he guessed, or plant dye — that looked similar to the writing in the very first volume. Only at the end was there a sign that the parson of St George's had finally acquired a modern steel nib and access to iron-gall ink. That was in the middle of the last century.

The current register ran from ARD 1411 to the present day. The writing of the first two parsons who had kept it was crude and in parts illegible. Then Father Lacy's hand took over: very small and neat, the script of an intelligent and meticulous mind. It filled many pages, unchanging over more than thirty years. Fairfax recognised some of the local names from the previous day's burial: Fisher, Singer, Gann, Fuente . . . The final entry was for a service of marriage between George Shorcum of Vine Cottage and Mary Creech of The Piggeries that had been performed three weeks earlier. He started with that and worked his way backwards, trying to find some clue in the tidy columns that might explain why Lacy had taken the precaution of hiding the registers. But he could see nothing obvious in the columns of names and dates, and after a few more minutes of fruitless searching, he sat back in the dead priest's chair, defeated.

There were scholars in the chapter house, cleverer men than he, who had devoted their lives to combing the Scriptures for hidden meanings. If there was a mystery here to decode, they would be the ones best able to find it. The prudent course would be to take all four volumes back with him to the safety of the cathedral and explain the situation to the bishop. It would probably be even wiser if he pretended he had never looked at the books himself.

He started packing them back into their plastic sacks. But when he came to the register covering the ancients' twentieth and twenty-first centuries, he paused. Outside in the passage, the long-case clock ticked heavily; the silent countryside pressed against the leaded window. Something stirred in his mind. He glanced across at the display cabinet and let his eyes travel up to the communication device with its inscrutable dead black mirror face. The period before the Apocalypse, not the present, was the old man's obsession, and it struck him that by concentrating on the most recent entries, he might have been looking in the wrong place.

He set the book down on the desk and opened it again. He turned to the final lines, and ran his index finger up from the bottom – up over the terrible record of burials of the autumn of 2025, up to the flurry of christenings and marriages of the summer that represented the final days of normality. He wondered who had written them. The writing had a feminine quality: for that brief period before God's wrath descended upon the Earth, when there had been women priests, perhaps the village had had a female parson? He imagined the unsuspecting parishioners going about their lives, making their arrangements – welcoming a baby, embarking on a marriage – with no inkling of what was impending.

His finger travelled on up, retracing time, back through the spring of that year, through the quiet winter and the preceding autumn of 2024 . . . He turned back one page, and another, and nothing stood out as significant until he came to July 2022, and then he experienced for a second time the strange sensation of a fingertip touching his face, for on that date a marriage had been solemnised in St George's Church, joining in holy matrimony a Mr Anwar Singh, 'computer programmer', of Clerkenwell, London, to a Miss Julia Morgenstern, 'web designer' – an occupation, surely, for a spider rather than a human – whose address was given as 'Durston

Court Lodge', and whose father's occupation was recorded simply as 'university professor'.

For several minutes he sat motionless, unsure what he should do. In the end, he took a sheet of writing paper from one of the desk drawers and dipped the nib of his pen in the ink pot.

> The Parsonage
> Addicott St George
> Thursday 11th April ARD 1468
> My lord bishop,
> I send you God's greeting and beg to inform your lordship that yesterday I fulfilled the charge you entrusted to me and carried out the burial of Rev. Thomas Lacy. By ill chance, a heavy storm that same afternoon closed the single road out of the village and obliged me to abandon my journey home.
> Today I was called upon to perform an urgent baptism of an infant on the point of death and secured her immortal soul. In addition, I have visited the sick and performed several pastoral duties that of necessity have been neglected since Rev. Lacy's death. I have found the parish to be in sore need of Christian succour. Therefore, I propose to

offer Holy Communion on Sunday before my return to the cathedral.

I trust this course of action will meet with your lordship's approval.

I beg to remain your lordship's humble servant in Christ,

Christopher Fairfax

He read the letter through carefully. He had left the content deliberately vague lest it fall into the wrong hands. He wondered what the bishop would make of it. With him, one could never tell. He might tear it up in a rage and throw the pieces at the dean: 'Can none of your priests obey even a simple instruction?' Equally, he might pass it across his desk with a nod of benediction: 'This young man shows a true sense of vocation.' Either way, Fairfax felt he could not remain absent from the cathedral for two more days without sending an explanation for his absence. He was conscious that committing such an act of insubordination entailed a risk: it gave him a stabbing pain in his bowels merely to think of it. But on his return, what a tale he might be able to lay before the bishop!

He folded the letter three times until it was small enough to fit into the palm of his hand, then flattened it and wrote 'The Right Reverend Bishop Pole, Exeter Cathedral' on the outside. He held the stick of sealing wax in the candle flame, twisting it as it melted, and sealed the packet with first one red blob and then two more. It bestowed, he hoped, a suitably impressive look of confidentiality and authority.

He opened the door a fraction. Agnes was in the kitchen. That was unfortunate: it meant it would be impossible for him to replace the registers in the stable without her seeing him. Yet it did not seem wise to leave them lying on the desk. He looked around the study, and in the end he hid them under the couch.

'Mrs Budd, might I beg a favour?' He tried to make his tone nonchalant.

She was staring at the plate rack, a dish and a cloth in her hand, seemingly lost in a reverie. 'What is it, Father?'

'To stay a little longer, if my presence is not too great a burden.'

She turned round. 'How much longer?'

'Three nights.'

He had expected she would readily agree: had she not expressed a hope that he might take over the living? Instead he was disconcerted to find her regarding him with even greater suspicion than before. 'First one night became two, now ye wishes two to become five?'

'Once again I seem to have allowed the time to get away from me . . .'

The excuse sounded feeble even to his own ears,

and there could be no doubting her distrust as she folded her arms and scrutinised him. 'But there's time to get to Axford, Father.'

'It's not solely a question of time. It must be some days since there's been an opportunity to worship here. I have decided it is my duty to offer the parish a service on the Sabbath.'

She could scarcely argue with that. 'Aye, well that's true. A communion would be welcomed.'

'Good, then it is settled. In which case, I have a letter that must be sent — today if possible. How is the dispatch of mail arranged in the village?'

'John Gann's boy at the forge takes a bag to Axford to meet the mail coach most afternoons.'

'Excellent.' He started to move away, and then turned back as if a fresh thought had just occurred to him. 'There is one other thing — I wish to pay a call on Lady Durston. How best to find her house? Durston Court, I believe it is called.'

'The Court lies a good mile outside the village. Just past the forge, there's a lanc to the right.' Suspicion was replaced by a look of undisguised curiosity. 'She'll be expecting ye, Father? If not, 'tis a good long walk for nothing.'

'I am invited, if not expected. She asked me to call on her if I happened to stay in the parish any longer.' Another lie: he would be busy in his prayers that night. 'Besides, even if she's not at home I shall be glad to stretch my legs now the rain has passed. Is her husband away? He was not in church, I think.'

'No, sir. She's widowed. Sir Henry has been dead the past five year.' Obviously she wanted to add something else, although it took her a moment to muster the courage. 'Forgive me, Father, for putting the matter plainly, but if ye's to lie under this roof for three more nights, it would be best if ye went careful with Rose. She's but a silly girl, and I fancy has an eye for ye. It could be a trouble for a man such as thyself, sworn to the pure path, especially one with an occasional liking for drink and dancing.'

So that was the cause of her dark looks! He was relieved it was only that, even as he felt himself colouring with embarrassment. He held up his hand. 'Say no more of it, Mrs Budd. The warning does you credit. I greatly regret my behaviour last night. I am sorry. It will not happen again. And as for Rose, I shall be on my guard against offering even the slightest encouragement.'

CHAPTER NINE

Lady Durston

I<small>T WAS IN</small> a spirit of considerable anticipation, albeit edged by a certain mild apprehension, that, a few minutes later, Fairfax set off from the parsonage to walk to the forge and thence to Durston Court. He was wearing the traditional wide-brimmed ecclesiastical black hat known as a saturno, much favoured by the rural clergy of an earlier generation, an example of which he had found in Father Lacy's wardrobe. He was glad of its protection, despite its lack of fashion, for the afternoon was warm and cloudless. The flag of St George on top of the church tower flapped in a breeze that he calculated by the position of the sun was blowing from the south.

He had gone no more than fifty yards along the lane towards the river when yet another boom shook the valley. It felt louder than the previous day's explosion — more menacing, as if the village was under bombardment and the enemy's artillery had moved closer overnight. He guessed it must have been amplified by the wind. It lifted the rooks from their nests in the high trees and distributed them like blackened fragments of debris above the churchyard.

None of the women in the row of cottages opposite the church appeared to have noticed. They were seated on their stools on their front steps in the sunshine, working their spinning wheels, entirely absorbed. It was the same tranquil picture all along the main street – no menfolk anywhere, just the women working their feet on their treadles, conjuring thin white thread out of clouds of pale grey wool, young children playing in the small front gardens or at the side of the road, a couple of babies in their cribs in the shade beneath the apple trees. One of the spinners looked up and nodded to him as he passed. He nodded back. She could be Jane Tunstall, he thought, whose stillborn son was buried unbaptised in 1597, and her neighbour might be Ann Shaxton, recently married to Thomas Turberville, or she could be Margaret Robynns with her baby Alice asleep beside her. More than a thousand years had washed over England since those days, a civilisation had fallen and another had been reborn, and life went on in Addicott St George as if nothing had happened.

In the spray beneath the bridge a rainbow arced. A glitter of plumage like a bird of paradise seemed to hover over the torrent and then, when he took another step towards it, to vanish. The phenomenon was so striking he paused on the embankment and repeated the process several times, summoning the brilliant colours and then banishing them, summoning and banishing, until he realised his behaviour was attracting the amused attention of some of the women, whereupon he crossed quickly to the opposite bank. He passed the entrance to the lane that led to The Piggeries and presently in the distance heard the clink of a hammer striking metal.

The forge was set back from the road at a crossroads. A horse in the forecourt stood tied to a wooden pole that was perhaps twelve feet high, from the top of which, suspended by chains, hung a large yellow plastic scallop shell of great antiquity, battered and much-repaired. The double doors to the smithy were folded open and the glow of the furnace silhouetted the squat figure of John Gann working at his anvil. In one gauntleted hand he wielded a hammer; in the other, a pair of pincers gripped the flattened tongue of red-hot metal he was beating into shape.

'Mr Gann!' He stepped into the heat of the forge.

The blacksmith looked up at the sound of his name, raised a glove to shield his eyes against the glare of daylight and squinted in Fairfax's direction. As soon as he recognised him, his expression cleared. 'Good afternoon to ye, Father!' He plunged the metal into a tank of water, sending up a great gout of hissing steam, and came round the anvil towards Fairfax. His torso was naked beneath his leather apron, although his hairy black arms and chest were so matted with sweat Fairfax thought at first he was wearing a woollen jersey.

'That were a merry night last night! Never seen a parson dance afore!' Gann grinned, showing big teeth – horse's teeth – stained brown by his strong tobacco. 'What can I do for ye, sir? Horse need a-shoeing afore ye sets off?'

'It is your other service I stand need of, Mr Gann. A letter of mine requires delivery.'

'To where, might I ask?'

'Exeter.'

'Well now, let me see about that.' Gann pulled off his glove and wiped his hand on the side of his apron. He took the letter and peered at the address. He made no attempt to disguise his interest and gave a low whistle. 'My lord bishop? Is there trouble, Father?'

'Not at all.' Fairfax was tempted to tell him to mind his own business. 'I merely need to let him know my plans.'

'That means ye'll be staying longer?'

'A few days, I think.'

'So ye likes it here?'

'Yes, I like it well enough.'

'Well then, let me cast your fortune: if ye don't leave now, ye never will.'

For a moment, Fairfax was not sure he had heard him right. 'That sounds an ominous prophecy!'

'Not at all. Just the way of things in our valley. Place tends to get a hold of folk if they stay too long, and then won't never let them go.' Gann's dark grin gaped again – friendly or menacing Fairfax could not decide. 'Good, then. Let's find the lad.'

He followed the blacksmith outside. Two large pits were set into the forecourt, each about eight feet deep – one half covered with planks – both shelved around the sides almost to the surface with boxes of tools, horseshoes and nails, and lumps of scrap metal. In the fully uncovered pit was a youth of about sixteen, who climbed a ladder when his name was called – 'Jake, come on up here, boy!' – and stood respectfully with his cap in his hands as Gann gave him his instructions.

'Take this here letter and give it to the mail clerk at the Swan and tell him to be sure it meets the coach to Exeter.' To Fairfax he said reassuringly, 'Coach ain't due till four, so there's time aplenty so long as he gets a move on.' He pretended to aim a kick at the boy. 'Well, go on, take the father's letter and get on that horse!'

Fairfax said, 'And the cost?'

'Five pounds for the coach mail. Four for the horse hire. And then whatever ye cares to give the lad.'

'Would a crown suffice for his trouble?' Silence. 'Ten shillings?' Silence. 'A pound?'

'Aye, I'd say that'd do well enough. Say something to the father, Jake.'

'Thanks, sir!' The boy touched his forelock.

Ten pounds! It was robbery. It left only ten to get him home. But the young priest was too fastidious to haggle, so he counted out the coins from his purse, then watched Jake swing himself up easily into the saddle, clatter over the cobbles and disappear into the road. Gann trickled his share of the money into the front pocket of his apron and patted it appreciatively, like a man who had just eaten a good meal. 'So, Father, will ye take another pipe with me? I'll find us something milder than the last.'

'It's tempting, but no, I must get on.'

Fairfax stepped off the forecourt and stood at the corner of the two roads. He eyed the narrow lane. He knew that Gann was watching him. He had an uneasy sense that he had trapped himself. So be it, he thought: by God's will he had managed to so contrive things that there could be no turning back now. *Narrow is the way which leadeth unto life, and few there be that find it.*

The blacksmith's voice called after him, ' 'Tis the wrong path, Father: the parsonage is back there,' but Fairfax pretended he hadn't heard and set off up the track.

The blackthorns were in full bloom. A froth of sweet-smelling white blossom washed over him. In the fields beyond the hedges a dozen ewes lay on their sides on the cropped turf, feeding the season's new-born lambs. He dawdled, beguiled by their soft bleats and the song of the skylarks hovering high overhead, until he recalled Gann's prediction that if he stayed too long he would never leave the valley, whereupon he forced himself into a brisker pace. After several minutes of gentle climbing, a pair of large stone gateposts appeared ahead on the left, surmounted by what must once have been heraldic creatures — griffins, perhaps, or lions — but reduced by time to formless shapes, like guttered candles.

The gates were missing. The drive was a track, no better than the lane. Waterlogged potholes, smooth as mirrors, held blue fragments of sky, and curved in a glittering archipelago for a hundred yards until they disappeared behind a pair of ancient cedars. To his right was a dense bed of waist-high nettles and this-tles. He assumed it must be where the lodge had once stood. He hunted around for a stick and started hack-ing away at the tall weeds, beating them down and trampling them underfoot. The crushed stalks and leaves released a sour, pungent odour. He stung his wrist and gave a yelp of pain. The poison was at its strongest in spring.

He threw away the stick and stood in the little clearing he had created, surrounded by clouds of midges and blue and yellow butterflies and sucked at the hives on the side of his throbbing hand. The foundations of the lodge must lie buried under several feet of topsoil. Apart from a couple of red bricks and a few lumps of concrete, there was nothing left to see. The air was hot, drowsy, still. Whatever had once stood here was long gone. He felt the impossible remoteness of the past and his earlier enthusiasm began to ebb.

He returned to the drive and picked his way between the puddles, towards the cedars, until the house came into view. He had to stop to let his mind absorb it. The spectacle it presented was not unique: such haunted edifices were common enough in England, usually to be glimpsed from the road – roofless, windowless and burned out, long since looted of anything that might be salvaged for shelter or fuel. Visiting them on a Sunday afternoon was encouraged by the Church as a means of stimulating reflection upon the transience of human glory in comparison to God's eternal kingdom. Fairfax had himself toured the magnificent gutted facades of Wilton and Longleat in the east, and Holcombe Rogus and Paignton in the west, and marvelled with his fellow sightseers at the civilisation that had produced them and the hubris that had led to their terrible fate. Durston Court, nestling in its own small dell about a quarter of a mile away, was not on the same scale as those ruined palaces, nor was it entirely abandoned, yet the effect was the same. He could see glass in the windows of the nearest gabled wing, and the roof above that section, at least, was intact. But the other three gables looked dangerously close to collapse, and at the far end only a great chimney stack remained, rising like a solitary tower to a height of three storeys. He wondered if he had misunderstood. Lady Durston might own this place; surely she could not possibly live in it?

He descended through the desolate park, past crumbling centuries-old oaks and a beech tree turned to charcoal by a lightning strike. A stone bridge led over a muddy lake choked by water lilies, with the rotted ribcage of a rowing boat upended in the reeds, and then the drive turned away from the water and swept up over an unkempt lawn, between rhododendrons, to an immense front door. He hammered on it with his fist and waited, and hammered again, and waited longer. Still receiving no reply, he made his way along a terrace of uneven flagstones to the corner of the house, and then along the western flank.

The shutters of the ground-floor windows were closed, the casements of the upper floors so overgrown with ivy it was impossible to make out all the rooms. The breeze ruffled the ivy and stirred in the ugly trees that had been allowed to encroach close to the terrace, and yet for a moment Fairfax saw the place as it might have been before the Apocalypse – music emanating from the ballroom, lanterns strung around the garden, couples strolling by a lake clear enough to reflect the moon, flying machines drawn up all the way along the drive to carry the guests home, oblivious to the disaster coming.

At the back of the house was a cobbled courtyard with a stable block in better repair than the house. Women's underclothes were drying on a washing line. In the far corner was the entrance to a walled garden. And there at last he saw a human figure – a gardener in shirtsleeves and a straw sunhat, bent forward slightly, using a scythe to cut a swathe through the weeds.

Fairfax walked across the cobbles and called out a greeting: 'Good afternoon!' But the figure was too absorbed to hear him, and it wasn't until he had entered the garden and was within a few paces that his presence was detected, at which point the gardener swung round in alarm and flourished the scythe blade at his throat. Fairfax recognised Sarah Durston at the same instant she recognised him.

'Mr Fairfax!' She lowered the scythe.

'Lady Durston.' He remembered to take off his hat. 'I'm sorry to have startled you.'

She was dressed in a man's white shirt with the sleeves rolled up, the tails tucked into a pair of heavy brown breeches, which were in turn tucked into a pair of old black riding boots. She was flushed from her exertions. Her face, her throat, her arms and even her shirt, unbuttoned at the neck, were wet with perspiration. She is a Ceres, thought Fairfax – who was prone to these flights of poetic fancy – a goddess of fertility.

'And you must forgive me for being startled,' she replied, 'but we are quite out of the way here, and wary of strangers.' She removed her straw hat. Her damp red hair was tied up at the back but had been plastered flat at the front and sides by the pressure of the brim. She used the hat to fan her face. 'This is a surprise, Mr Fairfax. I had thought you lost to us by now, and back among the smart folk of Exeter.'

'A mud fall bottled up the road.'

She ceased her fanning and studied him. 'Is the way not cleared?'

'I believe it is now, yes.'

'And yet you have not left? What brings you here?'

'There is a certain matter I wish to discuss, if it is convenient.'

'A matter concerning . . . ?'

'Your house.'

She frowned. 'What business is my house of yours?'

'It bears upon the death of Father Lacy.'

She stared at him a little longer. Perhaps it was his imagining, but there seemed to him a trace of reluctance on her part to continue the conversation. She fanned herself some more. 'I swear I am as cooked by the sun today as I was drowned by the rain yesterday. How odd our weather is these days. Was it always so, do you suppose?' She replaced her hat. 'I cannot imagine what might tie the Court and poor Father Lacy, but I am ready to learn it. Come. We shall take some refreshment indoors.'

It was more a command than an invitation. She shouldered her scythe and led him out of the garden. The house's rear elevation loomed ahead. But instead of crossing the cobbled courtyard, she turned aside towards the stable block. Setting down her scythe beside the nearest door, she indicated that he should go inside.

For the second time since entering her property, he was brought up short by the sight that met him. The space must once have been big enough to stable half a dozen horses, but the stalls and tack hooks and fodder racks had been removed and it had been turned into a sitting room – or salon, rather – using furniture presumably salvaged from the main house. A large, faded and elaborately patterned Persian rug covered the floor. Upon this stood a pair of gilt antique chairs upholstered in threadbare yellow silk, a two-seater sofa of matching fabric, and a low and rather ugly table with a glass top bearing a vase of daffodils. Three of the walls were hung with tapestries. The white-wash of the fourth was almost entirely obscured by paintings of elaborately costumed ladies, mustachi-oed soldiers in red uniforms, and a view of Durston Court and its parkland with children and hunting dogs in the foreground. The whole was lit by a golden blade of dusty sunshine thrusting down from a skylight.

Fairfax took off his hat and gazed around him. He felt as if he had been carried back in time to a more genteel age, entirely unlike anything he had seen before, even in the bishop's palace. 'What an extraordinary room!'

'When my husband died, I decided this would make a more comfortable home for a widow than that great tumbling tomb of a house.' Lady Durston dropped into one of the armchairs and unfastened her hair, then threw back her head and shook it. Red tresses tumbled over her shoulders. 'Sit down, Mr Fairfax. What refreshment can I offer you? Lemonade, or tea – or ale, perhaps?'

He thought this might have been a sly reference to his behaviour the previous night, but then he remembered that mercifully she had left before he started dancing. 'Lemonade, thank you.'

He settled himself on the edge of the sofa. She picked up a small silver bell from the table and rang it. Almost at once, a young woman in a black dress appeared at the doorway. 'Abigail, bring us lemonade.'

After the maid had withdrawn, Lady Durston began working off her riding boots, kicking repeatedly at either heel to loosen them, then crossing her legs and tugging the leather casings free of her feet.

She placed the boots carefully beside her chair and massaged her toes, which were clad, Fairfax observed with fascination, in slightly soiled white silk stockings. She glanced at him and he looked away.

'My manners are doubtless rougher than they should be. We are only women here, and have become unused to polite society – or society of any sort, come to that.'

'Only women?' The notion shocked him. 'Is that safe?'

'Oh yes, quite safe. Abigail acts as maid, Jenny cooks, Mary aids me out of doors. I have my husband's old musket. If heavy work requires a man, we hire him. The villagers leave us quite alone. I suspect they think us witches.'

'Surely not!'

'I am joking, Mr Fairfax. In future perhaps I should ring the bell to warn you when I am not to be taken seriously?'

He was spared the need to reply by the return of Abigail carrying a tray. Lady Durston moved the vase to make space for it. After the maid had gone she poured two glasses of lemonade from a curious metal jug with a lid and a long curving spout. 'You'll take honey for sweetness? We grow our lemons under windows taken from the house. We also have three hives. Whatever we don't use we take to Axford and sell.' She spooned out some honey and stirred. 'So we are quite sufficient unto ourselves – a regular little colony of Amazons.'

She handed him the glass, raised hers to his and drank it down in one. He followed suit. 'Very well,' she said, wiping her mouth with the back of her hand in a way that would have been considered in Exeter most unladylike. 'What is this about my house?'

Fairfax set his glass back on the table. Now that it came to it, he was uncertain how to proceed. Away from the parson's study, the whole affair seemed suddenly both far-fetched and fraught with risk, and nothing in his training had prepared him for such a conversation. Still, he took a breath. 'I shall give you the facts of the matter as straight as I can. This morning I looked through the old church registers. One, very ancient, records a wedding held some eight hundred years ago – thirty generations' distance from us by my reckoning, if one can conceive of such a span. At any rate, the bride's address is set down as Durston Court Lodge.'

There was a pause.

'So she was a Durston?'

'No, your ladyship, her surname was Morgenstern.'

'Really?' She gazed at him, very cool, but he detected the tiniest flicker of uneasiness in her eyes. 'I thought only Durstons had ever lived here.' She shifted round in her chair and nodded to the portraits. 'My husband's family built this place – a fact of so much pride to him, he flat refused to move out, even though the house was barely fit for pigs to live in.'

'The register is quite clear on the point.'

She gave a slight shrug. 'Perhaps her father was the gatekeeper.'

'His occupation is given as "professor".'

'And what was his particular study?'

'I understand it to have been physic – the study of natural phenomena.'

'Is that so?' She picked up the jug of lemonade, as if to cover his disquiet and offered to refill his glass. He held up his hand in refusal. 'But a tall tale, surely,' she continued, pouring some for herself, 'for why would the child of this professor of physic – and thus presumably the professor himself – live in so quiet a spot as this?'

'My mind ran along a similar course. It is possible they did not live here every day. People then had mechanical means of transport, much quicker than anything we possess. They could even fly. He might have been able to travel here from London in less than a day. In that event, he could have made his work in the city, and retired here for his leisure.'

'Less than a day – imagine! Well then, I suppose one must grant at least its possibility. But what has this to do with Father Lacy?'

'I have found the parsonage to be filled with a great many volumes devoted to the study of the past. Objects also.'

'He made no secret of his interest. What of it?'

'For one thing, they are beyond doubt heretical — although that will be for my lord bishop to determine.'

'What manner of books are they?'

He hesitated again, then unfastened the collar of his cassock and withdrew the small book he had taken from the old priest's bedroom. 'There is one volume in particular that he seems to have been studying just before he died.' He opened it to the marked passage. 'In it is printed a letter written by the same Professor Morgenstern. At least I guess he must be the same, for there cannot be many others of that peculiar name.'

'Ah! Now I am quite pulled in to your story. May I see it?' She held out her hand. Fairfax withdrew slightly. What did he know of her really? Nothing but a handsome face, a ruined house and a certain force of manner. She reached out further. 'Come, Mr Fairfax. Have some faith in my discretion, or I shall be insulted.'

'Of course. Forgive me.' He gave it to her. 'But I would indeed be glad if the matter went no further. I am in an awkward place. I shall have to pretend to the bishop I have never read it.' Although whether he will believe me, he thought, picturing that steely countenance, is another question.

He watched her closely as she read — her forehead creased in concentration, her lips moving as they tried to shape themselves around the unfamiliar words. For all his misgivings, he found it a relief to be sharing his discovery. Such information was a heavy burden to carry alone. When she had finished, she let out a long breath, and he was gratified to observe that she seemed to be at least as stirred by Morgenstern's appeal as he had been. She said, 'I do believe that that is the most remarkable thing I have ever read.'

He nodded eagerly. 'I am left rocked from top to bottom! More than twelve hours have gone by since I first read it, and still I cannot rid it from my mind. It seems so fantastical, I ask myself: can it be genuine?'

'How could anyone invent such a document? No poet ever conjured such a fancy! *Why* would they?'

'For the purpose of sedition. Because it undermines the authority of the Church and reduces the mysterious workings of Almighty God to various speculations – six possible forms of catastrophe, and so forth. It places humans at the centre of the universe and suggests that His supreme will could be thwarted by mortal foresight. It mentions none of the things the Church teaches. Where is the Beast of the Apocalypse with its seven heads and ten horns? Where is Babylon and the Lake of Fire? The letter is heretical – even diabolical. Merely to possess it is to invite the severest penalty.'

She stared into the middle distance. 'Imagine living in those days,' she mused, 'feeling oneself sliding into an abyss and yet being powerless to do anything to escape it.'

'Perhaps they did do something.'

'But too late to have an effect. Their world has passed beyond recall.' She turned back a page. 'His letter was written in March of their year two thousand and twenty-two. His daughter married when?'

'That same summer.'

'And when did the catastrophe occur?'

'Three years later, in two thousand and twenty-five.'

'In what season? Summer? Winter?'

'The exact month is unknown. The Scriptures point only to the year six hundred three score and six. Although,' he added tentatively, 'I could perhaps hazard a view.'

'Do it then.'

'No, I would prefer not.'

'Why?'

'Because it is contrary to the Church's teaching to dwell too closely upon such matters.' Yet he could not resist it. 'Very well, if you press me, I would say – judged on the number of burials held in the village in the autumn of that year – it was most probably sometime in the late summer, just before the harvest. People started then to die in the great numbers foretold in the Book of Revelation. Soon after that, the records cease. Whatever it was that happened was sudden and overwhelming.'

She flicked the pages back and forth. 'I wonder what became of Dr Shadwell.'

'Dead by now, one would conjecture, given the severity with which the heresy was suppressed. Although I had a notion—'

He stopped. He was talking too much.

'A notion? What?'

Reluctantly he continued, 'It is fanciful, doubtless – but a notion that the man who cried out at the burial might have been him.'

'Perhaps it was.' She sat back in her chair for half a minute, staring at the open door. She seemed to be trying to make up her mind about something. 'Can I trust you to be discreet, Mr Fairfax?'

'Of course,' he said, somewhat offended, 'seeing as I am most certainly trusting you to be the same.'

'Then we shall be bound together in jeopardy.' She rang for the maid, who appeared with such alacrity that Fairfax wondered if she had been listening at the door. 'Abigail, bring my shoes, and a lantern.'

CHAPTER TEN

Colonel Durston's collection

THE INTERIOR OF the great house was a shipwreck – dark, damp, silent, strewn with abandoned objects, its gloom tinged by an ethereal greenish light that seeped through the shutters and the layers of ivy. Where the rain had penetrated the ceilings the floorboards had given way, infesting the ruin with a heavy, spore-laden smell of mildew and rotted timber.

Fairfax followed Lady Durston from the rear of the house via what must have once been the domestic offices towards the state rooms at the front. Her white shirt danced ahead in the shadows as she moved from one exposed joist to the next. In the wavering gleam of her lantern, images loomed out of the darkness – a stag's antlers mounted on the wall of the passageway, a pink plastic figure without arms or hair propped up next to a door. In the dining room, a long, sheeted table was surrounded by two dozen high-backed chairs similarly shrouded, giving the effect of a feast of ghosts. In the ceremonial entrance hall, at the bottom of the staircase, weeds grew beside a rusted gong. Pale rectangular patches on the walls showed where the pictures had been removed. Hanging over it all was the stench of decay.

She opened one of the big panelled doors opposite the staircase. At the far end of the long room a latticework of subaqueous lime-coloured light pressed against the closed shutters. She tried to unfasten them, but the task was beyond her. 'Mr Fairfax . . .' there was a trace of irritation in her voice, as if it pained her to ask for his help, 'if you'd be good enough to assist me?'

She held up the lantern. The shutters were nearly twice his height, fastened by a long brass bar that he had to strike repeatedly from underneath with the palm of his hand until it became loose enough to lift. The hinges of the panels cracked as he dragged them open. Through the tall glass, fogged by grime, the drive and the lake lay still in the sunshine, frozen like a painting. He turned. The room had once been the library, but only a few torn volumes remained. At some time, birds had clearly invaded it down the chimney. An ancient layer of twigs and feathers carpeted the floorboards. The long rows of bare shelves and the top of the soot-stained fireplace were marbled by petrified droppings.

She said, 'The library was destroyed years back.

My father-in-law used to say nothing burned so well on a cold winter's night as a good book.'

Fairfax looked around at the empty, bird-limed bookshelves. Surely Morgenstern must have written a book himself, given his eminence? If so, might he not have presented a copy to the family in the big house, even if they, with their gun dogs and their hunting parties, could not have understood it? It would have been a polite gesture for a tenant to make. But it would have gone up the chimney on a frosty night along with all the others. How many volumes had been used for fuel – not just in Addicott but all over England? Countless millions. Hundreds of millions! How much knowledge had been lost?

One large item of furniture stood sheeted in the centre of the room. Lady Durston unveiled it in a single flourish: a library table with a peeling red leather top. She cast aside the sheet and pulled open the central drawer. She felt around inside and took out a key, then led Fairfax to the corner of the room, where there was a door, small and discreet, covered in the same faded and peeling crimson paper as the walls. No handle, only a small keyhole. She unlocked it and gave him the lantern. He looked at her, uncertain what was expected of him.

'Tell me what you think.'

The chamber was small and stuffy, barely sufficient for one person to move around. He guessed it must have been the muniment room, where the family had stored their documents. A circular window, heavily barred, admitted just enough light to show shelves crammed from floor to low ceiling with a profusion not of paper but of glassware: flasks and beakers, tubes and coils, rods and funnels, hundreds of pieces, few of them whole, all very fine and of a type he had never seen before. He picked up the largest fragment, a cylinder perhaps three inches in diameter and a foot tall, broken at the top but with its base intact. Nothing so precise and delicate could be manufactured nowadays. He shone the lantern through it. A toothcomb of lines and numbers was engraved in red along one side, and when he wiped away the dust, he saw that there were letters, 'ml' and 'cl', marked off in numbers: 10, 50, 100.

She called from the library, 'Look in the cupboard on the left.'

He hitched up his cassock, kneeled with the lantern beside him and opened the door. A rusted object, as long as his forearm, was lying on a piece of cloth — heavy, with a snub tube protruding from one end. Attempts had been made to clean it. Beneath the rust, patches of metal gleamed. But the attempt to burnish it had been abandoned and what must once have been moving parts were corroded into a solid mass.

'Do you see it?'

'Yes.'

'Well?'

'It appears to be some sort of firearm.'

'So my husband thought. He found several on our land. That was the best preserved.'

Fairfax cradled the weapon in his hands. It looked quite unlike the long muskets issued to the army, although guns were unfamiliar to him. As a priest, he was exempt from military service. He brought it up to his shoulder, where it rested cold and sharp against his cheek, and squinted along the barrel. He sensed something malevolent about it — useless rusted block though it was — and replaced it in the cupboard. He straightened, dusted off his cassock and stepped back into the library.

Sarah Durston was leaning against the table. 'Remarkable, no?'

'Beyond remarkable! I've never seen the like. Plainly the glass had no domestic purpose. Nor was it made for decoration, although some of it has a certain beauty.'

'It has flummoxed me for years. But now perhaps I understand. Might it not have belonged to a professor of the science of physic?'

He saw at once that she was right. 'Doubtless Morgenstern brought it here from London.'

'To do what?'

'That I cannot guess.' He looked back at the muniment room. A picture of an alchemist came into his mind — a wizard bent over bottles full of bubbling liquids and noxious smells — although it seemed unlikely, given the cool intelligence evident in Morgenstern's letter, that he was anything of the sort. 'How long has it all lain there?'

'Five years. My late husband collected it.'

'All of it?'

'All.'

'Why?'

'A question I asked a hundred times, but never could he give a proper answer. I suppose his hope was that he would one day find a meaning in it, and it would lead to richer treasure.'

'But it must have taken an age to gather so much.'

'Oh yes,' she sighed. 'Years.' She studied him, weighing him up. 'Have you heard much of Sir Henry Durston, Mr Fairfax?'

'Nothing.'

'No village gossip overheard? People do love to talk.'

'None.'

'Then I should tell you something of him.' She glanced out of the window. 'He was older than I — a colonel in the Wessex Regiment, wounded in the late war against the French. From that ill fortune all our others flowed. He came back from the fighting badly broken. The house was hardly better than you see it today. The income from our tenants was insufficient to meet the cost of our debts, let alone carry out repairs. We should have sold up and moved away. But the Durstons are a stubborn lot — they lasted here a thousand years — or were, I should say, for Sir Henry was the last of the line, the thirty-fifth baronet.' She turned to look at Fairfax. 'So he gambled all his hopes for our recovery on what might lie beneath the land.'

'What? In buried treasure?'

'I see your wonderment, and believe me, I shared it. But his fancy was not entirely idle. Family tradition held that objects of great value had been hidden on the estate. He was out in all weathers searching, like a man who had lost something and sought to find the spot where he'd mislaid it. But all he recovered was glass and weapons. Those, and the usual rubbish from the past — plastics and suchlike — objects entirely worthless. The glass meant nothing to him either, for he'd never heard of Morgenstern.'

'And yet he kept it?'

'Hours he spent with it, cleaning it and arranging it in different configurations, as if there lay in it a clue to something else. He believed the fact that guns lay near the glass had some significance — maybe a greater treasure required to be protected. But for all his speculations, it stayed old glass. He knew it was contrary to the law to keep it, yet he could never quite bear to part with it — nor, after he was gone, could I, for it was just about all of him that was left to me.'

'How long did he search?'

'Every day for two years.'

'Why did he stop?'

'He drowned himself in the lake.'

'Oh my dear Lady Durston — I am very sorry to hear it!'

She waved away his sympathy. 'I disclose all this in confidence. As far as the world knows, it was a tragic mishap, so that Father Lacy could bury him in consecrated ground. But now that I have seen that little book, I think perhaps he might have come upon something of value after all. I hope so, for I was often impatient with him and accused him of wasting his strength on idle dreams. I fear it created some bad feeling between us.'

'Well, it must be of historical value, certainly, if not — alas — monetary.' Fairfax could imagine the colonel's increasing desperation as, time and again, rather than jewellery or gold, he dug up pieces of glass. The wounded soldier, the young wife, the decaying house — what a tragic scene it suggested, like something out of a play! A thought occurred to him. 'Did Father Lacy know of the colonel's collection?'

'Not as long as my husband was alive. Henry was always very wary of the parson — he felt he talked too freely.'

'But afterwards?'

She looked him directly in the eye. 'We reach the point at last, Mr Fairfax. The truth is, Father Lacy came to see me a fortnight past and asked me if I'd ever heard mention of someone called Morgenstern in connection with my house. The name was an unusual one, so I have not forgot it. I told him truthfully I had not. That was all. He offered nothing further, mentioned no book, nor marriage register neither.'

'But you showed him the glass?'

'I did. I thought I could trust a man of God.'

'And what was his response?'

'He pretended indifference but I could see by the trembling of his hands when he touched it that his passion was aroused. He desired to know how the pieces had been found – separately or together.'

'And what was your answer?'

'The truth. That they came from one place.'

'From the ruins of the lodge, presumably?'

'No.'

'From the grounds of the house?'

'No.'

'Where then?'

'From the very edge of our land, high in the woods – a remote spot called the Devil's Chair.'

He recalled her distant and preoccupied manner at the graveside, the way she had removed her glove to trickle earth on to the coffin lid. Now he saw the reason for her brooding. 'The Devil's Chair is where Father Lacy fell to his death.'

She nodded. 'I saw no reason not to tell him. It was

only broken glass, and a few rusted weapons that had brought me nothing but misery. Let him look if he wanted. What reason should I care?'

'And afterwards, when his body was recovered – you told no one of why he was up there alone? Not the sheriffs, nor the magistrate?'

'I considered it.' For the first time she looked uncomfortable. 'But to tell a single part of the story would have meant to tell it all – to confess myself possessor of a criminal collection.' The tone of her voice altered. She held out her hands to him, entreating him to understand. 'We are clinging to the wreckage here, Mr Fairfax, and there are plenty in Axford and beyond who would like to see me out of this house. Besides, I thought his death merely an evil chance.'

'And now?'

She did not answer.

Fairfax stared at her for a few moments and then began to pace around the library. His mind was restless with possibilities. He could not keep still. At last he halted in front of her. 'I must tell you frankly, Lady Durston, I think that was an error.'

'Why?'

'You weren't to know it, but no sooner had he visited here and seen all this than Father Lacy changed the locks at the parsonage and hid the church registers. A stranger was seen in the village on the day he died.'

'That I did not know.'

'I believe you. But what does it all signify? He must have been fearful of something – and it would seem rightly, as it proved. Does anyone else know of his visit here, aside from me?'

'No.'

'Captain Hancock?'

'Certainly not.'

'What about your women – might they have seen him come or go?'

'If they did, they have not mentioned it. Your questioning alarms me, Mr Fairfax.'

'Believe me, that is the last thing I desire. But consider what befell him. He came here in the week before his death – what day to be exact?'

She thought it over. 'It was on the Sunday – in the afternoon. As I was leaving after the service that morning he asked if he could call on me.'

'So that was what – the twenty-fourth of March? And he died the following Tuesday week, on the second of April. Consider it: after thirty years of walking the length and breadth of the valley without mishap, nine days after coming here, he fell to his death. The bishop will reckon that a most sinister coincidence.'

She looked at him in alarm. 'You will not tell him any of this?'

'I have no choice. I must report what I have discovered.'

'Then I am ruined.'

'Oh, come now, surely not!'

'But I am! Sheriffs and priests will descend upon this house and our lives here will be finished.'

'I refuse to believe it. If the objects had been precious, or if some had been sold – yes, perhaps. But no judge would convict a woman, especially one of your rank, of the crime of hoarding broken glass.'

'How little you know of the world, and of the peril of a woman alone in it, with no husband to protect her!' She folded her arms and stared at the floor. Half a minute passed before she spoke again. 'Well then, make your report if you must – but at least make no mention of my name.'

'How can I not? All turns upon the evidence of Morgenstern's presence in this valley so many centuries ago, and how it came to light. Your talk with Father Lacy is the central fact.'

'Could we not perhaps examine this matter further by ourselves, and not involve the Church for the present?'

The brazenness of the suggestion startled him. 'Lady Durston,' he said coldly, 'I can hardly conceal from my lord bishop urgent information about the death of a brother priest.' He was aware of sounding pompous – cruel, even – but really, what else was he to say? 'I could not think to do it.'

'Oh, Father Fairfax,' she said, her eyes cold with

contempt, 'are you really so lacking in simple Christian charity?'

Afterwards Fairfax was to count it a great good fortune that their conversation was at that point interrupted. Had it not been, he was sure he would have clamped his saturno back upon his head and insisted on being shown off the premises. Instead, just as he was preparing to make a suitably cutting reply, he happened to glance beyond her shoulder to the library window, through which he noticed a now-familiar figure in a pony and trap coming up the drive towards the house.

'Captain Hancock,' he blurted out in surprise, 'and for the second time today!'

'What?' She swung round to follow his gaze, and let out a groan. 'He has invited himself to supper – I had clean forgot.' They watched Hancock drive past the front of the house and disappear behind the rhododendrons towards the stable yard. Suddenly it was as if their argument had never happened. 'You must join us, Mr Fairfax.'

'I would prefer not,' he said stiffly.

'But I insist on it.' And to his amazement, she reached out and clasped his hand. 'I would count it a very great personal favour if you would make the table three instead of two, but I beg you not to say a word to Captain Hancock of what has passed between us.'

CHAPTER ELEVEN

The supper party

H E CONTINUED TO protest that he ought to return to the parsonage, that he had no wish to interrupt a private arrangement – which was indeed the truth – but she would not hear of it. She was anxious that they should not be seen emerging from the rear of the house together, so at her suggestion they left through the front door. Its mortise lock, heavy bolts and huge ring handle were as big as those of the cathedral. As it opened, it dragged in tendrils of ivy that clutched at the doorposts as if the house was reluctant to allow these rare visitors to escape. She locked it behind her, slipped the key into her pocket, and together they made their way around the side of Durston Court towards the stables.

By the time they reached the courtyard, Hancock had descended from his buggy and was standing with his back to them on the threshold of Lady Durston's

sitting room. He was holding a bouquet of blue jacarandas pointing downwards, tapping it against the top of
his boot, oblivious to the falling petals. She called out,
'Captain Hancock!' at which he turned with a broad
smile of anticipation that shrank on seeing Fairfax. 'I
have been giving Mr Fairfax a tour of the grounds. He is
joining our little supper. I hope you approve.'

There was something heroic in the way Hancock
struggled to hide his disappointment. 'Not at all. A fine
idea.' He remembered the flowers, glanced at them in
embarrassment and thrust them into her hand. 'They
were not worth picking. Best throw them away.'

'I would not think of it.' She put her nose to the
jacarandas. 'How strange that something so beautiful
should have so little scent. I shall put them in water
directly. Come in, gentlemen. I must go and change
out of my gardening clothes. Take a little of our gin
while you wait. I shall have a jug sent in.'

She withdrew and left them sitting awkwardly in
the two gilt chairs. In the confined space, their knees
were almost touching. For some time, neither spoke,
until at length Fairfax said, 'May I trouble you for the
time, Captain Hancock?'

Hancock reached into his inside pocket and pulled
out a watch. 'A little after five, sir. The time for which
I was invited.' He returned the watch to its place and
stared at Fairfax. 'I take it ye have concluded your
"church business" – or did I interrupt it?'

'No, I have done all that needed doing. I shall conduct a service on the Sabbath and then I shall leave directly for Exeter.'

'So if it was not church business, may I ask what brought ye to this house?' There was aggression in the question.

'You may ask, although I regard myself as under no obligation to answer. However, if the matter is important, I happened to take a letter to Mr Gann to catch the post to Exeter, and then thought I would take a walk along the lane. I saw the gateposts and came in.' All of this had the merit of being true, even if it was not the full story, but it appeared to satisfy Hancock, who gave an upward tilt of his chin and a grunt. What a boorish fellow he was, thought Fairfax, and for the first time he felt glad to be staying for supper, if only to cause him irritation.

Abigail came in with a pair of jugs and three glasses, which she set upon the table. Hancock sent her away and insisted on doing the pouring himself: two large tumblers of gin, with only the merest slop of water for dilution. He pushed Fairfax's drink across the table towards him.

'Let us toast your journey home, sir. May it be safe – and quick.'

'Safe and quick.' Fairfax sipped the sour, oily liquid and grimaced.

Hancock drained his glass and poured himself

another. He stared at the open door and muttered, 'Why do women always take so long?'

'You're unmarried, I take it, Captain?'

'Never had the time for it. First the army, then my business. My sister keeps my house for me. Of course, the issue does not arise in your case.'

'Alas, no.'

'Alas indeed! Although in my opinion, a man should only marry when he reaches a certain stage in life. At that point it becomes a necessity. The parson – God rest his soul – would have had less time for that morbid passion of his, collecting bones and whatnot, if he could have had a wife in bed at night to keep him content. Mind ye,' he added with a wink, 'it's said that Agnes filled the role.'

'Captain Hancock!'

'I'm sorry, young man. I shock thee. Forgive me. I withdraw the remark entirely.'

Fairfax set his drink down on the table, folded his arms and glanced away, resolved to have no further conversation until Lady Durston returned. But as the silence lengthened, he found himself considering those aspects of life at the parsonage he had himself observed – the housekeeper's extravagant grief, the cramped living conditions, which required her to sleep with her niece, her resentment at the prospect of leaving her home – and he saw that there might well be some truth in the insinuation.

Inexperienced as he was, Fairfax was not a prig. He could understand how these things might happen. He did not presume to judge. He had passed too many hours himself secretly thinking of the young women of Exeter, sometimes even in the cathedral itself, might God forgive him. After a while, curiosity overcame his resolve, and he said, addressing his remark not to Hancock directly, but to the open door, 'Mrs Budd told me that you were with the search party that discovered Father Lacy's body.'

'Not merely with it,' replied Hancock. He seemed eager to make amends; his tone became friendlier. 'I raised the search myself and provided most of the men from my mill.'

'Really?' Now Fairfax turned and gave him his full attention.

'Aye. The church clerk, Keefer – who works for me when he's not employed on God's business – turned up late seeking help on Wednesday morning, said the parson had not been home all night, and Agnes was quite deranged with worry. I stopped half my machines so we could go and search.'

'And how long did it take to find him?'

'All day. We carried him off the hill at nightfall.'

'I heard his body was discovered in a remote spot.'

'Aye, indeed – the remotest! A place in the woods about two miles north of here, close to the ruined tower. The land is always very soft and treacherous up on the hills after the winter rain — a lot of springs rise underground. The earth must have given way beneath him. He fell into a ravine, his little trowel beside him.'

'It sounds lucky you found him.'

'It was. Fortunately Keefer had some inkling of whereabouts he'd been scouting lately, so we knew the area to look in first. Otherwise it could've taken days.'

Fairfax sat up at that. 'Keefer knew where to go?'

'Roughly speaking, aye. Most of the men won't go near that place, due to the local superstition. One mercy, though, Fairfax.' He put his hand on Fairfax's knee and leaned in, confiding, man to man. 'I reckon it must have been a quick death.'

'Why?'

'Because the animals in the woods had been chewing at him. They'd never have done that if he'd still been alive.'

Just at that moment, Lady Durston appeared in the doorway. Hancock gave Fairfax a warning look, withdrew his hand from his knee and briefly put his finger to his lips.

'What an intimate pair!' She sounded surprised, and even a little put out. 'Perhaps you'd prefer it if I went away? Otherwise, gentlemen' — she executed a mocking curtsy — 'supper is served.'

*

The dining room was further along the stable block, with a door through to the kitchen. Like the sitting room, it had been furnished with objects rescued from the main house: a pink floral carpet, its lozenge pattern faded almost to nothing; a table that could seat eight, with chairs that did not match; and a sideboard on which stood two large pewter candelabra. Lady Durston sat at the head of the table with the two men flanking her. Captain Hancock's flowers were in a vase between them. Her hair was tied up and she had changed into a long black skirt, a pale blue blouse and a brocaded jacket. Like the costume she had worn in church, it was clearly of fine quality, but old and mended, and although it took Fairfax a while to notice it, her neck, ears and fingers were naked, unadorned by jewellery. *We are clinging to the wreckage*, she had said. She asked him to say grace.

The food was good, if simple – a hot egg soup followed by boiled pigeon on a bed of spinach with a slice of bacon on top – each course served from the kitchen by Jenny the cook. The wine was a Devon red, although Hancock stuck to gin. He had carried the jug in from the sitting room and kept it beside him throughout the meal, frequently topping up his glass. He was the type of successful man Fairfax had often observed socially among the wealthy merchants in Exeter. Dominant and even (one might concede) entertaining when the conversation was to their liking, they lapsed into a brooding and impatient silence when the topic did not touch upon their own interests. Thus, when the captain held forth on the manufacture of woollen cloth and the way in which a single man working at one of his machines could produce as much in a ten-hour day as fifty using traditional methods, and how this would sooner or later transform the economy not just of the valley but the county, his voice was animated and Fairfax listened with interest.

'And how many days of the week do they work ten hours?' he asked.

'Six. On the seventh they rest, as the Bible decrees.'

'Sixty hours a week sounds a long time to work at one machine. Do they not complain?'

'They complain without cease! But I pay them more than ever they could earn by weaving in their own homes.'

'Not fifty times as much,' observed Lady Durston.

'No, but I must bear the cost of the machinery and its maintenance. I take all the risks and they take none.' He turned to Fairfax. 'Our looms are water-driven and break down often, mostly because we have no control over the size and force of the river. In the spring and winter it's too fast, in the summer sluggish. Nature is the greatest brake on our expansion.'

Lady Durston said, 'Well I for one am glad that

nature keeps your ambitions in check. I should be sorry to see the old way of life in the village disappear.'

'Aye, my dear Sarah — and that is why we sit down to eat in your horses' house while your real house falls to pieces beside us!'

She laughed at him. 'Hark at the way he bullies me, Mr Fairfax! Come to my rescue.'

'I believe you need no rescuing by me, or by anybody else, Lady Durston.'

'Ah, but she does, Father! She needs rescuing right enough. She's just too proud to face it. Listen: I employ close on half the men in the valley. Because they produce more, I pay more. They then have more to spend in Axford market, and the stallholders and the shopkeepers can extend their produce. Prosperity spreads. What objection can there be to that?'

'None,' said Fairfax, 'unless the pursuit of money becomes an end in itself. Then I should find plenty to object to. "Consider the lilies: they toil not, they spin not."'

'Indeed, sir, they do not — that is because they are *flowers*.'

'Enough of business,' said Lady Durston firmly. 'Tell us of yourself, Mr Fairfax. Was it always your intention to be a priest?'

The abrupt change of subject caught him by surprise. 'Mine? No — the intention was rather chosen for me. My parents and my sister were killed by the fever when I was young, and I was obliged to live with my uncle in Weymouth. He was a decent enough man, but getting on in years, with little use for a lively boy of ten, and so I was sent to the cathedral school in Exeter, and from there to the seminary.'

'So the Church has been both your mother and your father?'

'Yes, and all my other relations combined, since my uncle also died soon after he sent me away.' He felt a flicker of guilt. His behaviour this day had hardly been that of the Church's loyal son. 'Since childhood my vocation has been to serve God, and it is my honour to do so.' For the first time the familiar formula sounded vaguely hollow.

'There are too many priests,' pronounced Hancock, pouring himself another drink. 'That is my opinion. No offence, Fairfax, but they interfere too much in the running of things that do not concern them. Take my factory, for example. They come out from Exeter to inspect it in case I've broken some law or other and installed machines that are proscribed. Where is this decreed in the Bible? They should confine themselves to matters of the spirit and leave the weaving of cloth to me.'

'So Church and state should be separate?'

'It would be best for both.'

'Then surely we would arrive at a place where the Church would have morals without power, and the state would have power without morality. That is exactly what led the ancients to disaster.'

'So the Church maintains — but then of course it suits their interest to tell us such. But how are we to know if what they say is true, since they have made it a crime to investigate the past?'

'Be careful, John,' warned Lady Durston.

'I merely express my private opinion. I'm sure the father will not report me to the bishop for heresy.'

Fairfax smiled. 'Your opinions are safe with me, Captain. There are even some in the Church who hold similar views. I well remember an ordinand who said much the same.'

'And what became of him?'

Fairfax paused. 'Now you ask me, I do not rightly know.' And it was true: he did not. One day the young man had been dining with the rest of them in the chapter house, the next his place had been cleared and his belongings packed and gone. No one had spoken of it. Fairfax had forgotten the episode himself until this moment. It must have been three or four years ago. He couldn't even remember the ordinand's name.

There was a lull in the conversation. The sun was setting; it was beginning to feel cold. Hancock drained the jug of gin. Lady Durston rose and closed the stable door, then went over to the sideboard, struck a match and started to light the candles. Fairfax glanced up at the skylight. It would soon be dusk. He felt suddenly uncomfortable. 'I had best start back to the parsonage.'

'Not yet, surely?' Lady Durston sounded dismayed. 'The meal is not complete. We have a pudding of baked apples.'

'A tempting prospect, but the light is going. I must observe curfew or Mrs Budd will wonder what has become of me.'

'But it's a long walk and the way is unknown to you.'

'I shall find it well enough, I'm sure.' He folded his napkin, placed it on the table and stood. 'My thanks, your ladyship, for a splendid meal, and for the company.'

She swung around to Hancock. 'John, you'll give him a ride home? It's on your way.'

Hancock pulled a face at her across the rim of his glass. 'I do not see the necessity. The journey is easy enough.' He looked up at Fairfax. 'Through the park, turn right and then left at the bottom of the hill. There's an hour's light, at least.'

'I would feel easier in my mind if I knew Mr Fairfax was safe. Who knows what desperate characters may lurk in the empty lanes with night coming on? Please – as a favour to me – take him.'

Fairfax said, 'Really, Lady Durston, there is no need.'

'But think of what happened to Father Lacy . . .'

Hancock banged down his glass in exasperation. 'Lacy was an old man, wandering the edge of a dangerous hill. Fairfax is young and the way is safe.' His tone became uncharacteristically wheedling. 'Really, Sarah, I have no desire to leave just yet. There are matters I wish to discuss with ye.'

'Please, John.'

Hancock drummed his fingers on the tablecloth. 'Very well, Fairfax, if she insists, but I'd be grateful for a minute or two alone with her ladyship before we go, if ye'd oblige us.' He reached into his inside pocket, withdrew a folded sheet of paper – a legal document of some sort by the look of it – and laid it on the table.

Fairfax turned to Lady Durston to settle what had become an awkward impasse. She gave him a look that made him feel he had let her down in some way, but then she sighed and her expression became resigned. 'Would you mind waiting in the other room while I hear out Captain Hancock?'

'Of course not. Excuse me.'

He went out into the stable yard, closing the door behind him. He wondered what business it was that needed to be discussed so urgently. The servant women – Abigail, Jenny and a third, more mannish-looking, whom he assumed must be Mary – were huddled together whispering. Mary, who was in out-door clothes and bonnet, seemed to have just come back from somewhere. She was holding a large dog on a leash that growled when it saw him and strained to reach him until she tugged at it sharply and it settled down. He nodded to the trio and made his way to the sitting room.

No candles had been lit. In the gloom the Durston family portraits peered out at him with unnaturally large round eyes. How modern-looking they were, he thought. One might encounter them in any street or house in England, complaining about their servants or the state of the roads. Their clothes were more elaborate – military uniforms nowadays were a drab olive green rather than scarlet – but otherwise they came from a world recognisably similar to his own. It was as if the long recovery after the Apocalypse had stalled at the point civilisation had reached two centuries before disaster struck. Why? Was it that there were certain basic patterns of human behaviour that were irreducible – the need to grow food, to live in settlements, to worship God, to bear children and to educate them – but that beyond those essentials a great leap was required to achieve the sort of world described in Morgenstern's letter, and such a leap had never been attempted? Or had it been attempted at some point in the past, but had failed or been suppressed, and he had never heard of it?

He stood for a long time, perhaps a quarter of an hour, in the accumulating dusk until his meditation was ended by the sound of Hancock impatiently calling his name. He went outside to find him already seated in his trap, his body hunched forwards, his elbows on his knees, the reins held loosely in his hands, staring into nothing. Lady Durston was standing in the doorway of the dining room with a shawl around her shoulders. He sensed an atmosphere between them. Clearly they had said their farewells already. The three servants were nowhere to be seen. He approached her with his hand outstretched.

'My thanks again, my dear Lady Durston, for a memorable tour and supper. I hope perhaps we might have a final chance to say goodbye after church on Sunday.'

'It's possible, Mr Fairfax, although I must confess I am feeling very tired.' She did indeed look pale. She took his hand in both of hers, leaned in and added quietly, 'You must say whatever needs saying to the bishop. It was wrong of me to argue otherwise. If Father Lacy was murdered, his killer is at large and I am very glad the captain will escort you.'

'It's not I who am at risk, but you, in this isolated place.'

'I am well able to protect myself. Only don't think

too badly of me.' Her fingers squeezed his palm briefly then she released him and stepped back. 'Good night, gentlemen. Safely home.'

The buggy rocked as Fairfax climbed up on to the bench seat. Hancock released the brake, made a clicking noise with his tongue and shook the reins. They lurched across the cobbles and swept around the courtyard in a wide arc. Fairfax raised his hand in farewell towards the place where Lady Durston had been standing, but she had already gone inside.

Hancock did not speak and Fairfax did not feel inclined to start a conversation. They drove in silence, down to the lake and across the bridge. Frogs croaked in the dusk. Fairfax looked over his shoulder at the house. It seemed darker than the surrounding trees, as if its density absorbed the light, its high gables rising like four pyramids against the purple sky. Then it slipped behind the cedars.

'God damn this road!' muttered Hancock. He was staring straight ahead, concentrating on steering around the potholes. But although he handled the buggy with skill, it was impossible to avoid them all and several times the wheels jolted so hard Fairfax was almost pitched over the side. 'How often have I offered to fix it for her, and always she refuses!'

They clattered between the gateposts into the narrow lane and began to descend the hill. Hancock said through clenched teeth, 'Doubtless it's too much to hope ye might tell me the true reason for your visit to Lady Durston this afternoon.'

'So we are back to this? I have said what happened.'

'Aye, what happened, but not the truth that lies behind it. No one walks all the way out here without a purpose. Ye delayed going back to Exeter in order to see her.'

'Not at all.'

'Lie then, it does not concern me.' He took up his whip and flicked the horse's flanks. The buggy gained speed and Fairfax had to clutch on to his hat to prevent it flying away. It occurred to him that Hancock was slightly drunk. 'I've admired her ladyship for many years,' the captain went on, 'many, many years – since before her husband died, to tell the truth – so I well understand her attraction.'

'No such thought has entered my head, sir, I assure you. This is foolish talk.'

For the first time Hancock took his eyes off the road to look at Fairfax. 'Then why were ye there? And in the house together, if I'm not mistaken, because I swear I glimpsed her through the window as I came along the drive.'

'I'll answer no more questions, and would be obliged to be set down here. I would prefer to walk the rest of the way.'

'No, no, I'm a man of my word. I promised her I'd see ye home, and so I shall. She seems quite unreasonably convinced some mortal danger lies concealed in these harmless empty lanes.' He darted another look at Fairfax. 'And again I ask myself: why is that?'

They had reached the bottom of the hill. The forge was shuttered, although there was a light in an upstairs window, presumably Gann's home. The yellow plastic shell at the top of its pole gleamed faintly luminous in the twilight. They turned towards the village.

Hancock slowed the buggy and said casually, 'Well, none of it matters. What's past is past. Ye may congratulate me, Fairfax.'

'Congratulate you on what?'

'Just now, when we were alone, I asked Sarah — Lady Durston — if she'd do me the honour of becoming my wife, and she accepted.'

Fairfax stared at him. For a moment he was too surprised to speak. 'Well, then yes, of course, I do congratulate you, most sincerely.'

'It's not the first time I have asked her.'

'No?'

'Oh, she does not love me — I do not deceive myself on that. But she needs a man to protect her and restore her fortunes, and I have hopes that in time her feelings for me may grow.'

Fairfax could not stop himself asking, 'Did she say why she had changed her mind?'

'She did not. But in some curious sense I cannot fathom, I attribute it to ye.'

'Surely not!'

'I do. That's why I'm interested to know what passed between ye. But as ye clearly have no intention of telling me, I suppose I must concentrate on my good fortune and forget about the rest.'

There was no one abroad in the village. It was just as it had been on the night Fairfax arrived, which seemed to him at that moment a very long time ago — the quiet muddy road, the drawn curtains, the occasional lamp, the engulfing silence. Hancock drew up outside the parsonage, applied the brake, then reached into his inside pocket and drew out what looked to be the same folded sheet of paper he had produced at supper. 'This is our application for a wedding licence, signed by us both this evening. I believe notice of it must be read out in church before the ceremony can be held.'

'That's true — on three successive Sundays.' How typical of a man of business, thought Fairfax with sudden bitterness, to make sure he had the deal in writing and signed before the other party could change their mind!

'I thought ye might make the first announcement from the pulpit this Sunday — before departing.'

'Yes, it would be an honour. Congratulations again.'

'Good night, Father.'

'Good night, Captain Hancock.'

There was no handshake. Fairfax descended from the buggy. Hancock released the brake, jerked the reins, said, 'Walk on!' and trundled away up the lane that ran next to the parsonage, leaving the priest alone on the roadside, holding the paper and watching him until he disappeared.

CHAPTER TWELVE

The Devil's Chair

THE MOMENT HE walked through the door, Agnes came hurrying from the kitchen, Rose almost treading on her heels. 'Father Fairfax! Thanks be to God!'

He made an effort to put on a show of apology, smiling, taking off his hat, spreading his hands. 'I am sorry to return so late, Mrs Budd – good evening, Rose – Lady Durston pressed me to stay for supper.'

'But I've been worried sick, sir! It's but a week to this very hour since Father Lacy was carried home.'

'Is it?' He hung his head. 'I had quite forgotten. How thoughtless of me. I apologise.'

'Well, ye're safe, at least, and that's the main thing.' The irritation in her voice softened to relief. 'So ye'll not be wanting feeding, then?'

'Thanks all the same, but no. The day has been

long. A candle is all I require, and then I'll bid you both good night.'

In the old priest's bedroom, he sat on the edge of the bed to take off his boots, abandoned the effort, flopped back on the mattress and closed his eyes. He was affected by the fate to which Sarah Durston had just consigned herself – more affected than he would have expected, or cared to admit. He could not rid himself of the feeling that he was in some sense to blame – that if he had not embroiled her in the matter of Morgenstern's letter, she would have continued to resist Hancock's proposal, but that now, thanks to him, she felt in greater need of a protector. He recalled the pressure of her hand as she said goodbye. *Don't think too badly of me.* At the time he had read little into it, assuming she was merely referring to their argument in the library, but now he wondered if she was instead preparing him for the news that Hancock had taken such relish in delivering.

He turned it over and over in his mind until gradually the clarity of the day's memories began to blur, and he fell asleep to the image of her white shirt leading him through the darkness into the interior of the shipwrecked mansion.

He woke from his first sleep with a start a few hours later. He lay there for a few moments, listening for signs of movement. Neither Mrs Budd nor Rose seemed to be stirring. He sat up and finished the task of removing his boots, then collected his candle, went over to the door and opened it quietly. No sound came from the other bedroom. On tiptoe he descended the stairs and let himself into the study. The registers were where he had left them, beneath the couch. He pulled out the volume covering the century before the Apocalypse, unwrapped it from its plastic cover, laid it on the desk, placed the candle next to it and turned to the page that recorded the marriage of Miss Julia Morgenstern.

According to Sarah Durston, no one knew that the old priest had been to see her apart from him. If this page was excised and destroyed, the only physical link between Durston Court and Lacy's death would disappear. He could still inform the bishop of everything else that was suspicious. The circumstances of the priest's demise might yet be investigated. But she would be left out of it and would be able, if she wished, to extricate herself from her promise to marry Hancock.

He rummaged through the desk drawer until he found the parson's penknife, opened it and tested the blade against his thumb. As he would have expected of that avid collector, it was honed like a razor. He placed the tip at the top of the page, and pressed it close to the binding. He increased the pressure. The first few fibres of the thick paper began to separate. But then he stopped and lifted the blade away. He could not do it. It would be a sin against history. The strength of his conviction shocked him. As surely as a man might catch the sweating fever, he thought, I have been infected with the heresy of antiquarianism. He bowed his head and prayed to God to guide him to the light.

He closed the knife and replaced it in the drawer beside the bundle of sermons tied with black ribbon. Suddenly curious, he lifted them out, unfastened the knot and started sorting through them – two dozen at least, on brittle yellowish quarto-sized paper. The ink was faded and hard to read, full of crossings-out and added passages. In places the force of the nib had torn the paper. Arrows streaked across the pages to link to new material. Sentences in minuscule writing looped around the edges.

He rotated the pages and tried to decipher the tiny script. *And in those days shall men seek death, and shall not find it; and shall desire to die, and death shall flee from them.* He recognised the verse from the Book of Revelation. In fact, as he worked his way through the papers, he saw that all the sermons were based on Revelation. They appeared to have been revised endlessly over the years and presumably delivered on more than one occasion. What was it that somebody had remarked at the burial? *His sermons were of a peculiar sort . . .*

He retied the bundle and pushed it back in the drawer. Then he took the candle over to the bookshelves and stood before the forbidden texts. His gaze travelled along the spines until it came to rest on *Antiquis Anglia* by Dr Nicholas Shadwell.

He reached out and withdrew the heavy volume, carried it over to the desk, sat, and opened it to the title page.

Antiquis Anglia
A Record of Miscellaneous Surviving Structures
From the Late Pre-Apocalypse Era
by
Dr Nicholas Shadwell, SA
With Illustrations and Maps
by
Mr Oliver Quycke, SA
First Published by the Society of Antiquaries
London MCDXLIX

The frontispiece was an etching of a towering concave structure, with trees and people drawn in for scale, and a caption: *The Great Chimney, Gainsborough, Lincs.* He turned the page to Shadwell's Preface.

I have been inclined since my earliest years to a fascination for antiquities, and being born with some limited private means, and never having encumbered myself with the delights of a wife and family, I have been able to indulge my passion to a degree that perhaps no other man in England can boast. Mine has not been an entirely solitary life, I am glad to say. Throughout my travels, which have taken me the length and breadth of the country, I have been fortunate in the companionship of my secretary, Oliver Quycke, Esq., whose skill in draughtsmanship is evident in these pages.

I have not attempted to give a comprehensive account of every building and monument in England above eight hundred years old, for such a task would be impossible. Too numerous to count are the examples that have survived from the Pre-Apocalypse Era, most notably our churches and cathedrals, which, being constructed of stone, have proved more durable than structures erected many generations later. The same may be said of certain houses and other public buildings of what the ancients called their eighteenth and nineteenth centuries – now some thousand years old. There are even structures dating from far earlier times, such as the great Roman wall between England and Scotland, part of which once again serves as our fortified border against that ferociously independent northern people, even though it originated some 2,700 years ago. Stone – at least certain types of stone, such as granite, limestone and marble – is impervious to the ages.

However, the latter part of the twentieth century and the first quarter of the twenty-first present a very different picture. Paradoxically, what was supposedly the ultimate and most advanced phase of scientific technology has left almost nothing behind except plastic and fragments of glass. Who can now believe that at one time London alone is said to have boasted a dozen buildings rising to a height of more than six hundred feet, and one that rose to a thousand? No trace of them remains.

We do not know the precise processes by which these structures were destroyed so completely and so quickly. Some have proposed the theory of a terrible war involving explosives of unimaginable power. On the other hand, my colleague Mr Berkeley has speculated that it may have been due to the late-ancient era's reliance on the use of embedded steel in concrete: once the preponderance of glass that encased these structures was damaged (they must have been quickly abandoned by their inhabitants), rainwater was able to enter them. A combination of vegetative growth in summer and cracking caused by ice in winter in due course penetrated the concrete and caused the steel to rust. The rusted steel, in turn, expanded to fracture the concrete further, and the buildings eventually collapsed. This theory strikes me as the most plausible. What is sure is that within 150 years, when human beings began once again to record the world around them, only a few shattered mounds of debris remained, and even these have now entirely disappeared. (It may be noted in passing that sailors returning from long voyages in the West Indies have reported an area of ancient plastic flotsam, miles across, which not even eight centuries of Caribbean tempests have been able to disperse – the sinkhole down which an entire civilisation may be said to have vanished.)

The same is true of almost every structure of that period – apartment buildings, houses, 'shopping centres', factories, bridges, aeroplane ports . . . When we survey the tranquil moors and plains, the fields and farmland, the woods and forests of England, it is impossible for the imagination to conceive that they once teemed with buildings. And it is not merely buildings that have vanished. Maps exist showing a great system of wide roads and steel-tracked causeways carrying locomotive engines that has been crumbled to nothing by the remorse-less forces of nature, and whose very outlines are lost under many feet of roots and soil.

Not all is destroyed, however. Some edifices, for the most part constructed of concrete but without glass, have proved too large or too durable to be completely effaced, and it is these I have made it a large part of my life's work to catalogue, and which are the subject of this volume. They appear, for the most part, to be either the concrete supports of road bridges, the embankments of the same, or various chimneys and towers. What was their function? Of what mighty and intricate systems were they once a part? These questions we cannot answer. They stand strewn across the landscape – isolated, melancholy, mute – the tombstones and funerary monuments of a once-thriving civilisation of unimaginable sophistication that was felled with terrible and mysterious suddenness nearly a millennium ago.

The volume ran to almost three hundred pages. Fairfax turned them slowly. It was essentially a picture book. Each page consisted of an illustration of a structure, captioned with a few archaeological details and accompanied by a sketch map giving its location. Some sites were small, such as 'The Pillars at Boxley', showing six round concrete columns rising weirdly out of a field in Kent. 'The Arc, Huddersfield' was a delicate rainbow-like ellipse set against a background of wild moorland. 'The South Wonston Water Tower' was shaped like a torch-holder planted in the ground. Others were not really structures at all, such as 'The Stokenchurch Gorge', a vast, curving man-made canyon carved out of the Chiltern Hills. Perhaps the most dramatic was 'The Charwelton Tower', soaring needle-thin from a flat deserted plain with not a road in sight, and visible, according to Shadwell, a full day's ride away. The margins were covered in tiny scribbled notations, made in pencil, hard to decipher. The drawings themselves were precisely rendered. He turned the book to the candle to study them more closely.

What a labour it must have been, Fairfax thought, to scour the country and record all this. The book was a monument in itself. He had often passed similar ruins, albeit smaller and less complete: a megalith standing isolated by a roadside near Exeter without explanation; a lump of concrete half hidden by trees in the king's hunting woods around Yarcombe. He had never troubled himself to consider where they came from. They were merely a part of the English landscape. Once the mind began to worry away at their meaning, he could see how easily one might become obsessed. There were in truth two Englands: the everyday one, and this other, ancient hidden England, almost obliterated, through which most people moved without thinking.

He leafed to the index to see if any of the sites he knew had merited an entry. The structures were listed alphabetically by region. Wessex was particularly well served. He ran his finger down the place names and stopped when he came to 'The Devil's Chair, near Addicott St George'.

He stared at it for a few moments, then flicked back to the relevant page. Mr Quycke's illustration showed a featureless concrete cylinder surrounded by trees, not as impressive as some of the other entries, but formidable nonetheless.

> The Devil's Chair rises to a height of some seventy feet with a circumference of eighteen. If the trees that have encroached upon it in the past century were to be cleared, it would command extensive views to the east. The most plausible theory of its purpose, viz. that it might have served as an observation tower, is frustrated by the fact that there appears to be no discernible entrance, although rust marks rising at regular intervals along the NW elevation to the top indicate the possible existence in the past of a metal ladder. Local inhabitants are unclear whether the name refers to the structure itself or the ground upon which it stands, a depression girdled by steep hills, which does to some extent resemble a chair.

After he had made a copy of the map, sketching out the route from the village to the hill, Fairfax became aware of the sounds of movement above him. He did not wish to encounter Mrs Budd and explain what he was doing. Besides, there was nothing more he could do of any use except gather his strength for the next day. When he returned to bed, however, he found himself in that frustrating mental state in which one is too exhausted to think productively and yet too alert to sleep, and in this restless borderland he lay for the remainder of the night, twisting and turning between the old priest's sheets, until he heard a cock crow in the village. Soon afterwards, some time before six o'clock, the first faint greyness appeared at the window. He drew back the curtains and gazed upon a view as monochrome as one of Mr Quycke's etchings. Nobody else seemed to be up.

He splashed water over his face to revive himself. In the chest of drawers he found an old wide leather belt, which he fastened around his waist and used to hitch up his cassock so that he could move more freely. He carried his boots downstairs to avoid making a noise. At the last minute he remembered the pocket telescope in the study. He wrote a note to Agnes and left it on the kitchen table, explaining that he had gone for a long walk, that he would not be back for some hours, but that she was not to worry, and that he had taken the liberty of helping himself to some bread and cheese. He wrapped his provisions in a cloth and tied it to his belt, put on his boots, took a hickory walking stick from beside the back door and let himself out of the front.

The day was fresh, the village just beginning to stir. He nodded affably to a shepherd and a milkmaid as he passed them, but ducked his head to avoid conversation. He crossed the river and left the cottages behind. A brown pall of smoke hung over the fields close to The Piggeries. At the crossroads, the big wooden doors of the blacksmith's forge had been folded open, but the fire wasn't lit and he was relieved to see no sign of Gann or his apprentice.

He started up the lane towards Durston Court just as the sun broke over the trees. When he reached the gateposts with their curious melted stone figures, he slowed his pace. He was strongly tempted to call upon Sarah Durston. But the hour was unsociable, and after the events of the previous night he hardly knew what he would say to her. He pressed on up the hill.

The track became steeper and narrower. The hedges grew higher, turned into trees, and before long he found himself climbing a footpath through wood-land. The sound of a stream nearby reminded him he was thirsty. He scrambled down the bank, cupped his hands in the cold water and drank, then sat on a mossy fallen tree trunk and ate his bread and cheese. Wild flowers grew all around him — anemones, bluebells, irises — and there was an extraordinary profusion of butterflies — red admirals and holly blues, and others, purple and primrose-coloured, he could not identify.

The sight of so much wildlife and the sensation of food in his stomach helped restore his spirits (which were not, in truth, as robust as his decisive action might have suggested). According to his map, the lane should have continued for another half-mile until it curved round to the west and brought him to the tower. It might have been like that twenty years ago, or whenever it was that Shadwell and Quycke had visited the area, but it was not so now. Nature had reclaimed the place. There was nothing for it but to climb. Sooner or later he was bound to reach the crest, he reasoned; then he could work his way along it.

He set off again. The silence of the woods was disturbed by the chatter of parakeets; the marshy ground sang with the noise of the springs that bubbled up everywhere. He jumped the shallow streams. The hem of his cassock became damp and heavy. He started to sweat. When he looked over his shoulder, it was hard to pick out the path as it twisted between the trees. One could quickly become lost. He imagined Lacy following the same route barely more than a week ago, his tall, thin frame moving swift and oblivious towards its fate. An unpleasant picture to entertain in such an isolated spot. He tried to put it out of his mind.

A little higher up, a clearing at last afforded a view of the surrounding hills. Sheep were grazing on the slope leading up to the forest edge. He took out the telescope, extended it and scanned the treeline. Immediately his eye was caught by movement: a figure – possibly a man, a shepherd maybe – on the periphery of the wood. He lost him almost as soon as he'd found him. He adjusted the focus slightly, tracked a few degrees to his right and glimpsed a flash of something greyish white, motionless behind the trees, too big to be human. The tower? He lowered the telescope, wiped his eye and looked again. A structure of some sort, no question of it. He collapsed the spyglass and resumed his climb, but quicker now, eager to get it done.

He emerged from the trees on to the lower part of the slope, glad to be out in the open, where the ground was firmer and the light was clear. The sheep glanced up from their grazing as he approached and waited until he had almost reached them before scattering in panic when he came closer, their hooves drumming over the cropped grass. A pair of skylarks soared vertically hundreds of feet into the air and hovered, singing in alarm.

He paused to catch his breath, turned and looked back, and was immediately startled. A vast panorama had crept up behind him, as in a game of grandmother's footsteps, a view that took in the hills on the other side of the valley, and beyond them the empty moorland stretching to the horizon. There was a small smudge of human settlement in the centre of the plain, and when he trained his telescope upon it, he was just able to make out the spire of a church, no larger than a thumb-tack — Axford presumably.

When he turned his back again and resumed climbing, he felt peculiarly exposed. The view seemed to be watching him. Ahead, the tower was now half-visible behind the trees. But the route to it had become treacherous. Parts of the slope had given way, creating deep brown slashes of raw earth. He had an odd sense of instability underfoot, as if the firm downland might suddenly start to slide and send him tumbling in an avalanche of turf and soil and stones.

It was a relief to reach the solidity of the big trees and to feel their tuberous roots poking beneath his feet. He picked his way between them until he reached the clearing, in the centre of which stood the tower. Close to, its massiveness was humbling, like one of the great megaliths of Stonehenge – 'isolated, melancholy, mute', as Shadwell had written; the monument of a pagan civilisation, its purpose in their ancient rituals lost in time. Various species of vines and ivy had crept up from the forest floor to cover three quarters of it, which accounted for why it was so hard to detect from a distance.

He craned his neck to peer up at the top of it, shielding his eyes against the sun. He walked around it. He laid his hands upon it and felt its cold power. Here and there past generations of visitors had attempted to carve their initials, but whatever tools they had used had not been adequate for the task. They had merely scratched the concrete, and it was only possible to make out the occasional letter and numeral. In several places close to the ground he noted scorch marks. Fires had been lit against it. There were small holes in a regular line at roughly waist height, very old and weathered. He pulled back some of the ivy to make a closer examination. He poked his fingers into them. He remembered the rusted weapon in the colonel's collection, and it occurred to him that they were bullet holes. The thought made him pull his hand away and step back.

He made another circuit of the clearing. The wood was silent. No birdsong. All he could hear was the rustling of the wind in the tops of the trees. Now that he was starting to get his bearings, he could see that the tower was built on a flat area of ground, a kind of natural platform perhaps two hundred yards across and more or less the same in depth. Beyond this the land began to rise again, forming the arms and back of a natural chair. It was easy to see how the place had got its name. If one imagined it without trees, one could easily picture some great ogre sitting here, in this natural hollow, and staring out across the valley towards the distant moorland.

He scanned the wall of trees and wondered whereabouts Lacy had suffered his fall. Cautiously he began to climb the steep incline directly behind the tower. It bulged in places like a giant's forehead, overhanging the slope beneath. The ground was as Hancock had described it, soft after the winter rains. He could hear water running but could not see it. He prodded the ground in front of him with his stick before he took each step. Huge exotic ferns were growing in the damp earth. Weird fungus growths, some purple, some dead white, extruded from the trees, and where branches had fallen they were covered with emerald-green moss. In several places there had been mudslides, like the one that had closed the road out of the village. He could tell they were recent because of the lack of vegetation. There was a strong smell of fresh cold earth, such as he had only encountered before when crossing a newly ploughed field, or standing beside a fresh grave.

He dug his stick into the exposed earth, reluctant to go much further, and his gaze was caught by something pale lying in the soil. He bent to examine it, worked it free with his hand, held it up to clean the mud off it and cried aloud in horror when he realised he was poking his thumb into the eye socket of a human skull. In an involuntary reflex of revulsion, he flung it away and stood shaking for a few moments. It was only when he nerved himself to look for it again that he saw the other remains: arm bones and leg bones, a ribcage and more skulls; he was not afterwards sure how many — three or four, perhaps but enough for him to realise he was standing in some kind of burial site, and he turned and ran, stumbling in his panic, tripping and falling and hauling himself out of the clinging earth in his desire to get away.

CHAPTER THIRTEEN

Friday 12th April: in which Fairfax returns to Axford

IT WAS TEN o'clock by the time Fairfax reached the sanctuary of the village, barely four hours after he had set off. Never had he been more grateful to see a dreary muddy street, or the mundane normality of women spinning on their front steps. His descent of the hill had given him a chance to compose himself, and none who saw him that morning, striding with his stick across the bridge, would have guessed at the turmoil in his mind. He told himself that it was not uncommon to find human bones in England, that skeletons could last a thousand years, that they turned up in the fields at ploughing time, or in gardens, or when ditches were being dug − usually singly or in family groups, occasionally in the mass pits into which they must have been dumped in the chaos immediately after the Apocalypse. But he had never himself stumbled across a body, and the conjunction of the skulls, the tower, the remoteness of the spot and its association with Lacy's death created a feeling of foreboding he could not shake off. He was sure he would remember the sensation of his thumb running around the sharp edge of that eye socket for as long as he lived.

As he neared the parsonage, he saw there was a horse tethered to the fence. Someone must be visiting who owned a fine grey mare. He was sufficiently disinclined for company to consider altering his direction and waiting inside the church until whoever it was had gone. But curiosity as well as a determination to maintain a calm appearance kept him walking, and he went directly through the gate and over the threshold into the house.

Sitting in the parlour, dressed in a black riding habit, was Sarah Durston, a leather saddlebag on the floor beside her. She rose as he came in.

'Lady Durston!' She was the last person he had expected to see.

'Mr Fairfax.' She offered him her hand. 'I hope you don't mind my calling uninvited. Agnes was not sure when you would return.'

'I have not kept you waiting long, I hope.'

'An hour or so. It's no matter.'

'An hour! Can I at least provide you with some refreshment?'

'Agnes has already made the offer, thank you.' She lifted her bag on to the table. 'Forgive me, but I have not come to take tea, and time is pressing.' She opened the bag and handed him a sheet of paper. 'Jenny brought this back from town yesterday afternoon but didn't show it me till breakfast. Look there, at the bottom.'

It was a handbill, crudely printed, smudged, with tiny letters out of register, entirely devoted to advertisements – for livestock, agricultural tools, seedlings and suchlike – and public notices: a group of travelling players was offering a performance of *The Mystery of the Passion* at the Corn Exchange, a fair was coming to the common land, a public execution was fixed for one o'clock that afternoon: 'Jack Porlock, tomb robber'.

'Has the hanging some connection with Lacy's death?'

'Not the hanging.' She leaned across impatiently and put her finger on a couple of skewed lines that seemed to have been added at the last moment. 'That.'

Dr Nicholas Shadwell, the Celebrated Scholar, will be Honoured to offer His Famous Public Lecture on 'The Heresy of the Ancient World' at the Corn Exchange on Friday 12th April at 2 o'clock. Admission 10 shillings at the door, or apply to O. Quycke, Esq., c/o The Swan Inn.

'Such flyers are given out in Axford each Thursday afternoon. Now surely that is proof that you were right – it *was* Shadwell at Father Lacy's burial. He not only lives, he is in the locality!'

Fairfax read the notice through again. 'I'm amazed he should be so brazen as to announce a public lecture. Why run such a risk, even if he does disguise his obsession as a denunciation?'

'A risk for him – but for us an opportunity.' She delved back into her bag and carefully lifted out an object wrapped in a shawl. She loosened the cloth and set down on the table one of the cylinders from her husband's collection. It was the most intricate of them all – a foot long, the thickness of a man's arm, tapered at either end and containing within it a tightly coiled glass tube in the shape of a spring.

He looked at her uneasily. 'Is it wise to carry that around?'

'I mean to take it to Shadwell and ask his opinion.'

'But what if you are stopped? Captain Hancock said the sheriffs are mighty strict in Axford.'

'That's most unlikely – it's never happened to me yet. And what better chance to find out what it is? We can be in town by two, with ease.' He registered that 'we'. She noticed his expression. 'Something is amiss?'

'I have visited the Devil's Chair.'

'And so? What of it?'

'I saw human remains there – three or four skeletons. Exposed by the storm, most like.'

'But that's only to be expected. Where artefacts lie,

most times are graves.' She shrugged and smiled at him. 'Oh dear, Father Fairfax — is a priest of all folk to be afraid of a few old bones?'

'They make me cautious, I will admit.'

'You sound like a villager talking: "Oh, the place is full of devils!"' She started to rewrap the cylinder. 'Well *I* shall go and see him, and go alone if needs be.'

'No, no, I shall come,' he said quickly. The prospect of an afternoon in her company was alluring in itself, whatever the risk. 'Naturally I shall come.'

Upstairs, he changed back into his own cassock, newly laundered by Mrs Budd. He washed the soil from his hands and examined his face in the mirror. Gone was the pallor of the chapter house. His skin was burned by the spring sun. He looked more farmer than cleric. He made an attempt to smooth down his hair and shape his beard with his wet hands. After a few moments of indecision, he once again slipped the volume of *The Proceedings and Papers of the Society of Antiquaries* into the pocket of his undershirt. There might be an opportunity to discuss it with Shadwell.

The housekeeper was waiting for him in the passage as he clattered down the stairs.

'I am riding to Axford, Mrs Budd. Don't trouble Rose to fetch my horse — I'll saddle her myself.'

He looked in the parlour for Sarah Durston, but she wasn't there. He saw her through the window, waiting for him in the road: already mounted, sharp in profile, impatient for the hunt.

Their appearance on horseback together, riding through the village side by side, provoked a stir of interest. Heads turned to follow their progress. A pair of women washing clothes in the river stopped what they were doing and whispered to one another. As they passed the forge, Gann looked up from his anvil, and when Fairfax glanced back over his shoulder, he saw that the blacksmith had come out to stand at the side of the road and gawp at them.

Lady Durston turned to see what he was looking at. She smiled and settled back down in her saddle. 'I fear I am ruining your reputation, Father Fairfax. The village will talk of nothing else for days.'

'I cannot believe that.'

'Oh, it's true, no question of it. As I said – they think I'm a witch.'

'You also said that was a joke.'

'Indeed, but there's truth in jokes. They're super-stitious folk. They'll think I've cast a spell on you.'

'And on Captain Hancock?' he couldn't stop himself asking.

'Him too.'

They continued for a while without speaking. He felt he should make some reference to what had happened. 'I gather I must offer my congratulations.'

'Thank you. And yet your tone suggests disapproval.'

'Not at all.'

' "Judge not, that ye be not judged" – is that not what the good Lord teaches us?'

'Among other things.'

She seemed to find his reply very droll, and repeated it to herself, her chin pressed into her neck, in a solemn, deep, pompous voice that he presumed was meant to be a parody of his: *Among other things . . .*

The road led them up the side of the valley. They came to the place where the land had slipped on Wednesday afternoon and prevented his departure. The track was now clear. The rocks and earth had been dumped onto the lower slope to the left; the bulging land to the right was restrained by a timber palisade. Fairfax said, 'It was good of Captain Hancock to open the way out of the village.'

'It was not entirely done out of goodness – he needs the road to ply his business. And it suits him to use his power to perform a public service from time to time. It maintains his dominance. He is quite the king of our little country.'

'Come now, Lady Durston!' He was almost beginning to feel sorry for Hancock. 'There must be something to be said in his favour. After all, you have agreed to marry him.'

'Yes, sir, there is plenty. He is kind, after his own

fashion. He has courage. And I believe he is a man of honour.'

'And he loves you.'

'Aye, he certainly does that,' she agreed sadly. 'Any woman should be glad to have him.'

They had reached the top of the hill. Swaying in his saddle, Fairfax peered down at the village – the mushroom huddle of brown thatched roofs, the square grey church tower with its orbiting black specks of soundless rooks, the silvery glint of the river. He wondered what it might have been like in Morgenstern's day. Perhaps not so different. He could imagine the same suspicion of outsiders and eagerness to gossip, the same prejudices, superstitions, rumours. Of course, the inhabitants would not have been so isolated then. They would have been able to communicate more easily, and across vast distances, using their strange devices with the symbol of the bitten apple. But would they have had anything wiser to say, or would their local vices merely have been spread more widely? He let his eye wander up from the village and tried to search out the tower on the top of the opposite hillside, but either the density of the trees or the strange configuration of the Devil's Chair hid it from view.

The narrowness of the path as they descended along the tunnel of trees precluded their riding alongside one another. He invited Lady Durston to go ahead of him. She was much more skilled in handling a horse than he was. From this trailing position he was able to admire the straightness of her back, the set of her shoulders, the way she swayed easily with her mount as if they were conjoined. He had assumed Hancock's obsession with her was due to her house and her position in society – she had implied as much when he first met her at Lacy's wake – but now he could see it must arise also from her dauntlessness. For a man such as he, she must present an irresistible challenge.

When they reached the plain and were able to travel beside one another again, he complimented her on her riding. 'Your skill must have been learned young.'

'Not at all. We were far too poor to keep a horse. I never so much as sat in a saddle till I was twenty.'

'Ah, I thought . . .' He was unsure how to finish the sentence.

'That I was born rich? Alas, far from it. My father was a schoolmaster in Dorchester. I have not a drop of noble blood.'

'Do you still have people there?'

'No, like you I lost my family to the fever, though I was older – eighteen – and good at my books, so my godmother found me a position as governess in the house of a local widower. Now *he* was rich – which people, being cruel, maintained always was the reason I married him, but that was not the case at all. And now I can see I have said something even more outrageous.'

'No.' He tried to hide his surprise. 'Why should I be outraged?'

'Twice married to older men, twice widowed — I know how tongues wag. And now a third wedding in the offing? But if people think I've schemed to make myself wealthy . . . well, let me say it's a poor job I have made of it. My stepdaughters inherited their father's house and threw me out with nothing. I fled to Axford to escape their vile chatter and so met Sir Henry, who took pity on me, but then he proved to be ruined. And there is my full life story, all very neat, for use as a parable in your next sermon.'

Throughout this speech she kept glancing over her shoulder, and when she had finished, he turned to see what had been distracting her. There was a rider about half a mile behind them. 'Is something wrong? Do you recognise him?' He assumed it was a man, although it could have been a woman.

'Not at this distance. He must have come from the valley — the road leads nowhere else.'

'Is he following us?'

'Let us stop and see if he will pass.'

She pulled up her horse. He did the same. They both turned in their saddles. The mysterious rider also halted. For a minute they waited. It was an unpleasant sensation in that wild and desolate landscape to feel oneself a stranger's quarry.

Fairfax said, 'We should continue.'

'No, wait, look — he's moving.'

The other rider had turned his horse off the road and up on to the moorland, then began heading away at a right angle, trotting at first before gathering speed to a full gallop. They watched him dwindle until the land dipped behind a tangle of yellow gorse, at which point horse and rider disappeared.

Fairfax said, 'Maybe he was warier of us than we of him.'

'Maybe.'

She did not sound convinced. He had to concede it did not seem very likely. They resumed their journey in silence.

After another hour of steady riding beneath a vast sky, the wildness of the moor began to yield to signs of cultivation — vineyards at first, then small farmsteads, allotments, orchards, olive groves, fields with dry-stone walls, fish ponds, cow sheds, henhouses — evidence that people were confident it was safe to move outside the fortified walls of the town now that England had been reunified and pacified under King and Church. The first sign of Axford itself was its church spire, fifteen hundred years old, poking pale and spindly out of the ground like a sapling. They crested a slight rise and the rest of the town arose around it.

Dust hovered over the road ahead. There was a commotion. As they came closer, the cause became clear. The advertised hanging had just taken place on the common. A big crowd, cheerfully sated, was streaming back towards the town's gate – most of the population, or so it seemed by the time they caught up with it – men and women and a gaggle of excited children, who blocked the road and slowed their progress to a walk. From what he could overhear of their conversations, Fairfax gathered the condemned man had died contemptuous of his fate, *as if he were no more'n walking out of one alehouse and into another.* His bravado was recalled with admiration. *Gave the hangman his watch as payment to do a quick job and said he'd better have it now, for in ten minutes the taking of it would be a crime.* In the centre of the field, in full view of the prison, the hooded corpse of Jack Porlock, tomb robber, dangled from the scaffold. A cart was drawn up beside his gently swinging feet, its horse nibbling the grass, waiting to convey his remains to the gibbet.

Fairfax crossed himself and said a prayer for the dead man's soul, and then for good measure added another for Lady Durston's protection and his own. If tomb robbing and the looting of antiquities had been made capital offences to deter treasure-hunters, were they not in peril of the same fate? He glanced across at Sarah Durston and wondered if the thought had occurred to her. But she was staring straight ahead and her expression gave no clue to her feelings.

The river ran beneath the town's western wall and served, for that section of Axford's perimeter, as a natural moat. The press of the crowd carried them over the drawbridge and through the gate, where at once they were swallowed up in a noisy marketplace, bordered on the right by the prison and on the left by the assize court flying the red cross of England and the yellow dragon of Wessex. The local wine was being sold at a shilling a cup, and all manner of animals – chickens, rabbits, pigeons, piglets, lambs – were strung up dead, some skinned, some not, or caged alive, their terrified squawks and squeals as they anticipated their fate adding sharply to the din.

A man played a jig on the pipes; a girl dressed in a sailor's outfit danced in spasms, as if having a fit. An aged muzzled bear, with patches of missing fur, was chained to a stake. There was a pillory and a whipping post. A pair of sheriffs in black uniforms and helmets, their belts hung with truncheons and handcuffs, and holding two powerful dogs on short chains, stood talking on the prison steps. Fairfax noticed how they watched as he and Lady Durston rode past, continuing their conversation but obviously interested in the sight of a priest and a well-dressed woman together. It was a relief when they had threaded their way through the last of the stalls, passed out of the market and were on to the main street.

A row of shops fronted by wooden sidewalks – a haberdashery, an ironmonger's, a butcher's, a saddle-maker's, a barber's – ended in the town's main square, across which the Corn Exchange and the Swan Inn faced one another. In the centre of the unpaved space a circular stone drinking trough was surrounded by a post-and-rail fence to which horses could be tethered while their owners went about their business. It was here that Fairfax and Sarah Durston dismounted and paid a shilling each to the ostler. Lady Durston unstrapped her saddlebag and lifted it down. Fairfax offered to carry it – 'The sheriffs will be less minded to search the property of a priest' – but she refused: 'The risk is mine and I should bear it.'

They joined a queue of about twenty waiting to gain admission to the lecture. Just inside the door, a hefty, handsome dark-haired man of middling years was seated at a little desk, collecting money and issuing tickets. He was evidently surprised to see a priest, although he quickly recovered his composure. Fairfax guessed he must be Quycke, one-time secretary of the Society of Antiquaries and the illustrator of *Antiquis Anglia*. He placed Fairfax's pound coin in his cash box and said pleasantly, in an educated voice, 'Sit wherever pleases you, Father.'

They crossed the vestibule and entered a large modern chamber with a vaulted timbered roof and high windows. Benches had been set out on the flagstone floor and were already mostly filled. At the far end, beneath the town's coat of arms, was a platform on which stood a trestle table. Lanterns flickered on either side of it. Various bulky objects were covered by a green cloth.

They found a couple of places in the centre of a bench halfway from the front. People shifted apart to accommodate them, and Lady Durston pushed the saddlebag under the bench. Once they were seated, they were pressed together so tightly Fairfax could feel the rhythm of her breathing against his arm. He was conscious of her thigh hard against his and the scent of her skin and hair, perfumed with rose water and jasmine. He looked distractedly around the room. The chamber was full. There must have been more than a hundred in the audience, and he sensed that he and Lady Durston were the objects of some curiosity – the unknown young priest and the vaguely scandalous titled widow of Durston Court.

He felt her body tense. Captain Hancock was moving around the edge of the assembly, searching for somewhere to sit. He glanced over in their direction, staring at them for several moments – a hard look, full of suspicion. When he took his place, he sank from view, and almost immediately the door beside the platform opened and Dr Nicholas Shadwell, the Celebrated Scholar, emerged.

CHAPTER FOURTEEN

'The Heresy of the Ancient World'

THAT SHADWELL WAS the mourner who had shouted out in church was clear from the moment he opened his mouth. His voice, like his appearance, was peculiarly distinctive – reedy, elderly, old-fashioned, mannered. He was considerably below normal height, his thin frame clad in an eccentric form of evening suit made of shabby black velvet, with a red-dotted handkerchief protruding from the cuff, a brocaded waistcoat, a dark shirt with a matching cravat, and a black velvet cap pulled down low over straggling long grey hair. A pair of small, round mauve-tinted eyeglasses added a sinister final touch. He was some years past sixty. He stood at the front of the platform and spoke without notes, his fingers grasping his lapels, addressing his remarks like a blind man or a visionary to some indeterminate spot above the heads of his audience. He began without preamble.

'It is our good fortune, my fellow countrymen and women, to live in the Age of the Risen Christ, whose return to Earth eight hundred years ago was foretold in the Book of Revelation. But by the same token, we also live in the Age of the Fallen Man, whose violent expulsion from the blasphemous Paradise he had presumed to create was God's just punishment for his hubris.'

A woman in the audience cried out, 'Amen!'

'Amen indeed, madam,' responded Shadwell. He began to cough — a dangerous cough, it sounded to Fairfax, of the sort he had heard in many a death chamber. He fumbled for his handkerchief and turned away from his audience until he had recovered. 'Amen! How evil must have been their world to bring down upon its towers and steeples such a shattering punishment! According to the ancient sources, the population of England in the year before Armageddon was some sixty million. The census that our gracious lord the king has recently commissioned records our present numbers at roughly six million. And this is after years of stability and civil peace, during which the English people have grown steadily in numerical strength. How much lower must our numbers have plunged during what we call the Dark Age — that century when famine, plague and warfare devastated our island, and no one had the will, or even the means, to record it?

'And this calamity, the immediate cause of which no one understands, was not visited upon England solely. Otherwise we would have been invaded, and either rescued from disaster or made vassals by some foreign power. No, ladies and gentlemen: it seems clear that the whole world was struck by the same blow at the same time. Our government rightly watches the ports and strictly licenses those foreigners allowed to visit here, and places close restrictions on those few of our citizens who travel overseas. But from such enquiries as one is able to make, it appears that the peoples of France and Savoy, of Bavaria and Saxony, of Tuscany and Genoa and Rus, of Africa and China and Japan, of the fifty independent states of the Americas who were once joined in a single country – all the nations of the world suffered the same calamity. The blow – whatever it was and whatever form it took – was at once overwhelming, instantaneous and universal.

'Therefore, when I speak of "The Heresy of the Ancient World", I do so not out of any sense of admiration, let alone out of a desire to recreate it.' He looked directly at Fairfax, the only member of his audience wearing clerical dress, and held out his hand towards him, so that Fairfax felt himself again come under scrutiny from all corners of the hall. 'As the Church teaches us, any attempt to recreate the ancients' civilisation would be a grievous sin and an insult to Almighty God that would justly provoke Him to spread the same wrath across the Earth.' He bowed slightly, and then his gaze switched up to its former fixed trajectory. 'Rather, the purpose of my life has been to discover what errors brought the ancient world to ruin, with the sole aim of ensuring that we never repeat them. For this worthy – I might say noble – ambition I have suffered greatly.' He pressed his hand to his breast. His voice trembled. 'Poison has been whispered into the ears of the powerful by my enemies, and I have endured persecution and harassment such as few men on this island have ever known—'

'Careful!' hissed Quycke, but loud enough for all to hear. He had stationed himself next to the platform so that he could watch the audience, who were beginning to shift slightly with boredom at the speaker's highfalutin language.

Shadwell stopped and peered down at his assistant, then blinked around the assembly through his tiny spectacles as if remembering where he was. Hesitantly, he began again. 'So what ... ah ... was the source of their heresy?'

A man behind Fairfax called out, 'Aye, why don't ye tell us? That's what we've paid for!'

Some laughed, others shushed him.

'Yes, sir, that is what I'm about to do, although doubtless you will say I am describing a mythical kingdom. We know from drawings, and from extensive fragments of glass and plastic that have been discovered to the west of Hounslow, and which match those same drawings, that the ancients could fly, although the machines they used have entirely disappeared. We know that they had metal carriages that could move at tremendous speed of their own volition on cushioned wheels without the need for horses – although again these have rusted away entirely and barely a trace of them remains. We know that they had buildings in London, which was their Babylon, that were tall enough to touch the clouds—'

'Nonsense!' someone shouted.

'No, sir, it is not nonsense: their existence is well attested. And we also know that almost every person, including children, was issued with a device that enabled them to see and hear one another, however far apart in the world they might be; that these devices were small enough to be carried in the palm of one's hand; that they gave instant access to all the knowledge and music and opinions and writings in the world; and that in due course they displaced human memory and reasoning and even normal social intercourse – an enfeebling and narcotic power that some say drove their possessors mad, to the extent that their introduction marked the beginning of the end of advanced civilisation.'

This was too much for many. Exclamations of disbelief erupted around the hall. People swatted their hands at the speaker as if dismissing some bothersome fly.

'It is true, it is true,' repeated Shadwell calmly. He waited for them to settle. 'Allow me to give you two facts that are irrefutable. First, we know that compared to us the ancients were a race of giants, because the skeletons of people who died eight hundred years ago show they were on average a foot taller than ourselves. And second, we know they lived much longer than we do, because tomb inscriptions establish that a lifespan of ninety or even a hundred was not uncommon, whereas today a man is old at fifty. These are facts, ladies and gentlemen: facts, provable by bone and stone.'

The assembly was still again, height and length of life being concepts that everyone could understand.

'The question is: how were these marvels achieved — the miracle of talking to their loved ones even when they were many miles distant, and performing the work of a hundred men with the press of a lever? These people may have been taller than us, and healthier than us, but they were mortals just as we are. Their brains were of the same size: I doubt they were much cleverer. They ate, they drank, they slept, they reproduced, they dreamed. But clearly they must have possessed some secret we have lost. Somehow or other, in the tumult of its sudden collapse, the vital animating spark of their civilisation was extinguished, and has never been rekindled. I should now like to demonstrate what I believe that animating spark to have been. Ladies and gentlemen, may I ask those beside the windows to assist me by closing the shutters?' His breath gave out as he finished speaking, and he began to cough again.

Squeezed in the middle of their bench, Fairfax and Sarah Durston were obliged to remain in their places while the room was darkened. As the shutters banged shut, extinguishing the afternoon light one bright oblong at a time, there was an increasing chatter of anticipation. The occupants of the Corn Exchange seemed to be separating themselves from the everyday world and preparing to embark on a voyage to another. Sarah leaned in to Fairfax and whispered, 'What will he do?'

'I have no notion.'

'Conjure up the spirits of the dead, by the sound of it.'

He half twisted round in his seat, but it was now too dark to make out individual faces. 'I wonder what Captain Hancock thinks. It must have been he who followed us.'

'Is it of any consequence what he thinks?'

'Not at all.' Still, he was uncomfortable. It did not feel entirely proper to be out unescorted with another man's intended wife, nor as a clergyman to be seen at such an event – which for all Shadwell's protestations of piety trembled on the edge of heresy.

The one-time president of the Society of Antiquaries

had now been joined on the platform by Quycke. The glow of the lanterns provided the only illumination, casting their shadows as wavering silhouettes on the wall behind them. The daylight and the noises of the street had gone. Together they lifted away the cloth from the table. A curious collection of objects was revealed – a glass bell jar, a pump-like contraption with a small spinning wheel, two cylinders with a crank handle between them, a thin glass tube, various tins and boxes, and a white paper marionette of a skeleton that Quycke lifted up and suspended from a brass stand. Shadwell unbuttoned his jacket and handed it to his secretary.

'A natural force exists in the world,' he began, 'which the ancients taught themselves to harness, and which may be conjured into existence using this simple apparatus. The devices you see here have been manufactured according to the specifications laid out in a book in my possession that is more than a thousand years old.' He opened a box. 'First, I am going to place this piece of amber inside the jar.' He held it aloft and showed it right and left.

It was difficult in the gloom to see exactly what he was doing, which heightened the sense that something mysterious was about to occur. People stood to try to get a better view, but were implored by those behind them to sit again. From what Fairfax could make out, Shadwell seemed to have attached the pump to the top of the bell jar. There was a repeated whoosh and creak of leather bellows. The spinning wheel turned and hummed. Shadwell stood behind the glass jar, undid his cuffs, rolled up his sleeves and with a flourish placed his hands upon it. At once a strange blue glow appeared, cold and ethereal, unlike anything Fairfax had ever seen, lunar soft and yet bright enough in the darkness to light up Shadwell's face. Lady Durston clutched his arm. A great collective exclamation of surprise broke from the audience.

'This is what the ancients called "electricity" − from the Greek word *elektron* meaning "amber". This is the force that powered their world. Electricity was as real for them as the power of God is for us. Imagine, if you will, a house lit by this astonishing phenomenon − a street, a neighbourhood, an entire town!' In the eerie gleam his cadaverous skull appeared supernatural, as if he were an emissary from the spirit world. 'But that is only the beginning of its uses. In addition to light, this natural power can also be harnessed to provide motive force.'

He nodded to Quycke, who started to crank the handle, slowly at first but with increasing rapidity, until the cylinders were revolving at high speed. The machine began to emit a strange crackle, and then blue sparks appeared, arcing across the narrow space and filling the hall with the unmistakable aroma of sulphur. A woman screamed. A man shouted, 'Satan's here!' and there was indeed something satanic in Shadwell's smile as he once again placed his hands upon the glass. The jar glowed like a blue moon, and then – Fairfax afterwards conceded that he experienced a prickle of terror himself, all across his skin and down his spine – the paper skeleton began to twitch into life and jerk its limbs in a macabre dance. Somewhere behind him there was a crash, and a voice cried out, 'She's fainted!' The door at the back slammed two or three times as people left. But most stayed in their places, gripped by the spectacle of the buzzing flying sparks, the luminous glass, Shadwell's disembodied grinning skull and that ghostly swaying puppet of a corpse.

Shadwell said, 'Is there a lady in the audience who would like to volunteer to experience the invigorating power of electricity?' Nobody moved. 'Come now! It is perfectly safe, I assure you. I have tried it myself and found the effects most therapeutic. Remember the remarkable lifespan of the ancients!' Still the spectators remained in their places until, to Fairfax's alarm, Sarah Durston rose to her feet.

'No, Lady Durston,' he implored her, and caught hold of her skirt. 'This is not prudent.'

But she turned her back on him, grasped her skirt and tugged herself free. Her neighbours on the bench stood to let her by. She edged past them to the aisle and walked up to the platform. Shadwell clapped his hands in admiration and the applause was taken up by most of the spectators. He held out his hand to assist her up on to the stage.

'May I ask you, madam, to stand upon that square of carpet precisely and not to move, and be so kind as to remove your hat and give it to my secretary, and unpin your hair?' She did as he asked and shook out her tresses in the same gesture that had so struck Fairfax the previous day. 'And now, if you please, raise your arms so they are level with your shoulders, and turn to face our friends here assembled.' Again she did as she was instructed, smiling, entirely calm.

Quycke started winding the handle once more. After a short while, Shadwell picked up the long glass tube, which was glowing blue like a wand, and gently touched it to the side of Lady Durston's skirt. At once her long red hair stiffened and began to rise and stand out around her head. Clad in her black riding habit, with her arms outstretched, her face pale and surrounded by what appeared to be a fiery halo, the effect was ghostly and dramatic. Fairfax was mesmerised. Gasps and applause broke out across the hall.

'And now,' said Shadwell, 'which gallant gentleman will step forward to share the stage with this spirited lady?'

For long moments nobody spoke. Fairfax stared at Sarah Durston – shimmering, or so it seemed to him, like some ethereal vision, her breast rising and falling as if the electric force was drawing its life from her. And then to his amazement, his right hand seemed to ascend of its own volition and he heard himself saying, 'I shall.'

'Well done, sir!'

He regretted it at once, but by then he was already halfway to his feet, drawing murmurs of surprise from those around him, which gradually turned into a general round of clapping for his good sportsmanship – and he a priest! As he made his way to the aisle and approached the platform, someone called out, 'Well done, Father!'

Quycke put out a firm hand to help him up. Shadwell, who was leading the applause, smiled at him and bowed before turning to the audience and holding up his hands for silence. 'I have performed this demonstration many times, but never before with a man of the cloth! What could be more respectable, ladies and gentlemen, than if I invite this most upstanding of citizens to claim from the Electrifying Venus a chaste kiss? If I might ask you, sir, to face the lady and carefully to bring your lips into contact with hers?'

He placed his hand in the centre of Fairfax's back and gently pushed him forward, despite the priest's mild protests: 'Oh no, sir, no, really . . .'

Out of the corner of his eye Fairfax could see a large shadow that might well have been Hancock standing and watching him intently. Sarah Durston, without altering her pose, shuffled carefully round to face him, like a clockwork toy doll. Her expression was still amused. She tilted her head coquettishly and offered him her lips. He ceased to resist. Time seemed to slow as he stretched towards her. A yard became feet, feet became inches, and then the gap between them vanished altogether.

The instant their lips made contact, there was a crackle and a flash of blue. He felt a sharp pain, cried out and took a pace back. The audience gasped. He put his hand to his mouth and stared at her. The spectacle they presented must have been at once alarming and comic. People began to laugh. He turned and looked at them in bewilderment, which only made them laugh harder.

In the midst of all this amusement, it was not at first apparent that a separate commotion had arisen. At the rear of the hall, doors were banging, dogs barking, men shouting. Quycke cupped his hand to his forehead, peered into the shadows and called out a warning to Shadwell. Fairfax glanced over the turning heads to see a pair of sheriffs thrusting through the audience, another official in uniform behind them − bearded, pale-faced, a splash of gold on his sleeve indicating his rank.

'This assembly is illegal!' He stood in the centre of the hall. 'Open the shutters! I have a warrant for the arrest of Dr Nicholas Shadwell!'

Shadwell moved with remarkable agility for a

man of his age and evident poor health. He vaulted from the platform and lunged for the nearby side door. But in the few moments it took him to reach the exit, yet another sheriff with a rearing, snapping dog had appeared in the door frame to block his escape. Hands were laid upon him, from front and back, and his wrists were manacled behind him. Throughout all this he maintained a stream of complaints in his querulous, educated voice – 'This is quite unlawful . . . There is no need to be so rough . . . I shall hold you personally responsible for the security of my apparatus . . .' – and then he was marched down the aisle with Quycke behind him. As he was escorted out, he cast over his shoulder a look of bitter reproach at Fairfax, as if he held not just the institution of the Church but the young priest himself personally responsible for his treatment.

By the time he had been removed from the hall, the last of the shutters had been opened and the illusion of the ancients' magic had vanished like a dream at daybreak. Only the few inert pieces of equipment were left behind on stage, along with the astonished figure of Christopher Fairfax, and Sarah Durston, her mane of red hair no longer stiffened by the mysterious force of electricity, but returned to its natural shape.

CHAPTER FIFTEEN

Captain Hancock learns the secret

FAIRFAX'S MOUTH THROBBED as if it had been stung or bitten. He wiped his forefinger along his lips then brought it up close to his eyes to inspect it. He half expected it to be coated in some luminous blue residue. The ache wasn't painful; rather it seemed to pulse in rhythm with his heart, which — now that he placed his hand upon it — felt somewhat engorged even though he wasn't breathless. It was thumping in the way it did after he had been startled or had narrowly missed a fall. What in the name of Heaven had been done to him?

Oblivious to the hubbub in the hall, he went over to the table and began carefully examining Shadwell's apparatus, picking up the various pieces of metal and glass, turning the glass tubes and metal cylinders around and upside down, as if by a process of deduction he could somehow penetrate the mystery of what had just occurred. From these incongruous objects had been conjured the fiery blue substance that, according to Shadwell, had powered the ancients' world. Now that the demonstration was over, it seemed impossible, and yet he had not merely witnessed the phenomenon, he had experienced it; tasted it, even – the hard metallic flavour of electricity conveyed upon the soft lips of Sarah Durston.

He wondered where she was. He looked around for her and saw her standing alone in the centre of the crowded room, cradling the saddlebag to her breast, watching him. He jumped down from the stage.

'Lady Durston, I'm sorry – I fear my wits must have been fried to such an extent I have quite forgotten my manners. Are you all right?'

'Yes, quite well. I felt nothing more than a curious tingling in my limbs and hair, not at all unpleasant.'

'The feeling has now passed?'

'Entirely. You seemed to suffer more than I.'

'I can feel the throb of my heart.' He brushed his hand through his hair, a gesture he often used to deflect attention from his embarrassment. 'Forgive me for any unwanted intimacy. I had no conception of what would be demanded of me when I agreed to go on stage. If I had, I should have refused to participate.'

'My dear Mr Fairfax, don't say that!' She smiled at

him. 'I would not have missed it for the world! Although I doubt Captain Hancock will ever forgive us.'

Fairfax looked to the spot where he thought he had last seen Hancock. People were milling around. 'Where is he?'

'I believe he left straight after poor Dr Shadwell. Now no one is being allowed to depart till they have provided the sheriffs with their name and address and an account of what they saw.'

At the prospect of Bishop Pole being informed of his attendance – and not merely his attendance; his active participation – he felt a lurch of panic. 'We should find the captain quickly.'

'Why?'

He did not answer, but took her arm and steered her through the crowd. He noticed how some people drew away as they approached, as if they feared coming into contact with the couple contaminated by the electricity. Others tried to detain him to seek his reassurance. They were the town's more respectable citizens by the look of them – traders, freeholders: ambitious, crafty people with enquiring minds who now had cause to regret their curiosity. They had only come out of casual interest to hear Shadwell speak. Did he think they would be prosecuted? Fined? Would they – and clearly this alarmed them most of all – be investigated for heresy by the bishop's men from Exeter?

'Stay calm,' he advised them, although in truth he was anything but calm himself. 'There is nothing to fear. If you'd be kind enough to let us through, I shall sort the matter.'

'None of us has done anything wrong . . .'

'We have merely attended a public lecture . . .'

He nodded reassuringly. 'Once the facts are known, the matter will go no further, I am sure.'

'Ye will explain all this to the bishop, Father?'

'Let us pass and I shall speak to him directly.'

'We are godly, Christian people.'

'Yes, yes, I can see that.'

They reached the front of the queue. A pair of sheriffs manned the door. The younger of the two sat at the small table Quycke had used to collect the admission money. He was writing down the names of each person waiting to leave. The other guarded the exit with a slavering yellow-eyed dog at the end of a short chain.

'Names and addresses?' He dipped his pen in the ink pot.

'I am Father Christopher Fairfax, temporarily serving as priest-in-charge at St George's, Addicott. And this,' he added, conscious of sounding like Hancock, 'is Lady Sarah Durston of Durston Court.'

The young sheriff made a laborious note, his pen scratching across the rough surface of the paper. He seemed determined not to be at all impressed by their titles. 'Did ye witness any action this afternoon that might constitute the crime of heresy?'

'No.'

'Madam?'

'No.' She transferred her bag from one hand to the other and brushed away a strand of hair.

The sheriff stared at them. He tapped the end of his pen against his teeth, enjoying his moment of power. 'Others tell a different story.'

Fairfax said, 'Then the lecture they attended was different to the one we heard. Is this why Dr Shadwell was arrested – for heresy?'

'That is not my place to say.'

'Where has he been taken?'

'He will be up before the justices this afternoon, and will be remanded to prison to await trial at the bishop's court in Exeter.'

'In that case I must make a report to Bishop Pole at once.' He moved towards the door, but the dog growled and bared its teeth and he was obliged to step back.

'Hold on, Father, not so fast. We has to make sure no evidence is removed. What's in her ladyship's bag?'

'A broken vase,' she said. 'I brought it in to town to see if it could be mended.'

'Show me, please.'

Fairfax felt his heart begin to pound again. Sarah balanced the bag awkwardly on her knee and started to unfasten the straps. He put out his hand and stopped her. 'This is an insult not just to Lady Durston but to my own position. And you claim to be investigating an offence against the Church? The bishop will hear about this as well!'

'It is of no consequence,' said Sarah. 'If the officer insists on seeing it, I can show him.'

'Let it be, Jack,' said the older sheriff with the dog. 'I cannot vouch for the father, but I knew Lady Durston's late husband, God rest his soul, and I'm sure his widow would never break the law.' He gestured to them to leave.

'But ye'll be hearing from us again,' the young one called after them, in a final flourish of official dignity. 'Ye may depend upon it.'

They emerged into the April afternoon just before three o'clock. A couple of shopkeepers in leather aprons were out on the wooden sidewalks, already putting up their shutters in readiness for the end of the working day. Otherwise the centre of the town was quiet. Presumably people were either oblivious to what was going on inside the Corn Exchange or choosing to keep clear of it. At the end of the street, rising above the town's wall, the bright green hump of a hill was dotted with black and white cattle. That was the toll road to Exeter, and it crossed Fairfax's mind that his wisest course would be to leave Axford at once, ride directly to the cathedral and confess everything to the bishop before a report of what had occurred could reach him. He ran his tongue around his lips. The metallic sensation in his mouth still lingered faintly. I cannot leave, he thought: I am bewitched.

He asked, 'Where might we find Captain Hancock?'

'Why this urgent desire to speak with the captain?'

'He is a man of influence in the town, is he not? If we could enlist his help, we might yet be able to speak to Dr Shadwell.'

She looked at him, surprised. 'Is such a thing wise?'

'No, but we have come so far, it seems a pity not to make a last attempt, for we will never see him again – that much is certain.'

'Good.' She nodded once, decisive. 'I approve your spirit. He keeps a private room reserved at the Swan, for the conduct of his business. We might ask for him there.' As they set off across the square she took his arm. 'But we must be careful, Christopher – he will insist on knowing all, and he is a man of driving temperament. Once he sets his heart upon a thing, there will be no stopping him.'

Standing beneath the inn sign, smoking their long clay pipes and drinking, was the same group of idlers who three days earlier had tried to get Fairfax lost. Now that they saw he was a priest, and with a lady on his arm, they swiftly uncovered their heads and cast their gaze respectfully to the ground. He disdained them.

Inside the bar, they were seized by a noisy, crowded, masculine embrace of sweat and beer, tobacco fug and sawdust. He detached himself from Sarah and shouldered his way to the bar. A man, his arms darkly emblazoned with tattoos – the Wessex dragon, the cross of St George, a winged angel, a skull – noted Fairfax's clerical outfit with concern.

'Afternoon, Father.' He touched his forelock. 'Is something amiss?'

'Where might we find Captain Hancock?'

'Along the passage, sir. Up the stairs, the first door on the left. Shall I show ye?'

'No, we can find it.' He beckoned to Sarah.

A brick-floored passage reeking of spilled ale, followed by a flight of twisting wooden steps, brought them to a dingy landing. Fairfax glanced at Sarah, then knocked.

'Come!'

It was a small room – wood-panelled, cosy, with a leaded window looking out on to the square, a fire burning in the grate and candles lit upon the table. A pile of account books were stacked on the sideboard. Samples of undyed cloth were draped across an easy chair. From a hook on the back of the door hung the captain's heavy overcoat. Hancock himself was seated in the bay window, his legs outstretched, his chin on his chest, brooding. He acknowledged them with the barest movement of his head.

'Well look at this! If it ain't the Electrifying Venus and her Adonis!'

Fairfax said, 'I have apologised to Lady Durston, Captain, and I wish to do the same to you.'

Hancock snorted. 'Very gracious, Parson, I'm sure!'

'I had no foreknowledge of what would be asked of me.'

'Maybe not, but ye went ahead with it all the same.'

Sarah said, 'The fault is mine, John. Father Fairfax meant only to offer me support.'

'But ye kissed him! How the devil could ye have allowed thyself to be made into such a public spectacle?'

'It seemed harmless at the time.' She shrugged. 'It happened, and there it is: done. But if it's so shaming you wish to be released from our agreement, I understand.'

Hancock stared at her, his jaw working as if he was grinding some invisible piece of gristle. Eventually he muttered, 'I never mentioned ending our agreement. As ye say, it happened, it is over, and let us never speak of it again.'

An uncomfortable silence ensued. Fairfax was about to break it when Sarah Durston said, 'May I ask you a question, John?' She was looking round the room. 'Have you been in this place all day?'

'Since eight as usual. Fridays are when I sell my

cloth.' He grunted. 'Why? D'ye disapprove of my using an inn for business?'

'Not at all. It's merely that there was a man behind us on the road from Addicott — this would have been close to noon.'

'Well it was not me.' He looked from her to Fairfax, frowning as he realised the implication. 'Ye thought I followed ye to town?'

Fairfax said, 'It seemed likely, as you arrived at the lecture directly after us.'

'I went to the lecture because the subject interests me, not in pursuit of ye! I'm not such a jealous fool I wouldn't allow my future wife out of my sight to spend an afternoon with a *priest*.' Hancock pushed back his chair and stood. 'Now listen to me. I've been mulling matters over. Something's strange here. I knew Shadwell the moment I saw him. He's the man who cried out at Lacy's burial. So to my thinking, the question is not what *I* was doing there, but what were *ye*?'

He gathered up his lengths of cloth and gestured to the armchair. 'Sit down, Sarah.' She hesitated, still clutching her bag. He frowned at it. 'What's that? What's the secret between ye?'

She glanced at Fairfax. He nodded. She laid the bag upon the table and extracted the glass cylinder.

After another suspicious glance at them both, Hancock took it from her and carried it over to the window to study it better. In his massive hands it seemed even more fragile, its survival over eight centuries a greater miracle than ever. He held it to the light in wonder. 'How in God's name was such a thing made? A glass spring inside a tube of glass? What purpose does it serve?'

'It is a mystery,' she replied. 'That is why we went to Shadwell's lecture – to show it to him afterwards for his opinion. He may be the only man in England who could tell us.'

'Where did it come from?'

'Henry found it years ago, buried near the Devil's Chair.'

'So this is what the pair of ye were discussing when I arrived at the Court yesterday?'

'It was.'

'Then why in God's name did ye not tell me?'

'That was at my request. I wished to keep it private.'

'But why?'

There was a knock at the door. Hancock called out, 'Wait!' He gave the cylinder back to Sarah. As soon as she had replaced it in the bag, he shouted, 'Come!'

The tattooed innkeeper entered with a tray. 'Afternoon, Captain Hancock. I brought more for the lady and the father.' He bowed to them, set the tray on the table and started to unload jugs and plates.

'Leave it,' Hancock ordered. He gave the man a handful of coins. As soon as the door had closed, he lifted the jug of gin and offered it to each of them in turn. When they refused, he poured himself a cup and took a swig. A crafty expression had come over his face. 'Of course I know why it was ye didn't want to tell me.' He swilled the remainder of the gin around the cup. 'It's because the Devil's Chair is where old Lacy took his tumble. Isn't that the truth? And now I expect ye want my help.' He finished the rest of his drink, wiped his mouth and grinned at them. 'Let's eat.'

He laid out the plates and cutlery himself and filled their cups — this time he would not take no for an answer — with much-watered gin for Sarah and ale for Fairfax. He pulled out their chairs and insisted they join him at the table. He heaped their plates with cold tongue and pickled artichokes and at the same time as he plied them with food he assailed them with questions. How many pieces of glassware had Colonel Durston discovered? Who else knew of them? How had Lacy come to hear about them?

Fairfax set down his knife and fork, and unbuttoned the top of his cassock, pulling out the small leather-bound volume. He took a breath before he spoke. 'There was a man,' he said, 'called Morgenstern . . .'

After that, there was never much doubt that they would end up telling him the entirety of what they knew, and in consequence everything was changed, and all that was to follow made possible, for what Sarah Durston said was true: when Captain John Hancock set his heart upon a thing, no power on earth could deny him. And what he set his heart upon over lunch that afternoon in the Swan Inn, Axford, was discovering what might lie buried at the Devil's Chair.

Once Fairfax had finished describing the hiding of the church registers and the connection between Morgenstern and Durston Court, he located the passage containing Morgenstern's letter and handed over Volume XX of *The Proceedings and Papers of the Society of Antiquaries.* Hancock took the little book across to the armchair, lit his pipe and settled down beside the fire to read. During the next few minutes, Sarah continued to pick at her food, while Fairfax, who found himself for once without an appetite, stared out of the window at the Corn Exchange. From time to time its door opened and the well-to-do of Axford emerged, singly or in pairs, and always they put their heads down and hurried away, clearly anxious not to linger and draw attention to their shame.

'Here is the crucial sentence, surely.'

Fairfax turned to look at Hancock. He was leaning forward, his elbows on his knees, the book in his hands, his pipe gone out and discarded on the hearth beside him.

' "Our purpose is *not* to propose counter-measures to avert any of these potential catastrophes . . . but to devise strategies for the days, weeks, months and years following such a disaster, with the aim of the earliest possible restoration of technical civilisation." ' Hancock looked up from the page. His eyes were unnaturally wide and bright. 'Suppose a man saw an appalling calamity looming – what would he do? What would any of us do? Well, I'll tell ye what *I* would do. I'd lay up a stock of provisions – of all that was essential to maintain existence – and I'd block up my doors and windows and attempt to live through it. That was what this man Morgenstern did. I'm sure of it.'

Fairfax nodded. After the lecture, he too was starting to see it all more clearly now, like a landscape emerging as the morning mist lifted. A verse from the Book of Genesis came into his mind. He recited it aloud: *And God said unto Noah, The end of all flesh is come before me, for the Earth is filled with violence, and behold I will destroy them with the Earth. Make thee an ark . . .*

'Aye, an ark – well put – but he didn't fill it with animals, and it didn't float. He built it somewhere around the Devil's Chair – built it with his friends and buried it, I shouldn't wonder, so that no one else could find it save themselves.' Hancock threw himself back in his chair and stared at the ceiling. 'Aye, that's exactly what he did, I'd wager my life upon it. Consider what might be hidden up there! Consider whether it contains the secret of electrifying. And not just in a form for playing stupid parlour games, but in the way *they* used it, a way that would permit us to produce a big and continuous supply, and the means by which to store and transport it. *The earliest possible restoration of technical civilisation . . .* The world could begin anew! What I would not give for that!' Suddenly he pitched himself forward again, up on to the balls of his feet. 'We must talk to Shadwell.'

Sarah said, 'You think we can? Even though he is now in custody?'

'All to the good. It means we know where he is.' He grabbed his overcoat from its peg and placed it full length on the floor in front of the sideboard, then dropped to his knees beside it and pulled out his ring of keys. 'I've never known a prison yet that can't be breached with the proper tools.'

He unlocked the cupboard door and dragged out a big iron cash box, searched for yet another key to open it, then proceeded to stuff the contents — banknotes and bankers' drafts, handfuls of gold and silver coins — into his coat pockets. When he was done, he pushed the cash box back into the cupboard and from elsewhere within its depths retrieved a pistol and tucked it into his belt. Then he stood and pulled on his coat, buttoning it all the way up to his neck. Bulked by his day's takings, he looked even more than usual like a fairground strongman. He opened the door to the landing. 'Well? Are ye with me or not?'

Fairfax and Sarah exchanged glances. The young priest had a premonition of disaster. We have strapped ourselves to a force of nature capable of getting us all killed, he thought. Nevertheless, he said nothing as they rose from the table and followed the captain down the stairs, through the bar and out into the square.

CHAPTER SIXTEEN

Making the acquaintance of Dr Shadwell

THE MARKET IN front of the assize court was over, the stalls mostly packed away and gone. Already the ragged grey shadows of the poor had materialised from the side streets and were competing with the crows and stray dogs to scavenge through the rubbish, searching for whatever they could eat – for fruit and vegetables that were starting to rot and were not considered worth taking away, or for meat that was on the turn. Begging was against the law, but not even the fear of a whipping or a day in the stocks was enough to deter half a dozen of the wretches from crowding around Hancock, Fairfax and Sarah as they tied their horses to the rail outside the court entrance. Fairfax had no alms to give and was surprised to see Hancock dig his hand into his pocket and distribute a few coins. When the captain caught him looking at him, he said gruffly, 'I know what it's like to be poor.'

The courtroom was deserted save for a solitary figure slouched at the front, seated just below the justices' bench, who turned to stare at them as they came in. 'That is Mr Quycke,' whispered Fairfax. 'Shadwell's secretary.'

'Is that his name?' replied Hancock. 'I thought I recognised him from Lacy's burial.' He advanced down the central aisle of the court. 'Mr Quycke, ye may remember us from this afternoon.'

Quycke scrambled to his feet. 'I do indeed, sir. You were in our audience, and this lady and the father were good enough to come on stage. How tragic that our harmless entertainment should have ended up in here!' His voice was soft and somewhat theatrical for such a hefty man.

'Indeed, I feel shame that such a thing should happen in our town. That is why we have come, sir — to offer our support to Dr Shadwell. Captain John Hancock is my name. The parson is Mr Fairfax and Lady Durston is soon to be my wife.'

'Well, Captain Hancock, I am very glad to see you all, for I swear at this moment Dr Shadwell has no other friends upon this earth besides the people in this room.' He shook hands with each of them, raising Lady Durston's fingers to his lips. 'Your ladyship: an honour. You find us, I fear, in a most wretched condition. Dr Shadwell's health was poor to start with, and I am quite certain that another week in prison will be the death of him.'

'Where is he now?'

'In the cell beneath us, awaiting remand to Exeter as soon as a justice can be found to commit him.'

'Can we speak with him?'

'No, he is forbidden all visitors.'

Fairfax said, 'Except a priest, surely? I have never heard of a prisoner who was refused the comfort of the Christian faith. Indeed, it is a person's right under the law.'

'That is true, although – with all due respect to your good self, Father – I doubt Mr Shadwell would welcome such a visit. The Church has been the source of all his misfortunes.'

Hancock said, 'It's not our intention to preach at him, but to convey an offer of help.'

'And what sort of offer would that be?'

'That I am willing to stand bail for him.'

Quycke's head tilted back slightly in surprise. 'You'd do that for a stranger?'

'Have I not just said as much?'

'That is noble – very noble. But there must be some condition? There is always a condition.'

'Only one. We wish to ask him all he knows of a certain matter.'

'What matter?'

'A man, long dead, named Morgenstern.'

The effect was immediate. Quycke glanced from side to side. 'When he hears mention of that particular gentleman, I am sure he will refuse the offer, however perilous his situation.'

'Why?'

'If you know of Morgenstern, then you know why.'

'If we know of Morgenstern, is that not proof of our serious intention to help?'

'Rather the opposite. To put the matter bluntly, Captain: what proof is there you're not all government spies?' He nodded towards Fairfax. 'Or bishop's men? Forgive me, sir, but we've learned the hard way to be careful about whom we trust.'

There was a noise behind them, and three hooded men entered, entirely nondescript but oddly similar. They took their places at the very back, put down their hoods and sat in silence. Quycke tapped his finger briefly to his lips and raised his eyebrows as if his point had just been proved.

Fairfax said quietly, 'If you're so afraid of spies, why hold a public lecture and advertise it in a handbill?'

'The usual squalid affliction of the scholar,' said Quycke sadly. 'Poverty. We owe thirty pounds to the Swan and they have seized our wagon until we pay. Lectures provide our only means of living. Occasionally we must take a risk, or starve. By calling them

"The Heresy of the Ancient World", Dr Shadwell usually stays on the right side of the law.'

Hancock unbuttoned his coat and showed a handful of banknotes from an inside pocket. 'Help us, and ye'll not go hungry for a while.'

Quycke stared at the money. He passed his tongue around his fleshy lips. 'May I?' He took a couple of the notes and held them up to the light. It was only in the last few years that paper money had gained a wider circulation; forgeries were common. Satisfied, he returned them to Hancock. 'Well, that puts the matter upon a practical foundation, and in truth we're hardly in a state to refuse such generosity. Come with me, Father. I'll convey the proposal to Mr Shadwell and let us see what he will tell you. Although I should caution you the chances are poor.'

Sarah gave Fairfax her bag. 'Show him this. It may help persuade him.'

As Quycke moved away, Hancock caught Fairfax's arm and whispered, 'Make sure his promise is certain. I'm not risking my money for nothing. Tell him if he tries to break his word, I'll deliver him back to prison myself.'

Fairfax pulled his arm away – really, the fellow was intolerable – and followed Quycke to the front of the court, where there was a door beside the judge's bench. Quycke knocked, a key was turned from within and the door opened. An elderly sheriff peered out of the darkness.

'Mr Shadwell wishes to exercise his right to pray with a priest.'

The sheriff scrutinised them both suspiciously.

'It *is* his right,' said Fairfax. 'A heretic must be given the chance to repent. That is the law.' Seeing the man still hesitating, he added, 'I have been sent to the district on a special mission by Bishop Pole.'

'Well, if the bishop sent ye, Father, I suppose ye'd better come. On your own, mind.' He put his arm out to stop Quycke. 'Ye must wait here.'

He closed the door on the secretary's protests and locked it again, then took a torch from its holder. A flight of steps disappeared down into the gloom. 'Watch thyself, Father. 'Tis as steep a descent as the path to Hell.'

The sheriff led the way, holding the torch low so that Fairfax could see where to put his feet. It was awkward having to carry the bag with its fragile cargo at the same time as ducking to avoid the low ceiling. He put his hand out to the wall to steady himself. His palm touched dampness. From somewhere below came the sound of a man's hacking cough. They reached the bottom. At the end of a short passage was a heavy door with a small iron-barred window, a stool beside it, and another torch in a wall holder, its flame feeble in the damp air.

The sheriff checked the occupant of the cell through the window. 'Old man? Thou has a visitor.' He unlocked the door. 'Go on, Father, and good luck with him. I'll just be out 'ere when ye've saved 'is soul. What's in the bag?'

'Only what I require to offer communion.' Fairfax stepped into the cell. He could just make out Shadwell's figure, in his velvet suit and cap, seated on the straw in the corner, his hands manacled in front of him, his right leg attached by a chain to a ring in the wall. 'Could we not remove his fetters?'

'Against the rules, Father. But it won't be for long — magistrate's on 'is way.'

'Then might we at least have some light?'

'Aye, I expect I can provide that.' The sheriff fitted the torch into a holder and withdrew, locking the door behind him.

There was nothing in the cell apart from the prisoner and a chamber pot. Shadwell's back was resting against the wall, his arms wrapped around his knees. He regarded Fairfax briefly through his tinted spectacles and turned his head away. Immediately he started coughing again, and fumbled in his sleeve for the red-dotted handkerchief, into which he spat more blood.

Fairfax waited for the spasm to finish, then cleared his throat. 'Dr Shadwell, my name is Christopher Fairfax, and I am very sorry indeed to see you in this condition.'

Shadwell inspected his handkerchief. 'Are you indeed? Well, as it is your Church that has *put* me in this – this – condition . . .' He resumed coughing, a terrible convulsive fit, much more violent than the first, that shook his entire body. After it had passed, he leaned back against the wall, took off his spectacles and wiped his eyes. His voice, when he was able to resume, was a croak. 'As it is the Church that has persecuted me, I attach scant value to your sorrow.'

'I understand, but I am here to offer more than just soft words. A wealthy local man, Captain John Hancock, is prepared to put up the bail to try to free you.'

'His time is wasted. They'll never grant bail for heresy.'

'He is a man with power in this town.'

'More power than Bishop Polc? I doubt it!'

'Still, he is willing to try.'

'And why would he do that?'

'Because he believes in the importance of your work, as do we all. Only last night I was reading *Antiquis Anglia*.'

For the first time he aroused a flicker of interest. Shadwell turned his head to study him. 'I'm amazed a copy still exists.'

'Well, one does. And this morning I went up into the hills to investigate the Devil's Chair.'

'That's an odd construction, as I remember.' He

paused and then added, plainly curious despite himself, 'Was there much to see?'

'Human bones, exposed by the recent storms.'

'Clustered together, or separated?'

'Together.'

'Together? That's interesting.' He stared thoughtfully into the distance. The straw on the opposite side of the cell rustled and a large brown rat with a tail as long as Fairfax's forearm ran along the edge of the wall and disappeared into a hole. The sight seemed to recall the prisoner to his predicament. 'Well, please thank Captain Hancock on my behalf, but tell him I've no time for such matters now. Old Shadwell's work is finished, and old Shadwell with it.'

Fairfax glanced over his shoulder at the cell door. He lowered his voice. 'It is our belief that something of great significance may lie buried there. May I?' He took a couple of paces towards the old man and kneeled on the straw beside him, keeping his back to the door. How tiny Shadwell was, he thought, how frail, with those glittering dark suspicious eyes, like an injured bird cornered and at one's mercy. The fetters hung loose around his skinny wrists and ankle. 'It's also my conviction that Father Lacy's death was no mere matter of chance – as you rightly declared at his burial – but came about because someone wished to put an end to his searching.' He undid the straps on the saddlebag and lifted out the glass cylinder.

'This was found in the same spot some years ago.' He unwrapped it from the shawl.

After a final few moments of resistance, Shadwell looped the steel arms of his eyeglasses back around his ears. He took the cylinder carefully between his manacled claw-like hands and at once let out a long and appreciative sigh, full of strange wheezes and creaks that threatened to turn into another coughing fit. 'Oh my, sir, what an exquisite piece!' He stroked it with his bony thumbs. 'Such miraculous precision! What genius they possessed! Are there more? There should be many more, I think.'

'Yes, there are — dozens of them, all in the hands of a private collector. How do you know there are more? What are they?'

Shadwell continued to gaze at it, enraptured. 'If this is what Lacy wrote to me concerning, well then, I believe it to be part of what the ancients called a laboratory — a word we have lost: from the Latin *laborare*, "to work" — which may have been removed from an ancient site of learning called Imperial College in London.'

The guard banged on the door and shouted, 'Time's up, Father!'

Fairfax shouted back, 'A few more minutes, if you please!' He tried to retrieve the cylinder from Shadwell. 'Please, sir, I must stow it before he comes in.'

But the old man was reluctant to let it go. 'For well

nigh twenty years I have searched for this. Odd to see it now, and in such straits as these – cruel, one might say.' At last, reluctantly, he released it, and watched as Fairfax wrapped it in the shawl and replaced it in the bag. 'What do you propose to do?'

'I am unsure as yet. Search the area properly, I suppose. That is why we require your help. When did Father Lacy write to you?'

'Two weeks back, or thereabouts. He said he had that day made the discovery of the glassware. We came straight from Wilton directly I read it. But scarcely had we arrived in Axford than word reached us of his death.'

'And you believe the glass came from this Imperial College – the same place from which Morgenstern wrote his letter?'

Shadwell looked at him in surprise. 'How do you know of Morgenstern?'

'Father Lacy had a volume of the proceedings of the Society of Antiquaries by his bedside when he died.'

'By God, then I envy you even more! It was my belief that every copy had been tracked down and destroyed. They took my library, more precious to me than life itself, and burned it in Exeter marketplace.'

'I remember it. I attended the blaze as a boy. But clearly not all was burned, for there is a full set of the society's papers at Addicott Parsonage, and many other volumes besides.'

'Well, that is the best news I have heard in years.' Shadwell suddenly put his claw on Fairfax's wrist and gripped it with surprising force. 'Give them to me.'

'What?'

'If I walk free from here, give them to me, and in return I'll help you. That's my offer. They're no use to anyone else now that Lacy is dead — nobody would dare take possession of them in any case.'

'But they are not mine to give.'

'What will you do with them otherwise? Hand them to Bishop Pole so he can burn them? Would Lacy have wanted that?'

Fairfax finished fastening the straps. The sheriff hammered on the door again. 'Father?' His face appeared at the barred window and moved from side to side like a pale round pendulum as he tried to make out what they were doing at the far end of the cell.

'Pray with me,' said Fairfax. Shadwell looked at him with disgust. 'Pray,' he repeated, 'quickly.' After a moment or two the old man bowed his head and Fairfax placed his hand upon it. He could feel the narrow skull through the velvet cap. 'O Lord,' he said loudly, 'we beseech thee, mercifully hear our prayers, and spare all those who confess their sins unto thee, that they, whose consciences are by sin accused, by thy merciful pardon may be absolved.' He whispered, 'I'll give you the books,' then finished loudly: 'Through Christ our Lord. Amen.'

'Amen,' muttered Shadwell, 'and tell your friend I am at his disposal.'

It was not until he was out of the cell and halfway up the steps following the sheriff that Fairfax recognised the enormity of the sin he had just committed.

To have lied to the bishop was grievous enough; to have gone against the teachings of the Church worse still. But to have abused the sacredness of the penitential prayer? To have recited it without a thought of God, but merely as a means of whispering an illegal offer to a heretic? That was a mortal crime against the faith – and he had done it, moreover, without a qualm, without a moment's hesitation.

The revelation of how far he had strayed from his former life made him feel quite faint. When he reached the landing, he had to lean against the wall for support. *What have I become?* Had it not been for the presence of the guard unlocking the door to the court, he would have slid to his haunches and covered his head with his hands. *I should be down in the cell with Shadwell, down among the dead men, down among the dead men, down among the dead men . . .*

The sheriff opened the door and said something to him he did not hear. As he stepped into the court, he was conscious of a change in the pressure of the atmosphere, of a subdued noise, a blur of faces. Sarah Durston and Captain Hancock were where he had left them, seated at the front, but behind them the empty benches had filled. They were a rougher lot than the audience at the lecture. Word must have got around Axford that a heretic was in the building. There was an air of anticipation. First a hanging, and now this! They were expecting to see the accused emerge, the entertainment to begin. Instead they saw a man of God – or imagined they did – and some groaned in disappointment. What a fraud I am, Fairfax thought.

He walked across the well of the court and took his place next to Sarah Durston. Hancock leaned across her and demanded, 'What was his reply?'

'Oh, he will do it. Naturally he will do it!'

His inner turmoil must have been evident in his voice, because Sarah looked at him with concern. 'Are you all right, Mr Fairfax?'

He could not bring himself to reply. 'Where's Quycke?'

'Gone to settle their account at the Swan,' said Hancock, 'so he can retrieve their wagon and have it ready outside the court. Shadwell must be got away as fast as possible, before anyone can stop him.'

'He says they'll never grant bail for heresy.'

'We'll see about that. I'm told the justice they have sent for is Sir William Trickett. He keeps a thousand head of sheep at Yarnton and I buy nearly all his wool. I believe he will do me a favour, if he can.'

Fairfax turned away. Above the judge's bench hung

a portrait of the king wearing his olive-green military uniform hung with entrails of gold braid and rows of medals, a simple crown upon his head, his expression at once benevolent and stern. In his sacred personage was combined state and Church – the glory of Old England restored after the chaos of the Apocalypse, along with all its ancient machinery of justice. Beneath the painting was a board with the motto of the common law: *Life for life, eye for eye, tooth for tooth, hand for hand, foot for foot, burning for burning, wound for wound, stripe for stripe.*

The Church had its own tribunals of inquisition to try religious offences. Hence the reason for the hearing: to effect the handover of Shadwell from the sheriffs to the bishop's men. Let him be taken off to Exeter today, Fairfax prayed. Let bail be refused and let this whole business be ended here and now. And then he thought of the old man in his chains and he despised himself for his cowardice.

Presently, the door at the back of the judge's bench opened and a clerk appeared, followed by an immensely fat red-faced man in black robes and a tall brimless hat – Trickett, presumably. The court stood. Trickett thumped himself down in his high-backed chair. He looked flustered and irritated in equal measure – a man who had been summoned unexpectedly from his Friday supper for reasons he neither understood nor appreciated. Everyone in the courtroom resumed their seats. The clerk said, 'Bring up the prisoner.'

The sound of Shadwell's coughing could be heard before the accused himself appeared. His shackles had been removed, although the sheriff kept a grip on his arm as he walked him to the dock. The old man stepped up into it and looked around. Such was his short stature, the wooden sides came up to his chest. The clerk said, 'Uncover your head in the justice's presence,' and after a moment's hesitation Shadwell took off his cap and calmly folded it. A gasp of delicious horror went round the room. Branded in the centre of his forehead, darkened by the powder that was used to ensure the scar stayed visible for life was the mark of the heretic – the letter H. Fairfax had heard of the punishment, but it was the first time he had ever seen it. He wanted to look away, but his gaze stayed fixed upon it.

The clerk said, 'State your name.'

'Nicholas Shadwell.'

'Your address?'

'The village of Wilton in the county of Wiltshire.'

Trickett regarded him with distaste, as if something unpleasant had been deposited on his plate. 'What is the charge here?' Even his voice – hoarse and breathless – was fat.

The chief sheriff stood. 'Heresy, Sir William. The prisoner held a public meeting this afternoon with the clear intent of spreading sedition.'

'Not true, sir,' said Shadwell. 'Quite the opposite, in fact. My lecture was meant as a warning *against* the evil of heresy . . .' His voice trailed off into another fit off coughing and he had to duck his head and search for his handkerchief.

Trickett turned to the chief sheriff. 'Ye don't intend for him to be tried here, I assume?'

'No, Sir William.' He was a young man, thickly bearded, with a zealousness in his manner that reminded Fairfax of some of the fanatics in the seminary. 'We ask the court to remand him in custody in Axford until Monday, when arrangements can be made to transfer him to Exeter to appear before the bishop's court.'

'Have ye anything to say, Mr Shadwell?'

'Yes, sir. I stand ready to defend myself, as I have often done in the past. But my health is poor, as you can see' — he held up his bloodied handkerchief — 'and I would ask that I might be set free on bail, to surrender myself to the Church authorities when they come to fetch me. Otherwise there will be nothing to deliver to the bishop but a corpse.'

'Ye have the financial means to post a bail bond?'

'No, sir. After a lifetime of unpaid study, I am entirely without means.' He peered around the court. 'But I am told there is a person in this town who is willing to stand surety for me.'

'And who is that?'

'Me, Sir William.' Hancock rose. From around the court came a hum of angry surprise.

'Captain Hancock?' Trickett folded his short ham-like arms and looked at him in puzzlement. 'Are ye now a friend of heretics?'

'No, Sir William, but I am an enemy of cruelty, and I believe that a sick man such as this, accused but not yet found guilty, should be lodged in better comfort than is provided in Axford Prison.'

'And where, pray, would ye lodge him instead?'

'Under my own roof, Sir William. At Addicott Mill House.'

'Is he not a stranger to ye?'

'He is. As God is my witness, I have yet to exchange a word with him, though I did attend his lecture and saw nothing in it that smacked of heresy.'

'Well, never have I heard of such generosity — especially not from the owner of Addicott Mill! Sheriff — what do ye say?'

'I object, Sir William, most strongly. Bail cannot be granted in so serious a case. With all respect to Captain Hancock, we have statements from witnesses who will swear that heresy did indeed take place and that devilish spirits were conjured forth. Shadwell himself is a most devious and practised blasphemer — observe the mark upon his forehead — and I have no doubt that he will make a run for it the moment he gets a chance rather than risk a trial in Exeter.'

Hancock said, 'I'll lay a thousand pounds he won't.'

Gasps and whistles greeted this announcement.

Trickett looked affronted. 'This is a court of law, Captain Hancock, not a cock pit.'

'Still, my offer stands.'

Sarah whispered to Fairfax, 'He will lose it for us by his foolish boasting.'

Trickett said, in disbelief, 'And can ye lodge such a sum with the court this afternoon?'

'I can, Sir William. With thy permission?' Hancock rose from his place, walked to the table in front of the judge's bench and began emptying out his pockets. Every eye in the courtroom, including Shadwell's, was on the growing piles of banknotes and coins, and when he had finished, he pushed it all towards the clerk. 'There it is, sir. Ye may check it if ye wish, but I assure ye the sum is complete.' He returned to his seat and left the money lying there, as if such an enormous amount – which would have taken one of his weavers more than ten years to earn – was nothing to him.

Trickett gestured to the clerk to approach the bench. The two men held a whispered consultation. The chief sheriff was summoned to join them. Occasionally all three glanced across at Hancock. Finally, Trickett turned to address the prisoner. 'Nicholas Shadwell, ye stand accused of a most heinous crime against God and our sovereign lord, the king, as Supreme Head of the Church of England, and it is our judgement that ye must be rendered to Exeter to stand trial.

'However,' he continued with a grimace, as if it

pained him to utter the words, 'in view of your health, and the well-known character of Captain Hancock, and the fact that he is willing to give the court such a large guarantee of good behaviour, we are minded to grant bail' – someone cried out, 'No!' – 'on condition ye return here at noon next Monday, the fifteenth of April, and surrender to the court.' He had to raise his voice to be heard over the growing outrage. 'In the meantime, ye are to remain under the roof of Captain Hancock, except on Sunday, when ye are obliged to attend a service of the Christian faith and show due penitence by receiving the Holy Sacrament. Is that acceptable to yc?'

'Yes, sir.'

'And Captain Hancock – be in no doubt, sir, that if Shadwell fails to appear next week, not only will ye forfeit a thousand pounds, ye may be charged with aiding and abetting the escape of a wanted man. He is in thy keeping.'

'I understand that.'

'Stand down, Mr Shadwell. The court is dismissed, and will keep' – he had to shout to make himself heard – 'and will keep good order!'

CHAPTER SEVENTEEN

Return to the Devil's Chair

I T WAS TOO late to appeal for calm. The citizenry of Axford had seen the brand of heretic upon Shadwell's forehead and that was sufficient trial for them. Like the blue fire in Shadwell's demonstration, violence fizzled in the air.

Hancock called to Fairfax, 'Help me!' and as the accused came down from the dock, plainly bewildered by this turn of events, the captain took one of Shadwell's arms and Fairfax the other. But not even their combined authority could prevent some rough handling. People reached out to try to push him off his feet. Punches were thrown. He was jeered and flecked with spit. The sheriffs made no move to intervene; Sir William Trickett had already withdrawn. Hancock seized one young noisy fellow by his jacket — he was barely more than a boy, hissing and spitting like a cat — and flung him out of the way, sending him crashing over the benches as if he were a toy. After that the spectators drew back somewhat, and they were able to squeeze through the door and out into the square.

Shadwell's covered wagon was drawn up directly opposite the door, hitched to a team of four mules. Quycke reached down from the driver's bench to haul Shadwell up beside him at the same time as Hancock hoisted him from behind. Once the old man was in his seat, he turned. 'I haven't had a chance to thank you, sir—'

'Ride straight for the gate, Mr Quycke,' said Han cock, cutting him off. 'We'll catch ye on the road.' He struck the nearest mule on the flank. The wagon lurched forward. As it pulled away, he tugged his pistol from his belt and turned to confront the dozen spectators who had followed them from the court-room. 'Now ye'll leave 'em be, d'ye hear me?' He waved his pistol at them. 'Else ye'll have me to reckon with, and not one man jack of ye'll ever sell me wool, or anything else!'

The boy he had thrown to the ground was bleed-ing from a gash in his cheek. One of his companions, his elder brother by the look of him, shouted, 'Ye should be ashamed of thyself, John Hancock, for free-ing a heretic! By God, I'm not a-feared of ye!' He thrust himself towards the front. Hancock cocked his pistol, took aim at him, and suddenly the whole mob seemed unstable, like the hillside above Axford, threatening to descend upon them.

'Yes, he is a sinner!' cried Fairfax, finding a voice from somewhere. He stepped between the crowd and Hancock. 'And I am a sinner.' He held his arms out wide. 'We all are sinners, in the eyes of God! Remember Christ's words: "He that is without sin among you, let him first cast a stone." Any man who dares to raise a hand against Shadwell or anyone else will have to answer to the Almighty. Are you willing to risk His verdict?' Nobody moved. 'Then go back to your homes,' he said, with all the severity he could muster, 'and pray for forgiveness.'

For a moment he thought they might crush him. But angry as they were, they dared not lay a hand upon a priest. He held them penned by his outstretched arms as if by an invisible force.

Hancock stuffed his pistol back under his belt, untied Sarah's horse from the rail and held the bridle for her while she carefully placed her bag across the saddle. The instant she was mounted, he unhitched his own horse. Sweeping a final look across the mob, Fairfax risked turning his back upon them. It took him half a minute to untie May and swing himself up on to her, every second an agony of vulnerability, and then he was galloping after the others, through the gate and across the drawbridge. Once again he realised he had used the word of God to assist a heretic.

As he passed the walls of the prison, he looked up. A fourth corpse, that of the tomb robber, Porlock, was hanging naked in its iron cage, the white flesh partly hidden by a swirling black cloak of crows.

By the time they caught up with Shadwell's wagon, it was already lumbering past the furthest edge of the common land. It was a cumbersome contraption with a heavy white canvas roof stretched across metal hoops, water barrels and toolboxes attached to the back, and a profusion of pots and pans, buckets and shovels dangling from the sides that banged and clanked whenever the wheels struck a rut or a stone.

Fairfax slowed his horse, stood up in his saddle and twisted round to look back towards the town. Hancock did the same. There was no sign of any pursuit. Rather the traffic was all the other way, as people began to head back to Axford in good time before the curfew. Apparently satisfied that they were safe, at least for the present, Hancock resumed his seat, spurred his large chestnut mare and went ahead to walk alongside the wagon, leaning over to talk to Shadwell.

Sarah dropped back to ride alongside Fairfax. 'That was bravely spoken.'

'It served to carry us through the moment, though I doubt I could play the same trick twice.' He strained his gaze ahead, trying to overhear what Hancock was saying. His view of Shadwell was blocked by the canvas cover. 'And what madcap scheme comes next, I wonder?'

'Who can tell with John? I warned you what would happen if we joined ourselves to him.'

'You did. The fault is mine. What a trap we have made for ourselves.' And then he added bitterly, 'Had I foreseen three days ago when I left Axford what lay at the end of this road, I would never have set off upon it.'

'Well I for one am glad you did.'

'Yes, but you'll be safe whatever happens, with a wealthy husband to protect you. And if Hancock has the power to spring a heretic from prison, I am sure he will be secure as well. But can you not see that I have lost myself entirely? Renounced my past and ruined my future, lost God and Church – and all for what? For an impious curiosity!'

It took her a few moments to summon a reply. 'Well, I will say this for the captain – at least he does not lack for courage!' She spurred her horse and rode ahead, overtaking Shadwell's wagon and putting a hundred paces between herself and the rest of them. Damn her, thought Fairfax, although he regretted his harsh tone and had to suppress an impulse to go after her and apologise.

Presently Hancock finished his conversation with Shadwell and pulled up his horse to let the young priest draw level. 'So, Fairfax, the old man tells me ye went up to the Devil's Chair today and found human bones.'

'I did. What of it?'

'Have ye not noticed the sky?'

'The sky?' He had been too absorbed to pay it any heed. But now he saw that it was just as it had been on the Tuesday afternoon when he first left Axford for the valley – entirely pewter, without a glimmer of a sunset, and with the same curious pregnant silence in the air.

'There's like to be another storm,' continued Hancock, 'and Shadwell's of the opinion we ought to find your bones and mark the place while the land's still firm, lest the rain wash away all trace.'

'But will it be safe in such poor light?'

'There's still three hours till nightfall, and we have each other for protection in case of devils.' He grinned. 'D'ye think ye can find the spot again?'

'I'll not forget it in a hurry.'

'Good man.' For the first time Hancock looked at him with something approaching respect. 'I know a way through the woods that will bring us out close to the tower, and spare us the need to go near the village.' He spurred his horse and returned to talk to Shadwell.

Quycke flicked his whip and geed the mules up to a trot. Gradually the last vestiges of cultivation began to slip away. The road dipped and they were alone on the wild moor with its desolate dark green undulations and streaks of yellow gorse, devoid of life or movement apart from the occasional wild Wessex pony galloping alongside them. Miles in the distance Fairfax could see low clouds dragging heavy showers like steel flails across the ground. He wished he had brought his cape. He tried to imagine the landscape as Shadwell had envisaged it in *Antiquis Anglia*, a place once teeming with buildings, but the effort defeated him. This land was immemorial. Even the ancients, with all their industry, would have been unable to do much more than scratch a road across it.

Eventually a line of hills appeared to coalesce ahead out of the murk. The road started to climb, and they passed from moorland into woodland. As soon as they crossed the treeline, Hancock squeezed past the wagon and rode ahead to catch up with Sarah Durston. Fairfax watched him gesticulating to her in the shadows, presumably explaining his plan. It seemed to him full of hazards. He wondered if she might have the good sense to leave them and take the road back into Addicott. But they passed the fork he had missed on his first afternoon and she continued to ride with Hancock. It was not in her nature to turn around.

The mules struggled to drag the wagon up the rough incline. Their pace slowed. Fairfax dismounted to give May a rest and walked beside her. He recognised they were on the same path on which he had encountered Keefer pushing his handcart. In the semi-darkness of the forest he found it hard to calculate their direction. They seemed to be curving from the west towards the north and he guessed they must be working their way around the outer sides of the cauldron of hills that enclosed the valley. Unseen creatures rustled in the undergrowth. He could hear the hollow drilling of a woodpecker. A pair of parakeets chattered close by, then stopped. There was a profound silence. And then came the boom of an explosion in the quarry, near enough to tremble the ground. May reared up in fright and jerked at her bridle, wrenching Fairfax's arm, and as he struggled to pull her down, he saw Sarah Durston's mount go up on its hind legs and send her flying backwards. He let go of May's bridle and ran towards her.

She lay motionless, curled up on her side next to the road. Hancock was still dismounting as Fairfax reached her and dropped to his knees. 'Sarah?' Her face was white. She seemed not to be breathing. Dear God, he prayed, let her not be dead — let her not be dead, and I shall abandon this cursed quest and obey the teachings of the Church. He hooked his arm around her shoulders and lifted her into a sitting position. Her head lolled forward. He feared her neck was broken. He took her chin in his hand and turned her face towards him. Her eyes stared frantically into his. Her mouth flapped open, fighting for breath. He put his arms around her and drew her to him. She wrapped hers around him. He could feel the shudders running through her body, spasm after spasm, until at last, with a sound like the whooping cough, she sucked in air.

A hand clamped hard upon his shoulder. 'That's enough, Fairfax. Let me attend her.'

Hancock squatted on his haunches and shoved the priest aside. But when he reached out his arms to take her, she pressed her palm to his chest to fend him off. 'No, John,' she gasped, turning away. 'Let me breathe.'

After a few moments, Hancock stood. He could not bring himself to look at Fairfax. 'No bones broken by the sound of it,' he said in a thick voice. 'She'll be right enough when she recovers her wind. I'll just wait with her. Get her horse, would ye?'

As Fairfax moved up the road, Shadwell clambered down from the wagon. 'Is she injured, Father Fairfax?'

'No, Dr Shadwell — she seems merely shaken, thanks be to God.'

Her grey mare was calmly chewing at the undergrowth. He held out his hand and made a soothing noise. The horse turned to look at him without interest. He noticed the saddlebag lying in the ditch. The instant he picked it up, he heard the rattle of broken glass. He undid the straps and emptied out the fragments on to the roadside. None of the pieces was larger than his middle finger. Behind him he heard Shadwell exclaim, 'A disaster!'

Fairfax muttered, 'Better broken glass than broken bones.'

'Not so, Father. Bones can mend. Such glass as that is irreplaceable.'

'There's plenty more of the same at Durston Court.' He began to edge the fragments into the ditch with the side of his boot.

'Wait!' cried Shadwell. 'I cannot bear to see it treated so!' He got down on to his hands and knees and began to collect up the debris, laying it carefully on the shawl. 'Oliver – help me.'

Quycke came up and kneeled beside him, and together they proceeded to gather up every shard, however small. Fairfax watched them in wonder. Why? It was not as if the thing was repairable. He is quite mad, he thought, and we have all gone mad with him.

'Fairfax, what is this?'

He turned to find the captain with Sarah. Her step was unsteady, her face as pallid as a corpse's, her riding habit streaked with mud, but she was walking unaided.

'Lady Durston – you should rest!'

'I am fine, Christopher,' she said in a thin voice. 'A little winded – nothing more.'

Hancock looked past him. 'Why do they kneel?'

'Her ladyship's glass was broken in the fall.'

She said, 'It does not matter. Its purpose is served.'

'Exactly,' said Hancock. 'It has brought us this far. Leave it, Mr Shadwell, for God's sake. We must get on. We are almost there.' He took out his pocket watch. 'It's only just past seven. The sun will not set for an hour.'

Fairfax threw up his hands in exasperation. 'There is no sun! Lady Durston should return home and go to bed. For all we know, she may have done some damage to her brain. The prize is not worth the risk.'

'I'm right enough. Let's go on.'

'But this is folly! By the time we find the tower, it will be dark.'

'No, sir,' said Shadwell. He had finished collecting the debris and stood nursing it, bundled up in the shawl. 'See there.'

He nodded towards the trees on their right. They all turned to look. Above the topmost branches, some way off, yet vivid against the dull grey sky, was the unmistakable flat white concrete rim of the Devil's Chair.

They continued the rest of the way on foot. Hancock went first, leading his horse; then Sarah, limping slightly, holding on to her mare; followed by Fairfax, who kept close behind her in case she stumbled; and finally Shadwell and Quycke walking beside the mules. Sometimes the top of the tower was visible; mostly it was hidden behind the trees. There was no conversation. The birds were still. The tower seemed to cast some sort of spell that muted sound.

Presently the road forked again. Hancock held up his hand to bring them to a halt and gestured to the right. Obediently they turned into the track, but the path quickly became too steep and rocky for the mules to drag the wagon. They tied their horses to the trees. Quycke fussed around Shadwell, insisting he don an oilskin greatcoat with a hood, then unlocked the boxes at the back of the wagon and took out various tools: four long-handled shovels, the same number of trowels, buckets and sacks, a sieve, and half a dozen bamboo canes with torn red handkerchiefs attached at one end. He distributed them equally — Fairfax received a shovel and a bucket with a couple of trowels in it — and they resumed their climb, Hancock once again in the lead.

Gradually more of the tower became visible through the trees, and after a few minutes' effort they reached the crest of the slope and emerged on to the right-hand arm of the chair. The hillside ran all the way around to form the back and the distant left arm, and from the seat the tower rose directly before them like some ruined pagan temple festooned with vines. They contemplated the vista in silence. Even Hancock seemed briefly awed. But soon he was all business again. 'So, Fairfax, can ye remember where ye saw these bones?'

'Yes, pretty well.' He pointed with the end of his shovel. 'About fifty paces behind the tower, where the land begins to rise.'

Rather than work their way round to it, the easier way was to descend through the trees to the level ground. When they were halfway down, it started to rain. They could hear it dripping off the canopy of leaves above their heads, and once they reached the clearing there was no escaping it – the same soft, drenching mist that Fairfax had experienced on his first day in the valley. They skirted the base of the tower and he led them along the path he remembered, climbing again between the ferns and fungi and the mossy fallen branches. The ground was spongy. He stopped and gazed around.

'It was somewhere here.' He went on a few paces and used his shovel to poke the undergrowth. He began to feel uncertain. Everywhere looked the same. 'Surely no one can have come and moved them?'

Hancock said sceptically, 'Or maybe ye imagined it.'

'One must always mark one's finds,' said Shadwell primly. He had pulled up his hood and stared out at them from beneath it through his curious shaded spectacles. 'It is the first rule of the antiquarian.'

'Father Fairfax is not an antiquarian,' said Sarah.

Hancock said, 'We're wasting time. Let us each take a part to search.'

They separated, and for the next few minutes the

silence was broken only by the noise of their shovels hacking away at the undergrowth, interspersed by Shadwell's periodic spasms of coughing. This exposure to the rain will kill him, Fairfax thought. He was finding it uncomfortable enough himself, his boots sinking in the soft ground, the rain running into his eyes, the shaft of the shovel slippery in his hands as he battered at the ferns.

Suddenly Sarah shouted out. 'Here!'

She was fifty paces from Fairfax, further up the bank. He had been looking in entirely the wrong place. They waded through the wet undergrowth towards her. She was staring at something close to her feet. Shadwell, slower than the rest of them, called out to her not to touch it. A piece of ribcage lay in a shallow depression, pale on the exposed brown earth.

Shadwell came up and planted one of his bamboo poles beside it. Awkwardly, he lowered himself to the ground, picked up the bone and brushed away the soil.

Fairfax said, 'Is it human? It seems too small.' It looked as though it might have come from a dog.

'Yes, it is. A child's. See? And there are more remains there.' Now that they looked, they could make out various other bones. 'This place is a charnel house.' Shadwell handed the ribcage to Fairfax, who held it gingerly – the thing felt fragile enough to disintegrate between his fingers – and then the antiquarian began to run his hands across the earth. He pulled back his hood and bent his nose close to the ground. He seemed to be sniffing the soil, like a bloodhound. 'You were of the opinion that these bones had been revealed by the rain, I believe, Mr Fairfax?'

'I thought it the most likely cause of their uncovering, yes.'

'Well, you were wrong, sir!' He turned to look up at Fairfax, oddly triumphant. 'This exposure wasn't the work of nature. This hollow has been dug out by human hand. See here, at the edge – the teeth mark of a tool? Someone has been here before us.'

Fairfax nodded. 'Father Lacy.'

Hancock said, 'Ye don't know that.'

'Who else could it have been?'

'The flood washed away his workings,' said Shadwell. He held up his hand. 'Oliver – help me.' Quycke offered his arm, and the old man, wincing at his stiffness, hauled himself to his feet. 'We must dig a trench,' he said, gesturing to show what he wanted, 'inwards, towards this spot, along a line of twenty paces.'

'For what purpose?' asked Sarah.

'Lacy was a man of scientific method. If he dug here, you may be sure he had good cause.' He took the ribcage from Fairfax and replaced it exactly where it had been found. 'Oliver, would you be good enough to make a drawing of the site?' He glanced around at the others. 'Well? We must make haste. Dig!'

Fairfax measured out twenty paces down the slope, rolled up his sleeves and stabbed the blade of his shovel into the ground. He was not unused to digging: there was a vegetable garden in the grounds of the chapter house where the younger priests were expected to do their share of work. But the earth of the cathedral garden was well broken, whereas here it was covered with ivy and ground elder, both deeply rooted, that needed to be sliced through, and then, once that had been cleared, the soil beneath proved to be full of rocks. Nevertheless, his sense of mission lent him strength   that desire to serve a larger purpose that was instilled in him as a priest – and soon his warm sweat was mingling with the cold rain.

After a while he took a rest and looked up. He could see Hancock working furiously, Sarah and Quyckc also digging, Shadwell walking up and down, occasionally stooping to examine some fresh find. There were four flags planted in the ground.

He ignored the pain in his arms and went back to work. At a depth of about two feet, his shovel struck something softer than rock. He took the trowel from the bucket, got down on his knees and bent into the hole. Scraping away the loosened soil, he used his fingers to work off the clinging mud from the bone, and gradually, like a sculpture emerging from a block of stone, the earth yielded its occupant, or at least its top half, from the base of its ribcage to its skull. It lay on its back, a coverlet of soil drawn up to its waist, staring at the wet sky. A tall figure, or so it seemed to Fairfax, well in excess of his own height. He felt a peculiar shyness, as if he had woken someone from a long rest who had no desire to be disturbed. He touched his wet finger to the cold bone forehead and lightly drew the sign of the cross. 'Who are you?' he said softly.

The light was becoming too weak for them to continue. Besides, they were wet to the skin. Shadwell, the only one well protected against the rain, declared they had done enough. Hancock, whose strength seemed to be equal to all of theirs combined, had dug a second trench, at right angles to the first, and exposed two more skeletons lying side by side.

They stood among the bones and surveyed their work. Quycke handed Shadwell his sketch.

'It is well laid out,' said Shadwell, examining the figures. 'These people were not left to rot where they fell, but properly buried. By my account, we have found ten. I feel certain if we dug for longer we would find yet more.'

Sarah said, 'So it is a cemetery?'

'Exactly — and as such, proof of settlement, for why would anyone come up here from the valley to bury their dead? They must have lived close by.'

'In the tower?'

'No, your ladyship, there's too little room in it.

And where are the doors and windows?' He pointed around the clearing. 'Have you noticed the way the big trees all stop some distance from it? Something prevents their taking root. There is a structure underground, I'm sure of it.'

Hancock said, 'We should come back tomorrow and dig nearer the tower.'

'Such an undertaking will require a great many men.'

'I have men.'

'You have men,' said Sarah, 'but will they come up here?'

'They will.'

Fairfax said, 'I thought most refused to approach this place, even to look for Lacy's body?'

'Oh, they will come — they will come if I pay them well enough. How many would be needed?'

Shadwell said, 'My reckoning from experience is that a man can shift three cubic yards of earth an hour. But this land is hard. Say, twenty yards a man a day. That means that to make a decent mark we'll need twenty men at least.'

'Twenty I can find.'

Fairfax said, 'How will you bring twenty men up here and keep it secret? The village will talk. It will be known in Axford in no time.' He looked around. He pictured Lacy, digging in this isolated place — a mad venture for one man on his own. A suspicion was beginning to form. 'Where was Father Lacy's body found? We have seen no ravine.'

'Up there.' Hancock gestured with his chin over his shoulder to the back of the Devil's Chair. 'Just beyond the crest.' He studied Fairfax. 'I can show ye, if ye like.'

'Now?'

'Why not? We're halfway there. It's merely atop this slope.'

Quycke interrupted. 'I fear for Mr Shadwell's health if we stay much longer in this damp and cold. We must find him someplace dry.'

'Then why don't ye all begin your descent?' suggested Hancock. 'Leave Fairfax and me our share of the tools to carry and we'll meet ye at the wagon.'

Sarah said, 'Surely it must be dangerous in this bad light, John? Leave it till tomorrow.'

'It will not take above ten minutes. Come, Fairfax. I'll point out the spot.'

He set off, forestalling further discussion, striding over the rough ground, and after a slight hesitation — for there was something about the captain's eagerness he found unsettling — Fairfax followed him. Hancock moved fast for such a big man, nimble as a goat, jumping across the myriad of little springs that had emerged with the rain and were bubbling down the hillside, skirting rocks and fallen branches, hauling himself up by vines and trailing foliage. Fairfax was struck again by the land's resemblance to a bulging forehead, the way in places it loomed over the clearing. It was dangerous, he thought, unstable.

They reached the summit and Hancock turned and held out his hand to help Fairfax up the final part. 'He lay just down there, beyond those trees. Go look. I'll hold on to ye.' He gripped the priest by the wrist and ushered him forward.

The ground was loose under Fairfax's feet. He could hear a waterfall somewhere, hammering down on to the rocks beneath. He edged forward, parted the branches and found himself immediately swaying over space. At some time during the winter, part of the hillside had sheared away to leave a cliff edge that plunged at least a hundred feet to the narrow valley floor beneath. In the dim light it was impossible to make out much.

'Whereabouts did the body lie, exactly?'

'Just beyond a big rock, close to the stream. Can ye not see it?'

'No.'

He risked another half a pace forward, and suddenly he could feel the soil sliding away beneath him, his legs giving way. Rocks and loose earth tipped over the edge and crashed down to the bottom, and for a moment he felt sure he was about to follow. He turned and with both hands grabbed hold of Hancock's arm. It flashed through his mind that the captain meant to murder him, and for a second or two he hung suspended. But then Hancock grinned — 'I've got ye, Father' — and pulled him back to safety.

'Dear God,' cried Fairfax. He backed away from the edge. 'What a fatal spot!'

'Aye,' said Hancock. 'Ye can see why folk are afraid to come up here.' He seemed well pleased by the scare he had given the young priest. 'So now is your curiosity satisfied?'

'Almost.'

'Almost?' Hancock frowned. 'What more d'ye need to know?'

'The day his body was discovered — I believe you didn't come all the way up to the Devil's Chair.'

'No, we had no need — we came along the track down there and found him near the rock. Why? How d'ye know that?'

'Because if you'd come up past the tower — before the storm — you'd have seen the fresh trench he'd dug.'

Hancock nodded slowly. 'That's true.'

'Then don't you understand? He was not at the Devil's Chair that day for no reason. He had a task — digging bones. Why would he venture up on to the ridge? Something must have caused him to desert his work and clamber all the way up here — chased him up, I shouldn't wonder. Whether accident or murder, I cannot tell, but I surmise he was in terror of his life, and that was how he died.'

CHAPTER EIGHTEEN

*In which Mr Shadwell gives an account
of the Apocalypse*

THE SKY HAD darkened while they were talking — so much so that by the time they began their descent, it was hard to see where to plant their boots. Several times they both went slithering, until they reached level ground and the open graves. The trenches gaped like wounds carved into the undergrowth. The outlines of the ancients' corpses, their bones a lighter colour than the soil, were faintly visible in the shadows. It seemed an outrage to leave them out all night exposed to the rain. Fairfax bent his head to pray. *And though after my skin worms destroy this body, yet in my flesh shall I see God . . .*

Hancock, further on, gathering up the shovels, turned to see what had become of him. 'Oh come now, Fairfax, for pity's sake! We have no time for that!'

'Have you no soul, Captain Hancock?'

'I have a soul, but these corpses have lain eight hundred years in unconsecrated ground, and another night won't hurt 'em.'

Fairfax ignored him, finished his prayer, made the sign of the cross and then shouldered his share of the tools.

A wind had risen, rustling the branches of the trees, rippling the ivy clinging to the tower, as if the spirits of the dead were whirling all around them. Who were these people, born to live long lives, with inconceivable luxuries and wonders at their disposal? How had they come to die in such an isolated place?

The others were sheltering in the back of Shadwell's wagon. A lamp was lit inside. A carpet was spread out on the boards. There were cushions, two straw mattresses, chests, a rack of books. Dozens of Quycke's drawings were glued to the canvas walls — sketches of grave sites, artefacts, ruined buildings. It was plainly where the two men lived when they were on the road. Shadwell was huddled on his own at the back, draped in an old rug.

Hancock leaned in through the flap. 'If ye're agreeable, I propose we all pass the night at my house. It's closer than the village.'

'Anything to escape this rain,' said Quycke.

Shadwell started coughing.

Hancock said, 'It's settled then. Stay here in the dry, Sarah. I'll lead your horse.'

'No, I'll ride.'

He looked ready to argue, but then decided against it. 'As ye wish. I'll borrow that lamp, if I may.'

He mounted his horse and held the lamp up so they could follow him, then led them back out into the lane. He wheeled right and they resumed their journey in the same direction as before.

For the next hour, Fairfax's universe shrank to darkness and drizzle, the faint glow-worm of light up ahead, the clop of the horses' hooves, the trundle of the wagon's iron-rimmed wheels splashing through the puddles, the noise of the wind in the trees, the hollow cries of owls calling to one another in the forest. At length he sensed they were descending again, and not long afterwards, the lamp swayed off to the right and they entered upon a well-made drive. He could hear water rushing nearby and could just make out the black shapes of large buildings and a tall chimney stack silhouetted against the sky. A lighted window appeared ahead. A dog began barking. A crack of yellow light became a rectangle as a door was opened, and a woman's voice called anxiously into the foul night: 'John?'

Addicott Mill House, like its owner, was large, solid, prosperous and proudly devoid of anything that might smack of frills or frippery. The whitewashed walls were bare apart from horse brasses. The brightly polished spotless oak floor exuded a strong aroma of wax, as did the plain oak furniture. In the sitting room was a newly carved baronial stone fireplace, not yet blackened by smoke, with a tiny fire on to which Hancock piled armfuls of kindling and heavy logs so that it soon became a blaze. They shed their wet coats and stood before it with their hands outstretched while their host issued various orders – bring gin, bring ale, fetch food, draw up a chair for Dr Shadwell, set up a table in front of the fire, close the shutters, warm the beds – most of which were directed at the heavyset grey-haired woman who had met them at the door and whom he introduced, almost as an afterthought, as his sister, Martha.

Sarah said politely, 'Allow me to help you, Martha.'

'Spare yourself the trouble, your ladyship,' replied Martha. 'Ye're not the mistress in this house yet.'

Fairfax noticed how Sarah's face seemed to tighten. 'It really is no trouble to me.'

'That's gracious, I'm sure, but I know my place.' Martha withdrew, triumphant.

'Leave her be, Sarah,' advised Hancock. 'She likes to do these things herself.' He tapped his foot in irritation, then followed his sister out of the room. They could hear him shouting after her, 'Martha?'

An elderly manservant and a maid came in, carrying a table, which they placed in front of the fire. The man returned with chairs and the girl with jugs and glasses.

Sarah pulled a face. 'I hardly dare presume, Christopher – will you serve us?'

He poured them each a helping of gin and they all sat down at the table to drink, apart from Shadwell, still wrapped in his rug, who stayed close to the fire, his glass cupped in his hands, staring into the flames.

Presently Hancock reappeared bearing a large tureen of soup. 'Martha has retired to bed. She is unwell. She asked me to extend her apologies.'

The maid fetched bowls and cutlery, the man a board of bread and cheese, and afterwards a pair of cold capons and some pickles. Hancock lifted the lid of the tureen. He inhaled the steam with relish. 'Onion. Excellent. This will warm us right enough. Will ye favour us with grace, Mr Fairfax?'

'I thought you were not a believer, Captain Hancock?'

'It's your Church I don't believe in, sir. Your God I treat with respect.'

Fairfax bowed his head and said mechanically, 'Bless, O Lord, this food for thy use, and make us ever mindful of the wants and needs of others. Amen.'

'Amen.' Hancock began to ladle out the soup. 'Won't ye join us, Dr Shadwell? Will ye fetch him to the table, Mr Quycke?'

Quycke bent to whisper in Shadwell's ear, and with some reluctance the old man allowed himself to be extracted from his fireside seat and manoeuvred into a chair at the head of the table. His face was unhealthily flushed, whether from the fire or his disease Fairfax could not tell. His spoon rattled against the side of the bowl when he bent to eat, and shed most of its contents on its wavering journey to his mouth. Still, he ate, and not long afterwards he took another glass of gin. He shrugged the rug from his shoulders and Quycke, ever attentive, rose to drape it over the back of his chair.

Hancock said, 'So, Dr Shadwell, what d'ye believe we might discover when we start to dig?'

'That is impossible to know, sir.'

'But there's like to be an underground chamber of some description?'

'Who can say? What once lay there may have long ago collapsed under the pressure of earth and time. Or it may prove empty. Or it may be a treasure house from the ancient world.' He made a resigned gesture with his spoon. 'I cannot foretell.'

'What d'ye hope for?'

Shadwell sighed and set down his spoon. 'In my dreams?' He dabbed at his mouth with his napkin. Out of long habit he inspected it for blood, although Fairfax could see it was merely smeared with onion soup. Satisfied, he returned it to his lap. 'Well, you've read what Morgenstern proposed. It could be nothing less than the necessities to one day restore the ancients' way of life. That was his purpose, proclaimed in his letter, and the glass would seem to signify as much, though why it lay in the ground as it did is a mystery.' He turned to Sarah. 'Glass, for all its brittleness, Lady Durston, is like gold. It does not decay. Perhaps the rest has rotted. When we dig, we may discover, for often there are traces of wood and metal visible to the practised eye – mere stains upon the earth – that your husband most likely would have missed.'

She said, 'Do you really think there might be gold?' She could not disguise her eagerness.

'There might.' He nodded. 'Most of the ancients' business was conducted not with coin or even paper but with electric tokens of money sent flying through the air. When the Apocalypse overwhelmed them, their devices failed and their wealth vanished. A man as wise as Morgenstern would have foreseen the danger, and might well have had the prudence to lay down a store of gold – the only safe money since the beginning of time. Might I trouble you for more gin, Captain?'

Hancock leaned over and filled his glass. 'If the ancients were foolish enough to trade with airy tokens, 'tis no wonder they were ruined.'

'It both made their vast trade possible and rendered them beggars when it failed. Consider waking up one morning entirely destitute, with skills no longer of value or of any use in the struggle for life!

Their world was based upon imagining – mere castles made of vapour. The wind blew; it vanished.'

Fairfax felt obliged to object. 'Come, Dr Shadwell, it is possible for men and women to live without money.'

'For us, sir, with our simpler way of life – perhaps. The grass grows. The sheep feed. The loom turns. Captain Hancock takes his cloth to market and exchanges it for food. I share with him my learning and he gives me onion soup. But consider, for example, London – a city that on the eve of the Apocalypse is believed to have boasted a population of some eight million. We know from ancient sources that it had great areas of open spaces – parks and gardens. But none, that we can see, was given over to crops or farm animals. How were those eight million souls to eat? You will recall that in his letter, Morgenstern declares that London existed at any moment only six meals removed from starvation. Every morsel of food had to be imported, and at the same time as their devices failed, the supply of food failed also, for how could it be paid for? Who would move it? Once one thing failed, so did another, and another. Their society became harder to recover with each day that passed. It was like a ship that had slipped its anchor and drifted off, leaving its crew stranded helpless on the shore. And that was when the Great Exodus began – but this was an Exodus without a Moses to lead it.'

Sarah shivered. 'Eight million starving souls in flight from their homes! It is a most fearful vision you conjure.'

'It is. Sometimes I wish I had found a less melancholy subject for my life's study. And yet there is a certain wonder in it — the wonder that we see expressed in the grandeur of their ruins.' He looked around the table. The heat of the fire and the food in his belly had restored his strength. Plainly he was a man who enjoyed an audience. 'The things we have observed, my lady! We have seen the great mass graves beside the roads leading out of the city — at Redhill, St Albans, Chertsey, Dartford — where the bones still lie scattered over the fields like stones. We have made copies, Oliver and I, of the writings on the walls of the churches left by those searching for lost relations eight centuries ago — such pitiful messages! — for families lived much apart in those days, and if they were separated at the time the blow fell, and could no longer communicate, how would they have known where to meet again? Those abroad must have vanished for ever. I am sure that no greater calamity has ever happened in the history of the world. It would have been better never to have been born than to have lived through it. Starvation would have taken most. Disease and massacre carried off the best part of the rest.'

Fairfax said, 'And the cause of the catastrophe? What was that?'

'None can say for sure. For my part, I believe it was most likely what Morgenstern listed as his fifth conjecture: "A general failure of computer technology due either to cyber warfare, an uncontrollable virus, or solar activity." Human nature being as it is, warfare is my guess.'

'And yet the country rose again,' said Hancock.

'Indeed, after a long interval, little by little, life picked up. Man is a stubborn, cunning animal. And in this, Father Fairfax, I grant your Church was key, for amid the chaos, if nothing else, almost every village retained its stone-built church. We know from the ancient sources that even in those godless days there were still some thirty-seven thousand churches in England. That was where those who survived the Exodus gathered — at first no doubt for safety; then for fellowship, welfare, schooling. And it was in the churches, a generation or two later, when all who could remember the old way of life were dead, that their descendants found in the Scriptures a simple answer to the question of what had ruined the world. To their still numbed and fearful brains it could only be the Apocalypse — Armageddon, as foretold in the Book of Genesis. On that assumption our present state was founded.'

'But ye do not believe it?'

'No, sir. If I cannot say for certain what did cause their world to fail, I can at least state with confidence that the answer must lie in science and nature, and not in the appearance of a beast bearing the number six hundred three score and six! That is a tale maintained by the Church to keep the people tame. In my estimation, half of the bishops do not believe it either — among whom, I might add, I number Bishop Pole.'

Fairfax laughed. 'Bishop Pole does not believe that God sent the Apocalypse? What evidence do you have for such a charge?'

'The evidence of my ears, Mr Fairfax!' Shadwell drank more gin. 'When the Society of Antiquaries was suppressed and its officers arrested, the bishop visited me in my cell on several occasions. He was most interested in our work. He questioned me with regard to Morgenstern in particular — who he was, what he sought, what might have become of him. He made no attempt to deny the truth of Morgenstern's letter. Rather the contrary: he took pleasure in speaking frankly to a man who could not escape. He said that the very fact it rang so true meant that all trace of it must be destroyed — that the Church could not allow its teachings to be so baldly contradicted. "The path to Hell begins with too much seeking into the past. The story of the Apocalypse is the locked gate that stands across that path. It can never be allowed to be opened." Those were his very words. I had five years in prison to remember them.'

Hancock said, 'I'm surprised he didn't burn ye as a heretic.'

' "Burnings make martyrs" – that was another of his sayings. So he merely branded me and burned my books instead, and I was left to languish, forgotten. Oh, he is a most subtle, worldly man, is he not, Father Fairfax?'

Fairfax was almost too stunned to reply. 'If what you say is true, Dr Shadwell, I am not sure any longer what he is. But worldly, certainly.'

'And what of you, Mr Quycke?' asked Sarah, turning to his secretary. 'Were you imprisoned also?'

'My part was considered less, your ladyship. I served a year. But the society's officers were quite wiped out. Poor Mr Berkeley and Colonel Denny both died in prison. And Mr Shirley never recovered from the shock and fell into an acute melancholy.'

'Now tell us about Morgenstern,' said Hancock.

Shadwell eyed the table. 'May I take a little of your capon first, Captain? All this talk has made me hungry.'

There was a lull in the conversation while Hancock carved the two plump birds and piled their plates with meat and pickles. He sent out the maid to fetch more gin. Shadwell ignored the cutlery and tore his share of the carcasses apart with his hands, feeding the pieces into his mouth and gnawing on the bones, looking from side to side occasionally as if he feared his plate might be taken from him – like a man, thought Fairfax, who had been a prisoner for five years. He finished noisily, sucking the grease from each of his fingers in turn, dried himself on his napkin and drank some more gin. Then he sighed and sat back in his chair. 'That is better.'

'So,' said Hancock, resting his hands upon the table. 'Morgenstern?'

'I shall tell you all I know, which is little. Of Imperial College – the place from which he wrote his letter – nothing to my knowledge now exists, except a piece of stone tablet on which are carved the names of all those members of the college who were honoured with this Nobel Prize. It must have stood in the hall or some such place. Morgenstern's name appears upon it, beneath the word "Physic". I have not seen the tablet myself, but a friend of mine, now dead, who collected such artefacts sent me a drawing of it. So we may take it he was a scholar of great eminence.

'We may also hazard a guess as to his age. His daughter, Julia, was wed three years before the Apocalypse. Women of that era married mostly at an advanced age – a time when, for our females, the fertile years are almost past. Thirty was most common. So if we take that as the likeliest possibility, and reckon Morgenstern to have been perhaps thirty himself when his girl was born, we may speculate that he was sixty-three or thereabouts at the time of the calamity. We know of no family except this son-in-law named Singh: England at that time, before the massacres, was full of foreigners. Singh is of Indian extraction. Perhaps there was a grandchild – who can tell? Most likely there was a wife still alive.

'All else we know is thanks to the efforts of our colleague Mr Thomas Howe, whom Oliver will remember well.'

Quycke nodded. 'Indeed, I remember Tom Howe keenly.'

Shadwell said, 'I guess none of the rest of you has heard of Howe's *Corpus Inscriptionum Angliarum*?'

They looked at him, uncomprehending.

'It is as I feared, Oliver – we have fallen among barbarians!' He allowed himself a smile, and then his face was serious again. 'Just as I set myself the task of listing every surviving concrete monument, so Mr Howe undertook the transcribing of all the inscriptions made in the course of the Exodus – a labour of Hercules not yet completed at the time of his death. He would travel from church to church, sometimes visiting ten in a day, and copy down all the piteous messages carved therein, and in this way built a mighty catalogue containing upwards of fifty thousand names. The index to this great work made it possible, in rare cases, to follow a person or a family until they vanished. For the first time their stories flickered briefly in the darkness.

'Morgenstern's name appeared twice. Once was on the wall of the church of St Peter and St Paul in Thruxton, Hampshire. A message from his niece. The date was a week after the start of the Exodus: "I seek my uncle, Peter Morgenstern. I shall return here every day at noon." Something of that sort — I cannot recall the words exactly. Can you, Olly?' Quycke shook his head. 'So: nothing more.

'The second time was further north, in Pewsey, in the nave of St John the Baptist. The name of the writer cannot be made out, but that of Morgenstern is plain enough. The hand differs from that of the niece, so the seeker was someone other. The message similar, the date the same.'

Hancock, who had been listening eagerly, looked disappointed. 'That does not tell us much, Mr Shadwell.'

'On the contrary, Captain — to the antiquarian it tells a good deal. Thruxton and Pewsey lie to the west of London, so it tells us that those who sought him believed him to have headed in our direction. Remember his letter was discovered with the corpse of the man to whom it was most probably sent — Professor Chandler of Cambridge. He was buried near Winchester — again to the west of London. All the skeletons in the Chandler grave site bore marks of violence. Nothing of value was found with them. It seems quite likely they were on their way to meet with Morgenstern when they were waylaid, robbed and murdered. Forgive me.'

Shadwell's voice had become hoarse. He began to cough. Quycke rose to help him, but Shadwell waved him away. When he had recovered he resumed. 'Our belief – well founded, surely – is that Morgenstern had prepared a refuge at the Devil's Chair. Perhaps he was there when the Apocalypse struck. Or, more likely, he set out for it from London the moment he understood that what he had long predicted had begun to happen. He would have had a day's head start before the general fear set in. He knew better than any man the lawlessness and disorder that would soon descend. It seems to me impossible that he would not have wished to protect his closest family. That is human nature. They must have gone with him, as must the families of any others who had helped prepare their ark.'

Fairfax said, *In the selfsame day entered Noah, and Shem and Ham and Japheth, the sons of Noah, and Noah's wife, and the three wives of his sons with them, into the ark.*

'Aye,' said Shadwell, 'but as the Scriptures tell it, no one else.'

'That is true,' conceded Fairfax. He had never considered the implication before.

'Which is why the tale of the ark has always seemed to me the cruellest in the Bible, for Noah must have had many others in his family he would have wished to save, and so surely did his sons' wives – *they* lost everyone. But the number who can be rescued has a limit. The niece seeking her uncle in Thruxton, the unknown wanderer in Pewsey — you asked what we could learn from them, Captain Hancock? In my opinion, they were the family members Morgenstern had to leave behind to drown in the rising waters.'

CHAPTER NINETEEN

Two sleeps at Addicott Mill

SHADWELL LAPSED INTO silence and turned away from the table to stare once more into the fire. Behind his back, Quycke gestured to Hancock that it was time the old man retired upstairs to bed. Hancock nodded. 'The hour is late. We have much to do tomorrow.'

Fairfax said, 'You mean us to go back up on the hill so soon?'

'Indeed I do. When else? Mr Shadwell must be surrendered to the court on Monday. We cannot afford to lose a day.'

'But the day after tomorrow is the Sabbath. I have a sermon to deliver in Addicott. I need to prepare my text.'

'If it must be done, then do it. But I say it is a confounded waste of time.'

'Could we not argue about this in the morning,

gentlemen?' said Sarah. 'I for one am ready for my bed.' She put down her napkin and stood. Hancock, Fairfax and Quycke all made haste to rise politely.

Fairfax was grateful the supper was over. He was over-fed with Shadwell's theories and revelations. He needed to retire to digest them all, and to order his thoughts for Sunday. 'Could I trouble you, Captain Hancock, for pen and paper? I must make a start on my sermon — waste of time though it may be.'

'Of course. Pay no heed to my rough humour. I'll have a maid bring it to your room.'

Quycke helped Shadwell to his feet. Hancock went and spoke to his servants, who were waiting by the door, then picked up a candle. He led his guests out into the hall and up the stairs while behind them work began clearing the table.

It was a much bigger house than the parsonage — built, the captain informed them proudly, exactly to his own design. He pointed out the height of the ceilings and in particular of the oak wainscoting: 'A tall wainscot is always the mark of quality in a property, and these are half a yard.' Stout panelled doorways led off one side of the wide passage. Hancock opened them in turn. The first he designated for Shadwell and Quycke. 'I trust ye don't mind sharing. The bed is large enough for two. Candles are lit and the bedding warmed.' The next he chose for Fairfax. 'A fine room also. I have it in mind for a nursery one day.' He risked a wink at Sarah. 'Write well, Parson.'

'Good night, Captain Hancock. Lady Durston.' For the first time, Fairfax kissed her hand.

'Good night, Christopher.'

He lingered just long enough to observe Hancock throw open the final door – 'Now here is a chamber fit for a lady!' – and see the two of them step inside.

He crossed the threshold into his own room and stood listening to their voices muffled through the wall. He reproached himself for eavesdropping. What was the point of tormenting himself by listening to their intimacy? Yet he could not help it. The conversation was brief at least. He caught only the parting exchange, when Hancock returned to the passage.

'Well, good night then.' He sounded reluctant to take his leave, his words slightly slurred by gin.

'Good night, John.'

The door shut firmly, and after a pause, Hancock's heavy footsteps continued along to the far end of the house.

Fairfax closed his own door and took stock of his chamber – the whitewashed walls ochre in the candle-light, the floorboards pooled with slightly trembling shadow. A candle flame wavered on top of a small table next to a shuttered window. A water jug and goblet stood on the nightstand. The bed was large. Poking from beneath its coverlet was the long brass handle of a bed warmer. He folded back the blankets, removed the pan and laid it on the floor next to the chamber pot, then smoothed his hand across the warm linen sheet. Martha Hancock plainly ran an efficient household: her resentment at the arrival of a new mistress was understandable. He lay down, careful to keep his boots from the clean linen, and savoured the comfort of the heat.

A light tap at the door forced him to his feet. A maid stood in the passage. She handed him paper, pen and ink, curtsied and scuttled away. After the click of her heels descending the stairs, the Mill was silent. He closed the door again.

Too alert for sleep, he sat at the desk and confronted the blank sheet of paper. Now it came to it, he regretted his offer to conduct a service. His mind was churning with other matters. He dipped his pen in the ink pot and scratched across the top of the page: 'Sermon. Addicott St George. Sunday 14th April 1468.' But nothing more would come. A barrier composed of images of bones and earth seemed to have arisen in his brain. Normally he could reach into his memory and retrieve whole chapters of the Bible and recite them by heart. Now the verses seemed to slide away from him, random and meaningless.

An hour passed and still he was without even the semblance of an idea. It was as if God had looked into his heart, seen the state of his faith and decided to punish him. The thought induced a mild panic. He found it hard to breathe. He went over to the window, opened the shutters and lifted the sash.

The sudden draught caused the candle flame to bend almost double. The shadows lurched. He could hear the river rushing close by, the sound of its movement indistinguishable from the wind lashing rain against the massive trees, and in that instant he had a vision of what it must have been like eight centuries ago for people to be pitched from the safety of their former lives into a night such as this, with nothing to eat save what they could forage, nothing to warm them except what they could find to burn, and the constant threat of predators lurking in the darkness to attack them. The epiphany was so vivid he banged the sash down again in an attempt to block it out. He closed the shutters and kneeled by the bed. But it was not God's voice he heard, only Shadwell's: *If I cannot say for certain what did cause their world to fail, I can at least state with confidence that the answer must lie in science and nature, and not in the appearance of a beast bearing the number six hundred three score and six . . .*

Suddenly he cried aloud, banging his fists against the heavy wooden bed frame. He stood and snatched up his paper from the table and tore it into pieces. If Bishop Pole did not believe it, why must he? He should write a different sermon entirely. He should write a sermon that told the truth. He paced up and down the floorboards as he composed it in his mind. He should tell them there was no beast with the voice of a dragon, no whore of Babylon, no lake of fire, no rain of blood; that they did not live in the Era of the Risen Christ, that time had not stopped and been restarted. He should say that they lived upon the ruins of an ancient civilisation that had collapsed not through an act of God but for reasons that might be discoverable, and that it was no heresy to seek those reasons, but rather the duty of an enquiring mind.

He continued to stamp up and down, up and down, and he was halfway across the room, facing the table with his back to the door, when he thought he heard a sound behind him. He stopped and turned. It came again: a quiet knocking. He hesitated, retraced his steps and opened the door partway. Sarah Durston was standing in the passage, wearing a white cotton nightdress – presumably borrowed from Martha – that reached down to her bare feet. Her black riding jacket was draped around her shoulders. Her red hair was loose. She carried a candle in one hand and shielded the flame with the other. Her eyes in the light were wide with concern.

She whispered, 'Are you all right?'

'Yes,' he whispered back. 'Forgive me.'

'Are you alone?' She frowned and peered over his shoulder.

'Certainly.' He opened the door wide to prove it. 'Who else could be here?'

'I thought you must be arguing with someone – so much talking and banging about!'

'I was merely trying to compose my sermon. I'm sorry if I woke you.'

'Not at all. My mind is too much stirred up. I cannot sleep.'

'Nor I.' He glanced along the passage in the direction of Hancock's room. 'We will disturb the captain if we speak out here. Come in, if you like.'

'May I? I should be glad of the company.'

He stood aside to let her enter. She brushed past him. He closed the door. She set down her candle on the nightstand, slipped off her jacket and hung it over the end bedpost and climbed into bed. She pulled up the covers. 'Pay me no mind. Go on with your sermon.'

He sat at the table with his back to her. But if the task of composition had been impossible before, it was doubly so now. He stared hopelessly at the empty paper. He could imagine nothing except her, quietly breathing behind him. After a while he heard her shift beneath the bedclothes. She said softly, 'What are you thinking, Christopher?'

'I cannot think, your ladyship. That is the trouble. My thoughts are entirely disordered.' He turned to look at her. She was lying on her side, propped up on her right elbow, watching him. 'I do not understand what it is I am doing.'

'In your sermon?'

'In my sermon, in everything – in this valley, in my duties as a priest, in this room with you.'

Suddenly she reached over with her left hand and flung back the covers. 'Will you lie beside me?'

It did not occur to him to refuse her. He simply bent and unfastened his laces and started pulling off his boots. Later, he was to wonder at the ease with which he did it – the way this last and greatest step away from his old life seemed to follow naturally from all the others. She wriggled backwards, making room for him. He sat on the edge of the bed and swung his legs up on to it. She laughed and tugged at the sleeve of his cassock and whispered, 'Do you always go to bed so heavily encumbered?' He stood again and removed it while she watched him, and then – for there seemed no point in modesty, although he had never undressed in front of a woman before – his underclothes as well. Naked, he slipped under the blankets and turned to face her.

He put his arms around her. He stroked her face and kissed her mouth. He ran his hand along her body. He marvelled at the feel of her, at the miracle that flesh could be at once so soft and firm. She pushed him away and sat up. He wondered if he had done something wrong. But it was only so that she could ease the nightdress up above her hips, gather it at her waist and then pull it all the way over her head. He gazed at her arching body as it was fully unveiled in the candlelight. She shook out her hair, made a ball of the nightdress and flung it across the room, lay down again, stretched out her hands and beckoned him to come to her.

The first sleep passed entwined. In the sweetness of her warmth he dreamed of nothing; not of searching for a door to the waking world; not even of the bones in their shallow graves. All was blackness.

And then:

'Christopher!'

An urgent, piercing whisper.

Still half asleep, he nuzzled into her shoulder.

'Christopher!' she whispered again and shook him. 'Listen!'

'What, my love?'

'Someone is at the door!'

That woke him right enough. He sat up straight.

'Fairfax!' Hancock called out from the passage. 'Are ye awake?'

'Don't answer him!' Her words were as soft as breath, but her hand clenched his so hard it crushed his fingers.

'Fairfax!' Another round of heavy knocking – hammering almost.

He felt the awful vulnerability of their nakedness. He will snap our necks like fledglings, he thought. He looked around for a weapon to protect them. He could see nothing substantial enough.

'God damn it!' muttered Hancock. After a few

impatient taps of his heavy boots, they heard him clump off down the passage.

She said, still whispering, 'He cannot have thought me here, otherwise he'd have marched right in. I should go back to my room before he returns.'

'Wait.' He held up a warning finger, listening. 'Did you hear him go down the stairs?'

'No.'

He imagined the captain lurking at the end of the corridor to see if anyone emerged, cunning in his suspicion. 'Stay there.' He threw off the covers and started dressing. His hands were shaking.

'Where are you going?'

'To discover what he wants, wherever he may be.'

He sat on the side of the bed and pulled on his boots. She kneeled behind him and wrapped her arms around his shoulders. 'Don't go.'

'I will distract him, then you can leave.'

'Take care, Christopher. If he suspects us, he is capable of murder. And he prides himself on his skill for seeing into men's souls.'

'He will not see into mine.' He bent and kissed her forearm. 'Not least as I can no longer see into it myself.' He picked up the candle from the table.

At the door, he turned. In the half-light it was impossible to make out her expression. But he hardly needed to see her. He could smell her upon his skin, his hands, in his hair; he could taste her on his lips. I came into this chamber one man, he thought, and leave it another. He nodded to her with a confidence he did not feel, went out into the passage and closed the door quietly behind him.

He looked both ways. There was no sign of Hancock. He reached the top of the staircase and started to descend. He held out the candle in the darkness and groped his way along the banister. A noise rose from somewhere below him, a scrape of metal on stone. He reached the hall. In the room where they had eaten, a maid, so small she seemed barely more than a child, was on her hand and knees before the fireplace, a dustpan in one hand, a bucket beside her. She jumped up when she heard him.

He said, 'This is a strange hour to be working!'

'The mistress likes the hearths made safe and cleaned before the second sleep.'

'Where's your master?'

'He stepped out, sir.'

'To go where?'

'The weaving shed most like. He often checks it in the night.'

'Could you furnish me with a lamp?'

She fetched him one and showed him to the front door. He stepped out on to the forecourt. The rain had stopped but the wind was still strong. It had broken up the heavy overcast sky into fragments of cloud, edged a bluish silver by the moon, and was sending them racing overhead, casting just sufficient gleam to show him the massive outline of a building he took to be the weaving shed. He set off towards it. Halfway across, he looked back at the house. The windows on the first floor were shuttered. No lights were visible. He supposed she was back in her own bed now.

He walked on. The door to the factory was partly open. He held up his lamp and slipped inside. A huge space, like the nave of a cathedral, but instead of pews, hundreds of looms extended in rows, lit by pale shafts of moonlight shining through a sloping glass roof. Beneath the roof was a complicated network of shafts and pulleys to which the machines were attached by leather belts. The floor was bare damp earth. The air was heavy with humidity and the smell of cotton fibre, and filled with the sound of the fast-running river.

He called out, 'Captain Hancock!' and moved his lamp around, trying to find him. Once he was satisfied he was not in the shed, he went back outside. Across the yard, a terrace of buildings ran at a right angle to the factory – storerooms, presumably – and he made for those, walking carefully over the uneven cobbles. Now that he was gaining his bearings, he had the impression of a vast enterprise, unlike anything he had ever encountered. He glimpsed a light moving and shouted again, 'Captain Hancock!'

At once, a greyhound, barking loudly, shot from

the building and raced towards him. What it lacked in weight it made up for in a kind of devilish menace – all thin snarling snout, flattened ears and protruding eyes. He shrank back against the wall of the weaving shed, where it held him pinned.

Hancock's voice came out of the darkness. 'Who's there?'

'Fairfax!'

'Fairfax, is it? Fly!' he called to the dog. 'Heel, girl!' The dog loped back to her master. 'Come here, Mr Fairfax, if ye please, where I can see ye.' He held up the lamp to his own face to show him the way, and when Fairfax reached him, he held it out and shone it directly in the young priest's eyes as he scrutinised him. He will catch her scent on me, thought Fairfax. Some red hairs of hers will glint in the light. My manner will be different. He is like an animal, with extra senses. 'I knocked at your door,' said Hancock, 'and called for a while, but received no reply. Where were ye?'

'In my bed, sound asleep. I heard shouts but thought them part of my dream.'

'Shouts in a dream? Then it was not a dream but a nightmare ye were having.'

'And why should I not have nightmares, after what we saw at the Devil's Chair and then what Shadwell told us at supper?'

'Nightmares!' repeated Hancock with contempt.

'Ye'll need stronger nerves than that if we're to bring our enterprise to a fruitful conclusion.' But the explanation seemed to satisfy him. He lowered the lamp. 'Come, I wish to show ye something.'

He led Fairfax inside, where another lamp was burning. The store was filled with building materials – wood planks, roof tiles, bricks, window frames, sandbags. Half a dozen heavy-looking canvas sacks, each about half the size of a man, had been dragged out and lined up next to the door.

Hancock gestured with the lamp towards them. 'Tents,' he said. 'I had to import the craftsmen from Exeter to build my factory. They lived in them while on site. I've been thinking on what ye said – about the need to keep our diggings secret. Ye're right – if the men come and go from the tower to the village, word will spread in no time. But if we pitch a camp and keep them up there night and day, we can preserve our privacy till the work is done.'

'Surely the moment they return home the word will spread?'

'Aye, but too late to stop us. And once we've dug out whatever's up there – if anything *is* up there – we can hide it someplace of our own choosing, which none but us need know of. Then we may learn the ancients' secrets at our leisure.'

The scheme struck Fairfax as improbable. The Church and government had spies in every district.

News of such a sensational discovery was bound to spread. But he could not help but admire the captain's daring. 'It is a plan,' he agreed, 'and at this moment I cannot conceive of better. Although whether men who are fearful even to set foot on the Devil's Chair in daylight will agree to spend the night up there as well, I have my doubts.'

'They might,' said Hancock craftily, 'if a priest goes with 'em.'

He left the suggestion hanging.

'Ah!' Fairfax smiled into the darkness. 'So that is why you came a-calling for me? A parson has his uses after all.' He looked from Hancock to the tents. Despite his misgivings, he felt a stirring of excitement. 'Very well, I'll give my blessing to your expedition – mad though it may be.'

'Ye'll really do that?' Hancock sounded surprised by how readily he had agreed.

'Why not? I am as keen as you are to solve this mystery.'

'But what of your faith?'

'Faith that cannot withstand the truth is not a faith worth holding.'

Hancock cocked his head. A grin broke across his face, a gold tooth glinting in the lamplight. 'I have misjudged ye.' Suddenly he stuck out his hand. 'Henceforth we shall be partners. Come, let us shake on it.'

Fairfax took his hand. It was hard and calloused, a cudgel of flesh.

'That's settled then.' The captain threw back his head and yawned noisily, his jaws stretched wide, like a wolf about to howl. 'Nothing else can be done till morning. I'm ready for my second rest.'

They made their way in silence back across the yard, carrying their lamps, the greyhound trotting ahead of them. Once they were inside the house, she slunk off to her basket and Fairfax followed Hancock up the stairs.

'Good night, Parson. I hope your morning dreams are sweeter.'

'Good night, Captain.' He waited until Hancock had moved away, then let out his breath in relief.

The chamber was empty. He had expected nothing else and yet he was still disappointed. He set his lamp on the nightstand, took off his clothes and climbed back into bed. The sheets were still faintly warm from where she had lain. She must only just have left. He rubbed his cheek against the pillow. He wondered if she might return, but there was no sound of movement from her room, the door stayed closed, and after a short while, despite everything that had happened, or perhaps because of it, he once more fell asleep.

CHAPTER TWENTY

Saturday 13th April: the expedition is formed

H E WAS WOKEN by a vague impression of someone moving past the end of the bed, and then by the sound of a heavy object being set upon the table. The shutters were clattered open. He raised his head. In the dawn light stood the maidservant he had spoken to during the night.

'Yes, child?'

'Father.' She curtsied, her face turned away. 'The captain says to tell ye 'tis seven o'clock and breakfast's laid downstairs.'

She departed without another word. On the table she left behind a towel, a bar of black soap and a jug of water that was steaming hot enough to mist the window. Fairfax looked at them for a few moments and then fell back on to his pillow. He no longer felt quite the same bravado as he had the night before. Nevertheless, he summoned his courage and by an effort of will threw off the blankets and got down on to his knees beside the bed. *Heavenly Father, hear my prayer, and forgive my sins, which I know are grievous in your eyes . . .* The familiar words emerged readily enough but now they seemed to fall stillborn to the floor and he hurried through to the end. *I ask for strength this day to serve your glory. In the name of Jesus Christ our Lord. Amen.*

He stood naked before the table and poured water into the basin. He picked up the soap and dunked it and set about washing. Beneath his slippery fingers, his ribs and muscles, flanks and loins, with their ridges and hard planes, felt strange and unfamiliar. At the seminary, for the avoidance of lewd thoughts, the priests-in-training had been encouraged to ignore their bodies. But now he found himself deliberately conscious for the first time of this undiscovered country, and the memory of the evening came back to him. His desire to see her again was a physical ache, and yet the thought of being with her in company – of having to pretend that nothing had happened between them – filled him with dread. He scooped his hands into the water and threw it over himself and reached for the towel. A few minutes later, dried and dressed, he stepped out into the passage and went downstairs.

In the room where they had eaten the previous night the fire had been relit and food laid out on the table. A woman was bending over it with her back to him, and for a moment his heart jumped at the thought that it might be Sarah and they might have a moment alone together. But when she turned, he saw it was only Martha Hancock. He had to struggle to hide his disappointment.

'Good morning, Father.' Her heavy slab of face was hard and unfriendly.

'Good morning, Miss Hancock.'

'I trust ye passed a pleasant night?' The trace of sarcasm in her tone set him on his guard at once.

'I slept most comfortably, thank you. I hope you did the same.'

'No, sir, I did not.'

'I am sorry to hear it.'

'So many comings and goings in the night – I never heard the like. They drew me from my chamber *more than once . . .*' Her expression remained leaden, but something moved in her dull brown eyes – triumph? malice? disdain? – and Fairfax felt his mouth dry. She went on, with lethal politeness, 'Ye must be hungry, Father, after all thy exertions. Ye'll take some breakfast?'

'No. Thank you. I must go and find Captain Hancock, if you could kindly tell me where I might find him.' He could hear his heart thumping, his blood rushing in his ears.

'Find him thyself.' She turned her back on him and resumed laying out the plates. She had a female version of her brother's figure. He gazed at her broad shoulders, her thick waist.

'I fear you must have imagined something untoward . . .'

She did not even deign to turn round. 'And ye a clergyman!' She snorted with contempt. 'Tell her ladyship that this engagement must be over by night-fall, else I'll disclose to John that I witnessed her enter thy chamber. Tell her I'll not be driven from my hearth *by a whore.*'

'No, madam, she is not that.' It seemed pointless to deny what she had plainly witnessed, let alone attempt a defence of it. Nor did he wish to lie. That left nothing else to be said. 'She is not that,' he repeated, and walked out of the room.

The instant he was out of her presence, he hurried straight to the staircase, mounted it quickly, two or three steps at a time, and strode directly along the passage to her room. He knocked quietly on her door. There was no reply. He opened it cautiously. 'Sarah?' But she was not there. The shutters had been unfas-tened. Her borrowed nightdress, neatly folded, lay upon the empty bed.

As he was making his way back down the corridor, Quycke emerged from his bedroom. From behind him came the sound of Shadwell coughing.

'Good morning, Father.'

'Good morning, Mr Quycke.' He made an effort to seem cheerful. 'And how is Dr Shadwell today?'

'Not well, sir — not well at all. He sweated through

the night.' The whiteness of Quycke's face accentuated the dark crescent moons beneath his eyes. His hair was awry. He looked as if he had barely slept. 'I thought I would fetch him food. He should eat before he rises, and try to gain some strength.'

'If his condition has worsened, then surely he should stay and rest?'

'He should, most certainly. I have tried my hardest to persuade him. But he declares he would rather die upon the hillside than in a stranger's bed.'

As they descended the stairs together, Fairfax said casually, 'I wished to say good morning to Lady Durston, but knocking at her door just now it seems she has already left. Is that possible?'

'Now that you mention it, I believe I heard her pass our door before it was even light.' At the foot of the stairs he laid his hand on Fairfax's arm. 'Is there any way you can stop this business? We were living in such a peaceful, happy retirement in our cottage in Wilton. I had hoped the danger was behind us. But then came Lacy's letter – and now look at the peril we are in.'

There was genuine desperation in his voice. Fairfax patted his hand. 'I could not stop it even if I wished. Captain Hancock is dead set upon it. But need it involve you, Mr Quycke? Could you not step aside? I am sure Dr Shadwell would not wish to expose you to any danger.'

'He has made the same suggestion several times.

But I have been his secretary and companion since I was sixteen. He rescued me from wretched circumstances. He educated me and showed me an entire world. How can I desert him now?'

'Your loyalty is to your credit, Mr Quycke. But do not give in to despair. Captain Hancock is a man of some resource. He has conceived a plan that may yet carry the thing off safely.' Gently he pulled his arm free from the other man's grip. 'Let us see what the day may bring.'

He slipped out of the house immediately to avoid any further encounter with Martha Hancock.

In the daylight, it was possible to take in the full extent of Hancock's enterprise – the big weaving shed, the warehouses built of bright new red brick, the tall chimney stack rising from a separate building to a blackened tip. Beyond the mill, the river was wider and shallower than he had imagined from its noise during the night, tumbling down the hillside and channelled through a complicated arrangement of sluice gates. A pair of immense waterwheels was mounted on the side of the shed; a further set of paddles turned idly on some kind of boat contraption moored in midstream – evidence of Hancock's restless and ingenious determination to harness the river's natural power.

At the entrance to the weaving shed, the workforce had begun to assemble. More were approaching down the lane. They seemed disconcerted by the silence of the looms, and as Fairfax crossed the court-yard, they turned to stare at him. He recognised several from Lacy's burial. Even at fifty paces he could detect their unease at discovering a priest in such a place so early in the morning, especially with the machines not working.

A door banged and Hancock backed out of one of the warehouses with Keefer the church clerk. Between them they were dragging one of the canvas tent bags. They leaned it against the wall. Hancock straightened, saw Fairfax and raised his hand.

'Good morning, Father! Good morning, lads!' He beckoned to them. 'Come here, all of ye. Gather round me. There's something I have to tell ye.'

They glanced at one another and obeyed, arran-ging themselves into a rough half-circle around him. Fairfax joined them and stood slightly apart at the back. His guilt seemed to follow him like a shadow. Hancock waited until the last of the latecomers had arrived before he took off his hat and spoke.

'There'll be no weaving at this mill today. Instead there's other work – and better pay – for any who are willing to do it. I'm not a man for speeches. I've always been plain with ye, and I'll be plain with ye now. The work is digging and the place we dig is at the Devil's Chair.'

The instant the name was mentioned, there was

frowning and head-shaking. A low and hostile muttering arose.

'Now hear me out,' continued Hancock, talking
over them. 'I know all the old tales as well as ye. But I
have information there's something buried up there
that may prove of value to this business, and I have
made it my purpose to uncover it once and for all. The
work should take no more than a day or two, provided
we put our backs to it, and for every day ye work I'll
pay ye a week's money. And if we find what's said to lie
there, I'll award a bounty of twenty pounds a head.'

That quietened them. Someone whistled. Another
muttered, 'All right, master, what's the catch?' and
there was laughter.

'There is no catch, Paul Fisher, but there's two
conditions. One: we stay up there till the work is
done – sleep up there in tents if needs be. The other:
no man breathes a word of it – not to his wife or his
mother, his dog or any other creature. And if I find
out someone's spoken, I'll have my money back.'

'Aye, that's because it's against the law!'

'We have permission. The land belongs to Lady
Durston and she gives her authority to the search.'

'She may own the land, but not what's under't!'

'I shall deal with the law. All I ask of ye is your
labour.'

Keefer said, 'May I ask a question as church clerk,
Captain?'

Hancock grimaced. 'If ye must.'

He nodded at Fairfax. 'Why's the father here?'

'The parson's here at his own request because he gives the dig his blessing. Is that not correct, Father Fairfax? Come — step forward, if ye please, and give the men your view.'

They parted to let him through and he turned to face them. He had never addressed such an audience before. For a moment he was unsure what to say. 'Good morning, gentlemen.'

A ragged chorus of 'Good morning' rose in reply.

'My interest in this matter's simple. Father Lacy — the late parson, your priest for more than thirty years, whom you all knew and loved, and who loved you in return — gave up his life because he wished to know the truth about the Devil's Chair. For that reason, I desire to know it too. We should undertake the task in his honour. There's no sin in what's proposed that I can see, and therefore no crime, at least in God's eyes. He gave us hands to dig and brains to reason. Nothing in the Scriptures teaches otherwise.'

'But the place is cursed,' said one of the men. 'That's why the parson died. Some evil spirit dwells up there that kills when it's disturbed.'

'I don't believe in evil spirits. And if such exist, I am certain God will protect us.'

'God didn't protect the parson!'

'God does not protect us from our own clumsiness,

my friend. Father Lacy fell because the land was crumbling, not because of some spirit.'

'And will ye be digging there thyself, Father?' The tone was mocking.

'Yes, I shall dig.'

This seemed to impress the men more than anything else he had said.

Keefer said, 'Even on the Sabbath?'

'We do not know whether the work will extend into the Sabbath. Let us see how matters stand by nightfall, Mr Keefer.'

But the clerk persisted. 'Surely it is written that "on the seventh day thou shalt rest"?'

Hancock said, 'I believe the parson knows more of God's laws than his clerk, Keefer.' The remark drew laughter: Fairfax could tell that Keefer was not much liked. 'So then, we have talked enough. Who is with me?'

A dozen hands went up straight away, perhaps a third of those present.

Fisher, looking round, said, 'And those who choose not to come, Captain? What of us?'

'If ye are so anxious to have a day of rest, ye may go home and take one.'

'And our pay?'

'What pay? There's no work here till this is done. No work — no pay.' Hancock held up his hand to quell the protests. 'Why should I pay men to be idle? Come to the hill or go to thy home – it's all alike to me. For those who choose to come, I will have word sent to their families that the mill is working through the night to fulfil a special order and they'll not be back in the village for a day or two. All right? It's settled. Those who have the courage to follow me may come with me now and load the wagons. The rest of ye, go home.'

He jammed his hat back upon his head and pushed his way through the men. After some hesitation, most fell in behind him. Fairfax lengthened his stride to catch him up. He said quietly, 'Was it necessary to talk quite so harshly?'

'Men need to be led. Sometimes they must be taken gently by the hand, sometimes threatened by a blow, and sometimes – as today – both methods must be used at once.'

'But you have created ill will.'

'What of it? We have sufficient labour. That is all that matters to me.'

It was true that some two dozen men were now with Hancock, while the remainder stood in a cluster around Keefer and Fisher, discussing what to do. There was some gesticulating. Occasional sullen looks were cast in the direction of the mill owner and the priest. Eventually Keefer broke away from the group and came towards them.

'We have made up our minds to join ye, Captain, but on one condition, if we may.'

'And what would that be?'

'That if we are still on the Chair on the Sabbath, the father offers the men the rite of Holy Communion.'

Hancock shrugged. 'I am easy enough with that. What do you say, Parson?'

Fairfax instinctively recoiled from the suggestion. Who was he, in his present state of mortal sin, to perform the sacrament of communion, and in such a place? 'But I am not prepared. I would need vestments and prayer book, wine and wafers . . .'

'These can be fetched, can they not?'

Fairfax wanted to refuse altogether. And yet, when it came to it, how could he say no without disclosing his reasons? Perhaps it would be fitting if his last act as a priest was performed at the Devil's Chair? Reluctantly, he nodded. 'Very well. If it proves necessary, I will do it.'

The sky remained grey, the temperature rose; the stillness of the air held the promise of another storm. Fairfax rolled up the sleeves of his cassock, untied his stock and worked with the rest. Their preparations took them half the morning. The covered carts Hancock used to transport his finished cloth were hitched up to their teams of oxen and led round into the courtyard to be loaded up with tents, tools, buckets, blankets, food, cooking utensils, wheelbarrows, barrels of ale and water. The labour took his mind off his predicament. Soon he was sweating profusely. He kept an eye out for Sarah, but she did not appear. He guessed she must have returned to Durston Court. He did not like to ask Hancock in case he aroused suspicion.

Around ten o'clock, Shadwell emerged from the house leaning on Quycke's arm and came over to inspect their work. In daylight and out of the lecture hall he seemed an even more curious apparition, with his dark velvet outfit, his cap and tinted spectacles. Several of the men broke off what they were doing to stare at him, and Fairfax thought it was just as well he had not been present earlier or the vote to go up to the Devil's Chair might have gone the other way.

'Excellent,' he said, having examined the four wagons. 'I congratulate you, Captain Hancock. You have proved as good as your word. I doubt a better-equipped expedition to investigate the ancients has been assembled in England these last ten years.'

Hancock accepted the compliment with pride. 'Is there more we may require?'

'Indeed there is, sir. The ground is sodden after the winter and liable to collapse. Timber we'll need — long stout planks to shore up the trenches, and posts to support them. Sandbags, in case of flooding. And rope — one can never have too much rope, in my experience. Ladders, should we have to dig deep. Pegs and string for marking. Trestles and a tabletop, if you have such things.'

Hancock turned to Keefer. 'Ye heard Mr Shadwell. Timber, sandbags, rope, ladders, pegs, string, trestles – all that we have – as much as may be fitted in the wagons.'

After a final, suspicious glance at Shadwell, Keefer left them.

'And where is Lady Durston?' Shadwell asked. 'Will she be joining us?'

'She left at first light,' replied Hancock, 'without disclosing her plans. Her mood was odd – but then that is often the case with her ladyship, is it not, Mr Fairfax?'

'Really?' Fairfax could feel his colour rising. 'I have not found it so.'

'Have ye not?' Hancock sounded amazed. 'Ah, but then ye do not know her as well as I!'

Shadwell turned to Fairfax. 'You made a promise to me, Father – you will recall it – to give me Father Lacy's books in return for my help. I fear the time has come to hold you to your bargain.'

'What, now? At this moment?'

'When else? I have but two days of freedom left to me. Besides, they may be useful in our searches.'

'He can fetch them from the parsonage,' said Hancock, 'and meet us at the Chair.' To Fairfax he added, 'There's a quick way down to the village.'

Within the hour they were ready to set off, and Hancock gave the command. He went first on his great brown mare, sitting very erect in the saddle, like a general at the head of a ragtag army. Then came Shadwell and Quycke in their wagon pulled by the mules, followed by the four teams of oxen dragging the heavy carts piled high with provisions and equipment, and behind them the workmen, many carrying shovels or pickaxes, chatting happily amongst themselves. There was a general air of adventure, despite the fearsome legends that surrounded their destination.

Fairfax rode last in the convoy. As May carried him slowly past the doorway of Mill House, he saw Martha Hancock standing on the step with her arms folded. He chose not to look at her, but he could feel her eyes on him all the way up the drive. Her furious gaze seemed to burn a hole in his back, and it was a relief when the track entered woodland and the house disappeared out of sight.

CHAPTER TWENTY-ONE

The secret of Addicott Parsonage

THE EXPEDITION TURNED left into the lane. Fairfax reined in his horse just beyond the entrance gate and watched them go, then turned the other way, following the directions given to him by Hancock. He was surprised at how calm he now felt, given the scale of his predicament. He had no doubt that Martha would make good her threat and inform her brother of what she had witnessed. He had broken his solemn vows. His life as a priest – the only life he had ever imagined – was over. Yet these disasters seemed to impart a curious sense of freedom: of decisions taken out of his hands, of burdens lifted. A whole new world had been opened up to him in the night, and now another was about to be uncovered by the digging on the edge of the valley.

He was content to sway in the saddle in the humid morning air, listening to the spring birds and inhaling the scent of the wild herbs sharpened by the overnight rain. The muddy track curved and narrowed and began to descend. Over the crests of the hedgerows he could see a sweep of brilliant emerald pasture with sheep grazing. A shepherd with a crook climbed the slope, two dogs loping at his heels. The man raised his hand and Fairfax waved back. After a few more minutes there appeared, through the trees ahead, the square stone tower of the church, with the flag of St George shining like a battle standard against the dull sky.

He followed the lane to the bottom until he recognised the rear part of the parsonage with its orchard and paddock, chicken coop and stable. As he passed Lacy's study window, he was able to stare straight down through the leaded panes into the gloomy deserted room. He wondered how he would carry the books. At the front gate he dismounted, tied May to the post and walked up the little path to the door. He didn't bother to knock.

Inside, instead of the usual silence disturbed only by the ticking clock, there was a sound of women talking. It seemed to be coming from the kitchen. Their voices were raised in anger. It was obvious they hadn't heard him. His first thought was relief that he had not walked straight into another of Mrs Budd's anxious cross-examinations. He decided to collect his belongings before he faced her, and was halfway up the stairs when some instinct made him stop and listen. The argument showed no signs of letting up. He could not make out individual words, merely two distinct voices. One was Mrs Budd's; the other – younger, shriller – he did not recognise.

It was not possible, surely?

Quietly and guiltily – for previously it had not been in his nature to eavesdrop, and now he seemed to do it twice a day – he went back down the stairs and along the passage. The voices fell abruptly quiet, as if his presence had been detected. He reached the kitchen door and pushed it open – a crack at first, then fully.

Mrs Budd was seated, slumped over the table, her forehead resting on her crossed arms. Rose was standing with her back to the dresser, face flushed, breast heaving. The instant she saw him, she clamped her hand to her mouth. Agnes raised her head to look at him. She groaned and lowered it again.

Fairfax said, 'Rose? You can speak?' She kept her hand over her mouth. Her angry breathing turned into suppressed sobs. 'Dear Rose, do not distress yourself! I am only glad to hear your voice. It is wonderful.' He held out his hand. She launched herself from the dresser, pushed past him, ran down the passage and out of the house. The door slammed.

He stared at the housekeeper's bowed head in bewilderment. 'Mrs Budd? What is all this?'

She did not reply.

He pulled out a chair and sat opposite her. Her narrow shoulders were shaking. 'Tell me if you wish,' he said, 'or not, if you prefer. I have only come back to collect a few things and then I shall be off. I doubt we shall meet again. I assure you I will never mention this to anyone.' She muttered something into her arms. 'What was that?' he coaxed her. 'I fear you must speak up.'

She raised her head. Her wet, veined eyes reminded him of the shattered glass on the roadside. 'Why are ye here?' she said bitterly. 'I'd thought ye still in Axford.'

'We were returning across the moor when the rain set in, and we decided to spend the night at Captain Hancock's.' He leaned in closer. 'So she has always spoken?'

Agnes looked at him defiantly for a few moments longer, and then something seemed to break within her and she nodded.

'But how could you possibly have managed such a deception? *Why* would you?'

'She is my daughter,' she said simply. 'Mine and Father Lacy's.'

She started to cry again, and this time Fairfax did not attempt to interrupt her. The revelation of Rose's illegitimacy did not especially shock him. Now that she had told him, he could see how obvious it had been all along. He imagined there must be more than a few parsonages across England where such secrets, of necessity, lay hidden. But the fiction of Rose's dumbness seemed to him duplicity of a different order.

Eventually, when Agnes's flow of tears had abated, he said, 'I still do not understand how a child was able to play such a part for eighteen years.'

She wiped her eyes on her cuff. ' 'Tweren't eighteen year. 'Twere ten.'

'You told me she could not speak from birth.'

'I did. That were the story we put about.' She sighed and shook her head, and after further gentle prompting, he began to draw out her tale. It came hesitantly at first, but then by the end quite freely, as if was a relief to speak the truth at last. 'I were married to a man in Nethercombe . . . When he died, I were engaged to keep house for Father Lacy . . . One night the parson came to my bed . . . I knew it were a sin, but I was young to be a widow, lonely and in need of comfort . . . When I discovered I was with child, I went back to Nethercombe, to my sister and her husband, and spent the whole of my confinement in their cottage . . . They had no child themselves and were content to take on Rose and pretend she was their own . . . I visited her often – as her aunt, as she supposed – but then one day she heard us talking and discovered the truth of her circumstances. When the fever took both my sister and her husband, I begged Tom – Father Lacy – to take in our girl. He refused at first – said the facts were bound to come out and he would lose the living. In the end he did agree, but on condition she never spoke to any in the village for as long as he were alive.'

'And yet such a deceit sounds impossible to carry off!'

'Oh, 'twere not so hard as you might think. Rose's nature's always been a shy one. She were weak with the fever herself when she arrived, so none in the village came close for fear of catching it. She stayed inside for half a year. Never made no friends. Time came when she ceased to talk even in the house.'

'And all because Father Lacy would not leave this spot?' The cruelty seemed unfathomable. Once again he was forced to re-evaluate the character of the old parson.

'Aye. 'Twere always his digging he cared about more than anything – more'n us, more'n God himself, I shouldn't wonder. Said there was no place on Earth to compare to the valley for antiquities. Could not bear to be ruined and forced to live away from the site.'

'And now that he is dead, I presume she wishes to speak?'

She gave him an accusing stare. ' 'Tis your presence that has changed her.'

'Mine?'

'As I told thee t'other day, Father – ye've turned her head.'

'Well, I am truly sorry if I have caused her upset, but at least now she can give up this pretence. She'll not be short of suitors, Mrs Budd, of that I'm certain. I'm sure you both will thrive.'

She looked doubtful. 'But where can we go?'

'Why go anywhere? The new parson will doubtless need a housekeeper. Or you can weave like the other women.'

'And if Rose begins to speak around the village after her silence all these years?'

'People are struck dumb by tragedy. Why not the reverse?'

'Folk will not believe it!'

'You would be surprised by what people will believe.'

'She would still call herself my niece?'

'No, she should tell the truth.'

'But the shame of it!'

'What shame?' For a moment he was tempted to confess his own sin. 'No act that yielded Rose can be a shame in the eyes of God.'

He looked around the neat and spotless kitchen — at the range with its simmering kettle, the copper saucepans hanging from their hooks, the plain white plates in the dresser, the cupboards, the door with its heavy new lock. He could hardly bear to think what life must have been like.

'I must go now.' He stood. She did the same,

smoothing her skirt, squaring her shoulders. Her moment of weakness had passed. She was plainly keen to see him off the premises. She would survive, he thought. 'I wonder, Mrs Budd, if I might beg a favour? The books in Father Lacy's study – not the religious texts, but the others, about the ancients – it is unwise to keep them in the house. They are against the law. I would like to take them, if I may.'

She did not hesitate. 'Aye, take them – and anything else in there ye want. It brought him naught but misery, and us too. I wish to God I had never set eyes upon them.'

She fetched him a hessian sack into which he placed the nineteen volumes of *The Proceedings and Papers of the Society of Antiquaries*. To these he added Shadwell's hefty *Antiquis Anglia*, and the various other books about ancient artefacts and inscriptions, until he was satisfied he had removed them all. It seemed a dangerous weight of heresy for one man to carry. They would burn an H on his own forehead if he was not careful.

From the desk he took the penknife and the spyglass. He stood before the display cabinet with its coins and plastic straws and bottles, its eyeless plastic doll – the detritus of a lifetime's obsession. After some hesitation he took down the shiny black device with the emblem of the bitten apple and slipped it into the inside pocket of his cassock. Upstairs, his bag was already packed and lying on the bed. When he went down to the front door, there was no sign of Agnes. He wanted to ask her where he might find wine and wafers. They must be kept in the church. He vaguely remembered seeing some in the vestry when Keefer was searching for the registers.

He tied his bag and the sack together and draped them over the saddle, then led May across the muddy lane towards the lychgate. The sky was threatening. None of the women in the cottages opposite were out on their front steps spinning. The village seemed deserted. He hitched his mare to an iron ring and opened the little gate. He went past Father Lacy's grave – still unmarked by even a temporary wooden cross – and into the porch.

The church was unlocked. Tiny flames flickered all around the walls. Keefer must have been in earlier to light the votive candles. He paused in the centre of the nave. Apart from the obscurity of some of the icons, there was nothing unusual about St George's. Yet once again he found himself seeing everything for the first time, altered by a history he had never stopped to consider. Shadwell said the churches had become the main places of refuge for the survivors of the Apocalypse. He tried to imagine them gathered here before the altar – stunned by the turn their lives had taken. Morgenstern's daughter had been married here. Perhaps the professor had been a believer?

Suddenly the air seemed thick with ghosts and for the merest fraction of an instant he seemed to sense a presence in the cold grey light but it was gone before he could properly comprehend it.

He bowed to the altar, crossed himself, and hurried up the aisle to the vestry. He kneeled before the cupboard and searched among the candlesticks and prayer books until he put his hands upon a bottle of wine and a small jar of wafers. Moments later, he was walking quickly back down the aisle. He closed the church door behind him. It was only when he turned and stepped out of the porch that he noticed a slim figure standing silently beside the mound of earth over Father Lacy's grave. The spectacle made him jump.

'Rose!' he exclaimed. 'You surprised me!' She gazed at him without moving. He felt like a thief, with the bottle in one hand and the jar in the other. 'I must be on my way.' He lifted them pointlessly, as if they offered an explanation. 'Will you say goodbye to me before I go? I should like to hear you speak.'

She glanced around to check she was not overheard. Her voice, when it came, was barely more than a whisper. 'Shall I not see thee again?'

'No. I fear I shall not return. But I thank you for all you have done for me, most profoundly. I shall not forget you.' He took a step towards her. 'You must speak, Rose. God gave you a voice. Use it.'

'But it's only thee I wish to speak to!'

He looked at her. What an inexperienced fool he had been to mislead her with what he had imagined to be a harmless flirtation. He felt full of remorse for his thoughtlessness. 'I'm sorry. That cannot be. God bless you.' He turned away and began to walk down the path.

She called after him. 'D'ye not wish me to tell thee of the stranger who was here?'

That stopped him. Across the lane there was still no sign of life in the row of cottages. He swivelled on his heel and made his way back to her. 'And what stranger would this be?'

'Oh, but I had thought thee most anxious to depart?' Her voice, though little used, had acquired a distinct edge of sarcasm.

'This is the man you saw in the village on the morning of the day your father died?'

She glanced down at the mound of earth and muttered bitterly, 'My father ye call him. He never called himself so in life.'

'It is most important, Rose, that you tell me what you saw.'

'No, I mustn't detain thee . . .'

He ran his hand through his hair in frustration. With an effort he mastered his temper. 'It's true he was your father. There is good reason for your anger. But this is not the time to show it. His death was not at all what it appeared, believe me. I need you to tell me something of this stranger. What was his manner? Was he tall? Old? Young?'

His urgency plainly took her by surprise. Her brow creased. She raised her palm and held it flat above her head. She had not yet lost the habit of talking in gestures. 'Tall,' she said, then stretched out her arms. 'And large.'

'Fat?'

'No, not fat. Big.'

'And his age?'

'Somewhat between thine and my father's.'

'Where was it you saw him?'

She pointed over her shoulder. 'At the church door. Talking with my father.'

'Could you hear what was said?' She shook her head. 'Did they seem at all angry?'

'No.'

'How long was their talk?' She shrugged. He felt his irritation rise again. 'Come, Rose. There must be more. How did it end? Who left first?'

'My father went back into the church. The man walked down this path to his mule.'

'He rode a mule?'

' 'Twere a sight to behold – a man so big on a mule.' Despite herself, she smiled at the memory. 'Poor creature's back must've been half broken.' She looked at the grave again, then back at Fairfax. 'Ye think the man had a hand in the death?'

'Perhaps.'

She bit her lip. 'Then ye must take care of thyself.'

'I will. Do not worry yourself about me.'

Suddenly she darted forward and kissed him lightly on the cheek. He blushed as much as she did.

'Goodbye, Rose.' He nodded and smiled at her and stepped away. This time he did not turn around.

As he rode back out of the village along the way he had come an hour earlier, his mind was full of disturbance. For he could not help but reflect that her description of the stranger sounded remarkably like Mr Quycke – the only man he had seen in the locality, apart from Shadwell, in possession of a mule.

CHAPTER TWENTY-TWO

Mr Quycke provides an explanation

I T WAS CLOSE to noon by the time the young priest finally caught up with the others. They had turned down the track into the forest and had drawn up their wagons in the same spot that Hancock had led them to the night before, where the top of the Devil's Chair was just visible above the trees. The carts were being unloaded, the mules serving as pack animals to help transport the tools and tents up to the crest of the hill. About a dozen men were intermittently visible climbing the slope, laden with equipment. Others were making their way down again empty-handed to collect further supplies. As he rode past the wagons, Fairfax was struck by the speed and quietness with which they worked. None of the men was speaking. Their earlier good humour seemed to have vanished now they had been confronted with the reality of the task. They were plainly anxious to do the job, earn their pay and leave as soon as possible.

He tied May to a branch beside the oxen. Hancock's mare was close by. Another horse tethered further along was tearing with its teeth at the undergrowth. It was the mount that had thrown Sarah Durston. So she was here! He felt a twist in his stomach. He lifted his bag and sack from the saddle and yoked the heavy burden around his neck, hitched up his cassock, tightened his belt and set off up the trail.

The rain overnight had made the ground muddy. His boots sank, became clogged and hard to lift. The weight of the cord tying his burden cut into his neck, and one sharp-edged volume in particular – he reckoned it must be Shadwell's *Antiquis Anglia* – pressed into his back like a knife. Some of the men coming down cast him furtive looks. He kept his eyes fixed ahead and forced himself to continue climbing. At length he came out on to the ridge. He unhooked his burden, dropped it and bent forward with his hands on his knees to catch his breath. On the level ground below, the first two tents were being erected. The clink-clink-clink of metal pegs being hammered into the earth rang around the natural amphitheatre. A fire had been lit. Smoke rose vertically in the motionless air. Above it all, the tower stood – malevolent, implacable in its shroud of ivy, disdainful of all this puny activity that was disturbing its solitude.

He hoisted his load again and began to descend. A file of men was climbing the slope towards him. Beyond them he could see various clusters of figures, and as he drew nearer he was able to make out Hancock close to one of the tents, gesticulating to Keefer. Shadwell was standing some distance away with his hands on his hips, surveying the mass grave, with Quycke next to him. He did not recognise Sarah until he was almost upon her. She emerged from behind the tower, carrying a shovel across her shoulder, dressed in the men's clothes she had been wearing when he met her in the walled garden – white shirt tucked into thick trousers, a pair of heavy boots. Her hair was tied up and hidden beneath a cap.

She stopped and nodded politely, as if it were nothing more than a chance encounter in the street with a visiting priest. 'Good morning, Father Fairfax.'

'Lady Durston.' He returned her nod. 'I did not recognise you in your workman's garb.'

'What else should I wear? A ball gown?' She swung the shovel from her shoulder and leaned on it. Her voice dropped but retained its teasing note. 'You look troubled, Father.' She bent towards him. 'What is it? Tell me: do you reproach me for tempting you from the true path?'

There seemed no point in dissembling. 'You were seen last night by Martha Hancock, coming to my room.'

Her light-heartedness vanished at once. She drew

back slowly, her mouth twisting in contempt. 'That shrew!'

'She swears she will tell her brother unless you break your engagement to him by nightfall.'

'Good, let her tell him. She will spare me the task.' She frowned and prodded the blade of the shovel against the ground a couple of times. 'Or perhaps you would prefer if I deny it?' She looked up at him. 'Of the pair of us, you stand to lose the most.'

He replied without hesitation. 'No. The truth must be told.'

'Even though his anger may be violent?'

'I fear God's wrath more than Captain Hancock's.' He glanced across to where Hancock was standing. He was watching them intently. The moment he saw that Fairfax had noticed him, he started to move towards them. 'Take care. He is coming over.'

'I will tell him, but not yet,' she said quietly. 'Let me find my moment.'

'As ever, the two of ye are very thick with one another!' Hancock came up to them and planted his feet apart. 'May I join the conversation?'

Fairfax said, 'I was telling Lady Durston of some intelligence I gathered in the village just now.'

'And what might that be?'

'You will recall, when we had our talk at the Swan, that I mentioned Father Lacy hid the church registers in the stables of the parsonage.'

'Indeed.'

'He took that precaution on the morning of his death after the visit of a stranger. I now learn that this stranger bore a marked resemblance to Mr Quycke, right down to the possession of a mule.'

'What of it?'

'Why has Mr Quycke never mentioned this meeting?'

Sarah took her cue from Fairfax. 'And as I was just observing: why would his visit cause Father Lacy to hide the books?'

Hancock looked from one to the other. 'Well, this is quickly settled. Let us ask him.'

He marched towards the area where they had dug the previous night. Shadwell was holding a skull up to the light, pointing to various marks upon the cranium. Quycke had his sketchpad and was making a drawing. No one was near them: Fairfax guessed that Hancock's men were giving the grave a wide berth. He exchanged a quick look with Sarah behind the captain's back.

'Mr Quycke, sir,' boomed Hancock, when he was still a dozen paces from them. 'Will ye settle a question for us?'

Quycke paused in his sketching. 'Why certainly, Captain Hancock, if I can.'

'Did ye or did ye not meet Father Lacy in Addicott St George on the day he fell to his death?'

'I did, sir.' His expression was innocent. 'What of it?'

'Why have ye not mentioned it before?'

'Surely I did?'

'No, sir,' said Fairfax. 'I would have remembered it.' He laid down his bags and folded his arms.

'Well then, it is no great matter. I shall give the details now. I rode a mule first thing that morning from Axford to Addicott with the purpose of arranging a meeting between Father Lacy and Dr Shadwell. It seemed unwise for Dr Shadwell to make the journey himself, on account of his health.'

'And a meeting was arranged?'

'Yes, it was settled that Father Lacy would join us for breakfast in the Swan at Axford the following day. We waited for him but he did not keep the appointment, and on the day afterwards – the Thursday, I believe – we learned the circumstances of his tragic death.'

Hancock said, 'Is this your recollection also, Dr Shadwell?'

Shadwell was still examining the skull. He frowned at Fairfax, irritated at being disturbed. 'It is.'

Fairfax turned back to Quycke. 'Your talk with Father Lacy – it was friendly?'

'Yes, of course.'

'Did he seem uneasy?'

'No.'

'Why then, I wonder, did he take the trouble to hide the church registers directly you left him?'

Quycke spread his hands — an overly emphatic gesture, Fairfax thought, such as might be made by an actor on the stage to convey sincerity. 'How is one to know? A habit of secrecy, given the law against anti-quarianism? A sensible precaution, given what he thought he might find? I can tell you only that he was looking forward greatly to meeting Dr Shadwell, and expressed much gratitude that he had taken the trouble to come all the way to Axford from Wiltshire to talk to him.'

'You must have been one of the last to see him alive. Did he mention his intention to come up to the Devil's Chair?'

'No.'

'After making the arrangement for the meeting, did you return directly to the Swan?'

'I did.'

'Mr Shadwell — again, is that your recollection?'

Shadwell sighed and lowered the skull. 'Oliver returned to the inn before the curfew. The precise time I cannot say. Might I ask why we are being questioned in this manner? Is there some suggestion Oliver was complicit in Lacy's death? If so, you may dig without us. I would sooner go back to jail than listen to such slander.'

'Not at all,' said Hancock quickly. He smiled his humourless smile. 'The questions arise only because Mr Quycke — by accident of circumstance, I am sure – neglected to mention his visit to Father Lacy. All confusion over the matter is now cleared, is it not, Fairfax?' He gave the priest a meaningful look. Fairfax nodded, unconvinced. 'Good. We shall speak of it no more. Let us return to the task in hand.' He pointed at the skull. 'Ye have spent a long time examining that poor fellow's head!'

'The head is female,' corrected Shadwell, 'and indeed it is true – I have given it a thorough examination, for hers was not a natural death. Do you see?' He inserted his little finger through a perfectly round hole in the back of the skull. 'I missed the detail in the dark last night. Either someone took a drill to the bone *post mortem*, or more likely she was shot by a firearm from behind, which would explain the damage around the eye socket. That was where the bullet departed the brain. I have seen such wounds before.' He held the skull out to face them, his little white finger wriggling in the cavity like a maggot. Fairfax felt the bile rise in his throat.

Sarah said, 'Poor creature, to be murdered in such a spot.'

'Best say naught of this to the men,' cautioned Hancock. 'They are skittish enough already.'

Shadwell went on. 'Such violent deaths were not of course uncommon at that time. Perhaps she ventured too far from the others, was murdered, found, and then brought back here for burial. Or she was sick and suffering and this was thought a merciful end. More digging may provide the answer.' He broke off and eyed Fairfax's sack. 'I see you have kept your side of the bargain, Mr Fairfax, and fetched the books.'

'Yes, sir. All that I could find.'

'May I see them?'

Shadwell placed the skull carefully on the ground and watched closely as Fairfax untied the knot and opened the top of the sack. He put his hand to his mouth as if to stifle his excitement, then held out his palm. Fairfax took out a volume of the proceedings of the Society of Antiquaries and passed it to him. The old man kissed the binding and showed it to Quycke as if he could not believe it still existed. His hands shook as he opened it and turned the pages. No father, Fairfax thought, had ever beheld his long-lost child as fondly as Shadwell did that book. But as he leafed through it, his expression slowly altered from delight to suspicion. He took off his spectacles and held a page very close to his eyes, and when he took it away, his face was screwed up in bewilderment.

'But this is my book!'

'Yes,' said Fairfax, 'the book you published.'

'No, sir, this book is *mine*. It comes from my own library. These markings are in my hand. Am I not right, Oliver?'

He gave it to Quycke, who nodded in confirmation. 'These marginalia were all made by Dr Shadwell.'

Fairfax said, 'I had assumed the notes were made by Father Lacy.'

'No, Fairfax. If you please?' Shadwell flexed his bony fingers urgently, beckoning for another volume. Fairfax rummaged in the sack and pulled out the *Antiquis Anglia*. Shadwell rested the heavy book in the crook of his arm and quickly examined the contents. 'The same! Here – do you see? – and here!' He looked up, his eyes bright, his gaze flickering this way and that. 'Bishop Pole told me my books were burned in the public square, but that was a lie. He must have packed them up and sent them off to Father Lacy.'

Fairfax said, 'I thought it odd that a country parson should possess such a collection.' The more he considered it, the more baffling it seemed. 'And yet why would the bishop behave in such a fashion? He must have known Father Lacy extremely well to trust him so. They were at the seminary together. Some bond must have existed between them.'

Shadwell was exultant. 'Does this not merely confirm what I told you last night about the bishop, Mr Fairfax? When he arrested me he touched the forbidden fruit and acquired a taste for it. Clearly he could not bear to part with the knowledge. But rather than risk keeping my heresy in the chapter house, where some might see it, his preference was to store it far away in the parsonage of some obscure clergyman.'

Hancock had been listening with mounting

impatience, as he always did when he felt himself excluded from a conversation. 'What does it matter? Bishop Pole's a hypocrite, like most of his kind. Doubtless he reserves to himself all manner of pleasures he denies to others in the guise of piety. But time is pressing. Ye wanted the books, Dr Shadwell, and now they've come back to ye, and we should begin our digging. Tell us where to start.'

Now that the transfer of supplies from the base camp had been completed, Hancock gathered his men at the foot of the tower. It seemed to Fairfax that there were fewer than when they had started. Doubtless some of the more superstitious had taken fright at the sight of the exposed mass grave and had slipped away back to the village, where they would surely even now be spreading tales of what they had seen. The whole valley would know by nightfall. And then what? It seemed inescapable that their enterprise was doomed, and he and Sarah along with it. She caught his eye and smiled at him. He smiled back as reassuringly as he could, but in his mind he was already trying to devise a plan for them to escape.

'Listen to me, men,' said Hancock. 'This gentleman is Dr Nicholas Shadwell, a most eminent scholar of the ancient world, and that there is his secretary, Mr Quycke. They have much experience in these matters, and they will guide our labours. Dr Shadwell, will ye give us your instructions?'

Shadwell stepped up beside him. 'Thank you, Captain Hancock.' His voice was wheezing. 'First, I congratulate you all on your attendance here. This is a scientific expedition of the most singular importance, and I believe you will one day be proud to tell your children and grandchildren of the work you do today.'

The effort of addressing the few dozen men seemed to strain his lungs, just as it had done in the Corn Exchange. The wheeze turned into a cough, the cough into a convulsion. He doubled over from the pain of it as if he had been punched in the stomach, and fumbled with his sleeve. Out came the red-spotted handkerchief. He spat up blood. Quycke took his arm. The men looked at one another uneasily. It was a full minute before he was able to continue, and then he spoke so hoarsely they had to move in closer to hear.

'You may ask: what was the function of the tower? I cannot tell you. Its purpose is lost in the great fathomless mystery of time. But some place hereabouts, beneath the ground, I warrant lies another structure, and our task is to dig down and uncover it. I count three dozen of you, so my plan is this – to divide our labour into four groups of nine and make four trenches running out from the tower: north, south, east, west. Each trench to be two paces wide and thirty paces long. At a depth of six feet each trench to be shuttered by timber to prevent collapse.

'One further point. As you dig, you may encounter

various artefacts. In such a circumstance, send for me or Mr Quycke, that we may record both the object and the spot. The discovery will then be removed and stored according to its provenance: north, south, east or west. By these means, we may both make an estimation of the nature of the settlement, and judge which areas are fit for wider excavation . . .'

His voice expired into another coughing fit. Hancock regarded him with a mixture of concern and distaste and then addressed the men himself. 'Sort yourselves into teams of nine and choose your compass point. Father Fairfax, would ye be willing to step over here for a moment and bless our enterprise?'

'Of course.' It was the last thing he wished to do. The small crowd parted to let him through. 'Let us pray.' He expected them merely to bow their heads, but to his surprise, they got down on their knees – Hancock too, along with Sarah, Quycke and even, with some difficulty, Shadwell. The only sound in the silence of the Devil's Chair was the wind rustling in the trees. There was a curious sacredness about the place.

He surveyed their bent heads and searched his memory of the Book of Common Prayer for some appropriate words, and they came into his head as if the Holy Spirit had decided to visit him in his sinfulness. *O God, whose nature and property is ever to have mercy and to forgive, receive our humble petitions; and though we be tied and bound with the chain of our sins, yet let the pitifulness of thy great mercy loose us; for the honour of Jesus Christ, our Mediator and Advocate. Amen.*

'Amen.'

Afterwards, as the men congregated into their groups and chose their tools, Hancock drew Fairfax aside. 'That was nicely spoken, Parson.'

'Thank you.'

'The more we convince the men it's God's work we're doing, the more we may keep. I reckon ten have gone already. What did ye make of Quycke's story?'

'He did not convince me entirely.'

'Nor me. Ye know I have a nose for liars? There's too much of the female in him for my taste — big strong-looking fellow though he may be. We'd best keep an eye on this "secretary" of Shadwell's.'

CHAPTER TWENTY-THREE

The dig begins

KEEFER HAD TAKEN charge of the team that was to dig out from the western side of the tower. Fairfax went over to join them. The church clerk smirked at the sight of a priest offering himself for manual work. 'Thy hands are very white and soft, Father.'

'I am quite used to gardening in the chapter house, Mr Keefer.'

'Gardening? 'Twill be harder work than gardening!' Some of the men laughed.

'I know it,' said Fairfax, rolling up his sleeves, 'but I wish to do my part. Our Saviour was a working man. He is example enough for me.'

A small wiry fellow with a carbuncle on his cheek said, 'Ye cannot argue wi' that, George!' He handed Fairfax a machete.

He set to work at once, before the others started,

hacking away at the undergrowth, dragging clear the tangle of brambles and clinging ground elder. He worked in a blank fury, relieved to lose himself in the effort of hard labour. Of course, Keefer was right about his hands: they were soon bloody with scratches.

The afternoon heat was sullen, storm-threatening. Clouds of midges danced frantically in the heavy air. Some of the men stripped to the waist. Fairfax's cassock became damp with sweat. Mosquitoes whined in his ears and bit his neck. He gathered a heap of wet greenery in his arms, carried it to the big bonfire about fifty yards away, twisted his torso in an arc and flung it on to the flames. Through the haze he could see Sarah Durston on the other side of the fire raking stray leaves and branches back into the smouldering pile. *I will tell him, but not yet,* she had said. *Let me find my moment.* The wind caught the smoke and coiled it around his face. His eyes smarted. His hair and clothes stank of soot. He wiped his face on his sleeve and went back to work.

After an hour, when they had cleared their patch of ground according to Shadwell's direction, Fairfax went to where the equipment had been piled and collected stakes, string and a hammer. He began marking out the lines within which they were to dig. Even before he had finished, Keefer was handing out pick-axes and shovels. The church clerk shrugged in apology. There was none left for him. Fairfax went in search of spare tools.

The teams on the other sides of the tower had already started digging. A near-continuous ring of metal striking earth and rock echoed around the Devil's Chair. Hancock was working in the northern trench. He too had removed his shirt. The massive muscles of his back and shoulders flexed as he wielded his double-pointed axe as easily as if it were a walking stick. Fairfax noticed he had tattoos on his upper arms: a cannon on one, crossed swords on the other.

'We seem to be making good progress, Captain Hancock,' he said.

'Aye,' replied Hancock, raising his axe, 'and the men are happier now they have hard work to occupy them.'

He brought the blade down once more with a blow that shook the ground and buried the metal head up to the shaft. He was working it free when a voice called out, 'Captain!'

One of the men at the end of the trench furthest from the tower had stopped work and was holding up his hand. Hancock dropped his axe and wiped his palms on the sides of his trousers. Fairfax followed him as he picked his way along the trench. Half a dozen men were staring at an object in the ground. It was part of a sheet of glass, only partially uncovered. Even so, what was visible was almost a yard long and a couple of feet across. Hancock knelt beside it and wiped away the clinging earth with his fingers.

Fairfax said, 'I've never seen a piece so large. I'll fetch Shadwell.'

'Must ye?'

'He was most particular.'

'Aye, very well,' muttered Hancock. 'But tell him to hurry. We can't stop work every time we find a bit o' glass.'

The man who had discovered it protested. ''Tis more'n a bit, Captain! And nothing normal, neither — I caught her with the shovel and she didn't even crack!'

Fairfax walked quickly up the slope to the site of the mass grave. The top of Quycke's head was just visible above the shallow trench. He was on his hands and knees with a trowel. A row of half a dozen skulls rested on the lip of the excavation, as if the skeletons had all sat up together and were peering out of their grave. A seventh was in Shadwell's hands. He was examining it with a magnifying glass.

Fairfax called to him. 'Dr Shadwell!'

'Mr Fairfax — look at this!' He showed the skull to Fairfax and inserted his finger into the hole at the back, near the base. 'Another — and a man this time.' He gestured to the row of heads. 'All of them the same. This wasn't death by disease or starvation. This was murder — a massacre, in fact.'

Fairfax crossed himself. 'Poor souls. May they rest in peace.'

'Rest in peace they may have done, but there was

nothing peaceful about their way to it.' Shadwell glanced towards the tower. 'And now I am concerned for our dig.'

'Why?'

'Because if it was a mass execution of prisoners – which it surely must have been – it's more than likely that their sanctuary was ransacked or destroyed by their attackers. Which means we may dig here for days and find mere ruins.'

'We have in fact found something just now – glass: a large pane and very strong. Captain Hancock wonders, do you want to see it?'

'I do, most certainly. Oliver, bring pen and paper.'

By the time they reached the northern trench, the window had been freed from the soil and was being cleaned off. It was almost six feet long and more than two wide, slightly curved, and irregular in shape, the base being longer than the top. The glass was heavy, perhaps half the thickness of a little finger, and when the two men holding it up turned it for Shadwell's inspection, it was possible to see that not only was it slightly darkened, but it contained within it, almost invisible, a delicate wavy filigree of metal threads.

Hancock said, 'A window so large must be from a building.'

Shadwell didn't answer him. He pushed his spectacles up on to his cap, breathed on the glass and wiped his fingers through the mist, circling round

346

and round, as if he might conjure some spirit from it. 'Eight centuries it has lain there,' he said softly, 'waiting for us to find it.'

'Aye, but what function did it serve?'

'As a window at the front of one of their mechanical carriages, to protect the driver from the elements. In London I have seen them used in houses, despite their age. The glass is very strong.'

'Strong because of the metal threads?' asked Fairfax.

'No, I believe the threads were placed within the glass to spread electricity around it.'

'For what purpose?'

'To heat it, one presumes.'

Hancock said, 'What manner of people would pamper themselves with heating glass?'

'A decadent people,' responded Shadwell, 'which I conjecture was part of their undoing, as it ever has been in the history of civilisations. The Romans depended on slaves, the ancients on science. They made their lives too luxurious and in the end rendered themselves helpless.' Reluctantly he lifted his hands from the glass and settled his spectacles back on his nose. He addressed the workmen. 'As you dig, you will doubtless discover other pieces of the same carriage – glassware smaller than this, plastic objects, perhaps some larger rusted metal parts. There may even be the traces of a road that once ran up here.'

Hancock interrupted him. 'Ye do not want us to stop on each occasion, I hope?'

'No, sir. On another day I would say yes, but we have a larger prize in view. This beauty we shall store, noting the position of its discovery. Mr Fairfax, if you would help us?'

Fairfax took one end of the glass and Quycke the other, and together they carried it into the tent that Shadwell had requested be set aside for the storage of artefacts. A trestle table had been erected, and upon this Shadwell had arranged his books, a pile of paper, pen and ink and pencils. They leaned the glass against the table and the old man made a careful note in a large ledger. When he had finished, he looked up.

'See how the place begins to yield its secrets? A road, perhaps. A carriage possibly abandoned when it was no longer possible to fuel or repair it. And fifteen people – there may be more – slaughtered in cold blood . . .' He paused, glancing through the tent flap towards the tower. 'May I borrow your services again, Mr Fairfax?'

Shadwell led them outside and over to the tower. He stood with hands on his hips, between the northern and western trenches, and surveyed the surface, then reached out and began tearing away the strands of ivy. 'Would you oblige me, sir, by kneeling with your face up close to the tower?'

Fairfax did as he was asked, and found himself

staring directly into the line of small cone-shaped holes that pitted that section of the concrete. He felt the tips of two of Shadwell's fingers pressing into the back of his head, and heard him say, 'Yes, that is how it was done. Do you see, Ollie?' He raised his voice in his excitement. 'Here was where they were lined up and murdered, one after the other, by a bullet to the brain. As I thought — it was a massacre!'

Fairfax turned in alarm. 'Please, Dr Shadwell — speak more discreetly!'

But it was too late. Several of the men in the nearby trenches had already stopped their work to watch this curious re-enactment, and now one of them called out, 'Massacre? What massacre were this?'

'Nothing,' said Fairfax quickly, scrambling to his feet. 'Dr Shadwell was merely speaking of a possibility, nothing more.'

'But "massacre" he said — I heard the word distinctly!'

'Aye,' joined in the man next to him, 'I heard it too.'

They huddled together. After a moment, they threw down their tools and clambered from the trench and went to talk to their friends in the neighbouring trenches. Shadwell resumed his inspection of the concrete, dictating notes to his secretary, apparently oblivious to the effect he had produced. As word spread around the site, the noise of digging and sawing gradually diminished, until eventually it ceased altogether. Some of the men who had been working on the other side of the tower came round to find out what was going on, although they kept their distance. The rest stayed where they were, leaning on their picks and shovels.

Hancock jumped out of his trench and marched over. 'What is this tale of massacre, Mr Shadwell?'

Shadwell affected surprise at the grimness of his tone. 'It is the truth.' He looked around at the faces watching him. 'What are they – men or children?'

Fairfax said, 'They are men who have been told since they were children that this place is full of evil spirits.'

'Then the truth should reassure them.' Shadwell raised his voice enough for it to carry to everyone. 'This was not the work of evil spirits, but human beings – people just like us. For God's sake' – he laughed derisively – 'devils don't fire guns!' and then the laugh turned into a racking cough.

'Easy for ye to say!' someone shouted. 'Ye're half a corpse thyself!'

It was Keefer, once again, who spoke up for the weavers. 'We were persuaded to come out here to dig for objects that were buried. No mention was made of bodies or massacres. Yet look over there at the grave-yard!' The church clerk clasped his hands in prayer. 'This ground has been hallowed by death, and should not be disturbed.'

There was a murmur of assent.

'I'm not asking ye to dig where the dead are buried,' said Hancock. 'Let them lie over yonder, left in peace. Has any man here found a single human bone?' There was no answer. 'Good. Then let us forget the foolish talk and return to work.' Nobody moved. Hancock struck the tower with his fist. 'God damn ye – move!'

'We're not your slaves, John Hancock . . .'

'Ye tricked us . . .'

'This was my husband's land!'

It was a woman's voice – so unexpected a sound to hear in such a place that all heads turned at once towards her. Not that Sarah Durston at that moment much resembled a woman. Her hair was all hidden beneath her cap, her sleeves rolled up, her freckled arms and man's white shirt streaked with soot, her face wet and shiny with the heat of the fire. 'This was my husband's land,' she repeated, walking towards the tower, 'and he dug here for many years, searching for a treasure that might restore the fortunes of our family. The effort of it broke his health.' She stopped and stared around. 'You all knew Sir Henry – as good and brave a man as ever lived – and I for one am not afraid to dig in this spot, if only in honour of his memory.'

She jumped down into the trench, took the shovel from the nearest labourer and began to jab it into the

ground, criss-cross, breaking up the earth and fling-
ing it inaccurately towards a nearby wheelbarrow.
After half a dozen spadefuls she broke off, breathing
heavily, and stared at the workmen around her. 'Well?
Will you leave it all to a woman?' She fixed on one
young handsome half-naked fellow in particular.
After a few moments he nodded and grinned ruefully
at her, spat on his hands, lifted his pickaxe and swung
it. The men next to him reached for their shovels and
resumed work. The rest watched them for a while,
and then, one by one, they too began to drift back in
silence to their trenches. Within a few minutes the
noise of activity was restored around the camp, the
mutiny was over, and Sarah returned to her bonfire.

The hours passed. The sky darkened. The unearthed
mounds of soil and rock grew higher, the excavations
deeper. At Shadwell's suggestion, learned by years of
experience, the floors of the trenches were formed
into ramps, with the deepest section closest to the
tower, so that the wheelbarrows could more easily
cart away the spoil up the slope to ground level thirty
paces distant.

Fairfax took his turn in the lowest section of the
shaft, where the work was most arduous. He was
obliged to shed his cassock and work in his underclothes. Cold water pooled over his boots up to his
bare ankles and made each shovel-load of oozing

black earth feel twice as heavy. The strip of grey sky above his head seemed far away, and although the sides of the trench were shuttered with timber for safety, he sensed the pressure behind the thick planks and could not rid himself of the dread that they might cave in upon him at any moment. Whenever the man working beside him knocked into him, he imagined them buried alive together in this loathsome place, clawing and gouging at one another in their efforts to escape.

At every level the earth yielded evidence of human presence from centuries earlier, most of it plastic – translucent shreds of plastic bags that clung to the hands like torn-off skin; lumps of foamy white polystyrene; bottles of various sizes, both clear and coloured; fragments of moulded casings from the ancients' wondrous devices. Occasional reddish streaks in the soil showed the shape of objects that had rusted to nothing; apart from a few coins and unidentifiable flaking lumps that crumbled between his fingers, nothing that was metal had survived. Wood was black rot. Of glass there was plenty – fragments of bottles, delicately shaped bulbs, and more elaborate shattered pieces that might have come from the same hoard as Colonel Durston's collection. The most interesting find was made by a man working at the shallow end of the trench, who dug out a pair of spectacles, perfectly preserved, the frames made of brown plastic and the lenses still intact. He cleaned them on his sleeve and they were passed along the trench, the men taking turns to try them on. Someone declared they restored his vision perfectly, but when Fairfax settled them upon his own nose, his sight became blurry, as if he was seeing the world through tears.

He said, 'I should take them to Dr Shadwell. They may be of significance.'

The man beside him hawked and spat. ' 'Tis all a fearful waste of time and effort, Father, if ye ask me! We work like miners, half the hillside's dug away — and all for a pair of eyeglasses!'

Fairfax yielded his place to the man behind him and walked up the ramp to where he had left his cassock. The mood in the trench had deteriorated as the afternoon had worn on, from fear to sullenness to downright dejection. He could see it in their faces — in the slump of their shoulders and the sluggardly way they were working. The landscape around the tower, hazy with smoke, scarred by trenches and disfigured by the heaps of spoil, did indeed resemble an ugly open mine-working. From the distance came a rumble that he thought at first must be blasting in the quarry but then realised was the thunder of a coming storm. He wondered how much daylight they had left. An hour or two, no more.

Shadwell was seated at the table in his tent, writing in his ledger. Quycke was beside him, sketching.

Piled up on the table and arranged around it was the soil-encrusted litter of their discoveries, through which Hancock was picking gloomily, like a man who had travelled a long way to market in the hope of a bargain and had found nothing but rubbish. Fairfax gave Shadwell the spectacles. 'Western trench, twenty-five paces from the tower.'

Shadwell said, 'At what depth?'

'Two or three feet, no more.'

Shadwell made a note and tried them on. 'Made for a person with short sight. One of Morgenstern's scholarly colleagues, perhaps.' He offered them to Hancock, who waved them away irritably.

'I did not pay a fortune for such trinkets. I want the ark. Where is it, Dr Shadwell? Ye sounded so certain last night.'

'No, sir. I was never certain. I guessed that whatever lay underground – if it existed – was likely to be joined to the tower. But we may be digging in the wrong spot entirely. One can never tell.'

'That is not my memory of our talk. How much deeper must we go?'

'I should say to twenty feet.'

'Twenty feet! Soon it will be nightfall! And if we find nothing at twenty feet – what then?'

'We start again tomorrow, but this time we dig further from the tower, and make the trenches parallel.'

'And what if we still find naught that is significant?'

'Then that itself will be of some significance. Today, for example, we have found no farming tools – no evidence of cultivation. If we still find none tomorrow, then we may conjecture that the people who were here eventually moved on. Two acres are required to feed one person for a year. Where did Morgenstern's colony grow its food if not here?'

Fairfax said, 'Perhaps they did not survive long enough to grow food? Perhaps they were all lined up and shot soon after they arrived?'

'That is possible.'

'Then we are wasting our efforts,' said Hancock, 'for whatever they brought here would have been stolen from them.'

'That is true.'

' "That is true",' repeated Hancock in exasperation. ' "That is possible." I am starting to conclude that ye know very little, Shadwell!'

Shadwell was unconcerned. 'Indeed, sir. That is also possible – and true.'

At that moment the tent flap opened and Sarah Durston's head appeared. 'Dr Shadwell, gentlemen. Would you come at once, please? The men have found something.'

The discovery had been made at the end of the western trench, where Fairfax had been digging just a few minutes before. The men stood back to let them pass along the narrow alley. Hancock strode down the ramp, followed by Shadwell, Quycke, Fairfax and Sarah. Heads appeared above them, peering down at the source of the excitement. But there was nothing to see, merely a pool of dirty water reflecting the dull sky.

Hancock stared at it, disappointed. 'Well?' he said to the man who had raised the alarm. 'What is it?'

'That I don't know, Captain. Listen.' He plunged his shovel into the water. The metal blade scraped stone. 'Thought at first it might be a rock, but if so 'tis a big one, and dead flat. Hear that?' He demonstrated by prodding beneath the surface right and left, front and back, each time producing the same noise. Whatever it was that was underwater covered the entire width of the trench and extended in length a distance of three or four feet outwards from the tower.

'We must drain it off,' said Hancock. He shouted again to the men looking down from the surface. 'Lower some buckets so we may see what we have here. Fetch a torch as well.' He took the shovel and experimented himself, striking the sharp edge against the solid underwater platform. He turned to Shadwell. 'Might this be the road ye spoke of?'

Shadwell shook his head. 'The ancients' roads were shoddy stuff. None survives in such a state. Besides, it's buried too deep to be a road.'

Two large buckets were lowered from the top of the trench. Hancock bailed water into one and Fairfax the other. But as fast as they tried to empty it, the pool refilled. 'Sandbags!' commanded Hancock. 'And light, so we may see!' A torch made rapid progress along the cutting, passed from hand to hand, until it reached Quycke, who held it up for them. Sandbags followed in the same fashion, and were laid like bricks to form a foot-high barrier across the trench. Hancock and Fairfax resumed their bailing. When only an inch or two of water remained, Hancock drew his boot through the mud. A flat, smooth grey surface was briefly visible before the black liquid closed over it.

'Dr Shadwell — your opinion?'

Shadwell leaned over. 'The roof of an underground chamber, almost certainly, built of concrete. I believe we have found it, Captain.'

Someone whistled.

'Pass me that pickaxe,' said Hancock. 'Stand clear, gentlemen.'

Fairfax stepped back over the sandbags. Hancock planted his feet apart, lifted the axe and let it rest over his right shoulder. He paused to gather his strength, then his body seemed suddenly to expand as his muscles tensed and he swung the pick in an arc with all his force. The pointed tip struck the concrete and seemed to bounce off. The shaft almost jarred out of his hands. He dropped it, took the torch from Quycke and bent to inspect the result. 'God damn!' he muttered. He handed back the torch and tried again, and again – four, five, six times: massive shattering blows that left him panting. He leaned against the side of the trench to recover his breath.

Fairfax took the torch and flourished it above the water, then bent and ran his left palm over the concrete. 'Barely a scratch.'

They looked to Shadwell. He held up his hands. 'This is why it has lasted nigh on a thousand years. I fear we shall have to dig outwards from this spot until we find the entrance.'

Hancock glanced around the steep sides of the trench. 'We cannot shift ten thousand tons of earth. 'Twould take us weeks. We shall have to tunnel.'

Fairfax said, 'Is that not dangerous?'

'Not if we put in props and beams. We have sufficient timber, if we salvage from the other trenches. I take it we may abandon the other workings, Dr Shadwell?'

'Indeed so, Captain. This is where we must put our effort.'

Hancock took out his pocket watch. 'Just after six. Two hours of daylight left – though if we tunnel we may work by torchlight through the night. Is Keefer there?'

'Yes, Captain!' The clerk pushed his way past Fairfax and Shadwell to the front of the group.

'How many men do we have?'

'Thirty, or thereabouts.'

'Sort them, if ye please, into three shifts of ten. Those who are the least tired to work from now till ten, the next to work the period of the first sleep from ten till two, and the last to cover the second sleep, from two until six.'

'Aye, sir.'

Fairfax thought, half a dozen men have deserted already; how many will be left by morning?

Hancock went on, 'We'll dig out four shafts a yard high – one out either side from here, the other pair to start fifteen paces back. Timbered every yard for safety. Does fifteen paces sound right to ye, Dr Shadwell?'

'Yes, that should do it. Although tunnelling at night is not without risk.'

'We're Wessex men, not your Wiltshire faint-hearts. Good. Then let us waste no time. Those who are not part of the first shift should have food and drink.'

As they turned to make their way out of the trench, it began to rain.

CHAPTER TWENTY-FOUR

Captain Hancock learns the truth

KEEFER SAID, 'WILL ye take the first shift, Father?' He grinned. 'Or are those soft hands o' thine too sore?'

'No, they're fine, Mr Keefer. I shall willingly do my share.'

In truth, every part of his body was sore, and his hands — swollen and hatched with scratches — hurt worst of all. But he would not allow the church clerk to score a victory over him. Once again he took off his cassock and handed it up to one of the men, who put it in a canvas tent bag along with the others' outer clothes, to protect them from the rain. Then he helped remove the shuttering and pass up the long planks so they could have a yard cut off them.

The walls of the tunnel, freed from the constraint, began to bulge. A shower of soil mixed with rain fell over his head and shoulders. He bent as if he had been attacked by flying insects, and vigorously brushed it out of his hair. Someone said the noise of sawing from the ground above sounded like the making of a coffin. Nobody laughed. Finally, the carpenter came down into the trench dragging a pair of stout timber frames. Fairfax used the pickaxe to dig the opening of a mine shaft, a yard square, working back to back with a man who did the same on the opposite side, then the carpenter hammered the frames into place, and the shuttering was lowered and re-fixed to the trench walls. But these precautions did nothing to calm Fairfax's fears. They seemed flimsy barriers against the weight of the earth.

The carpenter left. Fairfax sank to his knees in the shallow water and felt the cold concrete beneath him. He leaned a torch beside him so that he could see what he was doing, took a pickaxe and, by the hissing light of the burning pitch, began to hack away.

It was slow, hard, awkward work. The soil and rock were tightly compacted, veined with fibrous roots too thick to tear apart. When he reached in to the opening and tried to drag them out, he brought down fresh clumps of earth upon his head. The space was too restricted to enable him to properly swing the pick. He had to grip the shaft in one hand, close to the metal head, and peck away at the lumps of stone, loosening them, and then working them free with his hands. Repeatedly shuffling back and forth across the concrete to throw the debris into the wheelbarrow on the other side of the sandbags rubbed his knees raw. The more he excavated, the further he had to venture from the trench, and the greater his terror that the roof of the tunnel would cave in on him — pin his arms and body so heavily that he would be unable to fight his way free, clogging his mouth and nostrils with suffocating earth.

After more than an hour, when he had dug out four or five feet of tunnel, the carpenter called to him to come out so that roof props could be fitted. He reversed himself into the trench. It was a relief to be able to stand. The air was cooler, the day's light almost gone. Rain was falling steadily from the narrow strip of sky. He stretched his hands up to it to ease his stiffness. The man who had been carting away the spoil in the wheelbarrow offered to swap jobs. Fairfax accepted at once, hoisting the handles before he could change his mind, and pushing the load down the gangway of planks that had been laid along the floor of the trench, past the other pair of tunnels, over the second barrier of sandbags and up the ramp to the surface.

He ran the barrow up on to the nearest pile of spoil and tipped it. When he righted it, he stopped to survey the site. What a spectacle it presented — the heaps of waste, black in the twilight, rising like burial mounds between the abandoned canals of the trenches; the white canvas tents pitched close to the treeline; the flames of half a dozen campfires, protected from the worst of the rain by the canopy of foliage. One fire was larger than the others. Men were silhouetted moving around it. A smell of roasting meat drifted up the slope and made his stomach growl. He marvelled again at the sheer energy of Hancock, at the force of will that had brought them all up here and conjured this teeming effort into existence. But the thought of Hancock reminded him of Sarah and of the imminent confrontation. He seized the handles of the wheelbarrow, grimacing at the pain in his hands, set his jaw and turned back towards the tunnel.

At ten o'clock the shift changed and a fresh line of men trooped into the trench, laughing and joking despite the rain and the prospect of spending four hours labouring in the mud. The source of their good humour was detectable on their breath — ale, wine, gin — and Fairfax realised he craved a drink to take the edge off reality almost as much as he wanted food and sleep. He said to the man replacing him, 'I hope you've saved enough for us!'

'Aye, Father, don't ye worry. The captain's woman's cooked enough for an army.'

Fairfax gave the man his shovel, stumbled out of the trench and went in search of the canvas bag containing his cassock. *The captain's woman!* He felt his jealousy as a kind of nausea. Once he was dressed, he trooped with the others through the wet darkness towards the beckoning light of the big fire. Half a pig was roasting on a spit, a cauldron boiling nearby, potatoes cooking in the embers. Casks of ale and wine and jugs of gin stood on a trestle table next to tin plates and beakers, knives and forks. Sarah Durston was washing dishes in a tub beneath a tree. She looked up as they approached, dried her hands and came over to serve them.

Fairfax stood at the end of the queue and watched her carve the pork. She did it dextrously, slicing through the meat, wasting nothing, joking with the men. He had not conceived of her as a cook, although her upbringing was ordinary, so why should she not have learned kitchen skills, or to talk easily with labourers? He thought again how little he knew her. When his turn came to be served she was still in joshing mood and laughed at his appearance. 'Why, Father Fairfax, you are as black as the Devil himself!' She heaped his plate with meat and added a potato. 'Rough fare, I fear, but the best that may be managed.' The others had moved away.

He said, 'Where is Hancock?'

'Gone to talk to Shadwell. He and Mr Quycke are sleeping in their wagon.' She frowned. 'Are you well, Christopher? You look out of sorts.'

'I am tired, nothing more. And this business with the captain weighs on me — more than it does on you, it seems.'

He took his plate, moved along the table, filled a cup with the local red wine and drained it, filled it again, then walked over to a tree, apart from the rest of the men, sank to the ground with his back against the trunk and began to eat. After a while, she came over to sit beside him.

She said, 'If the delay troubles you, I shall go and tell him now.'

'No, not yet. Wait until the morning.'

'I promise you I mean to set things straight between us. This constant deceit is beyond endurance.'

'Are you certain of that?' He spoke bitterly, to wound her. 'If you deny that woman's allegation, and I do likewise, what proof of our betrayal exists?'

'He will still believe it.'

'In his heart he might. But you know as well as I he loves you too much ever to admit it. He will pretend to himself that all is well so as not to lose you.'

'And that is what you want?'

'It may be for the best.' He spoke quietly, without looking at her, and despised himself. He felt as if some other man had taken control of him – hardly a man at all, he thought savagely, but some pathetic weakling youth. To his shame, he felt hot tears pricking at his eyes. He still could not bring himself to face her. 'Forgive me,' he said. 'I am very tired.'

'You are afraid of him.'

'It's true. I am.'

'I cannot love a coward.'

She got to her feet and walked away. He watched her go, skirting the fire, heading towards a tent on the opposite side of the encampment. She opened the flap and went inside. After half a minute he set aside his plate and went after her. He was conscious of the men in the firelight gawping at this private drama. He stooped to enter the tent.

She was standing with her back to him in the candlelight. He took in a few details – a blanket spread across the groundsheet, a heavy earthenware jug and bowl of water, a leather bag – his bag – lying in the corner. It was the sight of that, and the realisation that she had thought to take it in for safe keeping, that pierced him more than anything. He stood behind her and wrapped his arms around her. 'I should be the one to tell him.'

He felt her shoulders stiffen at first, and then relax. Her expression when she turned was calm – no trace of a tear in those clear green eyes. On the contrary, she seemed to stare straight into him. Suddenly her mouth sought his. After a moment or two she pushed him away. 'You are filthy.'

'I know it.'

She pointed to the bowl. 'Take off your robe.'

He did as she asked and kneeled on the blanket. She took the jug and tipped it over his head. The water in the bowl, inches from his eyes, turned black. He scooped his hands and splashed his face. She continued to pour, running her fingers through his hair, teasing out the dirt. She laughed. 'You've half the hillside on you!' The water was cold. It trickled down the back of his neck. He rejoiced in the touch of her fingers.

'What a scene,' said Hancock.

Fairfax's head jerked around so sharply he almost knocked the jug from her hands. The captain stepped into the tent. The flap fell shut behind him.

Fairfax groped for a towel. Unable to find one, he rose to his feet dripping water, half blind. He wiped the back of his hand across his eyes. He felt hideously exposed, standing there in his filthy wet underclothes. Sarah was frozen beside him holding the jug.

Hancock looked from one to the other. He wore a terrible half-smile. 'This is not what it seems to be.' He nodded, as if trying to reassure himself. 'Ye do not need to tell me. I *know* it is not what it seems to be.'

'No, Captain,' said Fairfax. His voice sounded high and feeble in his ears, lacking all conviction. But the moment had come, and he was glad, and he pressed on. 'I fear it is just as it appears to be.'

Hancock's expression was disbelieving. 'Come now, Fairfax! It is not!'

'I am sorry. I must tell you the truth. Sarah came into my bed last night.'

'No.' The captain frowned and shook his head judiciously, as if rejecting a low offer at market. 'No, no.'

'Your sister saw her. She will confirm it. She is determined to tell you.'

This information seemed at first not to register either. But then a change came over Hancock's features, a sort of slow collapse. He started to move towards Fairfax. Fairfax watched his slow approach with a curious detachment, as if the violence that was about to be unleashed would be directed at someone other than himself. Hancock stopped in front of him and reached out his right hand. He touched the side of Fairfax's face, caressed it. His fingers found the ear and tweaked it — not the lobe, the whole ear — then abruptly closed upon it like a vice and held him in position while his left fist swung round in a terrific blow to the other side of Fairfax's head. The tent lurched, dissolved, vanished.

When he came to, he was on his knees and Hancock had his hands around his throat, his thumbs pressing into his windpipe, twisting and lifting him, as a farmer breaks the neck of a chicken. His hands beat feebly at Hancock's arms. The pain was worse than the choking. He could hear Sarah shouting. The tent began to darken again. Something flashed in the air. There was a crash, and brown fragments of pottery exploded in a halo around the captain's head. The grip on his throat slackened and he toppled sideways.

He felt a thud. The ground shook. He thought at first the blow must have laid Hancock out flat. But when he struggled up on to his elbow, the captain was still on his feet, clutching at the wound in his head, tottering in a circle. Sarah was holding a handle – all that remained of the jug. And this was odd, he thought: all three of them silent and panting with the effort of their struggle, and yet there was a sound of screaming.

Hancock swung around, listening, streaming blood, swaying like a drunkard, then lurched towards the entrance of the tent and disappeared. Sarah held out her hand. Fairfax took it and managed to get up on to his feet. He tried to speak. She gestured to him to save his breath. 'The men are in an uproar about something.' They followed the captain out into the night.

Around the base of the tower torches were darting back and forth, casting the elongated shadows of panicking figures running towards the western trench. More were emerging from their tents. Fairfax and Sarah stumbled through the darkness. A narrow section of the ground had collapsed close to the trench. A shallow crevice a yard deep and ten feet long had opened up. Men were standing in it, digging frantically with picks and shovels. Some were on their knees using their bare hands. Others were in the trench. They cried out to one another. 'Here!' 'Over here!'

Fairfax took a torch and picked his way along the gangplank at the bottom of the trench. All he could see were men's backs. He held up the torch. Hancock was in the middle of the group, shouting at them to give him space. He dipped out of sight. When he re-appeared, he had the top half of a man's body in his arms. He dragged it out of the melee and lugged it along the trench. Two others were holding the feet. Fairfax pressed against the shuttering to let them pass. He glimpsed a white face hanging slackly, bulging eyes, a round black mouth, wide black nostrils.

He followed them up to the surface. The body was laid on the ground. He held his torch over it. Hancock dug his fingers into the mouth and gouged out earth, then clamped his own mouth over it and blew. He came up for air and blew again. Earth trickled out of the nostrils. Someone threw water over the face. There was no sign of life. Hancock straddled the man and started working at his chest with the flats of his hands. Now that he could properly see the face, Fair-fax recognised him as the handsome youth who had been the first to respond to Sarah's appeal to resume work. She was watching the attempts to revive him, her hands pressed to her cheeks.

Fairfax said quietly to her, 'Would you fetch my prayer book and stole?'

A little while later, after she had returned, and when it was obvious the man was beyond hope, Fair-fax gave her the torch and put his hand on Hancock's shoulder. But Hancock would not stop pounding the chest and blowing into the mouth as if his willpower alone was sufficient to recall the dead to life. Eventually Keefer said, 'Leave him, Captain. Let the father do his work.'

'No, he can still be saved.'

It took two men to pull Hancock away.

Fairfax kneeled and closed the young man's eyes and took his hand. It was still warm. Rain fell across his open prayer book.

O Almighty God, he began. He paused while everyone else got to their knees. *We humbly commend the soul of this thy servant, our dear brother, into thy hands, as into the hands of a faithful Creator, and most merciful Saviour* . . . The wind whipped the torches and flicked over the page. He trapped it with his thumb. *Wash it, we pray thee, in the blood of that immaculate Lamb, that was slain to take away the sins of the world . . . And teach us who survive, in this and other like daily spectacles of mortality, to see how frail and uncertain our condition is; and so to number our days, that we may seriously apply our hearts to that holy and heavenly wisdom, whilst we live here, which may in the end bring us to life everlasting, through the merits of Jesus Christ thine only Son our Lord. Amen.*

'Amen.'

The body was wrapped in a blanket and bound with rope. Two men took the head and two the feet. One went ahead with a torch. Hancock sat on one of the mounds of earth, his bloodied head bent forward, his arms on his knees, and watched as they started to carry the corpse up the slope towards the base camp. The others came out of the area around the tents holding torches and lamps and followed in procession. Hancock regarded them with growing disbelief. He rose to his feet.

'Wait!' he called after them. 'Surely ye cannot all mean to go at once?'

He launched himself in pursuit, ran past them and planted himself in their path, holding out his arms to stop them.

'Four of ye can take him home. The rest stay here.' His voice was desperate. With his head and hair all plastered with dirt from the trench and blood from his wound, he looked half crazed. 'We'll dig no more tonight, in honour of his memory. We need not start again till daybreak.'

They did not answer, but merely diverted their course to pass around him. He turned to watch the cortège go. His arms dropped to his sides.

He shouted, 'There'll be no pay for a job half done!'

Fairfax said, 'Leave it, Hancock. They'll not come back.'

The captain glanced over his shoulder at Fairfax and Sarah. He seemed barely conscious of who they were, let alone what had passed between them. 'If we use more timber, the tunnels will be safe enough. Our error was to work at night.' He looked back towards the torchlit procession, beginning to thread its way through the trees. 'I'll fetch 'em down. It's foolish to travel in the dark.'

They watched him go, hurrying to catch the men up. For a while they could hear his voice calling to them to wait – pleading, promising, threatening – until the ribbon of lights reached the crest of the hill. Then, as they began to descend the other side, one by one the darkness swallowed them, and after that the only sounds were the wind and rain.

CHAPTER TWENTY-FIVE

Sunday 14th April: Father Fairfax and Lady Durston
pass the night on the Devil's Chair

THEY SAT BY the fire in silence and waited for Hancock to return. Fairfax kept a pickaxe close beside him, just in case.

After an hour, when still he hadn't reappeared, they agreed he must have gone back to the mill. Either that, thought Fairfax, or *he is out there in the trees somewhere, watching us.* He rested his hand briefly on the axe.

Sarah said, 'Should we not inform Dr Shadwell and Mr Quycke of what has happened?'

'They must know it, surely? The men would have had to carry the body directly past their wagon.'

'Do you think they have gone as well?'

'Perhaps. There certainly seems little point in their remaining. If I were Shadwell, I would make a run for it, and to hell with Hancock and his thousand pounds.'

They stared into the fire. Rain hissed in the flames.
'We could return to Durston Court,' she suggested, 'and pass the night there.'

'If that is what you wish.'

But neither could find the energy to move, and in the end the issue was settled by their exhaustion. First Sarah kept nodding off, then he did. Finally they banked the fire in the hope of keeping it alight till morning and retreated to the tent, where they lay on the blanket, wrapped in one another's arms, and listened to the pattering of the rain on the canvas.

At some point in the night Fairfax heard a noise and woke. Sarah's arm was flung across his chest. The candle had gone out. The darkness in the tent was disturbed by a faint blue flickering. He lifted her arm. She stirred in her sleep, muttered something, pulled her arm away and rolled on to her side. He rose quietly so as not to disturb her. The stiffness in his muscles from his day's exertions and then from lying on the hard damp ground made each movement painful. He lifted the tent flap and peered outside. The sky above the trees flashed blue, lighting up the tower and the abandoned camp brightly enough to cast sharp shadows. A rumble of thunder sounded in the distance. Beyond the glowing embers of the fire he thought he heard a movement, and for an instant, when the lightning came again, he glimpsed the outline of a figure standing near the empty tents, seemingly watching him. By the time of the next flash, it had gone.

He moved warily towards the red glow of the fire. On the trestle table, amid the abandoned debris of the meal, he found the knife Sarah had used to carve the pig. He heard a rustle, the snap of a twig. He flourished the knife into the darkness and called out, 'Who's that?' There was no response. He glanced back at the tent where Sarah lay asleep. To retreat, or to advance and leave her unprotected? He weighed the choices and decided he dared not leave her. He waited for another lightning flash to show him the way back, and just as he reached the tent, the accompanying peal of thunder followed, louder and closer than before.

He picked up his bag and carried it over to the blanket, laid it down and sat with his back propped against it, the knife in his lap, determined to stay alert. He was still in that position when Sarah woke him the next morning.

'Christopher?' She was gently shaking his shoulder.

'What?' His eyes opened. For an instant he thought she was a part of his nightmare, which dissolved with the daylight.

'You were muttering in your sleep. And the knife?'

He glanced down at it. 'I heard someone moving in the camp last night.'

'Who?'

'I did not see.'

'John Hancock. It must have been.' For the first time since he had known her, she looked afraid. 'It's light outside.' She held out her hand. 'May we please now get away from this accursed place?'

He needed no persuading. He let her help him to his feet and hoisted his bag over his shoulder. Knife in hand, he opened the tent flap and gestured to her to wait while he checked outside. The site was very still. There was no dawn chorus. He beckoned to her to follow, and together they stepped out into the daylight.

The rain had stopped but the air felt moist, the clouds so low that the tops of the trees above the Devil's Chair were lost in a smoky grey mist. Part of the hillside had fallen away in the night. He wondered if that was what had woken him. A brown mudslide, narrow at the top and broad at the base, lay strewn across the green forest like a skirt spread out to dry.

It was possible Hancock might be asleep in one of the tents. He put his finger to his lips. They trod stealthily, careful where they put their feet. It was only as they reached the bottom of the slope leading through the wood to the base camp that the silence was disturbed by the familiar sound of a distant hacking cough. They looked up. Shadwell was painfully descending the hillside, leaning on a stick. He stopped to double over and spit upon the ground. When he straightened, he saw them and waved his stick.

'Wait there!' he called. He made as much haste as he could, grimacing with the effort, his feet skidding on the muddy slope. Before he had even reached them, Fairfax could sense his distress. He called out to them again. 'Is Oliver with you?'

'No, sir,' said Fairfax. 'We believed him to be with you.'

'He was beside me last night right enough.' He joined them – unshaven, agitated. 'But this morning when I woke he was nowhere to be found. I thought he must be here.' He cupped his hands to his mouth and shouted. 'Olly!' He stared distractedly around the abandoned workings. 'What a disaster it has all become!' He called again. 'Olly!' The name echoed forlornly around the wall of hills.

Fairfax said, 'I think perhaps I saw him last night.' Now he thought of it, he was sure. The figure had been too tall to be Hancock. Tired as he was, he grasped what it meant at once. 'I fear he may be gone.'

'Gone? Without telling me? Why would he do such a thing?' Shadwell made circles in the air with his stick, as if he might conjure his secretary out of nothing. 'He must be here somewhere. Where do you think you saw him?'

'Over there, near the campfire.'

Sarah said, 'Perhaps he went to the tent where you worked yesterday?'

Shadwell turned to her gratefully. 'Yes. Exactly. That will be it.'

They walked with him towards the tower. The workings looked uncommonly ugly in the morning light. They defiled the strange beauty of the spot. Shadwell paused to examine the collapsed tunnel. 'This is where the young fellow was killed?'

Fairfax nodded.

'That poor boy — to drown in the earth! I warned Captain Hancock of the danger. He would not listen. To tunnel in mud, in a rainstorm, in the dark, using men without experience — what sort of folly is that?'

He wrenched his gaze away and they resumed their journey. Inside the tent there was no sign of Quycke, just the finds from yesterday's dig, carefully sorted by type — plastic, glass, metal. The big window with its tracery of wire was leaning against the table. But the table itself was bare.

Shadwell went over to it. 'My records are gone. And my books.' He ran his hand over the surface, disbelieving. Behind his mauve-tinted spectacles his eyes were blinking rapidly. 'Someone has taken them. Surely it cannot be Olly? He would have asked me.'

Fairfax said gently, 'I fear Mr Quycke has not been entirely straight with you, Dr Shadwell. Quite what double part he has been playing I cannot tell for certain, but for sure there is more to it than we know. As your secretary, I assume he was privy to all your correspondence?'

'Of course.'

'The letter from Father Lacy, describing his discoveries – the appeal for assistance that brought you to Axford – can you recall what day it arrived?'

Shadwell raised his hands hopelessly. 'No. I would need to consult my papers. And they are gone.'

'You told me you left Wilton immediately you read it?'

'That very afternoon. What of it?'

'Lady Durston says Father Lacy saw the glassware on the twenty-fourth, a Sunday. You say he wrote to you at once. Yet there was an interval of eight or nine days between the dispatch of his letter and your arrival at the Swan. The gap has always troubled me. Who would have opened his letter first, you or Mr Quycke?'

Shadwell looked at him bleakly. His mouth flapped open. 'Olly. He dealt with all my letters.'

'Then is it possible he could have made a copy and sent it to Bishop Pole before he even showed it to you?'

'I suppose . . . perhaps . . . He has been out of sorts just lately.' He shook his head as if to clear it. 'No, no. It is not possible. Not Olly . . .'

'Then where is he, Dr Shadwell? And why has he taken your work? Does the evidence not suggest he has all along been employed as the bishop's spy?'

Shadwell's jaw worked soundlessly in dismay. He clutched at the table as if he might topple over. Sarah took his arm and guided him to the folding chair. He sat down heavily and stared straight ahead. Suddenly he made an awful retching sound, leaned forward and vomited blood.

Sarah put her arm around him. 'Fetch blankets,' she said to Fairfax, 'and bring some water. Quickly!'

As he went outside, he glanced towards the tower.

A figure, immense and bulky, was moving between the mounds of earth. It was Hancock, staggering slightly from the weight of the two barrels he was carrying, one under either arm.

Afterwards, Fairfax was to realise that of course Hancock had not returned home tamely to the mill, that he would never give in, that he would see the thing through to the end, even if it meant destroying whatever it was he sought and himself in the process. He had been to the quarry and had bought or stolen – Fairfax was never sure which – the black powder they used for blasting, and now he was placing the barrels in the tunnel Fairfax had helped dig close to the base of the tower.

Fairfax stood behind him in the trench and addressed his wide back as he laid the charge. 'Captain Hancock, this is madness.'

'Why so?'

'Surely you must see why? The effect of the explosion — the damage that may be caused . . .'

'We cannot dig the monster out — the men will never return, no matter what I pay 'em. Therefore 'tis an explosion or nothing.' Hancock withdrew from the tunnel and turned to face him. There was a touch of insanity about him, in the wildness of his eyes, and in the curious grin he wore. 'Well, Parson, will ye help me?'

'Help you? How?'

'Carry the other barrels.'

'There are more?'

'Certainly. I have another ten in the wagon.' He laughed at Fairfax's expression and clapped his hand on his shoulder. ''Twill take more than two to do a job this big! Even twelve may not suffice.' He looked around the trench and nodded. 'But in a narrow space, with ten good feet of earth on top, the greater part of the force should be directed downwards. The chance is worth the effort.'

'You speak of "chance"? You know nothing of what you are doing!'

'Wrong, sir. In the late war against the French, we cracked open one of their strongest forts using this same method exactly. Well? Surely we have travelled too far to abandon our journey when we can see the end?'

'Our situation has changed entirely. Mr Quycke has deserted.'

'Quycke! Good. We have no need of Quycke.'

'He has not left out of cowardice. Rather, I fear he informs for Bishop Pole. It's my suspicion we have walked into a trap.'

That news quietened even Hancock. But not for long. 'Then all the more reason to make haste while we can. Will ye help or not?' When Fairfax said nothing, he shrugged. 'So be it. I'll do the work alone.'

He lurched off down the trench like a drunkard, stepping around the tools that had been discarded the previous night, and made his way up the ramp and out of sight.

Fairfax squatted on his haunches and peered into the tunnel. He could just make out the squat shape of the barrels at the far end. Two looked menacing enough. Surely twelve would bring the tower down? Here was Hancock's ambition embodied: that force without which no city is built, no city destroyed. He withdrew and hurried back to Sarah and Shadwell.

She had fetched the blankets from their tent, along with the bowl, and had laid out the old man on the ground. He was lying on his side. Occasionally he gave a feeble cough. The bowl was half full of blood.

She said reproachfully, 'I thought you had left us too.'

'Hancock is back, with blasting powder from the quarry. He proposes to break in to the chamber by means of an explosion.'

'When?'

'As soon as he has carried all the necessary barrels from his wagon.'

'Does he know of Quycke's disappearance?'

'I told him. He is unconcerned.'

'But he must not blast! It will be heard for miles! This land is mine – I shall forbid it.'

'Forbid it all you like. He will not listen.'

'Then we must abandon the hillside before he carries out his plan.'

'And Mr Shadwell? We cannot leave him, or carry him between us. We will need Hancock's strength to help.'

Shadwell had raised his head and was listening to them. 'What is that?' he asked in a weak voice. 'He is blasting into the chamber, do you say?'

Fairfax said, 'Yes, sir, I am afraid he is quite mad.'

'No, no. It is the only way.'

Sarah said, 'Surely you cannot approve?'

'I do.'

'But the risk!'

'I have waited many years for this moment, Lady Durston. Now that I have almost no life left – and, it seems, no friend left in the world, either – I do not mind a risk or two.'

And so it was that they stayed.

Sarah persuaded Shadwell to eat a little food. His strength seemed to revive somewhat, although Fairfax suspected it was the prospect of the explosion that gave him the will to recover rather than the stale bread and cold pork she cut up and placed in his mouth as if he were a baby bird. Occasionally Fairfax stepped out of the tent to watch Hancock as he struggled down the hill with another pair of barrels tucked beneath his arms. He made no move to help. He would have no part of it.

After an hour or two, when Hancock had transferred all the barrels and had set them in the tunnel, he could be seen unwinding a spool of fuse wire all the way along the trench. Once that was done, he came over to their tent.

'Ye need to move from here to a safer distance.'

Sarah said, 'You have no right to do this on my land, John. I do not give my permission.'

Hancock could not bring himself even to look at her. He addressed them generally. 'I am giving ye all fair warning. Remain here and ye may be hurt. Stay or go — 'tis all the same to me.'

Fairfax said, 'Will you at least help me to move Dr Shadwell to a safer spot?'

'If that is what ye want.'

They lifted the tabletop from the trestles and placed Shadwell on that, covered in a blanket, and carried him out of the tent. Sarah walked beside the makeshift stretcher, holding Shadwell's hand. 'D'ye see the sort of man I am, Parson?' panted Hancock.

'I'll help ye, even if ye'll not help me!' They went up the slope beyond the trenches, past the uncovered mass grave, to a spot some two hundred yards distant from the tower. Once Shadwell had been placed upon the ground, Hancock set off down the hill to the western trench.

Fairfax took out Lacy's spyglass, extended it and put it to his eye. Hancock was crouching at the top of the ramp, fiddling with something. He seemed small framed against the great panorama of the Wessex landscape. The land fell away into trees and pasture, and then, beyond the wooded valley, like a great flat sea, the distant empty moor extended to the horizon, pricked only by the church tower of Axford. It was just possible to make out travellers on the road, a half-dozen tiny figures on horseback. Fairfax twisted the lens, but they were too far away to bring into focus. He trained the telescope back on Hancock. He had risen from his crouch and was standing, studying the floor of the trench. His head was moving slightly from left to right as he followed the progress of the lit fuse. He seemed to study it for a long time – certainly longer than Fairfax thought safe – then began walking towards them.

He had only covered half the distance when the land at the base of the tower quivered and a section of the earth erupted like a roiling black fountain, shooting higher than the tower itself. An immense wave rushed underground towards them, the surface rippling like the water of a lake. Hancock, running now, was thrust forward and off his feet – sent flying head first, as if he was diving off a cliff. Fairfax felt the pressure suck at his ears. He was blown backwards. Soil and small rocks descended from the heavens, blocking out the light. He heard nothing. All was muffled, silent.

CHAPTER TWENTY-SIX

The burial chamber

WHEN HE OPENED his eyes, everything was different. A crater the size of a fishpond had appeared beside the tower. The structure itself was leaning slightly towards the south, away from the hills, which themselves seemed altered. Those trees closest to the crater had been toppled, their roots ripped out of the ground and exposed. Further up the slope, it was as if winter had returned. Branches were stripped of leaves; new springs were bubbling from the reconfigured land.

He shook the soil out of his hair and looked around for Sarah and Shadwell. They had also been thrown backwards by the blast and were sitting up dazed nearby. Hancock lay motionless, face down, about fifty yards away, half covered by earth and surrounded by human bones that had been lifted from their common grave and deposited to the west.

Fairfax rolled over on to his knees and got unsteadily to his feet. By then Sarah was also standing, brushing off dirt. Neither she nor Shadwell seemed to have suffered any injury, although nobody was speaking. But then he realised that everybody was speaking, himself included, and that nobody could hear. She cupped her hands to his ear. Her voice seemed to come from a great distance. 'Are you hurt?'

He shouted directly into her ear. 'No. Are you?'

She shook her head.

When they turned to make the same enquiry of Shadwell, they found that he had already left them and was moving with the slow, strange gait of a sleepwalker towards the crater. Fairfax took Sarah's hand and they stumbled after him.

The old man passed Hancock without even looking at him. Fairfax was sure the captain must be dead. But when they reached him, they saw that he was moving slightly, unable to rise because of the weight of debris on his back. Together they began to clear away the small rocks and fragments of bone. A skull lying close by seemed to grin at their efforts. The back of Hancock's coat was cut to pieces, bloody and crusted with dirt. In places his bare flesh was exposed. And yet somehow he found the strength to push himself up with his arms and clamber to his feet. Like the tower, he was not quite vertical. His eyes were unfocused. They moved to help support him, but he shrugged them away.

Unsteadily, he turned to survey his handiwork, then lurched towards it.

Shadwell had already reached the lip of the crater by the time they caught up with him. They all four peered down over the edge. It was ten feet deep, a shallow inverted cone. At the bottom, the exposed concrete was split by a fissure perhaps two feet wide, the jagged edges pointing upwards slightly and held together by rusted metal rods.

Fairfax realised his hearing was returning. Birds were calling in the woods. But still nobody spoke. They were transfixed by the black crack and the darkness below it. Hancock was the first to move. He sat on the side of the crater and pushed himself off, sliding down the loose soil until his boots touched the concrete. He braced and leaned over the hole.

Fairfax called out to him. 'What can you see?'

When he did not reply, Fairfax followed his example and slid on his back down to the roof of the chamber. The metal rods, each a half-inch in diameter, were embedded in the concrete a hand's breadth apart. Bent upwards in the middle, they formed a barrier similar to the bars on a prison window. It was impossible to make out anything in the darkness beyond them. The concrete was a couple of feet thick. The force required to shear it must have been colossal, Fairfax thought. He would not have imagined that even twelve barrels of blasting powder could have caused such damage. He searched around for a small stone and dropped it into the abyss. It clattered onto a solid floor.

He shouted up to Sarah. 'Can you find us a saw?'

'And a ladder,' added Hancock. 'And torches. And rope.'

The saw, when she threw it down to them, at first made so little impression on the metal that Fairfax feared they were doomed at the last to be denied their prize by a half-inch of rusty steel. But Hancock was determined, and after a few minutes he had cut through one of the rods very close to the concrete. He kicked at it with his boot; it did not bend. He set to work on the other side. When Fairfax offered to take a turn, Hancock answered with a shake of his head. The last shred of steel gave way and the bar dropped out of sight and landed with a clang. Hancock set to work immediately on the next.

Thunder sounded in the distance. It started to rain again.

The saw was blunted. The second bar took longer. But when at last it fell away, Hancock had created an aperture two feet long and eighteen inches wide, just big enough for a body to pass through.

Sarah passed the ladder down to them. Hancock lowered it through the hole and leaned in after it. Fairfax held on to his belt to stop him falling. The ladder was stout and heavy, seven or eight feet long, but even so it seemed to be either too short or Hancock too exhausted to manoeuvre it properly. He twisted and turned, grunting with the effort, and then it slipped out of his hands. Fairfax heard the crash and the sound of the captain swearing. He hauled him back.

Hancock said, 'No matter. We can use the rope.'

He untied the coil, paid out a length into the hole, and tied the other end to one of the metal rods. He tested the knot, sat on the edge of the opening and dangled his legs. His hands grasped the rope above his head and he lowered himself into the space. It looked to Fairfax to be too narrow for him, and for a minute or more he seemed to be stuck at the waist, wriggling like a man trapped in quicksand, but then slowly he started to sink. His chest passed through the gap, his shoulders, and then very quickly his head and arms, and he was gone. The rope snapped taut. He landed heavily, with a cry of pain.

Fairfax leaned over the hole. From within there rose a strong, cold smell of mould and lime. He could just make out the figure of the captain, crouching. 'Are you all right, Hancock?'

'Aye.' The voice rang hollow off the concrete walls. 'A twisted ankle, nothing more. Drop me a torch.'

Sarah called down to Fairfax, 'Is he safe?'

'So he says.'

She slid down the side of the crater to join him, and so did Shadwell, coming to rest in a spurt of mud. It was raining heavily now. Water was running off the slopes of soil and pouring through the aperture.

Fairfax dropped a torch and Hancock caught it. They heard the rasp of a match being struck, and then the soft *whump* of the pitch catching fire, followed by a gasp of shock. They craned their necks, but the thickness of the concrete restricted their field of vision to a faint orange glow.

Fairfax said, 'What can you see?' There was no reply. 'Captain Hancock? Can you see anything?'

A long silence.

'I have not the words.'

They looked at one another. Fairfax said, 'I'm coming down.'

'And I,' said Sarah. They turned to Shadwell.

He nodded. 'If it is my last act on earth, I shall rest happy.'

Fairfax called down, 'We all are coming.'

He tested the rope, then slipped off the concrete and eased himself down into the gap. The fit was tight, even for him. The sharp edges scraped against his back and stomach. He experienced a moment of panic as he lifted his arms and clutched the rope, pushed himself free and committed himself to the drop. His body was too heavy, his grip too feeble. The rope shot through his hands. He had a flash of memory – of the pall-bearers dropping Lacy's coffin into his grave – then he let go and fell six feet to the floor. As he struck it, his legs gave way and he crumpled.

His hands touched earth then concrete. He was lying on his stomach across a jagged wide crack that seemed to match the fissure in the roof, as if the ground beneath the foundations had been shifted by the explosion and the subterranean structure snapped. He pushed himself upright. The chamber was large, about fifteen feet square. He had dropped through a corner of the ceiling. In the opposite corner was a metal door. At first, until his eyes became used to the dim light, he thought the walls were painted – dappled in patches of red, ochre and light brown – and that time or damp must have damaged the surfaces. But then Hancock held out the torch and he saw that the different-coloured patches were in fact drawings of hands – hundreds of palm prints, the fingers spread wide. Where one ended, another began. The density conveyed an impression of shrieking panic – of a crowd reaching up out of an inferno, clawing for air and light.

Fairfax said, 'It is like a painting of Hell.'

'Aye. And what devilry is this, d'ye suppose?'

Hancock was standing by a small table in the middle of the chamber – the only furniture in the bare room. Candlesticks were set on either side of it, like an altar. Frozen drips of yellowish wax had melted on to what must once have been a cloth but was now nothing more than dust and a few colourless threads. Between the candles was an empty picture frame of tarnished metal, propped beside a thicker piece of rotted material that had disintegrated into a mass of feathers, like the carcass of a bird. On it lay what Fairfax thought at first was a large coin but then saw was a medal of some kind, almost three inches across, with fragments of ribbon still attached. Hancock seemed reluctant to touch it, so Fairfax lifted it up.

It was remarkably heavy for its size, nearly half a pound. He rubbed it, and the gold began to gleam. Hancock held the torch closer. On one side was a pagan goddess, on the other a man's bearded profile. Latin inscriptions ran around the edge. Fairfax turned it to read them: *Inventas vitam iuvat excoluisse per artes* and *REG. ACAD. SCIENT. SUEC.* There was a name and date beneath the bearded man: ALFR. NOBEL NAT. MDC-CCXXXIII OB. MDCCCXCVI. And another name was also inscribed: P. MORGENSTERN MMXIX.

Sarah called down, 'May we join you?'

At the sound of her voice, Hancock scowled.

Fairfax retrieved the ladder from where Hancock had left it lying on the floor, and with some difficulty, for it was heavy, swung it into place. The top just reached the opening. He shielded his face from the rain and shouted up, 'Throw more torches!' There was a pause and she dropped three. He caught them, one after the other. 'Use the rope to help you.'

The sky was blotted out as she climbed through the gap and put her foot on the first rung. Fairfax held the ladder steady. Hancock carried away the torches and began to light them. Sarah came down slowly. Fairfax held out his hand to help her the last few feet, as if assisting her out of a carriage, then looked back up to the opening. 'Dr Shadwell? Can you manage it?'

Shadwell's head appeared, then vanished, to be replaced by a pair of tiny feet. They waved around blindly as he tried to find the ladder. Finally, he connected and began to descend. Halfway down, he missed his footing and swayed out, clinging to the rope. Fairfax was certain he must fall. But somehow he found the strength to haul himself straight, and with painful deliberation he came down the rest of the way. Fairfax wondered how they would manage to get him out again. But Shadwell seemed unconcerned. He took a torch from Hancock and moved around the walls to examine them.

Fairfax also took a torch. With four now burning, the chamber was suddenly bright, the walls more vivid. 'Well, Mr Shadwell? What do you make of it?'

'Remarkable. Remarkable.'

'How did they build such a place?'

'They did not build it. Such chambers were

constructed by the state, for the purpose of defence. They must have occupied it.'

'And the hands?'

'I have seen similar designs in a book describing primitive peoples who dwelt in caves – ten thousand years before the ancients.' He put his own hand over one of the images. 'Left hands mostly, do you see? They placed their painted palm upon the wall and then used their right hand to hold a pipe to blow more paint around it, thus creating the effect.'

'For what purpose?'

'How can we know? In a world where there was no longer ink and paper, it was perhaps their way of telling some future generation they once existed. And here we are, at last.' He surveyed the walls. 'It seems to have been a colony of some size. Children, too.' He glanced at Hancock, who was cleaning the medal. 'Now what is that?'

Hancock bit it, inspected the tooth marks, then handed it to him. Fairfax said, 'It was arranged on the table, on a bed of feathers – once a cushion, perhaps – with candles and an empty picture frame.'

'Solid gold,' said Hancock. 'Five thousand pounds' worth, or thereabouts.' He turned to Sarah. 'Ye have got what ye came for, Sarah Durston. The treasure to restore your fortunes.'

Shadwell took off his spectacles and held the medal close to the torch so he could translate the

Latin. ' "They who bettered life on earth by their newly found mastery" . . . It is Morgenstern's prize for physic. And the bearded man must be that Nobel, who gave it. Your courage is rewarded, your ladyship.' He presented it to Sarah. 'But do not have it melted, I beg you. It's too rare for that. Now let me see the picture frame.' He took it from Hancock and examined it with the same care he had bestowed on the medal. He turned it over, fumbled with it, prised off the back and withdrew a piece of shiny stiff paper. 'It appears blank, Mr Fairfax, but it is not. The ancients recorded lifelike images on such paper, but the portraits lasted only two centuries or so before they faded to nothing. And yet I believe there is still the ghost of a face to be seen . . .'

He offered it to Fairfax. Now that he studied it closer to the flame, he saw that there was indeed perhaps the misty outline of a head, but the features had entirely disappeared. 'Morgenstern?'

'Yes, presumably. That tells us something. Whoever arranged the chamber would not have taken the trouble to set up a blank portrait, so we may date this place to within two hundred years of the Apocalypse — probably much earlier. It seems they made a cult of the man who had led them to safety — he was their Moses after all. It is possible this is his burial chamber.'

Sarah said, 'Then where is his body?'

'This antechamber may have served as the shrine. The body is most like beyond that door.'

It was the first time they had paid attention to it – heavy and rusted, with a wheel for a handle. Painted on it in faded yellow, just discernible, were the words GAS-PROOF ROOM. Above it was a concrete lintel. Letters had been carved into this as well. Fairfax held up his torch. 'There is something written here, in Latin.' He pronounced the inscription slowly as he made it out. '*Mal . . . maledictus . . .*'

'Cursed,' said Shadwell promptly.

'*Maledictus . . . qui . . . intrare . . . hic.*'

' "Cursed be he who enters here." It is a quotation, again from long before the ancients' own time, that was placed upon the tombs of rulers.'

A brief silence.

Sarah said, 'Perhaps the warning should be heeded.'

'What nonsense is that?' sneered Hancock. 'We have come so far – a man has died. Surely we're not to be stopped at the very last by a childish superstition? Shadwell, Fairfax – do ye agree?'

Shadwell said, 'Of course. I set no store by curses.'

'Fairfax?'

He glanced at the door. 'I agree.'

' 'Tis settled then.' Hancock spat on his hands, seized the wheel and tried to turn it. It would not shift. He growled through his clenched teeth as he tried again. His neck turned red and bulged with the effort. His growl became louder. Something metallic cracked. He stopped and unbuttoned his coat, wrapped it around the wheel for a better grip and set to work again. Gradually, in tiny increments, it began to turn. When he had moved it as far as he could, he put his coat back on and tried to push the door open with his shoulder. Nothing happened.

He said, 'Rusted solid. Stand clear.'

He retreated a few paces, turned and ran at it. The whole chamber seemed to shake. Fairfax wondered how he didn't break bones. He went back and charged it again.

Sarah said, 'My God, John, you've cracked the ceiling!'

They all looked up. A thin black line ran all the way across the roof.

Fairfax said, 'It must have been there before.' But it seemed to him that the whole structure was shifting slightly.

Shadwell said, 'I did not see it.'

Hancock mocked them. 'That roof is two feet thick! D'ye think I'm Samson, bringing down the temple?'

This time he took an even longer run-up, and when he smashed into the door, the metal yielded part of the way. A pattering of soil dropped from the ceiling. The crack had widened to an inch.

Sarah said, 'This is not safe. We should all get out.'

She took Fairfax by the arm and tried to pull him towards the ladder. But he resisted. 'I want to see what lies next door. You go.'

'I'll not go without you.' She looked desperately from him to the ceiling and then to the ladder. 'Please, Christopher – it is not worth it.'

Suddenly the shaft of light at the top of the ladder darkened. The woodwork quivered. A pair of black boots appeared and began a cautious descent, feeling for each rung with care. It crossed Fairfax's mind to lunge for the ladder and pull it away. But his legs refused to move. A black uniform came into view. Then a thick leather belt festooned with manacles and a truncheon. Then one black-leather-gloved hand clutching the ladder, and another holding a pistol. And finally the bearded face of Axford's chief sheriff.

'All of ye – stay still!' The command was shrill and edged with fear.

As he reached the ground and trained his pistol on them, another pair of boots appeared above him and a second sheriff descended, followed by a third, and a fourth. They drew their weapons and formed a line, cutting off all chance of escape. After them came Quycke, shaking with terror. He kept his eyes on the ground and shrank into the corner.

Shadwell cried out. 'Oh Olly, Olly – what have you done?'

'Quiet!' The chief sheriff struck him in the face

402

with the barrel of his pistol. The old man yelped with pain. The sheriff stepped back a pace without taking his eyes off his captives. Standing at the foot of the ladder, he shouted up to the surface. 'It's safe now, my lord.' He steadied the ladder.

An elegant shoe caked with mud checked its footing. Then a long black cassock came into view, and a pair of hands, upon one of which glinted a large episcopal ring, followed shortly afterwards by the long white melancholy face of Richard Pole, Bishop of Exeter.

CHAPTER TWENTY-SEVEN

In which the quest is ended

FAIRFAX FELT SARAH take his hand. He glanced at her. She was staring at the bishop. He wondered if he would ever be allowed to see her again. The thought was unbearable. After a moment, she let go of him.

The chamber, which had once felt empty, now seemed crowded by the presence of ten bodies. The sheriffs stamped their feet to knock off the mud. Behind them the rain continued to fall.

No one spoke while the bishop walked around the walls, torch in hand, examining the paintings. At last he stopped in front of Fairfax, who had to struggle against the instinct, born of long habit, to go down on one knee and kiss his ring. He remembered Shadwell's description of the bishop's visits when he was in prison. This was what he enjoyed. Toying with his victims.

'So, Christopher,' Pole said affably, 'you do not

kneel, I notice. Dr Shadwell.' He nodded to the old antiquarian, who was clutching his bloodied cheek. 'It has been a long time since we talked. Captain Hancock. Lady Durston.' He bowed. 'You see, I know you all well.' He gestured to the chamber. 'Well then. What do we have here, Dr Shadwell?'

Shadwell took his hand from his wound and somehow managed to stick out his chin in a show of defiance. 'Morgenstern's ark, my lord – long believed in, long sought for, now discovered.'

'But is this all? It cannot be!'

'There is another room – most probably more than one.'

Hancock said, 'I have just at this moment broken through to it, my lord.' He sounded uncharacteristically deferential, as if the bishop was a merchant who might be bargained with and they could sort it all out man to man. He turned and touched the wheeled handle.

'Leave it!' ordered the bishop. The chief sheriff trained his pistol on Hancock, who drew his hand back quickly. 'This is as far as you will be permitted to go – and too far it is already! I alone will inspect the chamber and judge what is fit to be removed, and then it will be sealed and buried for ever. I believe we will copy your method, Captain, and use blasting powder to do the job. After that, you will all stand trial in Exeter for heresy. And this time, Dr Shadwell, there will be no leniency.' He half turned and raised his hand. 'Where is Mr Quycke?'

Quycke said, 'Here, my lord.'

'Step out of the shadows, Mr Quycke, and show yourself to your friends.'

Reluctantly, Shadwell's secretary came forward. He still made no attempt to look them in the eyes. The bishop rested his hand upon his shoulder. 'Did you never ask yourself, Shadwell, why this true penitent was released from jail after one year, while the other officers of your society served five or more?'

Shadwell was examining Quycke with a look of disappointment as much as disgust, as if his secretary were some object dug out of the ground that he had believed was valuable but had proved to be worthless.

'I shall tell you why,' continued the bishop. 'In return for his freedom, he agreed to swear an oath of loyalty and return to the true path. For eight years he has worked for me, keeping me informed of the wickedness and folly of your obsession.'

Shadwell continued to stare at Quycke. His breath was wheezing. With a shaky hand he reached up and took off his cap. He pushed up his hair to show the bishop the H branded on his forehead. Pole drew back slightly.

'An obsession with the ancients, as you call it — inscribed upon my flesh, according to your orders — is your sin as much as mine. The difference is, I wear it proudly. "Wickedness and folly?" You kept my books, my lord. You did not burn them as you told me. You are a hypocrite.'

'Show respect!' The chief sheriff took a pace towards Shadwell and raised his hand to strike him again, but the bishop waved him back.

'One does not *burn* knowledge! That is a show for the common folk. One *hides* knowledge – one keeps it close. The libraries of the Church hold truths you cannot dream of, Shadwell. No, of course I did not burn your books. I sent them to an old colleague for safe keeping. I believed he could be trusted. That proved an error. But it was of no consequence: Quycke here sent me a copy of the letter Lacy wrote you. I saw it two days before you did. I let you come to Axford in the hope you would lead me here. And so you have. Why else do you think you were granted bail except by my instruction? And now I shall know the truth of this place, and you will not. So which of us in the end has proved the more successful scholar?' He smiled and glanced at the ceiling. A narrow waterfall of soil and water was pouring through the crack. His face became serious. He beckoned to the chief sheriff. 'Take them up and bind them.'

Fairfax said, 'You had Father Lacy killed! If we stand trial, I shall expose you as a murderer!'

The bishop regarded him with contempt. 'I sent you to bury Lacy, thinking you a young, ambitious fool who would do as he was told. But you are an even greater fool than I thought if you believe I would countenance the murder of a priest.'

Quycke said, 'There was no murder. It's true I followed Lacy from the church to the Devil's Chair. He saw me, ran and fell. That's all there was – I swear it.' He looked hopelessly at Shadwell. 'I'm sorry, Nick. God knows, I always loved you. I begged you not to leave Wilton. I never believed—'

He stopped. From somewhere above ground came a loud rumbling. Fairfax thought at first it must be another thunderstorm. The floor shook.

Hancock said, 'That's a mudslide.'

The rumble grew louder. What followed seemed to happen slowly. Bishop Pole looked up at the widening crack and began to back away, all the while staring at the roof, transfixed by it, then turned and pushed his way between the sheriffs and seized the ladder. The moment he put his foot on the first rung, the floor gave way and he dropped out of sight without a cry. Or perhaps he did shout out and the sound was lost in the roaring wall of mud and noise and concrete that was travelling across the room. Fairfax felt himself grabbed from behind. He saw the sheriffs go down first; then Hancock, Quycke and Shadwell crushed. He toppled backwards, pulled by Sarah. Their combined weight struck the metal door, and together they fell sprawling over the threshold. He landed heavily on top of her. Burning pitch seared his skin. An instant later, the roof of the antechamber collapsed.

The entire hillside seemed to pass above their heads — a terrible, deafening grinding noise like the mills of God — and even when the avalanche ceased, the silence that followed was punctuated by muffled crashes and implosions as various pockets of space yielded to the weight. Fairfax could feel Sarah beneath him. She was not moving. At any moment he was sure the roof would cave in and pulp them. He hoped his body would give her some protection. He kept his eyes shut and tried to remember the commination, but could not get beyond the first line — *O most mighty God and merciful Father, who has compassion on all men* — which he repeated endlessly in his head. After a minute, when the banging and thudding seemed finally to have stopped, he opened his eyes. The dust was thick as smoke, swirling orange in the light of the torch that lay nearby.

'Sarah?' His mouth tasted of concrete and chemical. He lifted himself off her and put his hand to her face. She moaned. He picked up the torch. Her skin and hair were streaked with dust. There was a darkness spread around her like a shadow. He put his hand gently beneath her head. His fingers came away sticky with blood. He bent and kissed her forehead. Her eyes opened. He smoothed her hair. She tried to speak. He put his finger on her lips. 'Hush.' He laid down the torch, stood, took off his cassock and folded it. He lifted her head again and rested it on the pillow. 'I shall find a way out for us.' He felt a feeble pressure as she squeezed his fingers. 'Lie still. I shall not leave you.'

He took up the torch and stood. Her feet were close to the door. Beyond it was a solid and compacted mass of concrete, rock and debris. He flourished the light across it, then turned and tried to peer into the room. It was hard to make out anything through the fog of dust. The light seemed to reflect off it rather than penetrate it. He ran his hand along the wall. It was covered in crude drawings, executed mostly in the same colours as the hands in the antechamber – red and brown, with streaks of white and black. Human figures, buildings, faces, diagrams of strange devices. Arrows led from one illustration to another.

He felt his way along the wall, not bothering to examine it, looking for another entrance. He tried to count his paces. Three, four, five . . . The tenth brought him to a corner. The chamber was tiny. A storeroom perhaps. He turned along the adjoining wall. The drawings continued. In the far corner he found a second metal door, identical to the first, with a wheel for a handle. He set down the torch and tried to turn it, but it would not yield, however hard he tried. He needed a tool to use as a lever.

He turned away towards the centre of the room

and trod on something. He stooped to pick it up. A device with the symbol of the bitten apple, but larger, heavier, although still thinner than the width of a finger. It opened like a book. A pane of glass on one side; on the other, squares of black plastic, each inlaid with a letter of the alphabet. They made a curious pattering sound when he pressed them. There were other devices scattered around the floor. Dozens of them, he saw, now that he passed his torch across them — some similar to the one in Lacy's collection, others of an entirely different design. There were boxes of metal and plastic, glass screens, smooth white plastic objects with steel bases that seemed designed to fit in the palm . . . Now that he inspected them more closely they seemed to have been arranged deliberately in a star-like pattern, radiating out from a white steel box, about the size of a man, that rested on a platform in the centre of the room. It was deeper than a coffin — perhaps three feet — but a sarcophagus was the function it served, he was sure. The lid was heavy, hinged along one side, but it lifted easily — dangling threads — and by some function of the mechanism he could not determine, it stayed open. Inside was a mummified figure, its hands folded across its chest, the features of the face just discernible — a noble face, with strong cheekbones and nose, and a wide brow. There was even still some long grey hair. He lowered the lid.

The dust had started to settle. He could see now what this was. A burial chamber, as Shadwell had predicted, with the technology of the ancients arranged around it in tribute, as if to accompany the dead man into the next world. There was no tool anywhere that could open the door. The devices were too flimsy to have any practical use. Without the secret power of electricity to bring them to life, they were as dead as the man they honoured. The flint tools of the Stone Age had more value.

He went back to the wall.

The paintings were arranged to tell a story, he saw now, that seemed to start in the corner by the closed door, with a sequence of drawings of a heavenly body, a planet – the Earth, presumably – brightly girdled by lines of light. In the second drawing, the lights had halved in number. In the third, they had halved again. By the seventh, the planet was in darkness and was depicted held in the claws of the Beast of the Apocalypse, with its seven heads and ten crowned horns. Then came a picture of one of the bitten-apple devices, its screen blank, followed by another with a skull-like face drawn on it, hands pressed to its cheeks, eyes and mouth both wide with horror. A long, straggling column of people ran along the remainder of the wall – shadowy, hunched figures, winding in an endless procession – accompanied by smaller illustrations of incidents that seemed to have occurred on the journey. Buildings with flames pouring from the windows. Wheeled vehicles resting on their roofs. A flying machine, like the one he had seen the children playing with in The Piggeries, ploughed into the earth. Scenes of rape and fighting. Hangings. Piles of corpses burning.

He turned away.

On the opposite wall he recognised a drawing of the Devil's Chair, and another of the stone church tower in Addicott St George, and the yellow plastic shell outside the smithy. And then a curious, chilling picture, of a group of twenty captives with their arms bound behind them, yoked in a line at the neck. The centrepiece of the saga was a large drawing of a man's face, with MORGENSTERN written beneath it and heavenly rays shooting from his head. Grouped around it like disciples were other, smaller faces, captioned KIEFER, FISCHER, SINGH. He studied them. A memory stirred. They were like the images of the obscure saints in the nave of St George's. And the names – Keefer, Fisher, Singer – they still lived in the valley. Gann the blacksmith – was that name a corruption also? Was he a descendant of Morgenstern himself?

He saw the truth then, at the last. It was not the refugees from London who had been massacred against the wall of the tower. It was the villagers. The colonists had taken their land to survive. And then this place, no longer needed, had been turned into a shrine to the founder. Not at the time, he sensed, but perhaps later, during the hundred and fifty years of lawlessness, the Dark Age, when the old knowledge had been lost and superstition had taken its place. A sacred spot, its origins lost in vanished memory, that no one went near.

He swayed and almost lost his footing. He was beginning to feel dizzy. His thoughts were strangely disordered. He guessed they must be running out of air. He went back to where Sarah was lying. He propped the torch against the wall, and got down beside her. She was still awake. She smiled at him. He kissed her and took her in his arms. The light of the torch was burning very feebly now, he noticed: a pale yellow glow. Nevertheless, he felt no fear, just a great drift of peace and well-being.

He said, 'There is a door. We will go through it in the morning.'

He closed his eyes and rested his cheek against hers. The torch guttered and flared briefly, and went out while they slept.

An Officer and a Spy

Robert Harris

Winner of the Walter Scott Prize for Historical Fiction 2014

In the hunt for a spy, he exposed a conspiracy.

Paris, 1895: an army officer, Georges Picquart, watches a convicted spy, Alfred Dreyfus, being publicly humiliated in front of a baying crowd. Dreyfus is exiled for life to Devil's Island; Picquart is promoted to run the intelligence unit that tracked him down.

But when Picquart discovers that secrets are still being handed over to the Germans, he is drawn into a dangerous labyrinth of deceit and corruption that threatens not just his honour but his life . . .

'The fact that this novel is seriously riveting is a testament to Robert Harris's storytelling power; he conjures knuckle-blanching suspense from a very well-known piece of history.'
The Times, BOOKS OF THE YEAR

'Menace and suspense twist tight in a narrative of tremendous tension.'
Sunday Times, BOOKS OF THE YEAR

'Superb . . . Harris demonstrates his unique ability to recreate historical events and turn them into spellbinding thriller . . . Written with scalpel-like precision and the elegance we expect of Harris, there is a passion here that justifies calling it a masterpiece.'
Daily Mail, BOOKS OF THE YEAR

arrow books

The Cicero Trilogy:
Imperium, Lustrum & Dictator

Robert Harris

'**Laws are silent in times of war.**' Cicero

'Thrillers are supposed to thrill, but few really do raise
your heart rate and short-circuit your critical faculties . . .
Exhilarating . . . This trilogy deserves the highest
compliment that can be paid to a work of historical fiction.'
The Times

'Triumphant, compelling and deeply moving . . . the
finest fictional treatment of Ancient Rome in the English
language. They are distinguished by the mastery
of the sources, sympathetic imagination, political
intelligence and narrative skill . . . It's a wonderful,
dramatic, story, wonderfully told.'
Scotsman

'Contemporary echoes abound in this endlessly
fascinating exploration of power struggles.'
Mail on Sunday, BOOKS OF THE YEAR (*Dictator*)

'Harris's fascination with politics galvanises his impressive
knowledgeableness into compulsive fiction.'
Sunday Times, BOOKS OF THE YEAR (*Dictator*)

arrow books

Conclave

Robert Harris

The Pope is dead.

Behind the locked doors of the Sistine Chapel, one hundred and twenty Cardinals from all over the globe will cast their votes in the world's most secretive election.

They are holy men. But they have ambition. And they have rivals.

Over the next seventy-two hours one of them will become the most powerful spiritual figure on earth.

THE POWER OF GOD.

THE AMBITION OF MEN.

'Thriller of the year . . . with a plot so serpentine and sinuous that I could not bear to put it down.'
Daily Mail, BOOKS OF THE YEAR

'I have been waiting most of my life for Robert Harris to write a novel that is not gripping, insightful and entertaining. I am waiting still. His latest, *Conclave*, is superb.'
Ben Macintyre, *The Times*, BOOKS OF THE YEAR

arrow books

Munich

Robert Harris

Spying. Betrayal. Murder. Is any price too high for peace?

'An intelligent thriller . . . with exacting attention to historical detail.'
The Times, BOOKS OF THE YEAR

'A gripping and atmospheric account of the negotiations in the
Bavarian capital in 1938.'
Daily Express, BOOKS OF THE YEAR

'Electric with tension and engrossingly informative, it persuasively
brings out what was formidable and courageous behind
Chamberlain's Edwardian provincial civic dignitary exterior . . .
As always, political manoeuvrings galvanise Harris'
imagination into thrilling creativity.'
Sunday Times Culture, BOOKS OF THE YEAR

'A wonderful tale of personal relationships and political
drama . . . This is a very, very good read.'
New Statesman, BOOKS OF THE YEAR

'Ranks alongside the most moving fictional portraits
of a politician that I have ever read.'
Sunday Times

arrow books

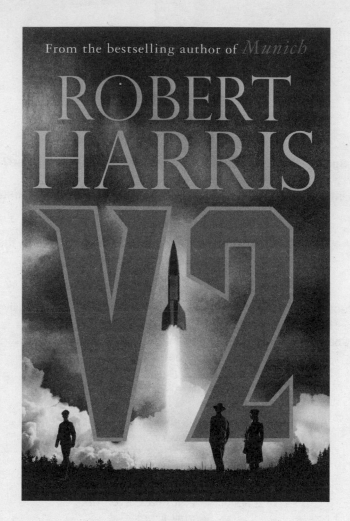

OUT
17 SEPTEMBER 2020

PRE-ORDER YOUR COPY NOW!